WHEN A BULBUL SINGS

HAWAA AYOUB

Published by Hawaa Ayoub
ISBN: 978-1-9996261-0-5

Visit Hawaa Ayoub's official website at www.hawaaayoub.com for the latest news, book details, and other information.

Copyright © Hawaa Ayoub, 2018

Cover design by Lieu Pham, Covertopia.com
Book layout by Guido Henkel

To the millions of voiceless child brides...
still girls or now adults

The fourteen-year-old, she no longer exists,
But her voice inside me still persists and insists,
Asking why, she had to die,
Please…please, tell her why,
She lives no longer, yet is not dead,
Her whispers and cries still shatter my head,
Can you tell her from your soul within
Her sentence began before her life did begin?
Yes, tell her, what she did so grim:
Born a girl—so guilty as sin.

CHAPTER ONE

I N THE BRIGHT, WHITE SUN, BORDERED BY PALM TREES WITH curved trunks and green heads that seemed to bow, and acacia trees whose green boughs shivered in the heat, men and women gathered in and around Uncle Faris' house made up of many rooms each standing separately around a large yard; most were locals from The Dibt (a semi-arid, semi-desert like area scattered with palm trees, Thorn of Christ trees and various euphorbias), and many had come in a procession of cars from the high southeast mountains which deceivingly looked like tiny mounds in the far distance from here. All were guests, dressed in their finery: men in white dresses with red and white shawls over their shoulder blades, curved daggers around their waists, rifles over the shoulder; women adorned with gold, in an array of coruscating fabrics, bright and dark, sequinned or glittered; all merry and in good spirit. Drums beat, reed pipes blared with an African-Arab descant and merry men danced in lines, the silver of their dagger Jambias glinting in the sun, outshone by the flash of teeth in laughter. The handsome groom, wearing black western trousers, a white shirt and black tie, who had come down from the mountains to take his beautiful bride by her delicate hand and lead her to her new home, danced and smiled; his fair countenance contrasted by his black hair, moustache and eyebrows now looked worried as the bride was not being cooperative, in fact his three relatives (two sisters and an Aunt) were dragging the poor girl across the length of a narrow windowless room, where they had been preparing her. Eve, small and slender, whose long loose curls of wavy brown-black hair and beautiful olive skin were concealed; fourteen years old (and usually intrepid and vivacious) and now afraid of what was happening looked around her, but her peripheral view was obstructed by the long black hood and veils forming the top part of her shiny black sharshaf; her brown eyes gleamed with tears from above the scarf they had tied around her face from the nose downwards, alarmed at the large crowd which had gathered around them to watch the giving away of the bride. Father's lips trembled and his nose ran as he took her small right hand and placed it into the groom's for the second time, as she had snatched it away the first. In Welsh accented English, jarring with the exotic Middle East environs and garb, she begged not to be forced to marry; Father, though his eyes betrayed unhappiness, bit his lower lip and pulled her forward towards the groom again whom now held her tightly using arm and elbow to keep the fey, finicky bride clasped beside him, whilst his sisters and Aunt helped keep her gripped. This simply could not be happening, she wasn't even supposed to be here and should have been long back in Britain instead of missing two months of school following the Christmas holiday. Automatic rifles were held above her shoulder by the Uncles in turns and the tremendous bangs left her ears ringing. Were they threatening her? Well they had succeeded, scared out of her wits she called out in English for her eldest brother to save her, but her voice was lost amongst the shrill vibrating screams emitted by all the women, ululations of an unwanted celebration. Poor Eve, she didn't know this was just celebratory customs, shooting into the air by guests were expressions of joy, his Uncles shooting from close proximity to her head signified their pride she was joining their family (never mind it worsened her already throbbing headache). Presently they were standing in front of a Land Cruiser with a driver already waiting behind the steering wheel, the groom got in and extended his hand towards her to join him, but she turned towards her father beseeching him from her heart, accompanied by a torrent of tears, to stop this madness. As she stared at him with her brown burrowing, hurt-doe eyes she remembered, and he remembered, how they got here and none of it made any sense to our bewildered bride.

*

2

SHE'D HAD A VERY HAPPY AND NORMAL CHILDHOOD, BORN AND BRED in Wales; she was Father's pride and joy being such a well-behaved girl and having an extremely high intellect, and he constantly rewarded her exceptional behaviour and studies with lavish gifts.

Always the first to awake in the family, she watched the light chase out the darkness from the window where she had pulled an armchair and plopped her law books, waiting to hear the first part of what she enjoyed, and there it was: the loud, incessant bird song coming from the crown of a large oak tree emerging from behind the houses opposite. Their music filled the air, and as she closed her eyes she felt their whistles, chirps and trills vibrate in her temples and soul, and resonate throughout her body—their melodies so clear, energetic and full of the promise of life—as was she. Father always joked that she awoke early so as to cram as many activities she could into one day, and it was true for she had zeal to do everything: study, read books of all types, newspapers (her reading age was much higher than her chronological age), she explored the city she lived in, its rich green areas and urban alike, played the guitar, rode bicycles and played with her friends. But more than anything her whole direction was aimed at getting into university, and she wasn't waiting until she got there to be enlightened; Mr. Halfspan (secondary school headmaster) and his deputy were in no doubt she would get into Oxford and were extremely proud of their star pupil; the brightest in One-Alpha-One (the highest set in her year), teachers were always impressed by her well of knowledge and the outstanding quality of her work. Now we don't want you to get the wrong impression of our Eve, she wasn't one of those nerdy children who are all study and no play, though she had been bestowed with, and nurtured, exceptional intelligence, she did not behave like an adult, but was a normal, popular girl with many friends, indulging in games and interests of her peers and pulling off practical jokes on her teachers. But there was nothing she wanted to be other than a lawyer. In the future Eve would ponder about many things in retrospect: she had begun to read law books while still in junior school; in both infant and junior school she had been advanced skipping whole years due to her high IQ; it seemed she was in a hurry to get to her future and the school was pushing her forward and she would have started secondary school very early had not the newly promoted headmistress put an end to it: citing, and garnering support, it would put too much pressure on Eve and be detrimental to her well-being (although little Eve was not under any pressure at all, she absorbed the curriculum and sailed through it with speed and ease, working at a much faster pace than the kids older than she in their class year) so she waited extra years languishing in Class Five until friends of her own age caught up with her. Although it would possibly not have changed the current course of things (well, who knows what knock-on effect one action has upon one's future), Eve often wonders if the headmistress hadn't interluded getting an early start in secondary school, if she would have made the same pace of progress and arrived early at University thus if she would have avoided the whole debacle she was in now (well, Eve—you'll never know so stop torturing yourself).

Father had surprised them all when he said they would be holidaying in the country of their origin—Yemen. For reasons obscure then, but obvious now, both parents had kept them in the dark about their roots; and had not corrected the children's misguided belief they were from Saudi solely based on receiving letters from their eldest brother from the Kingdom of Saudi Arabia—he lived and worked there. It was both surprising and intriguing to hear they descended from unheard of Yemen, and better still they were going to visit and experience the different culture—oh, this was a country not any of her friends had been to! The photos she would take, the stories she would bring back, and gifts for her friends. Lordy dordy, she could not wait to get there (if only she knew what was awaiting). Father chose the travel date for three days after her fourteenth birthday; brimming with eagerness and prepared for seeing exotic scenes, our fourteen-year-old had the excitement of a bus-full of tourists (safe to say that excitement has dulled considerably after the unfolding events not long after their arrival in Yemen). After leaving the small dusty and very chaotic Sana'a airport they swerved down wide dirt roads, swerving because the taxi driver engaged in conversation with Father would let go of the steering wheel and turn towards the latter emphasising with his hands what his mouth was probably perfectly imparting, while the children shouted at him in English to hold the steering wheel and watch where he was driving (he did not speak English, but understood the tone of panic).

Along the way they were stopped by a dark haired, bullet-strip-chested, automatic-rifle-shouldered young man; the children had only known the safety and security of stable Britain and were not used to seeing soldiers in the streets. Father handed over the passports, Eve guardedly glanced at the soldier and back at her father while another soldier was peering through the back-seat window; she had only seen people dressed like this, armed like this, on the news in some foreign country where guerrillas were rebelling against their government; and now Father had brought them to a country at war where guerrillas could stop people—maybe even shoot them. No amount of reassuring Eve would convince her they were soldiers, that they were not seventeen years old as she had estimated, but fully-grown men; there was no war it was only a check point. Eve wanted the taxi to turn around and take them back to the airport, but Father wouldn't have it, instead he translated her worries to the taxi driver whom found it hilarious, tilting his head backwards, laughing his heart out, and glancing at her through the rearview mirror before laughing some more.

It seemed they would never find a room as all hotels had been filled due to the exodus of Yemenis from Saudi Arabia. Finally they were in a stark marble floored room and while Father went to get lunch she convinced her brothers there was a war and they should leave (by pointing out if there was no war there would be no need for soldiers in the streets with all that ammunition (she knew nothing about the Middle East)) a terrible feeling (intuition my dear) from the pit of her stomach was screaming at her to go back home immediately, and upon Father's return even seventeen-year-old Yusef and fifteen-year-old Sami were clamouring to be taken back to the airport immediately. Father was able to reassure the boys, but Eve refused to eat and when Father extended a bottle of coke to her, she slapped it out of his hand; the brothers froze as the bottle shattered to pieces upon the marble floor. Mother's face greyed and grimmed with foreboding, for she had reason to dread: during Eve's happy, and unfinished, childhood there came a period of change in how Father treated her; she had gone from being his spoilt and beloved daughter to becoming his object of abuse: belting her, whipping her with tomato canes, calling her terrible names; and all unjustified for she had not changed, she had not done anything she wasn't supposed to do: affectionate Mother, routinely and concentratedly over many years inculcated upon Eve, from a very young age, that if she ever kissed a boy she would become pregnant, and, as if this wasn't enough, the warning always came with the consequence: her stomach would grow and grow with a baby inside and she would explode—and die! Of course, Eve, precocious little thing that she was, would eventually find out before she left junior school how babies were really made, and although she knew kisses could not bring about a pregnancy her mother's educational efforts had a lasting effect and she always rejected boyfriending in the amorous terms. But apparently psychologically scarring your child wasn't enough of a parental precaution, and as soon as her budding breasts started to take a more shapely form and fill her blouses in the thirteenth year of her young life, and as soon as she had swapped out wide pleated skirts for tight pencil skirts, Father became psycho-irrational, accusing her of being a slut; his undue distress at seeing her body begin to shape into a young woman was expressed through constant anger, but she didn't know this (nor could she do anything to stop her developing body had she known), and even worse were the beatings where she would do everything she could to protect her head as he angrily exclaimed he had to make her less clever. Social Services had taken her to a home where she found Father's beatings (though inexcusable) paled in comparison to the monstrosity of abuse some of her coevals had suffered. With her brothers and Mother along with Father crammed into a very small office where files were piled high on desks, during one of the rare visits he had been allowed at the home, and in a flood of emotional tears, in a blubbering display of his utter regret and compunction over how he had treated her, he promised if she retracted her statement and returned home he would never hit her again. She, not enjoying the stay at the home where no privacy existed, living with many other children of differing ages whom shared the facility, gave it serious consideration and, much to her Social Worker's dismay and disapproval, claimed in court that he had never hit her and wanted to live with her parents. Seemingly, the Social Services intervention had worked, he stopped beating her. Alas, this was to be the biggest mistake she had made in her young life, but one she would only realise after arriving in Yemen which was supposedly to be a brief, two-week holiday.

Having made their way by car from the capital Sana'a to the city of Taiz, they stayed overnight at the latter. It was there they were informed of being from a village to which they departed towards early in the dark morning. Asphalt roads ended and they travelled over dirt roads; nature was becoming more abundant and manmade structures ceased; they drove through rivers surrounded by trees on both banks and were told by the driver whom spoke English it was called Wadi Rushwan, parts of it were more swamp than river; they continued driving through the river for a long while with the murky grey water splashing up the sides of the car before crossing out of it and back onto dirt roads which then turned into partially rocky terrain. Eve noticed on some hilltops castle-like houses stood, some in clusters others solitary, and she assumed its dwellers lived lonely lives.

As the road became rockier and steeper the car shook along and soon they were surrounded on either side by exotic plants and shrubs they had never seen before, Eve and Yusef reached out and plucked different leaves to examine. It wasn't long before they ascended an even steeper path, to the children it seemed the car couldn't possibly go up such an inclination and uneven terrain, the area was void of vegetation and this path took them to a mountain of which the route tightly hugged to one side. From Eve's seat she could see how much they ascended and it was a breathtaking view of thousand feet drops and mountain tops left behind. The car no longer drove, but had become a crab clawing sideways, as the driver skilfully, slowly and carefully made his way up slabs of uneven stone and over rocks and rock outcrops, they only lost traction once and rolled backwards (a round-eyed goodbye-to-the-world feeling of expecting to die gripped everyone, bar the driver) and downwards, but still the children found this challenging, adrenaline pumping journey a thrill. Four and a half hours later the scenery had changed, rectangularish pieces of land, a giant's staircase, went up and down mountainsides in every direction. The mountains were jagged and grey, the plunging gorges fathomless, the paths filled with large scree, it seemed uninhabitable, but there were houses perched on peaks.

Eve got out of the car viewing the stunning environment, to her right a rocky hill with small shrubs in its niches, above it a derelict house built of stone. Behind it a high cliff rose with a wall erected at its top, the colour of the stone the same as the boulders. From behind the wall, the top half of two houses could be seen rising above, the first house looking much older and different than the second and beside them, massive boulders dwarfed the houses. Eve went to the other side, rocks moving under her Dr. Martens she held onto the vehicle with one hand to keep balance. A path led downwards towards the west, disappearing behind a rough outcrop of rock, appearing again further down then it disappeared behind a rocky hill. To the left, agricultural terraces of varying size, at different levels, went down and up, some bordered by the higher mountains, some bordered by a few houses. Palm trees, acacias, zizyphus spina Christi and plants unidentifiable were dispersed in areas. To the southwest a huge gorge before she saw large layers of land bordered by manmade lines of rock. She looked up and across the chasm to see mountainside to the higher southwest with three houses aligned together at its top, and behind them even higher mountains with several houses dispersed over them and then the sunny blue sky; a swell of breath inflated her lungs as she realised this was going to be a terrific start to travels which she had planned to make when she would be a few years older and be able to travel alone, her world had become even vaster and she was going to explore every beautiful part of it. Eve returned to the right of the car and opened her mouth to say something, but was cut short by the sound of loud gun shots, ducking as did her brothers, pressing their bodies against the car.

"Don't be afraid," said Mother, touching Eve's head, "They're not shooting at us."

Eve looked up the steep, rocky path to see four men in brilliant white dresses at the top, each man holding an automatic rifle; arms raised, shooting upwards while looking down at them, due to the hazy effect of the heated sun they seemed to shimmer in their brightness and whiteness.

"*Morad?!* My son Morad!" Mother exclaimed with delight.

Eve looked up to see her eldest brother whom she hadn't seen in years, also dressed in white, trying to come down a semi-worn path in the hillside below the old house. He lifted at his dress revealing white trousers made of the same material, as he slipped, twice, landing roughly on his bottom. Morad hugged Mother and kissed her on the head then turned to Eve, hugging and kissing her more than he had his mother for he loved Eve dearly; he constantly bragged about her success and probable future in front of his friends and colleagues in Saudi.

"I thought you were in Saudi?" Mother asked with a big smile, happy to see her eldest son.

"Things changed since Iraq's invasion of Kuwait and our President's statements," said Morad "It upset everybody and things turned for the worse for Yemenis so I decided to come home to my country." He held Eve's hand to help her up the steep path filled with rocking scree and looked back at Mother, "And I'm married."

"Married?! Married to who?" asked Mother, shock blanching her face.

The men continued to shoot as the family made its way up the steep, the boys kept falling so Mother helped Yusef and Father helped Sami. At the top of the steep known as Barh Salliya, Father hugged and kissed with the men, then Mother did the same. Morad introduced his siblings in Arabic, they recognised the mention of their names. One of the men, Uncle Salem, smiled at Eve; his silver incisor and gold front tooth glinted in the sun, he hugged and kissed her as did tall fat and white Uncle Yahya. Super-skinny Uncle Suleiman would not let go of her, hugging and kissing her, smiling at her with paternal warmth; you could tell he worked long and hard in the sun from his weathered skin. The fourth man, Abdulrazaq, was a neighbour; though he shook hands with the rest when Eve followed he just stepped back and looked away which she found to be rude, but this must be their custom here (if only all men, including your groom, would have ignored you so). Inside the newer of the two houses, while her brothers chatted, she noted there was no electricity as she examined a kerosene lantern hanging from a wire in the ceiling.

Now from this day forward and up until the wedding, there would be series of unforeseeable, and unfortunately inauspicious, shocks which would bombard our brave young naïve Eve, and her brothers. To begin with the mildest: they only became aware the only person, other than they, who spoke English was their elder brother

Morad—a disadvantage, especially if your parents had neglected to teach you, or even ever talk to you, in Arabic. The handshake consisted of someone extending to you their hand, they pull it forward and kiss the back of your hand, they push it back to you and you kiss the back of their hand, they pull your hand forward and kiss the back of your hand again before releasing your hand and kissing the pads of their own fingers; now repeat this with over two hundred visitors whom arrive within hours all excited to see you (how exhausting). The women, girls and children made rows on the ground all the way to the opposite wall; the older women wore zigzag dresses of different fabrics, tight at the top, but baggy at the bottom, a symmetrical zigzag pattern sewn onto both sides of the chest with a zip in the middle; the bodice seamed to a long flowing skirt, their hair completely covered by black veils either bound like a turban or tied around the forehead and over the ears. The younger women and girls wore square-cut neckline dresses showing cleavage, only the back half of their hair covered by a head veil, black, but with coloured or sequinned borders or corners, loosely hanging off the sides pinned into place by bobby pins, they all had their hair parted at the middle or from the side. Everyone wore green or blue rubber flip flops, many children walked barefoot. This wall of curious visitors crammed full of the Bawaba, gazed at the children without communing with them as if they were some odd spectacle; whenever the three British children tried to communicate the visitors laughed raucously at the sound of their strange, foreign language so Eve read the book she had been gifted by her brother at the airport, a supernatural novel, but this in itself caused a stir with the women pointing at it, and Eve, as if she were exhibiting some strange, unacceptable behaviour; but even the book did not cause as much stir as did her blousered body, trousered legs and uncovered, cascading dark brown hair.

Then came Uncle Aref, a thin dark young man whom swayed and sauntered as he walked, and had not an iota of the kindness and jollity of his brothers. Why, he furrowed his eyebrows and glowered at our already uncomfortable and out-of-place Eve; he didn't want her wearing trousers, he didn't want her wearing blouses (no he did not want her naked), he didn't want her reading books! In fact, he made such a hullabaloo out of her very modest attire she was begged to change by Morad and Mother, which led to her wanting a shower, which brought to the siblings' awareness there was no running water in the house, there was not even a bathroom, let alone a toilet as in the sense of a ceramic throne. Had Father prepared them, instead of lied, about the reality of the village: no water, no electricity, none of the basic norms you think you can't live without, it would have been kinder of him and the shock more gentle, but he had seen their extreme disappointment at the quality of the hotel rooms and worried if he gave them a true account of what he had described as a beautiful farm with horses (with the promise of choosing the best horse for Eve to ride (turned out she'd be the one ridden to the euphoric finish line)) and all the utilities and facilities of modern life they needed—well, he believed he would not be able to get them anywhere near the village and then all would be lost. It has to be said, they were lucky Morad had arrived a few months prior to their arrival, as when he'd returned after long life in Saudi there were only boulders to hide behind and hope no one trespassed upon you, which hadn't proven to be the case for Morad too many times with shocked, shy women peeping at his impressive exposure through splayed fingers covering their faces, hence the humble privy-cum-bathroom was built: a three by five foot building located outside and below a path: Eve felt how terribly wrong she had misjudged the toilets in the hotels of Sana'a and Taiz which were Asian style: basins embedded in the tiles of the floor, they were not holes, but this was definitely a hole in the floor complete with two jagged rocks on either side to place your feet on. Then came the day when Father informed them there was no going back home to Britain—this was their new home. Their passports had been stealthily confiscated, money surreptitiously taken away, and all vehicle owners and their families were given instructions that these three children were never to be allowed to board a vehicle unless accompanied by Father or an Uncle. The children had tried to discuss the situation with Father because rationale and discussion were the key to solving unexpected issues which suddenly popped out of nowhere with the threat of life-changing consequences, but when Father, with his newfound dictatorial attitude as there were no Social Services to answer to here, simply brushed off their oh-so important reasons pertaining to returning home: Yusef had college to return to; Sami and Eve school and exams; they had their friends to see, their lives to live; in exasperation Yusef said he would call the Embassy, in protest Eve said she would call the police—this only tickled Father pink, he laughed while telling them *here* in these mountains there were no embassies or police; and even if they had been in the city, well, this was Yemen: they were *his* children and not even the authorities have the right to get involved. The children were left with a disorienting feeling of being trapped: their minds and hearts still felt free, they *were* free, but they could not leave this village due to Father's instructions and the remoteness and perilous terrain; freedom, like good health, you don't notice it until it's gone—or, in freedom's case, taken away.

Eve quarrelled with Mother over Father's claim, and she demanded immediate departure, but after upbraiding her daughter Mother, looking much embarrassed, sat back with the other women, talking in Arabic as they turned their hands up and tutted, and held their cheeks in disapproval. Mother kept glancing at her with a lot of uncalled for disrespect, and it worried Eve that Mother be flustered because she wanted to go home, instead of being upset about her husband claiming they would not be returning. Eve threw herself onto the bed, crying, hating they had come to Yemen; she hated she had believed her father's lies; she could not stand the look of angry embarrassment on her mother's face and she hated that she was crying in front of a room full of strangers. A distraught Morad sat on the bed trying to comfort Eve, but all she wanted was to be taken home. At this point an old woman walked in, wearing a deep purple zigzag dress, a black veil tied around her head, turban style and unusually larger than everyone else's. She nodded her head and raised her hand towards them then sat with the women on the other side. She got up and stood a yard away from Eve, watching her cry; she turned her hands up and held her chin several times then turned towards the women saying something, very loud. Mother replied, giving Eve the stink-eye.

"What did they say?" asked Eve.

"She asked why you're crying," said Morad "And mother told her it's because you want chocolate." Eve felt insult bloat in her stomach, and the immense humiliation being accused of such a childish want had mixed with fright.

"I don't want *chocolate*!" she shouted in anger "I want to go home! *Take us home*!" and started crying again. When she calmed and lifted her head she was met by Purple Dress Lady whom had come closer, still watching her intensely and with much fascination as if she were something to be studied. The lady said something to Eve using a lot of hand movements, and every time she made her exaggerated gestures while talking her thick gold bracelets clanked and the waft of her sickly-sweet, strong perfume hit Eve in the face. Eve didn't care to know what she was saying: she felt lost and was more concerned about how soon they would be back home so she looked away, hoping the lady would leave her in her misery. Mother got up and spoke quietly to the lady whom turned to Eve, standing even closer, extending her arms, her hands almost reaching Eve as she spoke.

"Are you happy now?" said Mother angrily at Eve, "She says you're wild! She says you need to be tamed!"

Eve, though not a vulgar girl, rarely used swear words, unless in jest or in extreme anger; as you can understand being referred to as an animal causes the latter emotion; to put it into a less vulgar rendering than what she used, she asked her brother to translate to Purple Dress Lady to 'copulate away' (needless to say in this ultra-conservative culture, her brother did not translate his sister's message, but told the old hag his sister was upset about leaving home).

The sun hung low in the west, using Morad's binoculars tiny outlines of cargo vessels could be seen in the distance, silhouettes in a shadow-show. The children could make out a mass of land appearing on the curve of the horizon, Morad said it was the Horn of Africa. They watched the orange balled sun set in the sea from in front of the Second House, and still they didn't believe what had been said, that they would not return home. As it became darker, kerosene lanterns were lit and its yellow-tongued flicker gave a haunting illumination to Uncle Suleiman's face as he told stories of demons and beasts.

The next day more visitors arrived in the afternoon: women and children. Eve looked up from where she sat upon an elevated king-size bed covered by a sumptuous blanket with images of two angry, roaring tigers woven into it, to see a teenage boy walk in, to her surprise he wore extremely fashionable female black trousers with a colourful sash around the waist and a white Peter Pan-collared blouse. She did a double take and couldn't believe her eyes—he was wearing *her trousers* and *her blouse*! She jumped off the bed and demanded he tell her why he was wearing her clothes and how he had obtained them (had she known he was the local catamite for the paying non-locals at night, she wouldn't have requested their return), all he did in response was grin like a fool, while the guests laughed at her strange language. She went outside and called for Father and Morad, Uncle Suleiman followed them down wearing her baggy embroidered white blouse with engraved silver buttons seemingly unaware how ridiculous he looked with it too short on his long torso, too tight around his chest with the buttons ready to fly off. When Morad explained to him Eve's upset he merely smiled a yellow smile and embraced her in a hug more like a headlock and kissed her head; she could smell the not unpleasant brewy odour of a green substance stuffed in his cheek which was seeping onto his canine tooth; pointing to the shirt he wore he said something, then slowly shook his thick finger in front of her face; Morad translated: women don't wear trousers or shirts, she wouldn't be needing them. On inspecting her suitcase she found all trousers and blouses gone, given away to boys; her skirts and dresses torn to pieces, material had been sent for to be sewn into square-cut dresses, they were beginning her acculturation into becoming one with the nation of this village where all girls and women wore the exact same style of traditional clothing and hairdo.

Like all surprises, the greatest is better left for last: Father's final fateful changes to their lives imparted upon them was to be the most devastating. How does a girl who only dreams of playing with her friends, excelling in her exams and living a carefree life respond to being told she is to marry Uncle Suleiman's son whom she has never met before, currently working in Saudi Arabia? Well, first she thinks it's a joke, she and her brothers stare at Father bemused, their minds totally unaccepting what they have fully understood; then she goes on to enquire when they will be heading back home because she needs to resume her education and misses her friends; and when Father (brute of a man he's turned out to be) makes it unequivocally clear that she is to marry an adult, disregarding her tender age, an asthma attack hits you full force. And when you recover, you find out nothing has changed; you will still be forced to marry, but at least Morad provided comfort and salvation, with a worried and sympathetic face he told her if she did not want to get married all she had to do was say no right now, and he would not allow it to happen so she gave her brother the reply: an unequivocal, unmistakeable, absolute NO.

The following day Eve came to learn her family was moving to an area in the lower flatlands in the West called The Dibt; all, except Morad who would remain in the mountains, were leaving together; and she was left behind without being told why, to follow shortly after they arrived there. Sitting in the cool morning sun on the ducka outside, surrounded by both exoticism and eccentricity, Eve reading her book felt lonely without her brothers. Uncle Suleiman came out of the First House carrying a thermos flask of tea, Dawood his eight-year-old son (he had in total five sons and five daughters ranging in age from adults to toddlers) followed with three glasses and a can of condensed milk especially ordered because Eve didn't drink tea without milk. Uncle Suleiman squatted on the ground in front of Eve and watched her intensely, unnerving her with his stare; he was deep in thought, she could see that; his thoughts included her, she could feel it. He wasn't just watching her, but with quiet smugness measuring, looking at her and imagining, seeing what the future could be and how different his life would be as he stroked his short beard with the back of his index finger. A brief lupine-smile flickered in his eyes, on the corners of his lips, as if he'd won some prize, but he stifled it. Dawood poured himself tea and went off towards the stables. Uncle Suleiman smiled and smacked his lips as he drank the tea, when he finished, he spoke to Eve, she didn't understand though it was obvious he was trying to be very nice— maybe because her family had left. He reached into his pocket and pulled out a pretty small heart-shaped box and seating himself next to Eve, holding her right hand while he smiled and talked, he slipped a gold ring full of gem stones onto her finger. He pointed at it, lifting her hand with his closer to her face. She removed it from her finger and placed it in his hand, but he got up and bending over her tried to get the ring back on her hand by force, speaking loudly.

"No!" she said, hiding her hands in her armpits. He went into the Bawaba and returned with Morad and Dhalia.

"He wants you to have this ring," said Morad "It's from his son, the one they want you to marry."

"Tell him I don't want the ring, and I don't want his son." said Eve.

Morad translated. Dhalia frowned and walked away; Suleiman shook his finger at Eve and gave the box to Morad; glancing at Eve he spoke with half a smile, half a smirk before slowly walking away.

"He wants me to send it to Dad." said Morad.

Upon arriving at The Dibt she found though it was easier to walk around on level ground, it was actually a harsher environment with less food, less shelter, a more oppressive sun, an even more oppressive Father, and the unbearable heat and damned mosquitoes were a terrible combination. Not long after her arrival, her brothers were sent back to the mountains while she remained with Father and Mother at Uncle Faris' house in The Dibt. It was during these weeks before she would see her brothers again (and only glimpse them briefly at that on the wedding day), that he returned to violence in a bid to break her spirit, wanting her to marry Adam, Suleiman's son whom she'd never met nor wanted to meet, willingly (who needs pre-marital counselling for couples when you can beat them into compliance?). He beat her, threw things at her, belted her, took her out into the pitch-dark wilderness and left her there, but her answer always remained no. His last act of violence, making her believe he was about to cut her throat with her head pulled back asking her if she would marry Adam, and she would have said yes out of mortal fear had she been able to articulate, but all that would come out of her mouth was a strange "agh, agh" noise, and upon hearing Mother's screams Uncle Faris came rushing into the room shouting at Father to fear God and stop behaving like a madman. Father removed the knife from his daughter's neck and pushed her down to the ground where dirt stuck to her wet face, and he left the room. Uncle Faris scooped up the motionless girl and lay her on the bed, but Eve didn't notice falling asleep that night, the last memory she forever remembers of that terrible day was the taste of her tears mixed with the smell of damp dirt burning the back of her throat.

The next day Uncle Suleiman, his son Adam, both carrying a metal trunk full of presents for Eve: fabrics, perfumes, money, sweets and other trinkets; accompanied by a group of men including 'The Ameen', the person responsible for writing out official documents, arrived by car. From outside the door, Eve refused to say yes; nonetheless The Ameen (the noun which is derived from the word trusted, honest, integrity, safe-keeper) wrote out a marriage contract not only stating she had consented to the marriage, but also added three years to her age to take it well above the legal marriage age. Adam tried several times to get close to her, his mien was both excited and happy (Eve had had the same countenance when Father had allowed her to buy a kitten), as talking was out of the question with her not knowing Arabic and he not speaking English whenever he said whatever it was he was saying was followed by awkward silence; but whenever he smiled she reacted as if he'd flashed multiple rows of canines through an unlipped leer; and every time he attempted to get closer she would leave the room or area, but he kept appearing after her.

The day of the wedding her heart filled with worry as she poured water over herself and shampooed her hair and lathered her body, she couldn't stop fretting over why Morad had even allowed them to come and ask for her hand in marriage, he was going to object today. The Uncles Faris and Nageeb slaughtered a goat in front of her while she, seated wedged between two young female cousins on a bed which had been brought outside, covered her eyes, it was some sort of sacrifice. They proceeded to put goat blood on her forehead which she mistook as them wanting her to drink in some sinister Satanic ritual to which she leaned backwards on the bed and kicked with all her might to keep Uncle Nageeb and his sacrilegious blood away from her; Father and Mother laughed while Father explained they didn't want her to drink it—just to purify her by putting some on her forehead—they ended up having to wipe it on her feet as she continued to kick like a cycling kangaroo on drugs, before Mother soaped it off. The marriage convoy arrived with the men and women from the mountains. Uncle Suleiman's married daughters, Dhalia (married to Morad) and Latifa (married to her cousin Hammed), arrived in a cloud of perfumes, both wearing sparkling, brightly coloured dresses; donned with so much golden jewellery it could be mistaken for armour; the backs of their hands were covered in black patterns, their palms and finger tips dyed with henna, orange and dark brown. Smiling and emitting ear-piercing ululations, they took Eve by the arms as she asked about Morad's whereabouts, and they changed her into a dark green dress picked out from the large green gift trunk painted with golden mosques. They attempted to pattern her hands with black dye while two women sang in antiphony at her feet, one extolling the bride's beauty (highly exaggerated), the other praising the groom's handsomeness and wealth (slightly underestimated), while the child-bride wept in large sobs which shook her small frame; calming only when Morad entered to sit beside his bewildered sister, only to devastate her that he could not stop the marriage because Father swore to kill her if she didn't go along with the wedding. She cried until she could cry no more, and a different panic set in, whenever Dhalia and Latifa moved her from room to room she could not feel her legs, they belonged to someone else—it was not she that was walking, the eyes looking back at the bustling crowd, all gathered to celebrate the 'happiest day of her life', did not belong to her, she felt removed and though she knew her body was moving, her soul seemed to lag behind and follow it around instead of being in one being. She never knew a wedding could be this noisy and disarraying. They changed her again into a different dress, this time made of white fabric with three scalloped black frills going across the chest with tinsel green, pink, gold and silver flowers stitched into them, the remainder of the bodice and beginning of the skirt were white and the frills with tinsel flowers followed in layers from the knee to the hem; they sprayed her hair, neck and chest with so much Rumba perfume her head began to ache; Aunt Hasna brought an incense burner full of glowing, hot embers and broke pieces of bukhoor into it and with perfumed smoke anointed Eve's body, dress and hair until she coughed before they took turns incensing themselves; they piled heavy gold around her neck and pinned the rest to her chest, attached jewellery to her fingers, wrists, and she sighed as they affixed large, heavy earrings to her earlobes, as if the weight added to her already burdened soul, the dangles of golden beads of which tickled her neck every time she breathed heavily or turned her head. Women and girls took turns energetically dancing in pairs while the other guests threw money from over their heads. Mother returned to the room and leaning against the wall put a shaking hand to her own mouth and squeezed, her face red with sorrow, she cried painfully and it would be the only sign of regret she ever showed towards her daughter's marriage, giving Eve a faint glimmer of hope, maybe her mother would not allow this travesty to continue, but instead she told the others to get her ready. Latifa tied a large, flowing shiny black pleated skirt around Eve's waist; Dhalia threw over Eve's head a black hood made of the same material, it too was large and flowed overlapping her waist. Eve cried and trembled, still hoping Morad would prevent the marriage.

And now Eve stood facing Father beside the car, begging him with all her love for him, with all his love for her, for the sake she was his daughter, for her life, not to let this happen. But with a threat issuing from his mean thinned lips he and Morad lifted her and bundled her into the car next to the groom. And as the car rolled on, she saw her brothers standing under a rickety shelter with Mother behind them, all three crying; and she watched Father crying so hard his head and shoulders bobbed violently, and the two black chiffon veils sewed into the hood of the sharshaf fell lightly over her face and black tears rolled down from her kohl-lined eyes.

CHAPTER TWO

THE ULULATIONS AND CELEBRATIONS WERE IN FULL SWING, THIS was a smaller wedding in the upper southwest village from Uncle Suleiman's house in the mountains. Amongst the guests Eve, Dhalia and Latifa along with their younger sisters all sat on the rim attached to the wall which was for sitting on inside the rooms of houses in the mountains. Eve was amazed by the skill in how people built their houses using nothing other than what the mountains provided of rock, soil and timber, but she was also amused they made the 'sitting rim' only ten centimetres wide running along one wall of the room, and very low to the ground—it made a very uncomfortable sitting no matter how small your bottom, if only they made them as big and comfortable as the duckas, wide platforms running along the length of the outside walls used as seating. The bride was in her twenties, round faced, round bosomed, her golden coloured dress adorned with the single necklace she had been gifted for marriage, and with her dark eyes she glanced at newlywed Eve with her choker and many necklaces, her hands covered in coruscating gold; secretly the bride wished Eve hadn't come because the guests were assembled around Eve and staring at her as if it were her day; in all honesty Eve wished she hadn't come either because she didn't like being stared at and she was experiencing the psychological consequences which would ail her for the rest of her life: attending weddings, no matter how happy she would be setting off, where ululations, crowds and all the pomp and custom that goes with it threw her back into a state of dread, fear and fret as if it were happening to her there and then, followed by weeks of depression; the same if she ever caught a whiff of Rumba perfume, which they had almost drowned her in on her wedding day, now always gave her a terrible headache and all the symptoms of distress and alarm; even Yemeni songs she recognised as being played in the car which took her back up to the mountains while Adam tried to hold her hand or touch her arm, while she veered away from him towards the door not straightening up until she felt he had retreated a little into his seat, could offset headaches, uneasiness then melancholy. When they had reached the mountains, she had been carried by the groom in areas too difficult for her to walk along, the pitch black of the night disturbed only by a few lanterns to light the way, but everything had been a terrible black in her eyes even when the sun had been ablaze. Uncle Suleiman stood in front of the room that was to be Eve's, holding a sheep by its neck which he dragged towards them. Adam had stroked the sheep from its head to its tail three times, Uncle Suleiman gestured her to do the same so she lightly passed her hand over the neck before he dragged the poor animal along the path where he handed it over to the waiting Abdulrazaq; and Eve realised both she and sheep were being dragged along paths they did not choose, handed over to strangers, and things they did not want to be done to them would be done by these strangers. For dinner they had been served the cooked liver of the blessed lamb.

The current groom was around the same age as the bride and they were seated next to each other proudly, though not talking to each other. Eve recalled how on the second day of her wedding, which was as crowded and noisy as the first, people were shocked when she refused to sit next to Adam and instead had sat with the younger cousins and joined in playing their hand-games, until under threat of fetching Father she sat on the bed. Adam shifted nearer to her and held her hand, fondling it, caressing it, holding it tightly in his to show all the shocked women, those with gaping mouths and those speaking in lowered whispers from behind their hands, that everything was fine between groom and bride.

Currently, a relative of the bride entered the room and from underneath a pillow pulled out a large square white cloth, blemished with blood stains—the Subhiya (meaning 'the morning' with a feminine term); it was such a big deal in these villages proving the

21

bride had been a virgin on her wedding night: the groom after breaking her hymen and having slept with her would go outside the room and shoot a single shot into the night air, signifying two things at once: she had been a virgin and he was able to perform his manly duty; the Subhiya would be presented to her family whom arrived the morning of the second day of the wedding, and shown to the guests in the afternoon. The bride blushed and lowered her head with a coy smile (attagirl!), she had done her family proud.

On Eve's second day, she had been sitting in bodily and emotional pain when Latifa came rummaging around and asking her about the Subhiya, Eve didn't understand, Adam responded telling his sister where to find it. And as she pulled it out, smiling as she spread it open, Eve shuddered, upon this garment she had been raped the other night, she had fought and screamed, but it was a futile fight between a slight fourteen-year-old girl and a fully-grown man; he had stuffed the end of a shawl into her screaming mouth and continued to rape her until he came. With him still inside her, she cried atop a pink silk duvet covering several plush blankets on a high bed, surrounded by blue pillows with woven red roses all around her; red, gold, green and silver foil Christmas decorations hanging from the ceiling above her were the only witness to the rape. Uncle Suleiman had rapped on the door, but it was too late, not that he would have stopped it because to him it was just marital consummation. With Adam holding the door ajar, Suleiman ignored her plea for help, grave faced he kept his eyes on the floor and avoided looking at her, but he spoke in a serious tone to his son and pointed in her direction and shook his finger at Adam and the door was closed. From Adam's wish to approach her again later, with her fiercely shaking her head and saying "No", Adam would look towards the door as if contemplating what his father had told him, before backing off from her, she deduced Suleiman had warned him not to be too rough or excessive with her (if only from the beginning, Eve). Now Latifa was throwing her blood-stained Subhiya at the guests, the younger girls ducked and giggled too shy to look at it; the married and older women had two different ways of viewing it: the younger would hold it up spread out and comment to the lady sitting beside her as if studying a strategical map of attack; the older women would hold it with reverent delicacy, and their faces would show spiritual emotion handling it as would a devout Christian allowed to touch the Shroud of Christ (for God's sake put it down and out Eve's sight).

Adam would continue to rape Eve following their wedding night, but she sometimes feigned being asleep with her face and body as close to the whitewashed wall as she could get. And when she eventually fell asleep he haunted her in dreams: she dreamt of awaking in that bed, she would look to her left where Adam was sleeping and look away; the second time she would look at him, he had turned into a hideous werewolf whose red-iris eyes would suddenly open and she would scream. She then awoke and looked to her left and he was normal, only to look again to see his werewolf face awaken and she screamed again—then she awoke for real in the bed, breathing fast and shaking. She turned ever so slowly to look to her left where Adam slept, afraid to see a monstrosity—he wasn't— and she watched him in his deep sleep, his thick eyebrows, white skin and dark moustache: handsome, but he was a man: what was wrong in him so that he could marry a child? A stranger at that. She had seen many young women, beautiful women, why hadn't he chosen one of them as a bride? She sat silently in bed, afraid to go back to sleep in case she had the same dream; afraid to move, to avoid awaking the sleeping beast because if it awoke, he would want something from her.

He could not get enough of her and made love to her day and night, touching every part of her pubescent body with his muscled masculinity, his lusty caressing, his passionate gazes, nuzzling everything he could nuzzle, kissing everything he could kiss, and there wasn't an inch of her he could not reach. He stroked and held fistfuls of her lustrous soft hair inhaling it as if it were the essence of life, and he howled and grunted with pleasure making love to her, and though she an unwilling party at the start, the pain lessened day by day, her fighting ceased and her body disintegrated with flesh melting pleasure, only to be replaced by disgust and self-loathing when it was over. He spoke and she couldn't understand a word he said, she in turn tried communicating in English, but alas he did not speak the language of the lass. But through touch and senses they communicated in carnality through their skin, through bodies intertwined into one, where the throb and thrust of his lust tingled and sent waves throughout her as her tight body drove him to face convulsing orgasms, and when it was over he could not understand why she turned her sorrowful face away from him, pushing her face and body against the wall, her hand touching the cold whitewashed stone as she wept.

With every reason and emotion she could mention, she beseeched her parents to return her to Wales: this was not the life for her, nor was it fair she be forced to marry Adam, how would she ever get into university if she missed all this time from school, if *they* didn't want to return they could allow her and her brothers to leave, but all failed to evoke compassion in her parents hearts and they departed towards The Dibt with unhappy Sami and Yusef in tow, leaving Eve with her in-laws and only Morad to talk to in the grey mountains. And as her hope ebbed of an immediate egress, the solution presented itself effortlessly.

"He's going to take you with him," said Morad smiling, seated between his sister and Adam on the bed, "You'll like it in Saudi, it's much better than living in the mountains."

Eve smiled at Adam, or rather she smiled through him as she stared at the way back home. She wasn't going to Saudi, but as far as the British Embassy then no more husband: you can't marry a child—it's illegal.

CHAPTER THREE

THE ARGUMENTS BEGAN AS SOON AS ADAM ANNOUNCED HE wasn't leaving towards Saudi until he obtained a visa for his wife to accompany him. Suleiman's cheery face darkened, its creases seemed to develop creases, this would not do at all. Seated upon the ducka, he leant back against the wall and pulled the hem of his wrap-around skirt further down his tanned leg, his scowl getting tighter the deeper he sought a solution. He was the oldest in a long line of brothers, he had remained in the village all his life while Father, his brother through breastfeeding (if a child suckles from a mother's breastmilk a minimum of five sucks, he or she becomes a full sibling to all her offspring), went off to Britain; his brothers Salem, Nageeb and Yahya all went to work in Saudi; Faris remained in The Dibt at Nageeb's request to look after both their lands and families and he would pay him an allowance—it turned out to be a pittance and poor Uncle Faris would live impoverished for most of his life; but Uncle Suleiman had chosen to remain telling the rest of the brothers he would take care of their land and houses and be there for their families, but the brothers hadn't requested him to—the women would find ways to cope, as always. Father was his only brother to provide him financial support, but it was few and far between; Father had also sent him large amounts of money to buy more land and build him a modern house, which Uncle Suleiman chose to ignore, instead building a simple house for himself and spending the rest with nothing to show for it; his brothers in Saudi would only send him money if he repeatedly asked for it, whether in writing or telephoning from Taiz, which he couldn't afford to travel to most times so he had had to work as a foreman and builder whenever the opportunity presented itself in the mountains, and the rest of his income was from selling excess fodder from the harvests. Now God had sent him a gift and his son wanted to take it away, he simply would not allow it to happen.

"She'll leave you!" Suleiman shouted at Adam "She can go to the authorities and they'll listen to her." Adam, facial features clouded with irritation, remained unresponsive, staring at the vista of mountains ahead.

"She's not like our girls," shrieked his mother, Kareema with her oversized oily white cheekbones and gash of an unusually wide mouth, "Do you want her to leave you?"

"I want her with me," said Adam passionately "I love her, she's my life!"

"You can leave her here with us," said Suleiman "Like all men do! When you come back she'll be right here, waiting for you."

"I can't live without her," said Adam shaking his head slowly "I can't."

Suleiman had not taken into account his son's enchantment in such brief a period with a child-wife. This would not do at all. "She married you by force," said Suleiman spreading his hands upturning his palms as if opening a book to show evidence, and upon seeing a ripple of doubt run through Adam's face he knew this was the line to pursue, "Do you think she loves you? She'll run away as soon as you get there!"

Adam looked down at the ground, he couldn't deny she had been made to marry him, made to bed him, and though she seemed a sex kitten in bed, there was an accusation, a dislike in her eyes when she looked at him. Throughout the evening Uncle Suleiman endeavoured to drive this point through his son's troubled, love-sick mind and aching heart; and when he had finished with him Eve was no longer to leave, but Adam went to bury his sorrow along with his throbbing tumescence into her unwilling little warm body.

*

"MY SISTER HAS TO BE SERVED," SAID MORAD "SHE CAN'T CARRY water or firewood, she doesn't bake bread or grind grain and she can't shepherd."

"We'll serve her, but she has to learn." said Suleiman.

"She can't and don't forget," said Morad "It was part of the conditions you presented when you asked for her hand in marriage. It was *your idea and offer* that you would all serve her before my father would even consider marriage."

"You do everything for her and I'll send you an allowance." said Adam.

"You never sent a Rial all these years?" said Suleiman, feigning sternness.

"You fetch water, wood, serve her," said Adam "And I'll send you a lot of money every month, but I don't want her to lift a finger."

Suleiman smiled and laughed: what he had planned for, hoped for, was coming to fruition. He agreed they would serve her every need and let her live without needing to do a thing; Kareema eagerly agreed to this too, she wanted an income from her son, instead of having to hear her sisters-in-law count and list how much they had given them over the decades. This had been Suleiman's hope since he first set eyes on her: Adam would marry her and she would live with them as per tradition, and now his son had a wife, he would have to send money every month for her to eat and drink; now he had a delicate wife unaccustomed to this life whom needed to be served, he would have to send money for the whole family's needs. All those years his eldest son spent abroad had brought him nothing but bitterness: Adam wasn't like his peers of filial sons of the village whom worked and sent home the majority of their wages for their families to be fed and clothed. He had sent them nothing. Now Suleiman was eager to enjoy the money; he would not need to find labour in nearby villages, he could buy qat, which he loved more than food, as frequently as he liked; both Kareema and Suleiman would finally feel the benefit of having a son in Saudi like the other families in the past. They would no longer need hand-outs and help from his brothers, who had all been in Saudi until recently, and no longer go receive from their wives. He had a treasure trove in human form, this precious girl from Britain. When he had watched her a few months ago, sitting there reading her book, looking at the horizon, innocently smiling back at him, he was seeing wads of Rials, bundles of qat, easy food—and she was the guarantee.

*

TWO GREY HOUSES STOOD SIDE BY SIDE, SEPARATED BY A NARROW passage between them, the First House situated at a slightly higher level than the Second House. The former belonged to Father though Uncle Suleiman and his family were still living in it, it had been built before he left to Britain many a decade ago; its exterior was a dark weathered grey and had six huge rectangularish slabs of stone leading up to its arched wooden door with a large bar of metal nailed in its middle and a circular cast iron ring for a handle. Its internal walls were brown and had never been whitewashed, it contained a front room called Bawaba, a middle for cooking, and two inner rooms which resembled catacombs the ceilings of which had not been plastered with the brown mud-dung mixture so snakes were often seen weaving between the timber. The Second House was made of new granite, its rooms were rectangular with a Bawaba, a square middle, a dead-end corridor used as a pantry and two rooms adjacent to it—one was Dhalia's the other Eve's. The rooms were whitewashed and bordered with brown on the bottom few inches of the wall, the girls' rooms were carpeted with linoleum—Dhalia's black and white, Eve's green and gold. Its exterior had been decorated with white lines gridding the natural lines of the rocks used to build it, though built with Father's money the deed showed it belonged to Uncle Suleiman, Father and family would live in it for a while when finally returning to live in the mountains, but currently only Eve and Dhalia occupied their respective rooms. Two young trees (an acacia and Thorn of Christ) grew four yards away from the door, three feet behind the trees stood a low wall; the space in front of the wall where the First House ended, until where the wall behind the tree started had no obstruction and you could see the side of the abandoned house below them, part of the yard of the old house and the same view of the winding path disappearing behind the hill. In between, a breath-taking vista of the mountains and land on all sides; you could see chains of mountains and in the far, far distance peaks of lower mountains and stretches of flat land, minuscule in the distance, disappearing into the west horizon. Under these trees Eve now stood, looking towards the west path hoping her family were on their way back up to the mountains. Adam had departed in fits of tears and love making, Eve had remained dry-eyed throughout. Morad had left not long after and there was no consoling Eve, she loved him dearly, though her Arabic was improving, he was the only person she could really talk to and now he had gone. Eve, though intelligent, was rather naive, and the duplicity of adults surrounding her disturbed her. As soon as her brother departed, at night and every night Uncle Suleiman would place a big padlock on the large outer door of Eve's room and a smaller padlock from its inside, and he kept the keys on his person. Why? So you can't run away came the reply; sure she had to be harried to be married, but she was no Houdini. It was, of course, ridiculous she couldn't walk properly and without assistance in this rocky mountainous terrain, she wouldn't make it a thousandth of the way before being hurt by a nasty or fatal fall; if she tried to follow the car route, also rocky and winding, she would be caught up with in minutes at the speed she could go in what was considered 'easy' terrain. Kareema's kind attitude toward Eve dropped like a mask after both husband and brother left, Eve had sensed something lurking behind this lady's visage, but she never imagined a person could hate to this degree. The cruelness, rudeness and aggression she showed towards Eve, especially when Uncle Suleiman wasn't around, reduced Eve to a shaking, snivelling heap before she would run into her bedroom burying her face into a pillow, not understanding why this woman hated her so much when she had done nothing to be treated in such a manner. Kareema would throw insults at guileless Eve whom couldn't understand all the swear words but could feel the vibe of hostility, truculent Kareema never tired, but Eve never retorted (not even when her language was good enough to do so). If Uncle Suleiman was generous enough to send for fruit and vegetables with the vehicles, with money Adam had left specifically so Eve could be provided with edible food (her already slight figure had thinned greatly since arriving in the mountains due to lack of necessary food types), Kareema kept it under lock and key only letting Eve have a hard piece of bread (made of corn, sorghum or bulrush millet or white flour which she found difficult to swallow, even chewing it left her jaw aching) and tea, and sometimes not even that, then Kareema would have a jolly good meal with her children including Dhalia. Eve would pass in front of the First House or enter it and find them eating, they would frown, become silent and continue to eat without asking her to join them. Eve wouldn't sit down without an invitation, they had made it clear she was not welcome. Waiting, sitting quietly on a bed she stole glances at them as they hastily and greedily ate, the children sometimes snatching a morsel out of the other's hand, it was like watching animals fight over food, they didn't need to. How she wished they let her sit and eat, even a little. As time went by she cared less for food, you could get used to being hungry; her only wish and concern was to get out of this place, but the way they treated her, excluded her, did hurt her feelings. She wasn't a toughened adult, although they kept saying she was now a woman, but a teenager and had never been disliked and mistreated back home. But worse than starvation were Kareema's prompts and directions of her children to be rude and cruel to Eve, with which they had to comply (Kareema was a physically abusive parent) or be beaten; but they soon returned to their innocent and innate kindness, sometimes going out of their way on their return from shepherding to bring her gifts of figs and sugar apples to make it up to her. When guests arrived Kareema's kind and daughter-in-law-loving persona took over her features with such fluidity you would never guess the heavy and consuming hate she harboured for the young girl. Eve believed by being polite and pretending everything was alright would cause Kareema to be kinder, that or she would soon be leaving the mountains anyway. During Suleiman's absence in The Dibt for weeks on end, when darkness fell Kareema told Eve stories of her own and people's encounters with demons and monsters, emphasising it actually happened as if it were her duty. As if the realistic worry of venomous snakes and insects which were around the houses and regularly entered were not enough of a threat, Kareema also informed Eve of how the spot where Eve's room was built had been a demon-possessed area, where hideous demons had many a time been sighted. Eve would find her lantern mysteriously empty of fuel with the telltale signs of kerosene dribble running down its base; Kareema would not allow her to refill it so she would lie on her bed in the dark, alone and afraid, recalling the details of Kareema's bedtime story.

The in-laws had renewed Father's prohibition to the car owners that Eve not be allowed to board a vehicle unless accompanied by Father or Uncle Suleiman. When people became sick, and the sickness did not heal itself but chose to linger, those whom could afford a seat on one of the vehicles would have to go to Taiz because there was no hospital here, to put it in a nutshell—the only thing in the mountains were the people, their houses, land, cattle and the mountains, but Eve was never taken to Taiz no matter how ill she became; instead Uncle Suleiman would send for medicine using someone else's prescription if what they had suffered sounded close enough to her symptoms (sound medical practice), or he just borrowed any leftover pills from them. She missed her brothers in the Dibt and Morad in Sana'a deeply and had no one to speak to in English so she endeavoured to learn Arabic so when Adam would return she would be able tell him she wanted to leave both he and the village; she studiously copied out Bundar and Dawood's school text books, she didn't know what she was copying and may as well have been drawing patterns, but she continued to fill pages upon pages; she asked nine year old Bundar to teach her Arabic so both he and Dawood began with the alphabet, and while they taught her the correct diction of letters and words they laughed at her pronunciation of letters "kha, haa" and "taa" which they found particularly funny and entertaining, bringing into her room every cousin, brother and sister, asking her to repeat them so they could laugh too. It wasn't long and she could read what she was writing, she could pronounce it, but unfortunately not understand all its meanings. But at least she could talk in Arabic and understand what was said, mostly, and she noticed the words used in books were different than those used by the village people. Her Arabic wasn't perfect, she still pronounced words and letters incorrectly, but she could be understood, most of the time. Her in-laws and visitors roared with laughter when she feminised a masculine noun or vice-versa and found the way she talked highly amusing.

At first, she could feel time running past; she knew it was almost time for the final exams and felt great misery over an academic year lost. Soon, she lost track of time and date.

Dhalia or Suleiman would reply with a Hijri date or a month in their agrarian year according to the stars, where they needed to recount previous months on their fingers while their eyes looked upwards calculating, before telling her what month it was in that year, but it gave her no bearing on what date it was currently in the Gregorian calendar; but the unsettling disorientation she felt of time flying by was more distressing while being adrift.

A cow bellowed in the distance, Eve got up and went to the front of the house to watch women and girls driving cattle or carrying water in twenty or fifteen litre plastic containers on their heads, some carrying double, returning homewards and she wished her Uncle would let her go out to walk, maybe she would learn to be as nimble as they in this harsh terrain and have a chance at escaping, but this was not the case so she went from in front of the Second House to in front of the First House to behind them, watching people and animals with more freedom than she (they had all ignored and found amusing when she read to them Her Majesty's request inside her passport which Uncle Suleiman now withheld).

*

ALTHOUGH IT WAS HER PRISON, EVE COULD NOT HELP BUT BE TAKEN by the beauty of the village, its scenery and people. The houses were beautiful castles, built from rock broken from mountain itself, adorned outside and in; they kept their dwellings and person immaculately clean, with the exception of malevolent and malodorous Kareema. Men walked around in white dresses or wrap-around skirts and shirts; older men wore shawls wrapped around their heads around a small circular cap. Women wore colourful dresses made of fabrics brought from Saudi Arabia, silk, lace, brocade, velvet, sequinned and synthetic nylon fabrics. Married women, whose husbands were not abroad, put on their golden jewellery after lunch. Women smoked their dresses and hair with burning incense and sprayed perfume over their body and clothes; they did not wear skimpy clothing, but looked more magical and majestic in their swanning dresses and light, floating head veils hanging off the backs of their heads than princesses from Arabian Nights. The adults showed affection for the young, and the young respected their elders, the elderly were held and treated with the highest esteem and kindness. People visited each other and special visits were made to the sick. When a family member returned from abroad, gifts of fabrics, perfumes, cotton sheets, blankets and other materials were shared with the whole family, extended family and neighbours. Grain, flour and money were given to the poorest families whom had no breadwinner, and those without enough land to feed their family off, and it was given without making a show of it: for charity to be correct your left hand must not know what your right has given. There was hardly ever any trouble, people didn't fight with each other—except when gossip reached those concerned the adult women did quarrel standing far apart, one in front of her house and the other on a lower path, separated by a hill, and when women argued they enhanced what they had to say by clapping when shouting and holding their waist while tilting it to one side when proving a point, so much posturing was involved while quarrelling it was almost an art. When serious disputes arose and talking it out with each other didn't bring around a resolution, both sides would choose a villager as an arbitrator and accept his rulings—they were very harmonious for a whole community ungoverned by any kind of authority or police—traditional honour-based systems were working fine, their AK47s and Jambias were status symbols and adornment only. People sat down wherever they met each other to chat. The women and girls were natural beauties, but they came to Suleiman's house to stare at Eve and adore her; they wanted her silky skin, her shiny, long, thick unbroken hair; they wanted to be precious like her—sitting on a bed, not doing any hard work. They often came admiring the princess in the prison, and could not understand she was struggling from the harshness of the mountains; what they coveted as a comfortable life, to her was suffering. In spite of being forced to remain in the granite gaol, its nature, people and their traditions had a magical element to them which she grew fond of, but her want to leave still increased with every day.

The peoples' lives were dominated by what laborious chores needed to be done in order to survive, if in the cities it meant working to earn a living here it was still hauling water from miles away, girls and women carried containers on their heads, the boys and men carrying the plastic containers upon their shoulders; grain harvested from the land was stored for consumption and sowing; the grain manually ground on a rectangular stone similar to the metate and manos of the Aztecs; girls and women cut shrubs, trees and anything that could be ignited and carried it home bundled into a burdensome large faggot for firewood; bread was baked in an open top circular oven; most families had a milking cow, milk was left to curdle overnight and in the morning the yoghurt was poured into a dried hollowed squash that resembled a pumpkin with a long neck, it would be hung on the bed from the protruding handle of an axe and the mother would shake it vigorously until the fat separated, collecting the butter from the top and the rest would be diluted with water to make it enough to share; families whom didn't have milking cows were given a can of buttermilk every morning from the nearest relative or neighbour; women, girls and young boys took cattle, sheep and goats out in the morning and afternoon to graze within the borders of their respective lands. Even with the arduous work, with the hefty loads supported by slim necks, their smiles beamed when passing each other, or they stopped to chat as if the onerous weight was a feathered hat upon their heads.

After lunch women visited each other and men gathered to enjoy chewing qat bought from the only person in the villages whom traded in it. He could be seen appearing on the path far away, a tiny ant carrying a huge crumb, bent underneath the heavy sack of qat he carried from village to village, selling to men. Suleiman always watched out for him like a hawk, getting excited as soon as he saw him; sometimes he couldn't wait until he arrived and took off running to meet him on the way as such was his addiction to qat. He loved it and now he had money, he spent it on bundles and bundles of it; he even stopped ordering fruit, vegetables and rice so he could buy more qat. He would find any excuse to justify chewing in the morning: "I need a boost so I can break stones for the new room." he would say, or "I'm not feeling well, I need a little qat now to revive me."

He even tried to get Eve to chew, giving her a whole sheaf of the best quality qat. He smiled as he openly, and shamelessly, expressed he wanted her to 'get used to it' so she would 'ensure there was always money for qat'. Unfortunately for him, she was not skilled in the art of qat chewing: instead of keeping the chewed leaves in her cheek and spitting out the excess of strong juices, as they all did, she chewed the juicy, bitter-sweet dark green leaves and swallowed them, juice and all, like a panda. Her speech became feverish and she could not sit still, until afternoon came and she bawled in agony, writhing on her bed as her kidneys became moving rocks, tearing at her sides. The in-laws, Uncles and Aunts gathered in her room trying to figure out a cure, and whether they should send for her father, just in case she died, as she cried in pain then suddenly knelt on the mattress, eyes bulging, pointing to the opposite wall screaming: "There's a zebra in my room!"

They forced Canada Dry down her throat believing if she belched she would become better; they sent for fresh milk from a neighbour, saying it would soothe her stomach, but the only relief she found was after throwing up from being forced to eat a bitter, foul paste they made out of brown crystals mixed with a brown paste an old lady had provided.

Dhalia and Eve spent a lot of time together as both were at home most of the time. Eve spoke passionately about life in Britain and things in the world, and although Dhalia was intrigued, she didn't believe most of it: how could water and gas for cooking come straight out of the wall? Dhalia was pretty and young, her warm white skin, snub nose and full lips contrasted with the gold teeth she had chosen to have. When Eve and her family had first arrived at the village Dhalia had been peeping from the gap between the door and wall of the Bawaba and darting backwards not wanting to be seen; when she had hurriedly put on her best dress, jewellery and lined her eyes with kohl she had come out to be introduced; she was a slim lady in her early twenties, her hair parted from the side, a veil hanging to the back of her head; hair, hands and chest covered in ornate gold and her dress black and white sequinned. After kissing hands with the family Morad had said something and she laughed, showing two pairs of incisors, on the bottom and top row, covered in gold; she was so shy she didn't say a word and scurried back into her room, her behaviour gave the deceiving impression of a demure, kind character (she was anything but!) and with the years and help from her parents would drive a rift between Morad and his family. Morad provided her with everything and he loved her, she had more than what most women got from their husbands, but, unfortunately, jealousy ate her from the inside out. Envy she couldn't even mask, it clouded her face and changed her expression, pouting her pretty lips into an ugly frown every time an attractive girl or woman visited; if someone had more gold, or a bigger necklace than she—hers covered her whole chest up to the middle of her abdomen. Jealous Morad loved his sister. Jealous her sister Latifa had a loving husband, although her own loved and spoiled her. Other than occasionally treating Eve badly for no reason at all, she was pleasant company. Like Eve, she hardly did any work at all being able to pay her family instead of working and also paying some poor people in the village to fetch water when she couldn't be bothered. They talked and laughed a lot, except when Dhalia was in one of her moods, ignoring Eve completely, not even responding to a 'good morning'.

*

"HOW MUCH DID YOU BUY HER FOR?" ASKED A STRANGER THAT HAD passed by as Dhalia, Eve, Aunt Fulla, Aunt Khatima and Kareema sat in Dhalia's room passing the hot afternoon.

"Sixty thousand Rials, and that's not including what was given to her mother, or for the gold and clothes." replied Kareema proudly, both women turned their heads to look closer at Eve.

"You didn't buy me!" exclaimed Eve a little too shrilly, insulted by this outrageous lie, "You took me away from my family, but I wasn't bought!" the women laughed.

"Eve, girls are sold by their parents to the groom." said Fulla.

"We paid your father and mother their rights." said Kareema.

"This is wrong," said Eve "You can't sell girls! You can't pay money for somebody's life. It's disrespectful. And I wasn't bought!" There was a gasp and a little more laughter.

"If a man marries a woman and doesn't pay her family, then she's a slut or cheap." they all replied one after the other.

Eve explained why it was insulting to women, *to them*, to allow a price to be placed upon themselves, but all the women in the room laughed, smiled, and gave her looks which said she didn't understand; they were convinced there was nothing wrong in being paid for their own and daughters' marriage. In fact, the more paid, the prouder a woman could be; and if, God forbid, a woman married for no money, then she must have a defect, physically, mentally or morally. Eve found herself in a strange parallel world where wrong was right. How could they not see, being paid money for their marriage was like prostitution or slavery? And why if a woman married for no money was she considered a slut? As the women continued gossiping, Eve pondered why her mother-in-law had lied about paying for her to be married to their son. Yes, her father had forced her into marriage, but no way would she believe he accepted money in return and she wondered when she would see him again and prove to all those present today that she hadn't been sold. Grandmother Haleema arrived, and joined in the discussion, the others filled her in and she turned to the stranger and added:

"Eve's father asked for one hundred thousand when Suleiman requested her for his son, but Suleiman said his son didn't have that money...then Abdulkareem's son from over Maghaliba approached and said he would pay that and more for her hand, but Suleiman became angry and swore he wouldn't let anyone marry his son's bride. Abdulkareem's son offered one hundred and fifty thousand and Suleiman reminded her father that they grew up together and told him never to forget the bread and salt shared between them. Her father then asked for two hundred thousand and Abdulkareem's son agreed and Suleiman stormed off in anger because Adam had made an oath that he would never marry until you came to the village or he went to Britain since the day he saw a photo of you, which he stole from your grandfather, he kept it in his pocket kissing it all the time until it disintegrated," said Grandmother Haleema, puffing at the kooz, glancing at Eve and smiling kindly, "Of course your father was only teasing Suleiman, he rejected Abdulkareem's son's offer and Abdulkareem's son went off with a blackened face. He helped Suleiman out when he said his son didn't have enough money to pay what he was asking for so he accepted the sixty thousand Rials, but you were worth so much more, *and* they would have paid!"

"What's wrong with sixty thousand?" retorted Dhalia with a soured expression, snatching the pipe with both hands from Grandmother Haleema's lips, "That's how much her brother paid my family for me.", insulted by Haleema's mention of how much 'worth' Eve could have yielded. Eve didn't care how little or how much it was in their eyes, putting a price on a girl, or woman for that matter, was demeaning (in the future Eve would encounter a more demeaning experience when an educated female colleague would both calculate the exchange rate in US dollars and be aghast at the low price in comparison to what city dwellers charged).

It was dispiriting to hear the terms used in front of her by family and friends when a wedding occurred, or by strangers passing asking about her or Dhalia: they would say 'bought' 'sold' 'paid' 'she's worth it' 'they didn't pay enough'; it upset her it was used by the women themselves, as if they were talking about goods or cattle. When it was mentioned a father of a bride-to-be had asked for more than what was usually paid, one of the older women would remark: "Why? Does she have two vaginas?" Eve found it all extremely offensive, but the village women took pride in being paid in exchange for. What Eve discovered upset her more: they paid the father of the bride the bulk of money, the mother of the bride for her breastfeeding, and the bride for her marriage; it explained why she had found wads of money in her wedding trunk among the perfumes and clothes. In addition, it was custom on the wedding day the bride doesn't eat or drink until the groom gives her money before each action, she makes a number of stops on the way to her new home and sits on a rock, recalcitrant, not continuing on the journey until money is handed over; she isn't supposed to sit on the bed, take off her clothes until he hands over more money; she is not to have sex until the groom gives her even more money before the act itself, and this is payment other than that prepaid for her betrothal. To appalled Eve it sounded like prostitution, from paying the parents until the final moment, instead of the marriage being about love and the wedding event being full of romance. But it was normal here and nobody saw any wrong in it; and this is what Eve couldn't understand at the beginning, but with time she could see though it was wrong in her western opinion, this was a tradition gone on for generations. It was not degrading or insulting to women and girls here, but they took pride in what they were 'paid' in dowry and for everything, the more they were given—the more it showed respect and pride; there was no demeaning intent behind it, only Eve came from a world away and could not see it from their perspective, just as they could never see anything from hers. People didn't have income and lived on next to nothing so receiving money from a daughter or sister's marriage was valuable and helped, but more importantly it was a custom which signified honour and respect for the bride. A bride receiving money could use it to buy herself more gold, other than the gold gifted as part of her dowry on her wedding day, which in turn could be sold in the future if she needed to. It was not viewed as a sale and the bride had choice to agree or refuse the suitor, and it was categorically not a sale even if, unfortunately, they used sales terms when talking about marriage, it just came hand in hand with getting married. But forced marriage was frowned upon as they viewed it as unjust causing the bride misery; yet they didn't do much to stop it from happening when it did occur.

Adam sent his father large amounts of money monthly in order they serve Eve and keep her in the village. He also sent Eve five hundred Rials, she didn't know why he bothered as there was nothing to buy in this village. The only grocery shop sold white flour, tomato purée, matches, a bad tasting artificial juice full of harmful ingredients and preservatives, probably banned in most countries, which burnt the back of your throat instead of quenching the thirst; biscuits which sometimes tasted disgusting and disintegrated in the mouth upon entry, cigarettes (for men only (although both genders smoked the kooz, a spherical vase shaped sheesha made of clay with bamboo cane for pipes)), gum and Canada Dry. The only things Eve bought were gum, sweets and pop for herself and in-laws, and condensed milk for tea, and they cost next to nothing. As Eve drank from the bottle she wondered how people, especially children, grew up without regularly eating fruit, vegetables, meat, milk and dairy products as this produce was mostly non-existent in these mountains or extremely, extremely rare. Despite there being cattle and poultry, they were only slaughtered for a big event or the arrival of a guest. The milk wasn't enough to be drunk purely and cheese only came after long periods of time when cheese sellers came, travelling from different, far away regions, and so too was scarce; you could see them coming in a line from the farthest path in the mountains, sun-burnt bone-thin men and women carrying multiple layers of huge circular trays on their heads, filled with bowls of three types of cheese: creamy and soft, salty and hard, smokey and firm, all delicious, hoping they arrived at your village with cheese left to sell. They dressed and looked different than the mountain people too: the dress higher at the waist, the skirt and sleeves angular and not flowing; the head veil tied differently. The language though understandable (with great difficulty) was in a different dialect, but they told the most interesting stories and brought news from far away. As Eve contemplated how children developed normally, she began to worry if her own growth would be stunted, she missed real food.

It wasn't long before her in-laws began requesting she fetch water and wood, they wanted her to grind grains and bake bread.

"You have to, you're a woman," said Suleiman to the girl "I want you to start fetching water from the well and shepherding."

"I can't. Your son's sending you money to do these things and you're keeping me here against my will."

"You're not leaving this village. You will live and die here," he said, smiling as sweetly as if he'd said something kind, "This is the land of your father and grandfather! Go pour water in the bucket for the sheep and goats to drink from."

"Uncle, I can't carry heavy things."

"Alright, I want you to grind grains and bake the bread for lunch today."

"I can't do that either."

"How are you going to live? You have to work!"

"Uncle…you know, if you don't like it that I don't work—let me leave…"

"If I let you go, Adam will stop sending money. You're staying here forever."

Eve didn't believe this, she would be out of here as soon as she found a way to convince them to let her go or how to run away.

But it wasn't true, that she did no work at all: she always tidied and swept the floor of their house for them using a brush which was a branch from a date palm tree, when rancorous Kareema allowed her to; she even swept the outside of the house; she cleared the nits from their younger children's hair and removed the lice eggs and their parents gratefully announced it was the first time the children slept in peace without fidgeting and scratching; she washed the pans and pots, and always offered to wash her mother-in-law's clothes, when Kareema was in a good mood she handed over her dirty clothes with a reminder not to waste the water. She churned the milk, made tea and kneaded dough. The only work Eve ever did for herself was clean her room and wash her clothes. It wasn't as if she hadn't tried to do the hard stuff they were requesting of her, it was just physically impossible for her to accomplish. She had gone a few times to the well with the girls and needed help to get there, slowing them down; after being much admired by the congregation of women and girls around the well, they had put a ten-litre container full of water on her head, an immense pressure pushed down on her neck as if it was ready to snap and they had to remove it for her to stop screaming in pain, it left her unable to move her neck properly for days. She had tried to bake bread, but couldn't get her hand inside the oven from the immense heat. And she had no interest in herding sheep, goats and the cow and there was not a snowball's chance in hell to induce her to try mucking out the cow and goat's stables, she suffered more than enough from the fetor of Kareema and Huda, Suleiman's twelve-year-old, after they had performed this task, and that's after they had washed completely and thoroughly, it still stuck to them like—well, a bad smell. The rest of the day she spent reading school text books and sleeping, having read her lone English book four times and could remember each word of it.

She spoke constantly to Dhalia, Suleiman and Kareema, cogently explaining why she couldn't stay with them; why she had to leave; how she had things to do like school, university and life; how she could not live here, but to no avail. Sadness overcame her at the futility of her discussions, explanations—pleas. She entered her room, bolted the door from the inside, then lay on her bed for three days without leaving her room; not answering their calls and banging on the door.

*

UNCLE SULEIMAN SHOOK HIS HEAD AND LOOKED TO SALEM WITH an expression of quiet complaint, both standing outside the Bawaba where they could hear Eve. Breaking the only two cassette tapes of outlandish music her brothers had brought for the trip hadn't stopped her singing and dancing in her strange way. Uncle Suleiman could not yank out of her memory and soul, nor erase from her tongue the music she loved and grew up with, and now they were shaking their heads again as she '*Karma Chameleon*'ed and '*Dressed for Success*' laughing and dancing inside her room alone with as much energy as when she had been surrounded by her friends, enchanted in the zone of music while her body and heart danced. Smiling, her heart was as hope filled as the songs she sang. But (*my goodness!*) when she sang '*Those Were the Days*' her soul brimmed so much she could feel it trying to burst through her skin and felt for sure she would be back home soon. Suleiman sighed, telling her off to stop singing in English and stop dancing as if she was having an epileptic fit hadn't discouraged her, and he didn't want to beat her so he left her wanting to '*Break Free*'.

On a balmy morning Eve watched Suleiman as he broke rocks from the boulders next to the Second House using a big pointy sledgehammer. Despite being extremely thinner than all the other men he was strong from a lifetime of hard, manual work. When she bored of watching him she returned to the front of the Bawaba looking to the west, wondering if her brothers and parents were thinking of her, hoping they were on their way up to the mountains to take her away and back home. It seemed she could never give up on hoping they would still be protective parents although they had put her into this predicament. She wondered if her friends and teachers were looking for her; were the police searching for her and her brothers? Did they even know they had been taken to Yemen? Her thoughts were interrupted by a thud behind her where Suleiman had carried quite a big rock and dropped it to the ground.

"I'm building a bigger room upstairs for the men to sit in when they come for qat chews," he announced "When Adam comes back you'll be a bride again, and you can sleep upstairs when the weather's hot...get out of the way!" he shouted pushing her. They both jumped onto the ducka as an orange-brown snake passed below them and away, towards the area Suleiman had been working. "It must have come from the hen house." he said. He took a look and returned.

"You'll be a bride again when my son comes back, and the upstairs room will be ready for him. I've been thinking about this a lot and have discussed it with Kareema—I'm going to change your name for good luck and maybe you'll be tamed! I'll change your name to Haynama!"

Haynama meant 'madly in love'. If couples didn't get along well, they changed the name of the wife; sometimes they changed the wife's name on the day of marriage as a precaution, after consulting with a sorcerer, they believed if the couple's names did not align with each other's stars it caused them marital problems.

"My name is Eve." she said rather sullenly, they were always implying there was something innately wrong in her character, though she was good-natured and gregarious, and it hurt being constantly made to feel you were abnormal and needed to be corrected, little did she know this was just a gentle beginning of how they would work on her. She went to her room, closing the door behind her and threw herself onto the bed. It was taking too long and she still didn't know when she would be leaving the village and returning to normal life.

CHAPTER FOUR

D HALIA AND HUDA TOOK TURNS LINING THEIR EYES WITH KOHL from an engraved silver bottle, the lid of which was the rod applicator. Outside the Bawaba Aunt Ethe, an older version of Mother with wrinkled olive skin, surrounded by Suleiman's younger children (Fardoos, Akram and Eman), waited impatiently for the older girls, calling out for them to hurry up. Eve stepped out of the Bawaba in a red dress coloured with golden leaf prints, her red scarf covering the top part of her hair while the rest flowed freely from the back of her head to her waist, the white trousers trimmed with flowery black thread patterns covering her legs. Aunt Ethe frowned, told her to stop being improper and ordered her back inside to put on a long petticoat and head veil. It amused Eve how much they wanted women to wear: since returning to the mountains, she had been regularly inveigled to put kohl in her eyes, henna and black hair dye patterns on her hands; which they adorned themselves with by spreading around the finger tips and top half of the palm, the back of the hands decorated with patterns; they had drawn flowers and sorghum panicles among wistful twists on the back of a weeping Eve's hands on her wedding day, but as time went on she seldom relinquished to their requests. They wanted her to wear a small scarf covering only the back of her head, on top of it a head veil; underneath the dress, trousers with tapered legs that became such a mass of material as it widened around the backside, resembling an elephant's behind if you held it up as Eve did when first given a pair after all her western clothes had been torn up, and then it cinched at the waist by elastic band; and as if this hot air balloon, as Eve also liked to call it, was not enough coverage under the dress they also had to wear a long petticoat under the dress, longer than the dress, over the trousers. How lighter these women would feel going about their work, hard and heavy in itself, without being burdened by all these extra garments representing modesty and supposedly purported to keep them chaste. Didn't they realise if a woman was ready to give herself up to passion, all these extra garments needing to be peeled off only heightened the fervour of the foreglimpsed action? Eve refused to tire herself with all this additional attire, wearing a scarf indoors only if men not from the direct family arrived and wearing a petticoat and head veil only when going to visit, when she was ever allowed out. But it wasn't how she dressed which earned their disapproval: they constantly scolded her about how she walked, why she smiled so much and there seemed to be nothing about her that they didn't want to change.

"You bounce when you walk, it's not normal, stop bouncing."

"Your breasts go up and down. It's rude! It makes men look!"

"The bras I used to have are too small to wear." she said.

"Why do you slink like a cat? Are you a cat? Stop walking like that!"

"Why are you always smiling? Don't smile when you speak, they'll think you're looking for a lover or smiling at him!"

"Stop smiling all the time, they'll think you're crazy!"

"Stop sitting and playing with the children—you're not a child you're a married woman!"

The women repeated this to the young girl over and over again so she tried to be rigid when she walked, but they asked her why she was so stiff and eventually her walk changed. They incessantly praised her exquisite beauty, fondling her face, hair, hands, feet and skin as if she had come from another world, but constantly disparaged her character and behaviour—so they revelled in her beauty, but reviled her personality: her ways of speech, her curious questions wanting to know the origins of words, customs, sayings, questioning whether things were right or wrong, wondering how they had arisen, and her unwillingness to comply with their full dress code and traditions made her iconoclast in their eyes. Everything spontaneous and

45

normal, they made her come to feel was shameful. She knew there was nothing wrong in the way she walked and smiled, but the constant chiding of shame saturated words drilled into her head from every direction made her feel improper. Though she couldn't do anything to stop her spontaneous smile, every time she did she was guilt-ridden, as if she had done something unseemly. And there was nothing they could say to stop her from talking and playing with children closer to her age, naturally, they always attracted each other's company no matter how long the adults upbraided her to behave like a woman and that she was now a woman because she had married.

Eve drew the line when they requested she conform to extraneous rules: they wanted her to wear old women's clothes, she wasn't supposed to wash every day or put on perfume. Eve did wash and wore a different dress every day, and absolutely refused to wear old women's clothes—why should she when she was young? They always scolded her, Aunt Ethe and Kareema, but mostly Aunt Ethe. Grandmother Haleema, visitors and passers by all had something to say: her husband wasn't around so she should not wear nice clothes nor perfume; she shouldn't wear dresses of which the fabric was mostly white—what would the people say? Eve did not care. People would think she had a lover because she was always dressed so nicely and smelled so sensual while her husband was away. Eve wanted to know how was she to meet men or any lover to reach her, would he turn into a sheet of paper and slide between the gap of floor and double padlocked door? Eve do not talk like this! Their constant criticism and gratuitous conditions were starting to tell on Eve's patience, with a sigh she routinely replied washing and perfuming were routine and mundane; yet they continued for several months to haggle her until finally, and mercifully, they gave up.

*

UNDER THE SHADE CAST BY THE MASSIVE BOULDERS, DHALIA AND Eve were seated outside in their favourite spot watching people and animals moving around when two hawks flying in the sky caught their attention, they seemed to be dancing as they crossed each other diagonally. Eve left Dhalia in the shade and followed them behind the house. The hawks continued their dance then separated; one went far off into the sky, while the other flew over an outcrop of rock; the distant hawk returned at speed in a straight line. Eve watched as the closer hawk skimmed down, almost touching, mountain face and grabbed a fat rodent, then both perched on a rock and ate their prey together.

In licorice black evenings they sat outside the Bawaba, chatting, but if men arrived wanting to speak to Suleiman all the women and children had to go inside. The children fell asleep on their beds or mats on the floor, Dhalia would finish her last smoke and only Kareema and Eve remained awake. From inside Eve listened to her Uncle Suleiman give advice to Abdulrazaq about his land inheritance while a dozy Kareema gurgled at the kooz. He encouraged him to forcefully take ownership of the land in dispute against his half-brothers and sisters; he even told him what to say to justify doing so; he championed him, he was in the right and they were in the wrong. She heard Abdulrazaq leave full of confidence knowing what to do now that helpful Suleiman had shown him the way; she admired her Uncle's wisdom in inheritance rights, which was pretty complicated when family members were many. It was only minutes and Abdulrazaq's half-brother arrived, seeking guidance from Suleiman about the same dispute, this half-brother represented the remaining brothers and sisters all on the same side against Abdulrazaq. You can imagine how shocked Eve was to hear Suleiman tell him they were the rightful owners of the land and Abdulrazaq had no right to it; he went on to advise them what to do. Why was he doing this? Pitting family against each other, causing a divide which lasted for life and far beyond the physical land. Surely, in the weeks that followed, a great upset happened over the land and the brothers came to hate each other. And still they came night after night, separately, to Suleiman to advise them; not knowing he was spiralling them into greater problems. Tired of all the quarrels and hostility, Abdulrazaq suggested it was time to go to the Sheikh in a faraway land, to get him to resolve the issue between them, but Suleiman advised against this: why would he want to go the Sheikh? Yes he would solve their problems, but the Sheikh would want slaughter of sheep and goats, to be fed and given qat to chew for him and his entourage, and worst of all the Sheikh gets to take his pick of the best land from the whole inheritance once he resolves the issue for them. Why do this when he, surreptitious Suleiman, could resolve this issue, he understands inheritance and all he would ask for is a couple of thousand Rials and a bundle of qat, wouldn't that be better than paying for all those expenses and losing the best piece of land to a stranger who would tell them the same as Suleiman? Of course, Abdulrazaq was grateful and insisted Suleiman become the peace maker, but Suleiman requested Abdulrazaq talk to his brother so they both come to him requesting his intervention. So the meddler became the mediator—the double-dealer to make the deal. The issue wasn't resolved until after many bundles of qat were chewed, over many afternoons; and even after the matter was settled, family ties were cut forever: Abdulrazaq and his children became the unwanted family members, he and his siblings never visited each other anymore no matter what the occasion; he even banned his children from speaking to their aunts and uncles, and they were equally unwilling to talk with their nieces and nephews. Eve watched the ugliness play out, disgusted by Uncle Suleiman's devious ways in creating problems between families, and profiting from it too. Had he done this to survive when he had no regular income? But what was his excuse now his son provided for him? Needing money could never justify what he did, Eve could not ignore the elation he was in while explaining to Kareema everything, after they left him with their heads full of ideas and bad intentions. Couldn't he see the pain she saw in Abdulrazaq's sisters' faces when they complained to him and Kareema about the vileness of their brother's inappropriate and aggressive behaviour while Kareema plied them with more gossip and ideas against Abdulrazaq? Did he feel no remorse over their suffering? No wonder some of the village people had nicknamed him 'Two Evils'. But he was always so nice to Eve; although he was her captor, he was never cruel or rude to her like his wife. He always tried to make her laugh; when there was something nice to eat, he would ask his children to slow down so she could get her share because they fought and gobbled everything quickly while she ate slowly and had too many manners than to fight for her share; when he went to the far away Wednesday or Monday Market to buy nails and sheets of aluminium, or special qat, he brought her sweetmeats and savoury snacks which she shared with everybody, and he did care for and love her, almost as if she was one of his daughters (an old woman with a wart on her nose feeding a caged boy delicacies, before igniting the oven). Before leaving the village, visiting other areas, he would ask Kareema to be nice to her, to not let her sleep in the dark and make sure she eats (not that it made a difference to Kareema). When she became ill, he instructed Kareema to spare her a little milk while it was still warm from the cow so she could try to eat. She knew *he* was the reason she was being kept in these mountains, but she couldn't deny he was the kindest soul out of the in-laws she lived with, and could see two sides to him: the cunning, greedy person who pitted people against each other for his own gain which she didn't like to see. Then the warm, paternal side that was caring: she felt she was one of his children.

On a calm cloudless day Eve's family returned to live in the mountains permanently. They were to live in the Second House while Suleiman still occupied the First House, until they were ready to swap. She hugged and kissed Mother and her brothers, but only formally kissed hands with Father—the paternal affection and protection she had grown up with in Britain, were gone, and she no longer trusted him. Reunited the siblings were reinforced by each other's hopes and will to leave the mountains, their hearts ached with homesickness while they discussed possible ways out and upon trying to reserve seats with the vehicle owners they were faced with the reality they were banned to get on the cars without Father or an Uncle, and came to the conclusion walking was impossible as the boys had discovered through several attempts one could die in the desert, and the mountain range was very distant from the nearest city and perilous; all they could do was persist in their attempts to convince Father, and if any opportunity to get onto a vehicle arose— they would jump at it.

*

WHEN A BABY ANIMAL WAS BORN THEY ALL COOED, OOHED AND aahed admiring it, then praised God venerating how perfectly He created everything. Then a few days after a girl was born they would circumcise her, and the procedure wasn't even done by a doctor and in unsterile circumstances. A lady, Purple Dress Lady actually in this region, would go to the newborn's home and using a used razor blade, cut off the clitoris and labia minor completely. Why would they mutilate the poor girls you may well wonder as did our squirming Eve; well, they believed if the genitals were not removed the girls would always be craving sex and become wanton; they also believed it looked prettier without 'all those things dangling from it' they would say curving their hand downwards like a claw and wriggling their downturned fingers as if the uncircumcised vagina were a tentacled and excited squid. Mother had mentioned to Aunt Ethe and Kareema, Eve's lack of circumcision, and it is unclear how it came to be the topic of discussion while a group of visiting women were gathered in Dhalia's room one afternoon. A short lady with stubby fingers entered the room while they talked and laughed, her name was Ba'aad Sabih, a widow who'd brought up her three young children, now adults, alone; her husband had died from rat poison he purchased from the Monday Market and tied around his waist, somehow, as he walked back home, the powder escaped the package and he had inhaled the poison. Everybody in the villages feared her 'evil eye', they believed if she envied something she saw with someone else, something bad would happen to that person or thing such as falling sick, getting hurt, burning or breaking. Another thing they dreaded was her foul mouth; the thing she talked about most was the act of sex, but with much vulgarity and with the purpose of embarrassing her chosen target of the day and she would use any person in front of her as a subject for this topic, often finishing her visit by grabbing one of the ladies and pushing them backwards, lifting their legs above their head and pulling off their trousers, exposing them as underwear did not exist; she always did this to the middle aged women her age and never to those much younger or much older. Nobody found her funny, but an offensive harridan and people hated her busy bodying into others' business.

"Is it true Eve isn't circumcised?" said Ba'aad, as if other's private parts were for public perusal. The room fell silent as heads turned towards Eve, mouths dropped open while some women covered their mouths.

"None of your business." said Eve.

"Her mother told me she's not circumcised." replied Kareema.

"Your son must be upset!" said Ba'aad.

"He's never complained. They do it all the time so he must be happy." said Kareema, the women laughed, Eve frowned, appalled by the conversation.

"Adam *must* be upset," continued Ba'aad "I heard it feels like gravel underneath the man when he bangs a woman who isn't circumcised." she made vulgar hand movements with her palms while staring directly at embarrassed and riled Eve whom looked away.

"Ignore her," Aunt Khatima whispered into Eve's ear "She's a horrible woman whose husband died before she'd had enough shagging."

Some women whispered, glancing at Eve as if it were unacceptable to keep the organs God gave you. Thankfully, Ba'aad turned her attention to a pretty young wife.

"Haseema, how's your husband?" said Ba'aad training her beady eyes upon the brown beauty, "Is he keeping you happy in bed?"

"Did they wean you off milk with sex?" Haseema retorted. While the women laughed at the joke, Ba'aad left. Mother arrived shortly and sat next to Kareema on the doorstep. The women asked her why Eve hadn't been circumcised; she explained it wasn't allowed in Britain; Father wouldn't let her take her to the woman whom circumcised girls secretly and he forbade the woman from coming to their house—he said Eve would die if somebody just cut her with a razor; Father had even tried to bribe the GP, but the doctor refused (Eve is eternally grateful to you Dr. Dessi!); there was gasping from the congregated ladies, and with eyes open wide with warning and worry told Mother this meant Eve would always be 'hot' that she 'will never have enough or be satisfied' no matter how much and hard her husband rubbed her. All during this awkward conversation Eve alternated her gaze from wall to wall, to floor—they didn't know what they were talking about, but there was nothing wrong in having a healthy appetite in her view.

Eve noted from her observations and interactions with people that females were viewed as lesser beings, they were also to blame for anything that went wrong. Well, they did circumcision removing a girls' genitals completely, boys were circumcised for cleanliness only—if their argument to circumcise girls was to lessen the possibility of fornication and adultery then why didn't they chop off the boy's penetrating penis instead of just circumcising the foreskin for health reasons, did it not take two to tango? Boys had a less than rudimentary school which taught the basics, but for a girl to learn to read or write meant a shame associated with a belief she would find a way to get letters to and from lovers; many families didn't allow girls to wear watches as it would aid her in knowing what time to get to her lover (totally ignoring the fact many adults and children alike could tell the time of day by shade); whenever there was an affair going on, and there were constantly affairs being gossiped about (which belied female circumcision wasn't really working), the shaming and tittle-tattle was mostly about the gentler sex being a slut; when Eve pointed out that it wasn't fair to always blame the female partner and questioned why they always excused the male, Grandmother Haleema replied with a proverb "A man is like a dog—if the woman says 'gis, gis' (the sound to encourage dogs to come near) he will come to her lap—if she says 'haay, haay' (she lifted her arm in a warning gesture to the imaginary dog-man) he will run away with his tail between his legs"; Eve quietened thinking how their excuses for men allowed the male (to follow on with their analogy) to continue putting his tail between female legs, especially if they thought body mutilation was the solution when it was a moral one they should address with both genders.

Though it was assumed girls were taught to be subordinate to boys, it wasn't the reality at all as Eve witnessed in Suleiman's house and other places she visited, brothers and sisters played and fought as siblings do around the world, both genders were loved unconditionally and fairly received in equal amounts whatever was available to give; it was only in matters of when marriage was forced, especially when it was a girl-bride marrying an adult that the inequality stood out. Although many grooms chose brides they knew or had encountered, some marriages were arranged with the bride and groom not actually knowing each other until after the marriage, and (believe it or not) most lived happy, loving and content marital lives, but if the young woman did not like the man asking for her hand in marriage, she could refuse the proposal and that was the end of it, in fact it happened quite often, families didn't force their daughters into marriage—it hadn't been the whole village whom forced Eve to marry, it had been her parents and in-laws. Divorce initiated by a woman was taboo, unheard of in these villages so when Eve asked for divorce she was met with aggression in consequence of her abominable request and was treated accordingly as what she asked for was shaming both families, and they would never allow it to happen. How she longed for her big brother to return, believing after he saw how much she had suffered, how her mind was still set on leaving the village, he would take her back home.

The hubbub of many differing conversations rising in volubility from inside the Bawaba, which had been crowded with a flash flood of visiting women, reached Eve and her brothers whom favoured the peace and quiet outside in the white sun. An old man with a cane approached slowly and seemed to be just passing along the route. He stopped in front of the ducka and looked at them obliquely.

"Are you the children that came from beyond the sea?" he asked.

"Yes." replied Yusef.

The old man sat himself down between them.

"You need to go back to where you came from…you will not be able to live here." he said with much gravity.

"Our father won't let us. Can you talk to him?" said Eve.

"Your brothers can go back, but you're no longer their daughter—you're a man's wife, you belong to his family now." said the old man.

"I've heard when it rains and everything's green, that it's nice to live here." said Yusef.

"Who told you that?" said the old man "Son, when it rains and it's green—it's nice for cows to live here. If your father knows what's best for you, he'll take you back to Britain." And with that he got up and slowly carried on along the path.

CHAPTER FIVE

U NDERFOOT WAS COLD GREEN GRASS—A LITTLE MOISTURE came through the fabric of her light pink dress when she lay down and with every breath inhaled the dewy moistness. Eve's smile beamed as she twirled under golden ginkos, and stood inhaling the sweet air under the crimson-purple liquidambars. Among flashes of her friends' bright smiles and moving speckles of sunbeams coming through the foliage, Eve talked and laughed discussing anything from religion, to science, to fashion, music, back to what they wanted to be when they grew up, with her friends; jumping from adolescent subjects discussing it in a manner bordering adulthood, to fluidly returning to their carefree and pre-adolescent attitudes towards everything around them. She opened her eyes to see the whitewashed walls and timbered ceiling of her room on top of a hard grey mountain; memories were sweet, but contrasted to the harsh reality surrounding. No amount of rationale would bring reason to her parents, they had tried and failed; patience until she was allowed to leave seemed to be the only way. Friction was worsening between Yusef and Sami, easily irritable and readily angry, their fights were no longer boys messing around with each other, but they began to actually hurt one another whereas their sister had become inward and reticent.

Dhalia's screams were unbearable, Eve held Dhalia's hand comforting her while they both cried, never had Eve seen a person in such pain, nor a woman go through childbirth, and when she had been asked to fetch more pillows she'd returned to find Dhalia pushing again, legs wide open, where her vagina was supposed to be had been replaced by a swollen red bulge with a wet dark thing filling it painfully, and the same amount of pain was mirrored in Dhalia's face. It looked it was about to explode. The pillows fell to the floor from Eve's hands, it was the unsightliest thing she had ever seen. She closed her eyes and returned to her room, but could not unsee the pain of childbirth. Woozy, and worried over Dhalia, she lay cringing on her bed. Shortly a baby was crying. Grandmother Haleema appeared at the door, she was Suleiman and his brothers' stepmother, and Arif and Yahya's mother; she had been the second wife, both her husband and his first wife were long dead. Plump and brown skinned, she was a cheerful old lady; she loved to smoke the kooz more than anything in the world and had the habit of not paying back money she borrowed, often avoiding the paths which took her past her lender's house to avoid them, when cornered into repaying she'd count out the notes into your hand with a look of pain and insult on her face, as if parting with the money caused her physical harm. She was a tailor and also one of the only two midwives in the area, it was a reassuring presence that a member of the family could deliver the baby, although she had no medical training nor could she save a person's life, she merely received the newborn and cut the umbilical cord, tied the end still connected to the placenta to the mother's thigh with a piece of thread and waited for the afterbirth to follow. "You have a niece!" she said.

Smiling, Eve jumped off her bed. She peered at her baby niece and kissed her.

"She'll be pretty like you." said an exhausted Dhalia.

Haleema puffed smoke out of her mouth and said: "You'll have a baby like this soon. God will give you one."

Eve's face froze and she immediately returned to her room, knelt on the floor in front of the bed and put her hands flat together: "God, please, I never want to have a baby, ever. It's too painful—don't give me one."

Dhalia and her mother were a little upset because it wasn't a boy: it was preferred to have a boy as a first child and it was preferred to have a boy over a girl in general, something else Eve couldn't come to terms with. Aunt Ethe arrived the next day, the whole family was joyous to have a newborn child in the house. Suleiman entered the room and kissed baby Suha, swaddled in Mother's lap; Grandmother Haleema and Aunt Ethe smiled as they asked him if he now believed you could love a grandchild more than your own child.

"I don't love Dhalia's child," he said smiling "When Adam has a child I will love him!"

The older women laughed, and Mother kissed baby Suha and said to Dhalia: "Don't listen to him, he's only teasing you. *I love her.*"

To Eve's shock, he went on to say in terse verse:

"The son of a son is your son,

The son of a daughter is not,

The meat of a lamb you can eat,

The meat of a dog you cannot!"

Dhalia scowled and Eve was deeply affronted her niece, and entire gender, had been compared to dog meat, while the older women only laughed.

Aunt Ethe had brought with her frankincense and myrrh: translucent yellow, white and brown crystals; a big pot of hot coal was brought into Dhalia's room everyday. Frankincense was poured onto the embers and it fizzed; thick woody, spicy smoke filled the room, leaving everyone and everything aromatic. They used frankincense to remove the odours from babies' clothes, also a small piece was heated in oil and the oil dripped into one nostril to unblock a baby's nose when it had a cold. Myrrh was given to the mother to chew or drink, to alleviate the pains following child labour. Eve asked why they didn't just use the usual perfumed bukhoor which women anointed themselves with, Dhalia replied it didn't remove the smell of baby poop and went on to show Eve the difference after smoking two washed rags, one with frankincense and the other with bukhoor, and while the bukhoor smoked rag still retained the weird aftermath smell of the baby poop, the one smoked with the frankincense was only fragrant. She handed Eve a pile of rags to smoke and Eve smiled, pouring some frankincense onto the embers, no wonder the Three Wise Men had gifted this to baby Jesus, a present both valued and practical.

The seventh day a party was held in celebration of the newborn called (wait for it…) 'The Seventh'; a lamb or goat was slaughtered and rice was cooked for the guests; women came carrying baskets of grains, juice and *Abu Walad* biscuits and after kissing hands with the mother, some visitors opened the baby's palm and placed money into it or under her clothes. Dhalia counted the money and put it underneath the blanket each time; Kareema and Mother counted the number of packets of juice and biscuits before emptying each basket. Dhalia later explained to Eve: this money and presents given to the baby are called a 'debt', and the mother has to count and remember who brought how much and it obliges the mother receiving to pay it back or even more when the person who gave it has a marriage or newborn in the family; the same tradition was observed at weddings. The funds allowed the women to afford necessities, luxuries or medical trips.

The following day, Purple Dress Lady came to circumcise baby Suha, only eight days old. Eve, upset they would do this to the poor baby, tried talking Dhalia out of it, but they said it was according to Islam girls are circumcised, which wasn't true, Eve had yet to learn the people in these mountains didn't really understand their own religion and much of what they did was made up of their own superstitions, and traditions from generations past and pagan; almost everything they did came from ancient times, and as the world progressed around them in other rural areas and cities, their ways remained untouched because of the remoteness of the area and their unwillingness to change. It seemed the men whom went out into the world when they wanted, brought no progress back. Purple Dress Lady got up and pulled out a used razor blade from her pocket wanting to start.

"I've told you about sterilisation and diseases that are fatal," Eve whispered into Dhalia's ear "You can't let her use this on your baby, don't let her cut her, please Dhalia, *please.*"

"We'll buy a new razor," said Dhalia "Mama, shout for Dawood to go to the shop."

"I washed it with soap after I last used it," said Purple Dress Lady, begrudgingly stuffing her fibrous hand back into her pocket, "You didn't need to send for a new one."

Purple Dress Lady and Grandmother Haleema seated shoulder to shoulder took turns smoking the kooz a puff each in turn. Purple Dress Lady passed the pipe to Haleema.

"I'm here to circumcise the baby," she said, eyeing Eve, "And when I'm finished I might as well circumcise Eve…what do you say? She can be normal like all the women." The women in the room laughed.

"Let her circumcise you," said Haleema "You'll be better in a few days and before your husband comes back."

"Show it to me." said the violet vulviolator gathering her skirt around her and getting up towards Eve as the latter hastily jumped off the bed.

"Keep away from me!" said Eve holding her finger towards the woman and left them, locking herself inside her own room.

*

SAMI MADE FRIENDS IN THE BARIH VILLAGE, WHILE YUSEF BECAME fond of Aunt Hasna's company spending most of his time there with her daughters Mirsaam and Aziza, and the rest of his time sitting alone in Eve's room listening to Arabic music on her stereo. Eve spent her time bettering her Arabic through an English-Arabic thesaurus sent by Morad, and although it helped her greatly, most of the words were not understood by the village people. Father had installed a large metal, and padlocked, trunk which four people could comfortably be seated on into Eve's room for safekeeping; only he and Yusef had the keys. What did it contain? She asked. Books and documents, important documents, came the reply, which was sort of a lie as it contained much more than documents as would be discovered.

One morning Yusef couldn't be found, it was assumed he'd gone to Aunt Hasna's earlier than usual. While Shathi played with Suleiman's children in the afternoon (Aunt Hasna's fourth child whom had a peculiar fear of getting married (he was still only six) which had occurred to him the day he'd cupped the drooping, wrinkled cheeks of an old lady and asked her why her face was such a mess; the old woman replied it was marriage that made her so shrivelled; little Shathi shrieked and cried, as he ran towards his mother's safe hug, that he would never marry because he didn't want to wither like Obeida!), and with motherly concern for her favourite child Mother asked him if Yusef had breakfast and lunch at their house.

"No," replied Shathi "Yusef didn't come to our house today, he's gone to Taiz, he's gone to get…" the little boy stopped abruptly with the worried look and guilt of having given away information he knew was supposed to be a secret.

Eve and Sami looked at each other, their hopes high, he must have gone to get the police to save them. Excited throughout the evening, Sami and Eve whispered to each other, talking about seeing their friends again and finally resuming school. The car wouldn't return from Taiz until the next morning, it seemed too long to wait, but they fell asleep happy knowing that, at last, they were to be rescued from this harsh place they just couldn't adapt to.

CHAPTER SIX

E VE AWOKE AT THREE A.M. TO THE SOUND OF FATHER AND
Mother arguing with someone, assuming it was the police she
hurriedly put on a dress, but was severely dismayed upon
entering the Bawaba to find only her parents and brothers. Yusef was
back, with a box beside him. Sami seated on the end of his bed
looked perturbed as Yusef hadn't gone to Taiz to save them: he'd
gone with Uncle Salem to buy presents and gold to get engaged to
his daughter Aziza. Both parents argued long and hard with Yusef
and he responded back angrily.

"Where'd you get the money from?" demanded Mother. Yusef
ignored the question.

"You stole my money?" said Father rather alarmed and went
running to Eve's room.

It transpired Father not only had books and documents, but also
piles of wads of money in the trunk; Yusef having the key helped
himself with encouragement from Aunt Hasna; Father accused Eve
of allowing him; Mother came to her defence: Father had given the
key to Yusef so he shouldn't blame Eve for Yusef's actions. But Eve
was already: a) offended by Father's accusations and; b) also hurt by
Mother's repetitive red-faced exclamations of Yusef being too young
to marry—for she had participated in forcing Eve while much
younger after all. Father and Mother stormed out of the room in a
tempest of vexation at their son's impudence, and anger towards
Salem and Hasna's underhandedness in ensnaring him. An insulted

Eve asked Sami to help her get the huge, heavy box out of the room, but he declined saying Father would beat him, Eve though understanding his predicament expected him to have more backbone. Nevertheless, she opened both sides of the door and with great determination and difficulty pushed and pulled at the heavy box, using all her might to lift one end she raised it onto the doorstep then pushed at the other end until it came down into the square middle between her room, Dhalia's and the Bawaba. When the box was in the middle of the middle she could no longer make it budge.

"Take your box Dad, it's not in my room anymore!" she shouted defiantly in his direction and took the lantern from the Bawaba and went to the bathroom. Upon returning she hung the lantern on its hook in the Bawaba and dimmed the flame as her brothers were asleep, and walking briskly in the dark towards her room, tripped on Father's metal box and landed face down on top of it having forgotten in the dark she had just pulled it out there. She remained prostrate on the box, laughing at her own antics.

*

"ARE THE POLICE COMING TODAY?" ASKED EVE IN THE BRIGHT LIGHT of day, her hope shining even brighter.

"I didn't go to the police." said Yusef.

"What do you mean?" said Sami "What did you do all day?"

"I was with Salem buying gold and clothes for my fiancé." said Yusef in an unvaried voice.

"You still could've gone to the police or the embassy, why didn't you?" said Eve. Yusef didn't seem to be listening with his glazed eyes staring uninterestedly at the white wall.

"You crazy twat!" fired off Sami "You could've saved us!"

Yusef sat with them for a while then without a word picked up the carton and went to Salem's house, leaving his younger siblings in despair over the opportunity he had lost. They had lost.

Suleiman, Father, Kareema and Mother sat on the ducka outside the First House, discussing with much anger and shock, over many glasses of red tea, Yusef's sudden betrothal to Salem's daughter. Eve, Sami and Dhalia carrying her kooz, joined them and watched quietly.

"You know what she does," said Kareema looking to Suleiman "Tell them."

"Hasna has made papers for him...put him under a spell." Suleiman said gravely.

Father frowning and upset, suddenly grinned at the absurdity of spell-casting, but Mother's crumpled face tautened and reddened, her nostrils flared and she couldn't hide her distress over it being done to her favourite son.

"Nonsense..." said Father.

"She goes to the sorcerer's all the time," said Kareema as Suleiman nodded agreement "She's put people under spells before."

"It's true," added Dhalia in a whisper to Eve and Sami "She even tried to put a spell on Morad so he wouldn't marry me!"

"Why would she do that?" asked Eve.

"So he would marry her daughter Mirsaam." replied Dhalia.

"How do you know she puts spells on people?" Sami asked sceptically.

"Many people have seen her sitting in front of the sorcerer's house or coming back from that route." responded Kareema.

"And we found the burned papers she stuck in our wall." added Dhalia, with an expression of sheer contempt as if she could see Hasna standing in front of her. Eve rolled her eyes, they always looked for an illogical excuse when it was obvious Yusef wasn't coping well with the change of lifestyle; the vacuum left by the sudden absence of education, friends, parental affection (even a sense of direction for one's life) had suddenly been taken advantage of by Aunt Hasna, and through kindness and teasing a normal seventeen-year-old's horniness with the promise of pleasure with her pretty daughter, she had made him feel wanted, given him a purpose and provided him with what he had to do if he wanted to marry.

It turned out their parents' worry was soon to be over: Yusef one day returned to his normal self, with no explanations or regret for his past behaviour. Plonking himself between his sister and brother he monotonously announced he was breaking his engagement to Aziza, then passionately spoke of his need to leave. His siblings corrected him that *they all* needed to get out of here, but the question was how? Eve suggested he ask Salem to take him to Taiz again, but Yusef replied that Salem and his AK47 had not let him out of his sight, besides that Taiz was a huge city and he wouldn't know where to go and would have got lost (if Eve had been presented with the chance she would have weaved her way to freedom without hesitation like a fish taking to the sea). Sami criticised how Yusef had lost the perfect chance to get them all out of this predicament, but it was no use— again it seemed they were trying to move a mountain.

That same week a villager returned from Sana'a, bringing letters from Morad. This sparked an idea in Yusef's usually slow head—he would tell his parents Morad wanted him to come to Sana'a as he'd found work for him, Sami wanted to be included in the plan, but Yusef said it would look suspicious because he was too young to work. It worked, but Father refused to give Yusef any money still angered by his thievery so Mother gave him her three gold bracelets to sell. Eve and Sami drilled and grilled him with all the things he had to do when he got there to ensure their rescue: go to the British Embassy, tell them they were kidnapped British citizens and their passports were being withheld by Father and Uncle Suleiman, that Eve had been forced to marry, to tell them how old she was. They didn't need to tell him anything said Yusef, they would return to Britain together.

"Promise you'll come back for us." said Eve.

"I promise."

"Swear by God." said Sami.

"I swear by God." and with that oath Yusef left the village.

*

SMOKE WENT UP THE WALL, COLLATING IN ON ITSELF AT THE TOP AS if it were an otherworldly creature, and crept along the ceiling and out the door; the smell of hot oil and dough dispersed into the air and downwards, Mother stoked the fire at the landing at the top of the stairs, cooking bread fried in oil. Usually their stomachs rumbled at the smell of the delicious fried bread Mother made, but tonight

Eve and Sami talked excitedly about Yusef getting out of the village and how he would rescue them. It was a hot and humid night, so they decided to sit outside, but the ululating mosquitoes' rude stinging mouths drove them back in.

They waited impatiently. Every time they heard vehicles passing under the house they ran outside to see if it stopped; when a car returned from Taiz before dawn, Eve sat up in bed waiting to hear the sound of police coming to rescue them; sometimes she went to the Bawaba where Sami lay in bed, already awake, his face blanketed by melancholy. Waiting. "He lied." said Sami sullenly and turned on his side.

"He'll come back for us." said Eve.

Any hope of Yusef returning to save them disappeared as months passed without his return.

CHAPTER SEVEN

A LIZARD WITH A PHALLUS-SHAPED HEAD APPEARED ON THE LIP of the boulder outside Dhalia's room, Eve and the children watched in fascination from the doorstep, they called it the Wobbly One because its head shook and nodded up and down when it moved. It raised a foreleg at a pace slower than slow motion and took forever for it to step, then the second foreleg at the same speed—if it wanted to get somewhere, it was in no hurry. Eve watched the mini-dinosaur move slowly, slowly by until it reached the end of the lip, and all that remained was smooth rock, the sloth of a lizard suddenly darted upwards, scampering over the boulder in speed, and disappeared over the top in the blink of an eye.

Sami's melancholy had increased with fits of regular weeping; he bit harshly at his nails taking out against his cuticles the unfairness the world had laid upon him, while trying to figure out how he could use his mischievous intelligence which used to get him in and out of trouble back in Newport out of this current mess created through no fault of his own; and from somewhere in his brain he would be ejected out of the present, and without noticing, without thinking he would tear off a nail and spit it out. Eve, worried and watchful, hapless and helpless herself, watched the abnormal look on his face turn into a sick semi-smile that bordered on maniacal; in a trance-like state he couldn't hear her telling him to stop and she could see his mind wasn't where he physically sat; his eyes were seeing happy things, not happening here or now, but somewhere in the past, or who knows—maybe in an imagined, kinder future. While memories and the present state simultaneously gnawed at his mind, he'd dug into the fleshy nailbed until his fingers bled.

A traveller arriving with letters from Sana'a renewed their hope, Eve and Sami waited eagerly for Bundar to return. But all that was delivered totalled more than devastating disappointment: Yusef, instead of telling them when help would arrive, simply told of his work; they couldn't understand why he hadn't returned with help, nor why he hadn't moved onwards to Britain. Morad's envelope for Eve was thicker than just a letter, there was no consoling her when his happy handwriting and cheery card, which she had assumed meant a belated happy fifteenth birthday, was actually congratulating her on her sixteenth year (he'd even sent two cards recompensing the missed fifteenth's), driving a knife through her heart and twisting it, while two strong hands grasped her brain and squeezed. She had lost track of time, slow days and painfully long nights had turned into weeks, to months and without knowing, *without living,* two years of precious life had flown by while she futilely strove to persuade strangers and parents to allow her to leave so she could live and study. Oh, the way she cried, the wringing pain and wretchedness you would think the heavens would have opened up and God turned back the hands of time and given her back those two years which she agonisingly wanted returned, just as all people suffering injustice wish things to change based on the deep, soul destroying anguish they feel—and never does.

In whitewashed rooms filled with men and boys, in front of boulders so big they could qualify as mountains in their own right, and amidst the din of many conversations, or the lull of quietude when everyone was occupied by their own thoughts, the effect of the difficulties in coping with this way of life displayed clearly on Sami: after staring into the distance far beyond the closest wall opposite him, he would cry irrepressibly; irascible and unapproachable he would throw things at the wall in anger; worst still than his emotional outbursts, he became spontaneously violent: he would be sitting quietly, deep in thought, then he would get up and brutally beat whomever was sitting closest to him, without reason, without provoke; and after calming and returning to clarity he would sit down and cry painfully, begging for forgiveness. Surprisingly, they always forgave him, not only because he was usually a gentle and nice guy, but mainly they excused him because they knew he was losing his mind. You see, there was a saying in this village 'Don't cry for the one who has died, cry for the one who has lost his mind'.

*

THE USUAL AFTERNOON GROUP IN DHALIA'S ROOM: AUNTS HASNA, Fulla, Khatima, Kareema, Mother and Grandmother Haleema were in a buzz about Adam to be returning soon, cracking jokes about Eve getting 'lucky', while the unlucky star was in a cloud of disbelief, he had gone for two years and she was still here unable to make her break-out. She was not prepared to share the room, let alone the bed, with him again, yet she knew it would come to be while she dreaded his arrival. Always one to look on the bright side even if it was black hole staring her straight in the face, she saw it as an opportunity: she would do her best to be loving, nice and obedient and convince him to take her to Britain to live.

Gunshots from in the front of the First House in the middle of the night marked his welcome home; lying on her bed in short white silk négligée (which Aunt Kareema said would send her straight to hell when she'd purchased it from a travelling pedlar) she heard Dhalia greet him in front of the Bawaba, and apprehension rose in Eve's chest and her breathing laboured as the strongest emotion she felt for him overcame her, she hated him, she should show him how much she detested him and he should allow her to leave, but how she felt was never an element of his consideration: being dragged across the ground to be handed over to him, to be dragged across this room to be raped by him—her refusal and feelings had not been enough to deter him in the past. Thick nausea moved like black smoke from her stomach to her chest, she took three deep breaths and there was a knock at the door. Slowly, hesitantly, she walked to it and stood staring at the green metal, ambivalent; with another deep inhalation she slid the bolt open and there stood the man who had raped her at fourteen. He smiled, and she walked back to the bed feeling his smiling presence upon her. Holding her face, he kissed her long and hard, his smokey mouth and perfumed face pervading her senses; she stepped back to break the kiss, he smiled again and went to close the door as she grimaced and wiped her mouth against her shoulder; it was going to be harder than she thought as real emotions surfaced stronger than any pretence could be, but even the negative feelings were already subsiding in the wake of an aroused strong physical need tingling her extremities, aching in her depths. Our yearning couple didn't sleep until dawn, and even then Eve remained awake, her body satisfied, her mind disgusted with herself. Returning from the bathroom, she sat on the corner of the bed, her slim shoulders shiny and moist, hair dripping as she watched Adam content in his sleep; she studied his handsome face, he had money and women found him attractive, and she found herself wondering again why he hadn't married an adult, a willing woman? Over these years Eve had discovered women were eager to be wed bordering on desperation from a young age, they didn't mind if it was a stranger so why had he interrupted her life just to be his pleasure and wife?

They'd hardly understood each other when they had parted so he was surprised at Eve's fluency in Arabic; he was even more pleased with the developments in her body for she had grown taller, still slender, her breasts fuller, lips lusher, her long, thick eyelashes curled upwards naturally and her beautiful brown eyes drew him in, and her insatiable appetite for love-making drove him to euphoric extremes. Now she understood why she couldn't understand him before, more than the others, when her Arabic had been only broken, mispronounced words—he spoke with a Saudi dialect; he would only be here for three months and go back to work in Saudi. Between kisses and caresses he told her how beautiful she was and how much he loved her; he asked her about life in Britain and she asked the same about Saudi; she told him how difficult life here was in the village. He went on to tell her childhood stories about teenage mischief, he even had a surprising tale to tell about the village men and women not kissing on the mouth like they did (which she found hard to believe (especially at the rate of lusty affairs happening)), but only kissed on the cheek and forehead; when she insisted he must be mistaken, he went on to tell her how he and a friend of his used to sneak out at night and through an open window watch one of the men from the Barih village make love to his wife, they did everything, but kiss on the lips (maybe one of them suffered halitosis?). Then how come he kissed on the lips, Eve wanted to know. Watched films in Saudi. Had he seen this she asked, and showed him how to tongue, then laying supine showed him spots where she wanted to be touched and caressed; allowing her body to be her muse she allowed her femininity to teach him how to be gentle, rough, passionate, to take things slow and when to hasten. With all these delightful sensualities they spent most of his vacation in the bedroom, where he learnt to be more sensual, and how to make love in so many different ambiences. Drowning in delight, his body close to hers, he ran his palm up and down her silky arm and looking lovingly into her eyes said: "I love you and what you do," becoming quiet for a moment, his expression became that of concern before he continued: "How do you know how to move like this?"

"What do you mean?" asked Eve, smiling but surprised by the strange question.

"I've never been with a woman who moves like you or makes sounds like you…I'm your husband and I want to know how you know how to do these things." Eve let out a laugh, followed by a childish giggle and replied: "My body's reacting with yours, you're making love to me—it's normal…What you do to me makes me move like this." He became quiet again, his face though not accusatory was troubled.

"Do you mean the women you've been with don't move?" said Eve "That can't be normal."

"They don't move and don't make sounds." he said, his fingers now making exploratory slides up and down along her hip then cupping her hairless hillock. Eve found this hard to believe, for how could something biological and spontaneous be missing from such an intimate activity, but she would be surprised by what she learned from women later.

"Well, you obviously haven't been around many girls," she said "Or you'd find they do move and make sounds." In her mind, she wondered if he was lying for if this self-enforced restraint by women was practised here, she doubted all women he had sexual relations with elsewhere were as animated as an inflated mannequin.

"I've seen women move and scream in films," he proceeded with his curious doubts "But how do you know how to make your body move like this? Did you watch porn films in Britain?"

"*No, of course not!*" she said sitting up, mystified by his question, "What happens is a normal reaction between a boy and a girl." Now *she* was getting upset by his strange questions and what he was implying; how on earth could he interpret physical, sexual reactions as porn? They were not trying to imitate or assemble into impossible positions, but his questions were based on how vigorous and responsive she was to his virility, the tantalising touches she maddened his already excited body with; her lithesome, sliding, interlacing legs and slender smooth arms, the way she pulsated and thrust her pelvis, her strong back arching and pushing her up, the erotic sounds which his efforts stimulated, parting from her sweet open mouth.

Convinced she loved him, immersed in insatiable desire, by the end of the month Adam was intent to seek a new life in Britain with his young wife, where life would be better, and they would be blissfully happy living together (where she could end this sham marriage). He madly enamoured, both their desire to make love several times during the day and night left her slim body even thinner. She would rather not be with this man, but seeing she had no choice, she may as well enjoy the physicality (let the mentality torture you later, dear). Beneath her smiles her brain went over the list of possibilities: leave him as soon as she set foot in Britain and head back to Wales? Or notify police of what happened so they could deal with him and she resume her life—she did have two years to catch up with after all! Or just get to the British Embassy and have them deal with him, maybe she wouldn't have to tolerate him accompanying her to Britain.

Just when things seemed to be running smoothly, Suleiman and co. would show how much sway they held over their son, for the day he broke the news to his parents, all hell broke loose in the house. "I'm going to Britain with my wife!" he shouted and they yelled back they wouldn't allow it; they would put a curse on him; he would go to hell in the hereafter if he took her to Britain and left them. The argument continued for days, but this time he would not listen, he was going to take her out of the mountains for he was madly in love and would not part with her, intoxicated by lust.

Eve startled from her daydream (she was already running over dark green grass; walking down the polished halls of her beloved school) when Adam entered the room, consternation drawn on his face.

"I've changed my mind, we're not going to Britain." he said, lighting a cigarette.

"Why?" asked Eve, turning to him, troubled.

"No reason, I'm going back to my work in Saudi—you're staying here." He paid close attention to her facial expression, trying to detect something he was unaware of previously.

"But Adam, you said you want to go to Britain so we can live together and be happy," said Eve, but the angered look in her eyes gave her real distress away, "Why do you let your parents tell you how to live your life?"

"I have to obey them or they'll curse me, and then I'll be damned for the rest of my life. Anyway…it's not because of my parents, I've ignored what they say," He paused for a sigh "But your father told me everything…"

"But you said you never want to leave me, you can't live without me," continued Eve "That's why we're going there. If you don't want to go to Britain, let's go Saudi instead!"

"Your father explained everything," said Adam, a gleam of tears and tinge of anger ruddying his face, "He said you want to go to Britain because you want to divorce me, and you will divorce me as soon as we get there. *He said our marriage is illegal in the eyes of the English and they'll be on your side*! You were trying to trick me so you could get away!"

"It's not true! I just told you…forget about Britain, take me with you to Saudi." she knew her only shot was to reach Sana'a and the British Embassy.

"Your father knows you well…you're his daughter. He knows how you think and he warned me about what you're planning," he said looking much confused and anguished "I love you, I do want to take you with me, but I can't risk you running away and making me a joke in the village. You're staying here and I'll always come back," he paused a moment then said "Come here…" pulling her closer towards him he stuck his hands up her dress and down her trousers, first gently caressing her smooth buttocks then aggressively squeezing them while his mouth sought the sweetness of her parted lips (great Eve, you've created a sex addict for nothing).

Through eyes steaming with resentment she watched Father and Uncle Suleiman seated on the ducka in front of the other house, whispering together, glancing in her direction where she stood at the doorstep of the Bawaba leaning against the wall; what right did they have to collude against her, keep her from freeing herself from a marriage she had never agreed to and was too young to be consumed by.

Despite continuing to please Adam, her efforts to leave with him to Saudi were rejected as he was now convinced she wanted to be rid of him as soon as she set foot outside the village, and the more she tried to reason, the more she nagged, the worse the situation became between them.

"You can't keep me here!" she said.

"You're staying," said Adam, putting out a cigarette, "And I can do what I like—you belong to me."

"I don't belong to you! I'm not staying here."

"I bought you with my money. *I own you!*"

"You don't own me! How dare you say that?" Eve shouted; how she hated how he said it with proprietary possession. She was nobody's and nobody owned her no matter what cage they kept her in. "Leave me alone. You're sick!" she said and weeping threw herself onto the bed as Adam stormed out of the room.

Going repeatedly to Father for help was as frustrating and futile, asking for a divorce was fiercely rebuffed.

"No woman gets divorced here, it's shameful." Mother said vehemently, getting up.

"You can't get a divorce," said Father calmly "Only men have the right to divorce their wives so if he doesn't want to divorce you—you remain his wife."

"It can't be true," said Eve "Women must have a way of getting divorced if they want, right?"

"No, no," said Father "You're not in Britain where women can do what they want."

"Then tell him to divorce me. *Make* him divorce me." said Eve.

"You're his wife, I can't tell him to divorce you." said Father.

"I'm your daughter," she said. Eve talked at length explaining how unhappy she was, but her parents would not hear of it; they cared more about 'what will the people say?' than they did about her well-being and distress over dashing her chances of ever making it into university.

And no matter how hard and ferociously they argued Adam begged for sex, though he could overpower her he wanted her to come willingly, to enjoy and participate instead of crying.

"Go find yourself a prostitute," she would reply "Like the ones you use all those years you spend in Saudi."

After a stormy last few weeks of his holiday, he left in tears over their parting, with Eve tearful over her remainder but relieved he would no longer be around to pester her. Even his parents were happy with his departure because while he was in Yemen he spent the money instead of sending it to them, curbing Suleiman's qat spending, and Kareema had to be nice to Eve the whole time while he was here; they all ate the same food—no hidden meals and she didn't sleep in the dark. Eve never told Adam how badly they treated her while he was away, but who knows if she had complained of mistreatment maybe he would have been more understanding and been emboldened to carry her away to the west or to the east (either way would have taken you to the doors of the British Embassy) but her naivety in refusing to come between family though both adorable and commendable—was absolutely stupid, for all she wanted was to leave the mountains and resume her life which had been put on hold.

*

A CLOUD OF TINY TAWNY BIRDS FLEW OVER THE GRANITE HOUSE and grey boulders and across the blue sky following an invisible trail, tilting her head to follow them, Eve knew they were probably from a different country, migrating and only passing through.

"We need to get out of here soon." she said to her brother.

Even with Eve providing him with money both vehicles in the village were still banned from allowing him to board, Sami decided to use the unoriginal, but successful method Yusef had employed; he would tell his parents Morad had sent for him to work in Sana'a. Eve burst his bubble pointing out no one had returned from there so there could be no letter. Not to worry, he would take care of it. Yes, but if it worked for him—great, but how was *she* to get out of here? Why, he would come back for her of course! That was exactly what Yusef had said. But he wasn't Yusef, he would get help and return for her, he even swore by God (exactly like Yusef).

Having written a letter himself in his own hand, Eve informed Mother a traveller from Nagraba village had returned from Sana'a and sent word for letters to be collected. Mother, eager to receive news of her distant sons, urged Sami to fetch them. Two hours later Sami returned carrying the fictitious letters which he unashamedly shammed to have collected from the very real Nagraba village, and in two day's time he was ready to leave with his parents' blessings. Awaking at one thirty a.m. Eve went to the Bawaba to find Sami already wide awake and ready, so anxious to leave he couldn't sleep the whole night. Sitting outside on the ducka, Eve wept while she spoke to her brother, begging him over and over again to return for her, and he reassured her every time while tapping his foot nervously on the ground wanting the car to arrive. Through saturnine eyes Eve compared Sami's drastically changed appearance, he'd arrived in these mountains a happy chubby light-skinned fifteen-year-old, doing well in school, both clever and mischievous he'd had a bright future ahead of him; now she stared at a psychologically troubled, bone-thin sun-and-stress dark skinned, tormented soul. Car headlights shone from the nearby village, both siblings snivelled, there was nothing to say in such a painful separation for they had arrived together, but one by one been pulled apart.

"Don't leave me here," she said when they got up and hugged, sorrow pouring out with her body warmth—an eagerness to take flight and anguish over leaving his little sis trembling his core, "You have to come back for me or I'll die."

"I'll come back for you Evez. I swear, I'll come back." The car honked at the top of the north path.

She watched her brother walk away into the darkness, he never looked back. He disappeared into obscurity and she called out: "Come back for me, okay?" but there was no answer, and Eve felt the icy cold touch of how wrong her situation was take hold of her. Against the headlights his wispy figure silhouetted, and Eve was overcome with worry for she was to be left behind in the mountains. That was it! She had every right to leave this terrible place, and made her way in the dark towards the light, stumbling and falling on the rocky surface, full of determination to get in the car. Sami stepped out when he saw her.

"What are you doing here?" said the car owner "Go back!"

"I'm coming too, Sami has enough money to pay for both our seats." said Eve.

"Your father gave permission for Sami only." said the car owner.

"He forgot to tell you about me." she said.

"Your father-in-law warned us never to allow you on the car unless accompanied by him or your father. You're his son's wife, I need him to tell me to allow you on or they'll cause me trouble," said the car owner, he glanced at Sami and continued "Anyway, if you had permission you'd be wearing a sharshaf. I think you're trying to run away. Now go back or I'll cancel today's trip."

"Eve go back," Sami said in English "I said I'll come back for you."

Two lights moved from in front of the Bawaba and the First House, the lanterns swung to the corner of the Second House and Suleiman hollered: "Is Eve in the car?"

"No, she wants to get in," the car owner shouted back "But we won't let her—come and get her before the monster does, we're leaving." They got back into the car closing the doors, leaving Eve outside pulling at the locked door wanting to be let in. And they drove away.

Suleiman, and Father shining the way with lantern in hand, reached her, "Hmmmhh, trying to run away…I'll discipline you!" said Suleiman as they dragged her back to the house as she cried in anguish. Suleiman locked her inside her room, leaving a rusty empty can for her to urinate in; morning and evening they opened the door, placed a glass of tea and piece of bread on the floor and locked it again. Every time they returned they found the tea and bread untouched, Eve lying on her side, waiting for Sami to return with help: she wasn't going to eat until he came back. Suleiman picked up the cold tea and bread. "You'll eat when you're really hungry, you haven't seen anything yet." he said.

The fourth day after Sami's departure Mother opened the room "Look, I've boiled an egg and brought you fresh milk, not buttermilk! Eat my daughter, *eat*."

"Mama, get me out of here," said Eve, eating and crying, "If you love me, help me. I can't stand it anymore."

"Hush, hush, you'll get used to it. This is your country, your father's country and the country of your grandfather! You can't run away from your country. This is your *destiny*." This, Eve had been told repeatedly, she'd heard it so many times but it still made no sense. Her destiny. What destiny? To become a vegetable? Waste into nothingness?

For weeks Suleiman kept her locked inside the room allowing her to leave only for the bathroom until one day he decided it was enough.

"Come out, I need you to help me with something," he said. They stood in front of the ducka. Nails were scattered on the ground next to wood and a thin sheet of steel. "I'm making a door for the path," he continued "So we can close it at night to stop dogs passing through here. Hold the wood for me."

The banging of the hammer against the steel annoyed her, but at least she was outside. Sami had fled for himself and not returned, with lowered eyes she looked at the path he'd crossed to leave as if it were covered with the same bitterness coating her innards.

"We're swapping houses tomorrow," said Suleiman, the cheeriness in his voice needling the compressed vexation in her chest, "We're moving in with you and Dhalia, into the Bawaba, and your father will have his house back!"

CHAPTER EIGHT

I T WAS STILL DARK OUTSIDE, SHE COULDN'T SLEEP, STILL AWAKING in the early still morning where the air seemed to be fresher and its nip, cooler; she usually enjoyed the serenity, but today was agitated by a restlessness which she knew would only increase as the day progressed. Closing her eyes on the bluish black day outside which still seemed to be night, she recalled the same hue when Father had accompanied her to school play rehearsals in the evenings every year of small school. Eyes still closed she smiled remembering how they walked along cold lamplit streets then pitch-dark parks, unafraid because Father was near no matter how many paces she advanced or lagged behind. The white of her teeth flashed here and now, seeing Father's beaming face, there and gone, and enthusiastic applause after finishing her solo song back then when she was little. The upwards corners of her mouth settled into a neutral position and she opened her eyes not wanting to recall when he'd dragged her out into the pitch-black wilderness and left her there. What was this rattling in her chest and not allowing her to have peace? She looked around the room, there was nothing to do so she went outside to sit in the crisp ether, until everyone else eventually, groggily awoke. But all the while she sat alone in the dusky morning inhaling the earthy air, her mind kept turning to her friends and classmates, she could still feel that sunshine beam emanating out of herself and each of her friends, a ray of energy, hope, youth and infinite possibilities to become what you wanted, shape your future, enjoyment of life without even thinking about it; she could still recall what each of them wanted to be in occupation; out of them all she had stood out as not just the one to be most likely to achieve better than the rest, but the one who would most definitely do so. Sitting with her back straight against the cold stone wall she imagined them working hard—which is what they were most probably doing (she was under no illusion that the world stopped because her life had ended, and knew perfectly well the world would go on fine without her taking any part in it), getting closer to becoming whatever and whoever they wanted to be; her whole body cored and hollowed out at the distressing thought that she, the most intelligent, successful and most determined, would never even 'be'. How dreadful when one feels time passing, making no progress in your life, and she who was so keen to do so many things every single day, leaving no waking moment unoccupied, unfelt, unused, uncherished now made to sit idly as life and opportunity rushed past.

Her parents had a hard time fixing the mess Kareema had left their house in for decades: cleaning, whitewashing, burying the floor with gravel then soil; it was well known even her married daughters, Latifa and Dhalia, only came to learn of hygiene after marriage. With Suleiman's family now in, the Bawaba filled with beds and utensils, clothes scattered all over the floor and grime accumulated.

Kareema was a strange person with multiple singularities which alas, amusing and disturbing as they are, cannot all be delved into, but one of her peculiarities was with food: when feeling greedy, which was most of the time, she would not share food, not even with her young children; Eve recalled when once talking with her brothers-in-law Kareema had fried eggs, laid the pan and bread on the ground while her children watched with salivating eyes; she proceeded to eat, and out of fear none of her children dared join her; it became too much for little sun-faded, shaggy haired Fardoos so she sat down without invitation and picked up a piece of bread, no sooner had she reached to dip it into the eggs than her mother shouted "GET UP!" at such a monstrous decibel everyone jumped and Fardoos fell backwards like a stunned goat and kicked away. She always claimed she never ate, except she always did which was normal, but she always ate a meal twice, a bit gluttoness but still normal, but the second time she would eat hiding in the most unusual places, Eve and Dhalia always at home would startle her, or she'd startle them if she hid in the dark. Eve awoke from a nap in the morning and opened the door of her room to go through the Bawaba to get to the bathroom, only to find it dark, someone had shut all the windows and door; the only light now shed from Eve's room. She walked past the stairs and through the middle, passed the dead-end corridor next to it which was made from the ceiling of the stairs leading to the roof and the wall of the stairs below. She heard a movement, stopped and looked towards the dead-end corridor used as a pantry, to see Kareema squatted over a steaming pot her mouth and cheeks stuffed so full she could hardly chew. Eve wondered what could have happened to this woman that she had to hide when eating, and be unloving towards her children (most families allowed their children the lion's share of meat as it was a rarity to have such a nutritious meal), without saying a word to the crouching, much in need of a glass of water squirrel, she carried on her way to the bathroom outside. When Eve came back up the rock path of the outhouse, she heard Suleiman singing on the roof refreshed from his nap, she hurriedly closed the Bawaba door as it had been and ran through the Bawaba, now he was walking down the external stairs. Eve knew he was coming down to get money for qat from his trunk in the pantry, she rushed into her room and closed the door behind her, leaving Kareema in the dark as she had been before interrupted. Suleiman came down the stairs, singing. Eve waited. He screamed like a woman out of fright tripping over Kareema and her pot with a clatter and a bang while Eve covered her laughing mouth (even angels have their horns).

It was a beautiful sunny morning, Eve seated on the ducka in front of the Bawaba enjoyed the serenity. Kareema was in a good mood too, she came out and sat on the ducka in front of the First House giving Eve a "good morning" which was pleasant in itself as Kareema's usual greeting for Eve would be pelting her with insults 'Slut', 'City woman', 'Good for nothing whore' were some of the ways Kareema greeted her. A hen led its tiny bobbing coloured-cotton-balls of chicks, searching for anything to eat in the ground. Eve went in and returned, throwing a handful of grains for the hens to feed. The hen pecked at the grain without slowing down or stopping, leaving nothing.

"This hen's greedy!" Kareema laughed and beamed "Instead of picking and dropping the grain to show its chicks, it's gobbled it all up! This isn't normal, mother hens usually allow their chicks to feed first!"

Eve laughed loudly, Kareema joined in laughing harder, thinking Eve's amusement was solely derived from her comment, but Eve was amused by the sardonic parody (curtesy of the plump plumed poultry) of the subject and commentator.

As if living with her in-laws wasn't enough, dangerous creatures, big and small, constantly worried Eve. She often encountered snakes, they got into rooms, slithered across paths causing children and adults alike to jump away onto the highest surface. Scorpions with dark bodies and opaque yellowy claws were always visiting, indeed Eve had covered herself with a cotton sheet to take a nap one mid-morning when she felt something trying to clutch to the chest of her dress, sitting up she brushed it off only to find it a hand-sized scorpion before screaming for her Uncle Suleiman. While doing the evening prayer a loud, rhythmic tapping sound running along the green plastic covered floor passed by her, interrupting her prayers, which she wasn't supposed to do, she followed the direction of the sound to find a millipede its many legs like yellowed teeth, its shiny brown body over an inch thick and at least thirty centimetres long, had invited itself in and was making its way towards the bed "UNCLE!" she screamed, Uncle Suleiman came running with axe in hand as it scurried under the bed; it took a lot of battering its hard exoskeleton to bring its journey to an end. One morning Eve awoke feeling a terrible burning sensation on both her legs, she raised her gown to find across both shins her skin had reddened with a terrible burn and filled with small blisters. In Dhalia's room she showed her sister-in-law and a visitor.

"It's a wadheen," said the visitor "It crawled over you while you slept." A wadheen was a small centipede with luminous legs, it left a glowing fluorescent path after it in the dark; crumbs of incandescent matter fell from its legs like drops of molten lava, leaving a lighted mini-landing strip in its wake. The children would poke it gently with a stick to make it move faster, marvelling at its neon white or neon green legs. Though Eve had seen them before, they were many, she didn't know they caused blisters.

Three things kept Eve awake all night and troubled during the day if they came into or were around her room. The first and least harmful was a gecko, these small lizards often entered rooms, she would call for her uncle to kill it; if he couldn't, she spent all night watching it, making sure it wasn't exactly above her, and why, you may well ask, would she be afraid of a teeny-weeny little lizard? Well, she had been told by everybody if it spat on you it caused leprosy; and she believed what she was told by adults, and a spitting, leprosy-causing lizard above her bed made her sleepless, as she was unable to kill anything and relied on her in-laws to eliminate the threat. The people believed if you killed this creature with one blow, God would give you a hundred good deeds in your 'righteous balance' and the more blows and pain you cause to kill it, the less good deeds you receive in reward. Why would you get good deeds for killing this creature? People told religious stories of an evil, tyrant king trying to burn the prophet Ibrahim alive, and geckos blowing on the fire to increase its volume. The second creature which kept Eve worried and awake was a hideous looking furry spider called a Fa'ar; many people acknowledged it was dangerous and its bite caused a wound which became pus-filled, resulting in amputation or death (It's up to you, said the doctor.). Eve had met two people with missing body parts who had been bitten by this spider and she had seen it in body diameters ranging from the size of a fifty pence coin to the size of a side plate; its legs were elbowy and long, at the front, two hairless rod-like limbs were always folded, at the tips of the rods were three hairy pointy claws which Eve believed it bit with as she had seen it extend these rods that looked like bobby pins; and when one made itself a comfortable guest in her room and they couldn't kill it, she'd spend a hellish night, watching it, hardly blinking an eye just in case it attacked.

The third regular menace also kept Dhalia awake when it arrived. Thankfully it never entered the house because the doors were closed at night. Regularly, during hot evenings, a rattle snake utilised the walls and path behind their rooms, but there was also a much larger snake going back and forth behind their rooms during sultry, sleepless nights: they heard it moving from in front of Eve's room to in front of Dhalia's and back, a lover begging to be let in (a real tight-hugging Casanova), its body against the ground the sound of rushing wind or rustling leaves, something heavy and continuous being dragged; sometimes you could hear it as if it was in the wall; they would both stay awake until it went away. Rattle snakes caused a debate between the women during an afternoon gathering: Eve claimed it made the noise by shaking the rattle at the tip of its tail, but the village women insisted it made the rattling noise with its tongue; the discussion was only settled after Fakhriya, Latifa's mother-in-law, had seen a documentary while in Taiz for medication.

"I really believed it made the noise with its tongue, until I saw the film!" laughed Fakhriya.

*

"IT'S ALMOST THE TENTH OF MUHARRAM, IT WILL BE EID WUZOO soon!" said Huda excitedly.

Fardoos jumped up and down with pure glee, younger Eman emulated her sister.

"What's Eid Wuzoo?" asked Eve.

"We'll collect shughaff and the boys will collect firewood and light bonfires on the hills!" replied Huda.

"And they'll get sweets and juice and give us some!" said Fardoos hugging Eve's thigh, looking adoringly up at the latter.

"Where will our bonfire be?" asked Eve.

"It's only boys, not girls, but we'll light the house!" said Huda. She paused, her eyes widened, "Oh Eve—will you ask my father to let us have our own bonfire here? He'll say yes, if you ask!" Eve agreed. "I'll collect firewood—it will be better and bigger than the boys!" said Huda "We'll have our own bonfire Fardoos!" Fardoos was so excited she hopped from foot to foot.

The boys and girls all around the villages began collecting wood and sacks of shughaff—a small light easily ignitable bush. Huda hid her sacks and wood in Mother's house so her brothers couldn't steal it to add onto their own bonfire collection. The tenth of Muharram arrived, Grandmother Haleema decided to celebrate it at Suleiman's house, arriving with a carton filled with juice boxes and honey sweets carried on her head. Dhalia had ordered many packets of sweets and

Eve had ordered two whole boxes of juices and packets of boiled sweets. It was the same as Halloween and Bonfire Night all in one, but without the ghoulishness. When the veil of night lowered, the boys gathered into different groups and went from house to house chanting: 'Oh Night of Light, Tasuu' and A'shuur, Oh Happiness enter! Oh, Scowler leave!' at the tops of their voices, stopping at each house and calling from outside the door: "Oh dwellers of the house, do you want your wishes to come true?" The women would answer: "Yes!" and the boys asked what they would get in return if their wishes came true; the women would individually reply, listing what they would give in return in specific amounts of money, juices, biscuits and sweets, then each woman would stand in front of the door and say: "Pray for me pray, to God for me pray, if what's in my mind comes true, for you from me a present a year from today!" then close her eyes and make a silent wish and the boys would shout: "Aameen!"

Grandmother Haleema, Kareema, Dhalia, Eve and Huda took turns standing in front of the door: Haleema wished her daughter-in-law, Aunt Fulla, be carrying a boy; Kareema wished for wealth; Dhalia wished for a son; Eve wished to return home and Huda wished for a groom. They watched the boys, carrying their goodies (of last year's both realised and unfulfilled wishes) and sacks of kindling, go off into the darkness; the houses in the lower villages and higher peaks began to light up.

"Come on Eve, quickly!" said Huda. They ran up to the roof of Father's house and lit the kindle on the perimeter of the wall, which they prepared earlier in the day by planting the bushes into balls of mud. What a sight! Every dwelling was a beautiful house-sized celebration cake lit up by dancing flames at regular intervals bordering the walls of the roofs. They took a look to the lower north east, Aunt Ethe's house and all the villages in that direction were glowing, decorated with flames, too; on many hills and peaks boys had already lit up their bonfires. The girls ran down and stood in front of the boulders with the women looking up to the north where Bundar's gang would light their bonfire, it was huge, when fully ablaze they could see the boys prancing around it.

"Come on Eve," said Huda "We're lighting ours!"

Eve looked back at Dhalia and excitedly said: "Dhalia, come with us! Light the bonfire!" Dhalia laughed, her gold incisors looked like missing teeth in the dark.

"I'm not a child! You're happier than the children!" said Dhalia.

Eve, Huda carrying Eman, and Fardoos ran back to the roof of the First House. Huda extended the matchstick to Eve, but Eve would not deprive Huda the thrill. The kindling ignited and sticks caught alight, as the flames leapt higher licking the logs and increasing in height, the four girls danced around the fire, throwing in more bushes as they chanted: "Oh Night of Light, Tasuu' and A'shuur, Oh Happiness enter! Oh Scowler leave!"

*

IN DAYS OF GRANITE GREY AND BRIGHT SUNLIGHT EVE FOLLOWED Uncle Suleiman, still building the upstairs room, to where he worked, breaking rock off boulders, beneath another larger boulder. In fascination she watched how he broke off large sections using just his strength and a pointed sledgehammer and then pound it to break up, before fracturing it into rectangularish building pieces; sometimes the sledgehammer wasn't enough to break a slab into pieces so he'd use a chisel like a massive nail to place on the stone then hammer the chisel until the fracture appeared along the rock; he'd once hit his finger badly, it blued until the nail eventually, painfully, fell off.

"Hold this, so I can split the rock." said Suleiman extending the chisel to her.

"No, you'll crush my hand just like you did to Dawood." said Eve.

"Hold this or you'll be staying inside your room."

"No."

He took her by the arm, pulling her to her room then bolted the door from the outside. She remained standing in front of her bed, arms crossed, staring at the door. Seconds passed and he opened the door and with a toothy smile asked: "Are you going to help your uncle or do you want to spend the rest of your life locked inside?"

"I'll help you." she said and smiled.

He yielded the sledgehammer and brought it down repeatedly, and with every hit on the head of the chisel, vibrations went through her palm and travelled to her elbow. Scared of the possible pain, her heart leapt and she shook every time the sledgehammer went up and back down, and when the crack elongated in the rock, she let go of the chisel and took a deep breath. So she held the chisel to rocks, held down wood as he attached nails to aluminium sheets for many mornings while he told her stories of the past and gossip while she watched him work, only becoming quiet when he got tired and the sun became hotter.

Before Morad left, he'd given his sister a suitcase of Arabic books about religion and science and religion, hoping one day she would be able to read Arabic and pass her time (which he knew she would have too much of), knowing how much she loved to read books. And once she had mastered the language she dove into this literature, emerging with the understanding that her fellow villagers neither understood nor practised their religion correctly. From what she had observed most of what they did and believed had been passed down through ancient traditions and superstitions, they believed what they knew and had done for generations and anything new was disbelieved, rejected and viewed as disgraceful; and more importantly they stuck together against things deemed not allowed. She came to learn it was not a religious concern which had made her parents and in-laws force her, for they were breaking religion by forcing her into marriage; it was not the villagers being cold-hearted or uncaring that caused them to be aloof to her issue keeping her prisoner, but their respect for familial privacy prevented them from intervening and by abiding to cultural rules with regards to guardianship and male escorts, they could not allow her to board a car alone and take off. Eve lifted her head from the book, tilting book forwards in her lap and her head backwards against the wall, where she surveyed the mountains with her eyes and its people in her mind: it was not cunningness keeping her imprisoned, but unwillingness to intervene, being in the mountains where no authorities existed, no transportation she could use, and no people whom thought like her, and therefore could not understand her predicament (little did she know fathers and husbands spoke with their families at home of the unfairness of Eve being kept like a bond, or clusters of women exchanging pities over the

'Girl from Beyond the Sea' as they called her, that she live with such monstrous in-laws and be so unhappy; unfortunately the opinions were only expressed within family and friends), coupled with Uncle Suleiman's shrewdness ensured she could not escape by using her intelligence. Leaving her with only one option: to get out she had to persuade them to allow her to leave. The more time passed, the more her inner peace grew, fretting and shouting and begging would get her nowhere, and her patience knew no end, she had been gifted with the Patience of Job, so now Kareema could swear, starve, insult her as much as her energy could allow her—and Eve would no longer run inside like a trembling rabbit, nor flinch an eye; the negative flow and malicious mother-in-law vibes would sail over her head as if a domed protective bubble bent them upwards, over her head and away; it didn't matter Kareema never tired, it mattered that Eve never responded—it left Eve feeling, well, righteous—spiritually and morally. Similarly she had learnt to keep her face emotionless while hurt, anger and embarrassment raged through her chest during the years of afternoons listening to others around her speak about her lack of circumcision, the way she walked and talked as unnatural, their strange stories of people having sex in the streets of Britain, inconsiderate they were implying the home she loved was the Land of the Depraved; it took a lot of willpower and many jabs of injury for her to become impassive, to actually not feel hurt, or at least not let it show on her face, when they talked that way. But on languid days when the cruel sun would not set quick enough, seemingly stretching more than the twenty-four hours they contained, every second passing were heavy, piercing stabs of slow death to Eve; nothing could occupy her mind and take it off the tick-tock of time wasting by, racing by she knew, but today was making every second seem to last twenty, where the fabric of her patience frayed and the present she was supposed to have been living tore at her heart, and behind closed doors she cried in pain over years passing, education lost, time wasted from her life, a great lover mourning a greater love.

They'd had breakfast, the morning was clear and bright, as were all mornings here, and Eve followed her Uncle to where he busied himself into hammering at a large slab of stone.

"You know the Nasser brothers have bought this thing," said Uncle Suleiman "It makes a loud noise—doogadoogadoogadoog -

and it breaks into boulders easier and quicker than this sledgehammer! And they rent it to people to use…but it's expensive. I'll tell Adam to send money so we can rent it when we'll build him a house in the future."

"What's it called?" said Eve.

"I don't know…a coombre-ee-ay…a combree-ee-ash…a combreeshoor." he said. Eve smiled as her uncle stretched the word he was trying to pronounce.

"A compressor?" she offered, from his description she remembered workers using a jackhammer on the roads in Newport.

"I don't know what its name is." he said and broke at a boulder, and when he got tired stopped and wiped the sweat off his forehead with his forearm. "You know…we're Muslims," said Suleiman "But God loves the Disbelievers more than us." Eve's head tilted backwards, laughter as bright as sunlight and warm as sunbeams erupted from her small pink mouth.

"Why do you say that?" she asked, wondering if he knew he was blaspheming.

"He gave all the books with how to make things to the Disbelievers." and he said it without jealousy or enmity, just an observant matter of fact remark, like saying the sky is blue—the grass is green.

"What things?" asked Eve, not understanding.

"Cars, radios, airplanes, combreeshers…those things." he replied. Peals of laughter shook Eve's body, her small hand was now slapping her slim thigh before her laughter turned into a cackle at the funniest thing she'd ever heard said with conviction.

"Uncle, God didn't give a book with instructions how to make things."

"Yes He did! How else were they made? God gave those instructions to nations in a book and he didn't give us a book!" he was serious. Eve was now doubling over with mirth, she had to sit and her hand was now slapping the doorstep of Dhalia's room as she tried to mitigate the pain of side-tearing laughter, Uncle Suleiman was exceptionally hilarious when so serious. When she was able to speak, between chuckles and tears, she said: "Uncle, things like cars, machines, airplanes were invented by people."

"Are you telling me some man just sat down and the idea came into his head and he made those things?" said Suleiman.

"Well, not like that," said Eve "But they all tried to make things and they tried over and over again and when they succeeded the people coming after made them better. Uncle Suleiman, you're joking in what you say, right?"

"Impossible!" said Suleiman "There is no way cars and radios came out of somebody's head, impossible! If it was true, then why can't I just sit down and think and then make a car?"

"Uncle, it's not that simple," said Eve "But there was no book of inventions from God. Inventions are made by people."

"Impossible! No way!" he said, and later in the day whenever someone passed by Suleiman would tell them how preposterous a claim she had made.

People believed special families descending from the Prophet Mohammed existed; these people were considered closer to God, that God answers their requests because they were special; Eve debated this, to the elder female relatives' displeasure, pointing out where the Quran and Hadeeth stated not even the Prophet had the power to cause another person harm or good, and everybody is equal in the eyes of God, nobody has an advantage over anybody when asking God for help; she questioned their lineage as to how they could know they were descendants of the Prophet, as he existed about fourteen hundred years ago and there were no birth certificates in the village even now and over all those centuries; she asserted God answers everybody's prayer without a need for mediation from 'the special ones'. Her in-laws, Aunts, and visitors were appalled by Eve's comments, these so called "Saadaa" had no special closeness to God and did not have special gifts to cure the ailed or bring good fortune. Indeed, most men in the village seemed to have long abandoned belief in Walis and Saadaa, but many older women still held on. But the mountain people believed the Saadaa were so special to the extent they worshipped their dead, who became a 'Wali' after death, apparently it was when their power became stronger. Men and women travelled distances, presenting sacrifices of sheep and goats to be slaughtered at the grave of the Wali, ghee, honey and money were offered too. They argued, if it wasn't true then the offerings wouldn't have been accepted! They asked if it wasn't true then where did all the things they left for the Wali go? Eve pointed out (what was unambiguously obvious) it was probably the live relatives of the Wali whom took them. After presenting their offerings they circled the grave many times, led by a family member of the long deceased in some kind of mini-pilgrimage, first circling slowly, but the speed increased as they entered a mob mentality euphoria, some crying out the name of the dead Wali as the adulating rapture increased, their bodies jerking up in a possessed dance, as they swung their heads side to side and flipped it back and forth as floppy as a rag; they cried, screamed, and threw themselves at the grave which was not a normal ground level grave, but with a tomb built around it similar in design to a mosque, but in other areas they were just whitewashed, egg shaped domes; the shrine inside was shoulder length with a window at the ground, painted with whitewash and the best material streamed all over it. Those whom wanted to be 'blessed' by the Wali raised their hands and asked the dead Wali to help them, to make their requests come true. What surprised Eve most, they ate soil from the grave, also considered to have healing powers and spiritual advantages; the believers put their hands through the window at the bottom, taking soil in their fingers, wiped it over their heads; they even claimed it tasted sweet, but our clever cleric (with a bone to pick) suspected it was a case similar to the 'Emperor's Clothes'.

"You know what you're doing is prohibited?" said Eve with a smile, this was her chance to chastise (though she didn't really care about, and had nothing against what they believed in and worshipped)—for everything normal and natural she did, or the way she was, they always told her was prohibited loosely and unfoundedly tying everything into religion, always lambasting her about things she was pretty sure God was okay with: walking, smiling, keeping the body parts you were born with, and yet they committed the biggest of sins according to their own rules. Regardless of Eve's teasing castigations, they believed the Saadaa and Walis could help them, even though there was drought and they didn't bring rain; illnesses they did not cure; infertility they couldn't reverse for those whom sought from them offspring. Eve knew this was a form of paganism or idolatry, but was perplexed at how such rituals had been twisted into their Sunni Islamic beliefs, it must have existed long before Islam in this region, and with the remoteness of the area maybe the mountain dwellers had never fully understood the religion, and just as superstitions and ancient traditions had been incorporated into religion, such as female circumcision, Wali idolatry had too.

CHAPTER NINE

H ER FINGERS RAN NOSTALGICALLY OVER THE BROWN WOOD of the shield-shaped plaque, the now dented metal centre still bore her name, school and the year she was presented as 'Student of the Year', her last at Junior school. With wistful eyes she recalled Father had kept it and brought it to show her Uncles and relatives how brilliant she was; not long after the wedding whilst spending an afternoon in her room with girls, Latifa had become frustrated with one of the square green metal shutters of which the hinges were loose and kept swinging shut that she took the plaque from an admiring Aunt's hand and shoved it between the gap and the wall like a doorstop; now that is where Eve returned it where it had been put to use for years, denting when she accidentally tried to close the window while it was still jammed there. Fortunately, Eve's appearance had not succumbed as the trophy's, but the unseen effects internally would show up later on in life, for no matter how patient and resilient, inside her mentality was as battered as the thin metal of the plaque—she just couldn't feel it yet; and although affable she was as determined as ever to get out of the village and return to her life, her life with all its richness and possibilities still on hold. When would she ever get out of here, fed up with everything being forbidden for girls; a football she had ordered and gone to play with Bundar and Dawood had caused her in-laws and parents to physically intervene and allow her to watch only; dancing was frowned upon unless there was a wedding or gathering of girls—but both Huda and she discovered there was only so much pleasure in dancing without an audience or a group, in her room behind closed doors; women didn't sing unless there was a wedding and it was more chanting in whiney voices than singing; she had fallen in love with Arab songs Adam had brought with him: Yemeni, Saudi, Kuwaiti and other Gulfan artists, but had been rudely silenced while she was doing her best Mohammed Abdo just because (unbeknownst to her, until her Silencer came to shame her) Adam and Uncles, seated outside behind Dhalia's room, had been joined by some young 'stranger men' (stranger men being men without marital or blood relations to the female concerned) and were embarrassed by her wailings (in her opinion—singing) of the wounds left by love. Notwithstanding, there were some very interesting and enchanting songs sung off-key when doing work or trying to get an uncooperative baby to sleep, these songs were actually beautiful stories about kings and princesses, marriage and children, cows and goats, milk and neighbours, people and problems; there was even a song she often heard about a parent refusing to marry his beautiful, coffee-bean, young daughter to the rich and powerful Sultan—they had wisdom, a moral message to them. Which in turn made her wonder, if such wise stories were orally passed down over the ages, with this age being the more modern, what on earth had happened to these people, making them so backwards and closed minded? (She had no history of Yemen and how the Imams, dictatorial rulers of Yemen, had closed the country off from the outside world (and to be honest, the mountain people she lived with had done the same to themselves out of the harassment they'd received from the Imam's soldiers, whom to them were from the outside world)). She felt herself living in Medieval Europe, but exotic instead of grey and dreary, perfumes and scented smoke instead of unhygienic and rank, but still a land where time did not pass as progress froze; leaving its occupants in the darkness of ignorance, relying on superstition and ancient customs, shaming and rebuking anyone who dared talk, behave or believe differently than their way (let alone allowing a little Welsh girl longing to return to emerald green hills and brown walled educational institutions, go free).

All Eve had to do was close her eyes to recall the scent of books; the sound of vehicles on busy roads; flashes of friends' faces; the morning song of birds free to hop from branch to branch or leave the tree, or even the country if they desired; Judas tree branches sleeved in lilac-rose flowers pointing at something (or someone), the warm caress of sun coming into the back hall of home where she opened the back door and lay on the carpeted floor with closed eyes in some child play in warm sunlight; even dust particles dancing in a shaft of light seemed to be joyful in her recollection of random memories; oh, the golden and green waft of hot apple pie, its sweet and mellowed sour taste on the tongue; the crunch of sugar granules of welsh cakes; and none compared to the warm, beaming smile of Father playing with her in the park, carrying her on his shoulders, spoiling her, urging her to sample more fragrances before choosing the perfume she wanted, the confectioners he would take her to, to her hearts delight; Father looking down at her with kind, loving eyes, smiling face, checking on her satisfaction while waiting to pay at the till and all the sunlit, fuzzy with paternal warmth and affection reflection would now be met with a vigorous cold shiver—the reminiscent warmth escaped like heat from a living room opening directly onto the street on a cold winter's day as she opened her eyes at thirty-thousand metres high in her granite and sunlit room and could not believe (who could believe) he had one day in a humid climate held a knife to her throat, its cold metallic threat competing with the fiery anger in his eyes, while she was still his pet, *she was still his pet*, and had not changed. But how his eyes viewed her had.

*

MOST WOMEN AND GIRLS WERE NOT MARRIED AS CHILDREN, IT rarely happened—but it did happen, no matter how rare. There was news of a young man who lived in the houses on the higher peaks to the south west who was to ask for the hand in marriage of a girl from one of the lower villages—she was only seven years old. To Eve, analysing the unfairness, here is where the injustice of child-brides stood out, how can a child willingly consent to marriage if she has no idea what marriage truly is, the physical and psychological demands that it takes; it makes no difference if she was forced or went happily lulled by the glittering gold, sweet perfumes and sparkling fabrics— she has no idea what it truly is she is entering into, nor what effects it will have on her young life from a too early pregnancy, to misery as her true character emerges when she is in her twenty-somethings but has to be subdued to fit into the marriage when she finds she doesn't love this man, now that she is old enough to discern. Eve, though from her western point of view knew it was very wrong, still knew these men were no perverts, no paedophiles as some would like to claim, as they had no interest or fetish in a child's body—but they preferred the wife to have a woman's body and enjoyed it more when she grew, but it was a cultural problem: although they were troubled by it when a young girl was to marry, they saw the other side that this man would continue to love, protect and provide for her even as she grew and most would live a long and full life. But, thought Eve, what about all those whom suffered, and the fact that choice had been taken away, even if given with regards to those whom consented, how could they not see the famous Arab proverb 'a mother brings up a nation', how is the female before she was a mother to become her best as a person, whether educated or not, if she wasn't allowed to finish forming into an adult mentally and physically? Whom would she have accepted or rejected when she was old enough to make a choice of husband? Who would she have become had they allowed her to live her childhood and enter adulthood when she had matured and not been taken fruit vert? And so the debate whether the man is a pervert or not means nothing to the girl-bride as she is suffering from life, opportunities and childhood lost at the wish and demand of adults, including her family—not just the groom. But who was going to educate or change culture in these rocky, rural, far-flung, hard to reach, remote regions; and how were cultures not to be insulted by attacks and insinuations because they too abhorred rape and rapists, even child-brides were protected from sexual abuse by conditions put upon the husband and his parents that he is not to sexually touch the girl until she comes of age and specified in the number of years to pass in the marriage contract. It was said this fiancé himself was forced to marry the child, under unyielding pressure from his insistent mother wanting her niece from her sister's side as his bride—an environment where obedience to parents is tantamount to honour.

"They'll be an unusual sight on their wedding day," said Grandmother Haleema "She's as short as a hen and he's as tall as a palm tree! I mean he's unusually tall."

"Who is she?" said Dhalia "I don't think I know her."

"You saw her at Adam's wedding," said Huda "She was the little girl in the red dress, playing outside with Fardoos."

"My God!" exclaimed Dhalia "That one?! She's too young, she's as small as Fardoos! How could her mother and father agree?" Eve's face crumpled, was it size that mattered, not age? An urge to cry came on, but she swallowed it down, for she had been forced to marry as a child too, but no one had cared; she hadn't wanted the clean shaved, perfumed cheek of a man rubbing and resting against her smooth cheek so what if she was taller than a seven-year-old? She hadn't wanted his panting face, delirious in delight as he thumped his loins against her bruised thighs which he kept on trying to spread wider as if he expected her hips to be able to expand out of her narrow pelvis to accommodate his girth; so what if her breasts were visibly filling her chest, she had only turned fourteen and didn't want a man's giant paws squeezing and palming them.

Grandmother Haleema explained, the girl's family had put conditions to the marriage because the mother of the groom had refused to wait until the bride grew into a young lady: they had stipulated though the girl would be sent to his home to serve his mother, he was not allowed to have sexual intercourse with her until she began menstruating, but girls menstruated early some from twelve years old or even younger; this was more like Medieval Europe than Eve thought, where it was common for girls twelve years old and younger to be married. Intelligent but ignorant Eve, upset with her own people at what she thought was their singularity for allowing and not preventing child-marriage no matter it had only happened twice in her presence, had no idea that up until recent centuries it was normal even in countries now advanced, and was deemed reasonable that girls twelve years old, and younger, to be married to men (she had no idea, nor would have believed, even currently USA law allowed child-girls to be married, where across tens of states tens of thousands of underage girls per year were married to adult men—all in accordance to the law, albeit an abuse of human rights according to America); nor did she know in other religions adult men were allowed sexual intercourse with three year old girls—yet Eve was upset with the Muslim villagers around her, knowing it had nothing to do with religion not even from their perspective; Eve didn't even know it was not only she and this child bride whose unusual young age at marriage was more common than she thought—many girls in Yemen were married before they reached the age of eighteen; if she'd have known would it have worried her how common it was globally that girls were married at such a young age and there was no outcry over this practice until the Twentieth Century? Would it have worried her that it was not just a specific religion, not just a specific region that had practised this? Or would it have given her hope that just as it had been stamped (seemingly) out of the developed worlds, it could one day cease to exist in developing countries too? Truth be told, all this would have meant nothing to Eve except a troubling fact that across the world it had happened, was accepted, and was still happening, and that it had happened to her—fuelled by her existentialism trapped in her solipsism, where she had been the only one in the whole world it had happened to—until today it was happening to another. With her back against the sun-warmed stone wall she frowned upon the whole scene, the whole village, everybody and everything in it for not stopping what had happened to her—and now to this poor girl who would be driven to her marital home not as a bride, but a maid for the mother—unaware that between every two beats of her saddened and troubled heart a girl was being forced to marry somewhere in the world. On the wedding day, Eve, Dhalia, Grandmother Haleema and the others sat on the outside ducka watching the marriage procession, the ululations and gunshots echoed around the mountains.

"She looks like his daughter—not his bride." Dhalia laughed. Eve frowned, watching a little girl wrapped in black, walking hand in hand with a man over six foot tall.

A few months later there was a great uproar in the village: the lanky groom had had sex with his child bride, breaking the conditions of the marriage. The infuriated family took their daughter back to their home to live with them, threatening he had to divorce her, angered because he had molested a child—*their child*. Elders of the villages were requested to mediate a solution, and after a few months of head-shaking revilement of the groom over his abhorrent behaviour, the bride's family were talked into returning her to the husband's house—as she was still his wife; although he had committed a monstrosity she was still his wife, but that he should refrain from his desire and not touch her again and she sleep beside his mother; they wagged their fingers and reprimanded her parents as this was their fault and *they* should not have allowed the wedding while she was so young.

A year later, the child-bride passed by Dhalia's room one afternoon, on her way to visit a relative; Dhalia and the others watched her, their eyes and facial expressions hiding laughter. Fardoos sat on the doorstep, smiling and looking expectantly towards the visitor, waiting for her to get up and go outside to play with her; soon Fardoos' expression turned into confusion—this was not the same girl she had played with, it was her, but she seemed totally different: she wasn't behaving like she had when they played and shared sweets not that long ago; her eyes seemed to only see the adults and skim over Fardoos, she only spoke with the women. Eve could not help but notice the girl didn't behave like an eight-year-old, but had picked up the traits and acted and spoke like the adult women of the village. It was abnormal, she was hardly taller than the length of the cuboid cushion she sat upon, but she broke off leaves of qat, puffed at the kooz and patted her clothing and spoke and moved with the mannerisms of older women. Dhalia and Aunt Fulla seemed amused by the girl's peculiarity while Eve and Fardoos were disturbed: a woman in a girl's body—it hadn't taken long for it to set in—being told she was now a woman because she was married.

*

A HAWK GLIDED THROUGH CLOUDLESS SKY, THE CONGREGATION OF Aunts, Uncles and their children behind Uncle Suleiman's house watched silently as it gently, majestically, rose on invisible searing heat. It hadn't rained in years, Eve relied heavily on the description given by the locals how verdant these mountains became in times of rain, yet this was not the longest dry spell for they had suffered drought to the degree of famine during her grandfather's generation when her Uncles and parents were still young children—in a bid to fight the sharp pangs of starvation men and women had tied flat slabs of rock against their stomachs, tightening it as their waists emaciated and the hunger increased; and when it rained they fervently and lovingly worked the land and were happy because fortune and food was soon to come, children's hunger would be satisfied, adults would be strong again, bone-thin animals would be fed and plump. The desperate expectancy Eve saw on Uncle Suleiman's sun-wrinkled face was no different than what she saw in Grandmother Haleema's laugh-creases, or even passers-by, an urgent begging in their eyes for clouds to burst, but even the unkind clouds refused to congregate over their mountains; in despair and anguish they watched the darkening clouds gather over regions miles and miles away until they formed a circle around them creating the division of hope-filled shade and the abandoned in light and they remained in their halo of hell while it rained on every area around them, leaving the mountains high and dry; and as the dark sheets of pouring rain came heavily down over those regions while their mountains basked in the hot, dry, demanding sun—their bodies baked in the heat, their mouths asking God for mercy and rain, and their hearts steamed in despair and frustration. But they never lost hope that God would save them and send the Saylah and they would be crying in joy "Wa Saylah! Wa Saylah!" but while their hearts hoped, their eyes groped at the sky, *their need*, trying to wilfully, wistfully entrance the clouds to come nearer. But no 'saylah' running water stream would come, and not one raindrop would plop.

*

THERE WAS TOO MUCH PAIN LIVING HERE, EVE REFUSED TO DO WORK she was physically unable to cope with, to her in-laws' distaste, but it was still a slow, painful endurance which she smothered underneath smiles and pleasantness. Deep within her being she knew she would leave these mountains, a hope mixed with anguish of years lost without it happening, but she knew she would leave—eventually they would have to let her go. She never stopped trying to convince everyone she should be allowed to leave the village and she always spoke with common sense, trying to appeal to their hidden rationality, always giving compelling reasons why she had to go, and only cried in exasperation from unexplained rejections of her pleas. And when the strangling situation became too much, heavy hearted, with a body like lead she locked herself inside her room, not eating or leaving, constantly weeping as she lay on her bed for days in a row, drowning in wretched sorrow.

She suffered from bouts of depression more often; it overcame her while the usual gathering of ladies in Dhalia's room chatted; she didn't know what would trigger it: the same old story told for the umpteenth time, sometimes the colour of the day and sometimes even a scent of perfume redolent with a long-gone memory, or the stillness of the air. Feeling suffocated by an agitating sadness, she would get up without a word and lock herself in her room for weeks; drowning in something thick and bleak, no matter how long they banged on the door and eventually tried to coax her to come out and eat, she remained silent, hating the sound of their voices. Why couldn't they leave her alone in her unhappiness? If they just left her alone…after a few days maybe she would die from melancholy on this bed and never have to live this unbearable limbo. She would cry for hours and wish she was back home, but it wasn't just sadness, but utter despair: she had been here for so long, she would probably never leave—and so much of her life had gone, and this thought crushed the remaining life out of her. Halfway dead, she lay on her bed waiting, feeling death would surely come because there was no point in living; gloom surrounded her, there was only darkness in the future. Losing hope was the worst feeling she had ever encountered, it made her feel so heavy. Dead. Even the laughing sunshine coming through the windows was terribly wrong; how could it shine and be warm and light when everything was dark? It purposely poked at her wounds and she grimaced as she closed the shutters and lay still in the dark and what little light made it through the gaps could still hurt her eyes. And soul. She felt something akin to anger trembling inside her wanting to grow and growl and explode, but by virtue of trained patience it was caged and was no longer raging anger—but drenched in dolefulness and her soul flopped. How tired she felt despite doing nothing all day; what cumbersome sleep now enveloped her; it was heavier than sleep, she could feel it shrouding her insides before her eyes shut. Maybe it was heavy handed death, she hoped. It was the only way to escape the pain, let herself give up and slip into this weighty slumber. Why had Father done this to her? It was his fault, all his fault, if he hadn't forced her into marriage she wouldn't be immured in these mountains. Now all she wanted was to be dead.

Hunger, she no longer felt. Only this painful semi-existence. Alive—but not allowed to live. The more she stayed in her room not moving, not answering, the more reluctant and harder it became to get up and go out, the sadder she became, and the more exasperated she felt when they banged at her door, awakening her from heavy sleep, and called out for her; even when Uncle Suleiman's voice had turned into genuine concern; even when they had sent for the young Aunt Khatima to knock and talk to her from outside the door. All she wanted was, to be left alone to die. When they rudely roused her from hibernation by coming around the outside of the house, knocking and calling from outside the closed windows she still could not and did not respond. Why wouldn't they leave her alone, to be asleep where she could not feel this pain? Her thoughts were painful, remembering everything back home. The longing, the pain. The hope that had been crushed, the pain. The bright future all her teachers and headmaster had predicted for her, now her life was nothing but despair. Everything in her eyes was grey and drab, agonisingly, dreadfully slow. They were now banging on the windows from the outside calling out her name, to "come out", that they were "worried", "what is wrong?", she might have answered their calls if she had the slightest belief they would let her leave, but she knew they would never let her go, and this thick, drowning, downwards dragging sleep still had hold of her so she closed her eyes, and their voices slipped away as she entered oblivion. Prone to being optimistic she had always told herself she would leave and return home, but when she had lost this hope all that remained were tortured, devastated fragments of her mind and soul, memories of a happier life, feeding anger and anguish. After days of sobbing and anguished torment followed by heavy insatiable sleep, she would emerge from her room: calm, peaceful, affable Eve. Her soul still dragging on the ground behind her young form, but with hope she would leave this awful place soon.

It wasn't just the hard living conditions she couldn't bear, but also the mind-numbing boredom; the repetitiveness of the day with nothing to stimulate her brain. She had loved to read as a child, to walk and explore, experience different things; her days had always been full and now, nothing. Nothing. No real nutritional food, no education or books or even television to occupy her. In fact Eve had been here so long and become so bored every time one of the neighbours or family went to Taiz for medication, when they came to her with their plastic bags of medicines for her to read what it's for and what the doctor had diagnosed which would be jotted on the top of the doctor's prescription, at the beginning Eve just read it to satisfy their curiosity, but the longer she stayed with nothing to read, and Eve had loved reading books and now she was book deprived, she eventually looked forward to reading the inserts of medicines. First, she read every side of the carton, including the tube or vial, then opened up every box and read the insert from top to bottom, leaving nothing unread. First in English, then in Arabic and intensely as if reading a plot of some great novel, enjoying it and becoming slightly worried for the patient by the possible side effects (a wonder anyone takes medicine after reading it), while the person who brought it watched with a worried and expectant face, but all she translated was what it was for.

Haleema had a nerve which constantly twitched in her face making her left eye shut strongly and repetitively, she laughed reminiscently as they passed the kooz back to her to smoke, Eve always enjoyed Grandmother Haleema and Aunt Ethe's company, they had an abundance of interesting stories from the past to tell, it was as close as she got to entertainment (besides Eve singing songs from the eighties out loud in her room). From their reminiscing and the middle aged and older folk, Eve saw how drastically the environment of the mountains had changed, despite the fact its people had not altered their ways that much: there used to be an abundance of rain and in turn crops, grain, cattle, forestry and vegetation; Wali and other pagan worship was practised more, not everyone knew how to pray; clothes were different, trousers did not exist for men or women (nobody wore underwear even currently (the women were amused and found it odd that Dhalia and Eve wore knickers and bras during periods and husbands' presence)), both genders wore one type of dress: rectangular, like a robe, and dyed once a year with indigo; women wore fringes, they didn't part their hair like nowadays. From their stories it was evident women and men were not segregated as they are now; women and men (even unrelated) travelled by foot in pairs or groups, taking their produce to sell and barter in faraway areas; they spoke of feasts, where everybody gathered around large fires to eat, drink and socialise, women danced with men.

"It wasn't like you dance these days," said Haleema "It was energetic and we would dance until we couldn't anymore."

"It wasn't rude or shameful like they say today," said Aunt Ethe "We'd have so much fun doing the hakfa!" Hakfa was the dance.

"Did you know how to do the hakfa?" asked Dhalia.

"I could ihkaf all night, I was strong." said Aunt Ethe.

"We were young," said Haleema smiling dreamily "You could go up to anyone and ask them to dance with you. Up and down, up and down."

"Show us the hakfa." said Fulla. Aunt Ethe and Grandmother Haleema laughed.

"We're too old now," said Haleema "My knees and hips won't be able to handle it."

"Come on, let's show them how to dance the hakfa!" said Aunt Ethe enthusiastically as if suddenly imbued by youthful energy.

Eve smiled, Aunt Ethe was much older than Grandmother Haleema, yet the memory had sparked a desire to dance. Grandmother Haleema chuckled and got up, Aunt Ethe shook her hips, Eve couldn't tell if it was part of the dance or she was just warming up.

"I'll be the woman, you be the man." said Grandmother Haleema. They both started to make sounds: "Tst, tst, tssst. Tst, tst, tssst. Tst, tst, tssst." They faced each other, Grandmother Haleema lunged down almost reaching the floor in a squat, and jumped back up; Aunt Ethe, dancing the male part, followed and as their 'tsts' got louder, their squatting and jumping became faster, everyone in the room concealed laughter and smiled as the old ladies defied their age and tired bones, up and down, up and down they went, one purposely slightly lagging behind the other. Their lunging synchronised, Aunt Ethe stuck her right arm out, holding her open palm downwards, fingers straight together, above Haleema's shoulder and as they went down Haleema splayed her knees outwards and Aunt Ethe thrust her hips forwards as she went up. Khatima held her cheeks with both hands, Fulla's eyes widened, every face in the room displayed shock.

"What are you doing?" Khatima finally squealed, there was no mistaking what this dance represented, and the women in the room laughed, Haleema sat herself heavily down on a cushion, Aunt Ethe breathing hard sat on the bed beside Dhalia.

"You didn't feel embarrassed to dance like that? With men?" said Fulla with disgust looking askance at Haleema, her mother-in-law, "I'd die in my skin!"

"No wonder they banned this dance." said Dhalia.

Haleema regained her breath and said: "It started when some people returned from Saudi. They started to say everything was shameful."

"It used to be so different then, we'd have so much fun," said Aunt Ethe "We could talk to men, but they said it was forbidden and everything we used to do became rude."

Maybe the men going and returning from Saudi had brought changes in culture over the decades, evidently not just importing fabrics and fragrances, but religious prohibitions both authentic and fictitious.

*

EVE'S FATHER-IN-LAW, WHOM BY TRADITION IS CALLED UNCLE, stopped putting a padlock on the inside of the external door of her room, only padlocking its exterior. When she needed the bathroom at night she had to go through the Bawaba where all the in-laws slept, a few on beds and the rest on the floor, Suleiman and the boys only slept outside when the climate was hot. They had tried convincing her to urinate in an empty can during the night, as many women did, because once she was about to step out of the bathroom when she noticed two small black snakes intertwining around the top frame of the door, too scared she would be bit she remained there for hours, not daring to scream for help; after a long time hoping they would slither away it became obvious they were in no rush so she stood in the corner crying out for her uncle who came to her rescue.

"You should pee in a can and in the morning pour it out," said Suleiman "It's dangerous, you could be bitten, or the monster might eat you."

She'd heard many stories, from many people, they inhabited the mountains decades ago, but the numbers of these 'monsters' dwindled as more houses were built and also the monkeys and other animals became less too, and as the trees and vegetation became scarce, cut down for firewood, the animals eventually disappeared completely, but still every now and then a few people claimed seeing a beast called the Tahsh. At first Eve thought they were mixing it up with tigers, which were also witnessed, but there were great differences between how both animals were described making them stand out as two distinctly separate creatures: the tiger was described exactly as a tiger is: big cat, reflective eyes, walking on all fours. On the other hand, the Tahsh was said to have an elongated mouth with many teeth, standing high on its hind legs, shaking its head slowly side to side as it roared and was monsterly in their depictions, but was also considered an animal. Eve had insisted they were maybe seeing a tiger and out of fright had misidentified it, but the older people whom had seen and encountered both creatures in their past insisted they were two very different animals—the tiger was a tiger and the tahsh was a tahsh, and a much bigger animal than the tiger, but they all agreed they would rather accidentally meet a tiger than the latter.

Eve always woke up before the pre-dawn call for prayer, if there was no moonlight she took her lantern with her. Her morning routine was to go to the bathroom, come back up, get her soap, toothpaste and toothbrush and squat at the stepping stone under the ducka outside, brush her teeth, wash her face and finish the ablution for prayer. Today it was moonless in the early hours and dark. Suleiman sleeping inside the Bawaba muttered and turned in his bed as she walked past him with the lantern, and did the same when she came back up from the bathroom and fetched her things. It was silent in the darkness as she squeezed toothpaste onto her toothbrush, but dogs broke the stillness, barking from the lower village to the northwest. More dogs were now barking from in front of the three houses across the chasm opposite Barh Salliya, and even more dogs barking from in front of the houses high up in the southwest. Eve stopped brushing her teeth, realising the dogs were all barking towards one direction—rushing towards one direction. The barking neared from three different directions as the dogs ran in haste towards the steep below the house she lived in, wondering who the burglar might be, which is what she believed they were chasing, she began to brush her teeth slower. The dogs were almost underneath the steep path now, and had become one pack, their frenzied barking non-stop. Eve froze and turned slowly to her right as she heard loud thuds coming from Barh Salliya: THUD, THUD. THUD, THUD. THUD, THUD. And for whatever reason in her mind, thought she would see a lion coming towards her from in front of the First House, but luckily the thuds went down the steep head-on in the direction of the canine frenzy. Her mind began to rattle as what animal could make such heavy, loud thuds? It must be large. The thudding and the barks met below her on the path and with an abruptness as if cut with a knife all the dogs became silent simultaneously. There was a pause. Then a tremendous roar ripped into the darkness sending the dogs whimpering back down the path, and Eve scrambling into the Bawaba slamming the door behind her. She had moved before she even realised that she was moving, fear had kicked in and she was inside without knowing how she got in. Suleiman was already twirling the shawl around his head, awakened by the roar.

"I told you to pee in a can!" he said with anger and warning to a wide eyed, fast-breathing Eve, "Get out of my way," said Suleiman in bad temper and eagerness "I want to see it!"

"*You are not going outside to be eaten by the monster! I won't let you!*" Kareema said with passion and finality, pulling at his arm, holding him back with all her strength. Eve didn't move away from the door, scared out of her wits unable to believe she had made it in safely. What if it had chosen to cross the path in front of the houses instead of beneath them down the steep? She shuddered at the possibility, she could have been eaten alive and become a 'monster' story told in the afternoons on a repetitive basis, like all the stories told by women passing time. Villagers already awake, or awoken by the barking, had heard the roar, but no one was outside to see the animal so Eve had experienced the closest encounter. She was extremely upset with herself, if only she had been brave enough to go take a look down at the path before running inside, she would know and have seen if it was a tiger, she would know what 'the beast' the villagers talked about was, and satisfied her own curiosity. The thuds and the roar emanating from a tunnel of a throat were so clear in her mind, but her curiosity to know for sure, wishing she had seen what this animal really was would nag her forever. The encounter was very persuasive and at night she urinated in a can for a week, but as the fear diminished, she returned to using the outside privy—except, every time she woke Suleiman up, under his strict instructions, and he would sit outside on the ducka with the rifle across his lap and only go back to sleep when she was safely back inside. Sometimes he drowsily complained: "Why don't you just pray after the sun comes up? Why don't you just pee in a can?"

*

PEOPLE BELIEVED MALES WERE SUPERIOR TO FEMALES, THEY NEVER said it outright, but their proverbs and comments announced it. For they all loved their daughters dearly, kissing and hugging them with equal affection shown to their sons, but it was at the birth of a child when the cultural perception was made clear by both male and female adults: they celebrated with much joy from the moment of receiving a newborn boy; when a girl was born a visitor was bound to dampen the joyous atmosphere with: "you'll have a boy next time", "it's alright—she's still from God", "you have someone to serve you" or "you'll get money for her when she comes of age". Women were scrutinised if the firstborn was a female and shamed if all her offspring were girls. In these mountains, marrying a second wife while still married to the first rarely happened, but it did in hope of getting a boy as if it was in a wife's control to determine the sex of her pregnancy. If a couple didn't become pregnant, the wife was blamed of being infertile; she would be treated as if she was defected and, of course, the husband would marry a second wife, but more often than not, only after divorcing the first. There was one incident in the history of these villages where a man married and kept the first, second, third and fourth wife, blaming the first three of being barren; when all his wives failed to become pregnant, he and the village came to the conclusion that he was unable to impregnate them, which was considered more shameful than a woman being unable to bear a child, and now it was his four wives whom cursed the day he had chosen them for marriage and left them childless. Talking about sexual intercourse was taboo and only close friends diverted about experiences to each other. Sex was only mentioned without embarrassment if they were talking about a bride-to-be to lose her virginity, or part of an engaging long funny, lewd story and never was it mentioned in front of men or boys. Eve noticed young couples let go of each other's hand if a father, mother or brother entered the same room. Once Morad and Dhalia had an argument and made up, Dhalia's uncovered head rested on Morad's chest. They heard Mahmood, Dhalia's teenage brother whose scowling fair face was contrasted by a shock of dark unruly curls no matter how much cream and combing he tried to tame it with, approaching the room. Dhalia tried to separate from Morad, but her hair was tangled to his shirt button. Morad hurriedly tried to free her, but Mahmood's voice was close to the door so she violently yanked her head and broke free wincing, eyes watering, and rubbing her scalp. As Mahmood spoke to Morad, his eyes rested on the tuft of hair on the shirt button. It was unacceptable and considered immoral to hold hands, hug or even sit too close to your husband in front of male relatives and even in front of women such as aunts and cousins. Eve wondered at their way of thinking: adultery being immoral she could understand, but husband and wife not being allowed to publicly show affection seemed too much. Then again, nothing seemed to make sense in these mountains, its people and their ways were full of contradictions. You would imagine being so strict to the extent of not publicly expressing pleasure between husband and wife, adultery didn't exist, add to that adultery and relationships outside of marriage are one of the biggest shames, but adultery occurred and no matter how secretly lovers tried to keep their trysts, it was always exposed by others—it was difficult to keep under wraps when everybody lived and worked at different vantage peaks. They always gossiped and told stories of others' adulterous affairs, past and current - why they couldn't they see their act of female circumcision wasn't really working and stop mutilating their daughters, Eve could not understand. But she came to the conclusion that with no entertainment the only pastimes for the villagers were to be loquacious and lascivious. A young married lady sat next to Eve, while the others gossiped about the meetings of two adulterers.

"Do you know why women sleep with other men?" the young lady whispered to Eve.

"Why?" said Eve.

"Because someone else's always feels sweeter." she replied giggling.

They jabbered at length about the treacherous sins of adultery and its unbearable punishment in the afterlife yet there was an alacrity in how fast they pulled down the elastic waistband of their trousers that she found their ideology to be but a verbal façade (all for religious warnings—but no knickers).

For some reason which remained unknown to Eve, the whole village believed people in Britain were all without religion, women walked around stark naked and people did nothing but fornicate, even in the streets. The villagers somehow tied this belief with the cause being women were taught to read and write, educated. Eve had begun teaching Dhalia and some young girls from the family to read and write Arabic and to learn by heart verses of the Quran which upset some people from the village, they did not differentiate between literacy and education, in their book both were bad if women had this 'power'—it was good for a male to be educated, but nebulously negative for the fairer sex (what's good for the gander is not good for the goose), but Suleiman and a few parents were agreeable to their daughters learning to read and write as it would help them read the Holy Quran and ignored the others' objections.

Everybody feared demons, believing you could be possessed by them, and many stories of possession were told. The exorcism was performed by a pious person using verses from the Quran and debating with the demon in the 'possessed' patient while beating him or her with a sandal. It was said, the screams and voice of the possessed persons were unearthly and demonic because it was the demon's voice, not the person's, coming through; the person wasn't being beaten, but the demon—although the bruises left on the skin of the patient said otherwise. The exorcist both negotiated and punished the demon inside the human body, demanding it leave the person by exiting through the anus or the big toe. Otherwise it would damage the person's body if it left through anywhere else. Some of the biggest arguments between demon and exorcist were over the demon wanting to leave the body going through the eye, which was unacceptable because it would cause blindness to the person. A glass was placed on a can next to the door and the story goes, as the demon leaves the possessed, the glass tips over and breaks, indicating the successful exorcism. Haleema and some elderly ladies swore by God they witnessed possessions and exorcisms, but Eve preferred to believe it was trickery, mental issues—so she could sleep at night (poor Eve, superstitions and myth have already infiltrated into your subconscious). There was an amusing story of a woman from a southern village who was being regularly raped by an invisible demon; Eve suggested maybe she was suffering epilepsy, when this was dismissed by the others, laughing she suggested maybe they had interrupted her while masturbating so she had to come up with a ridiculous story…Shame Eve! Do not talk like that! Well why accept logical theories when the 'truth' be the nonsensical incubus got her caboose?

Eve's in-laws insisted she learn to work like them, but she was no longer interested. She had tried and pushed herself to do things she couldn't do, but Kareema always mistreated her and it became obvious she would always treat her badly no matter how hard she worked and how much she loved them, she hated her daughter-in-law for merely existing. Eve didn't want to be there and was intent on leaving the mountains so there was no point in learning how to bake bread in a clay oven or grind grain on a slab of stones. Twice she tried, out of curiosity, to bake bread. The round clay oven was about eighteen inches in diameter and twenty-four inches high, mounted on slabs of rock. Each house had one or two ovens side by side, situated outside, or in a separate small hut or by the stairs going up to the roof so the smoke wouldn't blacken all the walls of the house; its outside cemented with a mixture of soil, water and cow dung, used to plaster almost everything including the inside walls of houses and floors. They piled logs and branches into the clay oven, an easily ignitable bush was placed at the bottom of the firewood and set on fire. As the branches burned, whoever was baking pressed on their tops, pushing them down; more branches were fed into the fire until the inner of the oven was white in colour and a red-hot bed of coal piled on the bottom, you could feel the heat yards away. The patted circles of dough, on a circular tray made of palm leaves, were placed near to the oven. The person baking the bread, most of the time, was the mother, wife or eldest daughter. Next to the oven, a metal bowl of water was placed, the mother splashed water over her arm and face between sticking each piece of bread against the oven. When the inner wall of the oven turned an ashy white, it was hot enough to cook the bread, and depending on the type of grain being baked, the pieces of dough had to be applied while low flames still burned. A piece of dough was picked up and its face wet with water by palm of the hand, the mother bent into the gruelling hot oven and pressed the piece of dough against the hot wall, not letting go until it stuck to it, until all the pieces of dough were in a circle in the oven, then a light branch was placed in the oven and its flames gave the crust a nice colour. It was one of the toughest daily tasks for girls and women as they puffed and recoiled; groaning when scorched or singed: not only when their hand or arm accidentally touched the inner side of the oven, but from the intense heat they had to stand directly in front of to feed the fire, then bend over and reach into to apply the dough. When it was time, the lady went back to the oven and removed the baked circular loaves of bread. The hot embers remaining would be used to burn incense and light tobacco on the kooz for the rest of the day.

Kareema brought the oven to the intense heat it should be. Eve, Dhalia, Huda and Dawood waited at the bottom of the stairs watching her.

"Come, it's ready," Kareema said "Like I showed you." Kareema placed a wetted circle of dough into Eve's open palm whom neared to the oven and backed away.

"It's too hot aunty." said Eve.

"It's supposed to be or the bread won't stick and won't cook." said Kareema. Eve tried to near again, but stepped backwards driven back by the heat. "Quickly!" said Kareema "It'll cool and we'll have to use more firewood." Eve stepped next to the oven, her face was on fire. She leaned backwards instead of forwards, trying to keep her scorching face as far as she could from the mouth of the oven. She proceeded to put her hand into its wide-open mouth, but it scorched her before her hand even lowered below its rim, and her hand snatched backwards in polysynaptic withdrawal reflex to the heat, letting go of the dough into the hot coal. The smell of burning dough rose and filled her nostrils.

"Try again." said Kareema, slapping another piece of dough into Eve's hand.

"I can't aunty, it's too hot!"

"Your skin will only toughen if you do this all the time. Go on!" Eve approached the oven again, but the heat was too much so she threw the dough against the oven's inner wall thinking force would make it stick as if she was in a pie throwing contest, to its peril in the red-hot bed. Kareema pushed her away saying: "You're not a woman! Women know how to bake!"

Dhalia, Huda and Dawood laughed, amused to see Eve trying to stick the bread to the oven wall while trying to keep away from the heat. The second time she attempted was under Suleiman's insistence and supervision she could do it, regardless of his wife's objection that it was hopeless. More family members gathered to watch her bake the bread. She forced herself to stay in front of the oven, bending over its intense heat, feeling her face cook before the bread, extreme pain going up her fingers and hand as she reached into it, the material of her dress wanting to ignite. It wasn't as easy as watching Kareema and the others, when she pressed the dough against the oven wall it would not stick, and to her disappointment, slipped off the wall and into the fire, and besides that she wasn't supposed to be applying dough to uncooperative, primitive ovens—she was supposed to be applying to universities by now.

"Look how red her face is!" the elder boys and girls laughed.

It felt she had been standing inside the oven and still she couldn't manage to do what they so quickly and aptly achieved. Eve, smoke and fumes imbued in her clothes and hair, hand aching to the bone, walked out to cool in the open air as an angry Kareema kneaded a new batch of dough because every piece of the first had fallen or slipped off the oven wall to the bottom of the oven where it smoked in a heap.

CHAPTER TEN

F ROM IN FRONT OF THE SECOND HOUSE TO IN FRONT OF THE
First House, back below the boulders and returning to in front
of the First House, Eve paced back and forth with the agitation
of a caged tiger, she had in what seemed to be now a previous life
drawn a picture of a restless tiger behind steel bars based on a poem
she'd read and loved and now she was feeling its aggravation; the
restrictions of tradition, and rules set by greedy people taking
advantage of her vulnerability were more of an obstacle than had she
needed to gnaw through steel bars with her teeth. Sick of confined
walls, begging to be allowed out with the children shepherding she
could not understand their caution, after all, there was no way *or how*
she could escape the mountains by foot: she had proven this with
deep cuts in her palms and gashes across her shins when she had
taken advantage of a sleeping Kareema and slipped away only for her
Uncle to find her not that far away from the Gayra village following
the car route northwards, limping while passionately telling him she
was leaving and going back home and that he couldn't stop her. He
had humoured her walking alongside her, the same when she climbed
up a steeply inclined slab of rock as if she were scaling Everest, while
he without as much as changing his straight posture walked
effortlessly up it with his hands behind his back, before she exploded
into tears, tired and hurt, the sticky blood drying and pinching at the
skin around her ankles and he helped her return to his lair. Any
attempt she would fall off a cliff and die, or she'd fall and be injured.
If, somehow, she was able to keep from falling they would catch up

with her within less than ten minutes at the pace she could walk in the 'easy' terrain made for cars. She had watched with Kareema, Haleema, Dhalia and Suleiman when a young couple had been caught trying to elope: they had left early in the dark morning, by mid-morning they had been spotted and news spread like wildfire. The lad's family had refused to allow him to marry Sahira so they had tried to run away; after being caught up with she appeared on the path carrying a few sparse branches on her head (a cover suggested by her uncles that she had gone to collect firewood to deny the scandal towards the villagers) with her brothers, uncles and father surrounding her, their heads lowered in shame. A short while later the male lover and his male relatives appeared, walking slowly to keep a distance. While her lover was merely rebuked and told off by his family, her family beat her day after day and kept her under lock and key for months, unable to show their faces in public because of the dishonour she had brought upon them. They'd even gone to the length of bringing in a woman from a faraway village as an independent inspector to silence gossipers whom would destroy her chance of ever getting married now to a decent person, to check her virginity: after checking with her clouded eyes and thick calloused and cut fingers the woman announced Sahira *virgo intacta* although she was no longer a virgin in facta.

Eve explained to her in-laws if they allowed her out more often, she would be able to adjust and learn how to walk in the difficult terrain just like they could, but she was only allowed to the Uncles' and Latifa's, and to visit the sick with a group. She only went to Aunt Ethe's when Eid came, with a procession of family and relatives, but though she was excited most of the way, there were heart stopping, dangerous places to cross where a slight slip on a perilous precipice or misplacement of foot would ensure a plunge of thousands of metres with nothing but mountain face and rocks to smash against. Kareema promised to take her out when she went to land with easily accessible routes, and one morning Kareema did take Eve with her. They went over the usual path above Barh Salliya southwards and along the path below Latifa's house situated below an unusual black cliff whose hexagonal columns rose like sprouting stems from the ground. Eve was surprised how easy the route and different the colour of soil in the land and noted the many paths worn out by people going back and forth this way. People came out of their houses to stare at Eve, Kareema whipped at the hind of her cow to keep it moving.

"Where are you taking the girl from beyond the sea?" one woman shouted out, looking down from in front of her house perched on a cliff, they still referred to her as from beyond, not her name and seemed unaware she could now speak their language and be directly addressed.

"She has to learn how to work," Kareema replied "This cow will be hers one day!" Eve laughed, she certainly did not want a cow, now or in the future—another thing to put on her list to ask God not to give her. She continued to follow Kareema up and down paths. Finally, they reached the land where the cow was to graze; there was scarcely anything green in this piece of land.

"What's she going to eat?" asked Eve looking around at the dearth.

"When she finishes everything left in our land, we'll just soak grains for her until it rains and the land will be back alive and green for her to eat from," said Kareema "This is the worst drought in a long time."

Shortly, a woman arrived with her cow in the land above them where she left it grazing and sat with them on the raised soil border. Most of their conversation focused on Eve: how soft her skin was, how her fingers and toes looked and felt like a baby's, how beautiful and long her hair is, how strange it is she can read and write, why she wasn't pregnant; an absence of husband to impregnate her was not accounted for in the conversation, but maybe she was infertile or ill was determined to be the cause.

"You must take a sacrifice to the Wali and she'll become pregnant." said the woman.

"She doesn't believe in the Wali," said Kareema "So he probably won't help her no matter what we present."

"She might have been taking pills not to get pregnant when she was in Britain—you know what they do there all the time without shame in the streets. Maybe the effect lasts forever." said the woman, as if Eve was not there. Eve turned in anger to look at the stupignorude woman.

"No, she definitely was a virgin," said Kareema "I saw her morning cloth and I asked my son."

"Are you stupid or just rude?" Eve finally said to the woman who in turn just laughed, and the conversation turned to their cows. Eve wandered off to the other side of the land. She looked down, more steps of land crisscrossed by narrow paths and further away mountains going up to the sky. Two men came down the path above Eve and greeted her: "Good morning."

"Good morning." she replied.

"What are you doing here?" said one of the men squatting to look down at her while he spoke, but Kareema interrupted before Eve could reply, shouting: "Eve come over here! Come over here!" Kareema lifted at her dress as she cut across the land in wide strides looking ready to fight, "Why are you talking to my daughter-in-law? Have you no shame? Do not talk to her!"

Eve walked away, towards the strange lady still sitting on the soil as her mother-in-law came down on the men whom dared converse with her. Kareema shouted at them in vulgarity, heard by all those shepherding nearby. The men walked away hurriedly, their heads bobbing as if trying to duck her insults as she described their sisters as sluts, hollering at the top of her voice. She finished her vulgar attack and came back.

"Eve you have to stop smiling," Kareema reprimanded "People will think you're a slut!"

"But aunty they didn't say anything bad, they just said good morning."

"They shouldn't talk to you, they're strangers and you're Adam's wife!"

Eve sat on the sun warmed soil, digging at the compacted brown earth with a stick, she couldn't put together the contradictions she observed in the village: she wasn't supposed to talk to men, but she saw all the women in the family and extended family kiss hands and talk with 'stranger' men, as they described anyone who wasn't related to the family so why wasn't she allowed to talk to people? If men passed by in numbers, women hopped away like shy rabbits, but if they passed in ones and twos they just stood there, kissed hands and talked with them. Women walked off the path and climbed a hill to face rocks if a vehicle approached, they hid behind boulders if more than two men were seen walking towards them and they didn't come out and continue on the path until the men had well passed. When stranger-men approached the Second or First House, the women and girls scurried inside; Suleiman would tell Eve to go inside before she was seen so she followed her female family. More to it, why were they being so overprotective of her, she was chaste and wouldn't fall if men tried to seduce her—funnily enough it was Adam's cousins and brother-in-law whom fixed her with lusty gazes and slipped love letters underneath her door which, though her heart pounded harder because she was alarmed more than excited, she found disgusting— did their relationship to Adam have no bearing upon what they desired? What Eve was too innocent to understand was that although women and girls did hide if large crowds of men were passing, the reason she wasn't allowed to talk to men was Uncle Suleiman's precaution that she never find an aide to help her out or give her ideas how to escape his dominion, for the same reasons she wasn't allowed out that much unless to a relative's dwelling and accompanied at that.

*

FINALLY IT RAINED, TO LET ALL THE VILLAGE AND HAMLET'S OCCUPANTS' spirits rise in anticipation of good crops. Water came in from under the doors and windows even though they had holes to let it back out. The metal doors of windows and its bolts shook as thunder rolled and you could feel its vibration travel in your body. Eve stood outside in the rain, but they pulled her inside, fearing lightning. After the rain, the mountains were a beautiful sight: the water cascaded down every possible line in the mountain face, over land, down paths; the land arranged in steps were overflowing, beautifully architectured waterfalls. The Dibt usually unseen in the far distance could be made out, as large swathes of land bordered full with water could be clearly seen. Shortly, the rain water flowing down from the mountainous region would appear as thin lines in The Dibt, of course the people there saw it as a large rushing river, but from up in the mountains all Eve could see were glistening lines. The rain water had arrived suddenly in the mountains, ran over the rocks and soil and made its way out and away from this village. She hadn't, still here and unable to leave. The happiness of Suleiman and his family with the rainfall collided with her own sadness. It was a beautiful scene to see the mountains come to life and watch water weave around and converge, flowing downwards, reappearing in a land where lifestyle was different. Some of the irrigation was hand made by placing rocks to make a path of water flow towards specific pieces of land and a few individuals irrigated while it rained, placing rocks to change the direction or block the flow to their land. Water came down from the north end of the steep and also down from Barh Salliya, both flows met converging into one and went downwards, winding down the path, westwards and behind the rocky hill. All the routes and paths had turned into raging rivers. But as soon as the dramatic scenes faded and the lines of water dissipated in the distance, all she could feel was an emptiness; damp like the air she inhaled, her soul withered, weathered by the years spent here. The ammonious stench of the wet bunker made her queasy, reminding her it was made of dung; she made the faintest smile when Dawood kicked the tree trunk and jumped out of the way, making Mahmood scream like a girl as the cold water fell from the leaves and down his back.

After the rain the sky was azure clear; the houses and mountains stood more clearly defined against the sky. The little shrubbery there was, looked greener. People were buoyant: with the local well replenished they didn't have to wake up extra early or worry about going over the dangerous path to the next nearest well. The cattle would have something to eat, and if crops were successful so would the people from their land instead of having to buy white flour, which most families found unhealthy. Eve stood in front of the house watching trickling water make its way down the mountains, her mind wandered off and she remembered the old man telling them it was only better for bovine when it rained. How true. Here she was. Stuck. It made no difference to her if they were dry or covered with green crops. She stepped onto the ducka, walked to its end where she stood and gazed morosely towards the top of the steep where the car had stopped for Sami; the point where her brothers had left, leaving behind their promises and oaths to come back for her. She sat on the damp bunker, the sorrow she could not leave like they had sculpting a change in her soul which would remain forever.

"Why are you crying?" said Suleiman loudly, and with much excitement, "Now it's rained you'll like living here. You'll see!"

"What difference is the rain going to make? Uncle please, *please* let me go. I can't live here. *I can't*."

"You will live and die here," said Suleiman cheerfully "This is your country. This is your origin! The land of father and grandfather of grandfather! You can't leave your country!"

She let out a sigh as Suleiman repeated she would like living here now that it had rained and everything would be green. Eve shivered as distant thunder rolled over a different area while she stood behind the house watching lightning and rain go down on a village far away and unknown to her, the dark clouds as gloomy as her pained heart, pining to go home.

People, eager and excited, were preparing to sow their land, they had to wait for the excess water to evaporate from the soil. Using one cow, or two bulls, and a wooden plough with a sharp chisel-spear like head attached to its bottom, they turned the soil over in lines several times before returning another day when the soil was less water logged to do the same. When it was time to sow seeds the men controlled the movement and pace of the bulls, keeping the lines steady and a man or woman followed the plough-spear, taking a handful of seeds planting them into the dug open line behind the spear head by opening the index finger outwards sending a straight line of seeds into the soil. Skilled farmers of mountains, their forefathers had turned steep mountainside into terraced agricultural steps architectured to allow higher land to fill up with rainwater before flowing down into lower pieces of land, capturing every needed drop, and they were so skilled at upkeeping these terraced, walled steps that one rainfall could yield three successive crops—they knew what to sow and how to get maximum productivity from what was once a bare rock and had been made into a fertile land, and generations had survived and thrived on the fortune of the land without there being any rivers to irrigate from—wells and underground cisterns were for drinking and daily use only and needed to last until the next rainfall, and in this seemingly uninhabitable terrain Eve could see the tenacity and ingenuity of its people making it a home and an unchanged way of life spanning back from thousands of years and unknown antiquity living on into this current day. Eve, Dhalia and Huda stood underneath the massive boulders next to the Second House, watching a neighbour control Suleiman's cow pulling the plough while Suleiman and Kareema took turns sowing seeds. They laughed as Suleiman and Kareema argued.

"You're wasting the seeds!" Suleiman shouted at Kareema.

"Uncle, let me try." Eve shouted down.

"No, you'll waste the seeds." said Suleiman.

"Come on Uncle," said Eve smiling "You say you want me to work, but you won't let me learn."

"Alright," he said "Huda, help her down."

Suleiman demonstrated to Eve how it was done. Giggling and jumping she took a handful of seeds carried in a basket by Suleiman walking beside her. It looked fun while she had been watching, it looked easy too. It was neither. First, she couldn't walk properly over the furrows because one line was uplifted and in between the lines the soil was much lower, she couldn't find balance with the soil giving way under her foot, and the back half of her soles constantly slipped off the rubber flip flops.

"Quickly!" said Suleiman, with much irritation, "You have to follow the plough and get the seeds into the line directly after the spearhead."

Eve tried releasing a stream of seeds by extending her index finger, but nothing came out. She opened two fingers and seeds scattered over the outsides of the dug line.

"No! No!" Suleiman shouted "Like a line! Like a line!" he gesticulated the move.

Eve stumbled after the plough taking handfuls of seed from the basket throwing them in front of her, none landed in lines, but sprayed all over the place.

"You're wasting seeds more than Kareema," said Suleiman, disappointed "Step away, let me do it." She moved away and watched him do two lines.

"Please Uncle," she said, for he made it look so easy, "I've seen how you do it properly, I can do it now."

They switched places. She tried to send a line of seeds, but very few came out. She caught up with the plough and again attempted to send a line of seeds out of her palm, stepped on a pile of soil which gave way under her foot and fell face down and arms ahead into the soil. She looked up to see seeds scattered over the ground, Kareema and Huda laughing. She turned to see her uncle's exasperated face and she laughed. He helped her up saying at the top of his voice, amusement having replaced his vexation: "Oh my God! My son's wife will never be a farmer! She'll never be a farmer!"

*

WITH NOTHING TO ENGAGE HER BRAINS, EVE BECAME PAINFULLY bored, finding something to do became a necessity for her sanity so she found ways to keep herself occupied by teaching more girls Arabic; teaching Dhalia Arabic and English; she told stories: fairy tales, Greek myths, Aesop's fables, and books she had read, plays and films she had seen; telling them in Arabic to her in-laws and the children whom gathered in her room, captivated by stories they'd never heard before as she told them theatrically and enthusiastically—her young audience could never get enough of these stories and asked for them repeatedly (oh Eve, is this your future? All you need is to sit on branch in tree with lute in lap). She would babysit her niece Suha; the supernatural novel was taken out of the trunk and read repeatedly, but she had read it so many times she knew every sentence off by heart, it became mental torture reading it to kill time so she returned the book to its burial ground in the metal trunk, under clothes, hoping by the next time she dug it out she would have forgotten the words and find it interesting again. Oh, how she missed books and reading terribly! Over the years, she had passed time by making dozens and dozens of cushions and pillows out of unwanted dresses which she sewed by hand and stuffed to the brim with the spongy part of a plant she paid children to collect sacks of; it looked like the spherical crumbs of broken foam packaging, except they were softer and spongier to the touch; the pollen of which came off when she stripped it from the stems sent her into coughing fits. Bundar came running home from school one day, excited to tell her one of the teachers had brought rabbits to sell.

Eve immediately bought two and both she and Bundar built a spacious pen for them to live in, situated behind the Thorn of Christ tree at the front of the house; if they were to reproduce, half the litter would belong to Bundar. Sitting in her room she sang the songs she could still remember from the eighties, but noticed she had forgotten the words to many; it always left her sad, remembering a decade where she had once been happy and fully alive. She sang songs from school assemblies, later asking God to forgive her when she felt they contradicted her religion; she sang every song she had learnt for school concerts and plays, Christmas Carols. She even recited nursery rhymes. She longed for books other than the Arabic, religious ones left for her by Morad, many years ago. When falcons, eagles and other birds of prey landed nearby or flew above or below, she sat outside her room and watched them in fascination, particularly enjoying a huge black eagle that sometimes came, as it cruised, aiming towards a lower house on a cliffside for the neighbour's lambs then swooped, Eve marvelled at the span of its spread wings and she could see the black and white feathers from her vantage point. She washed Kareema's blackened pots and grimy bowls, returning them to the stainless-steel colour they once were to have Grandmother Haleema state in shock they looked brand new. She built a small garden behind her room and helped Dhalia make one too, using small rocks unusable by Suleiman, and paid the children to bring up cans and buckets of soil; then she visited Latifa who gave her stems of the aromatic plants she grew in her own garden, which Eve planted as soon as she got home. A wall climbing plant with large juicy spade-shaped green leaves had popped up and spread on the ground and up the two-metre wall she had been carried down on her wedding night; she didn't know when, but Suleiman had placed stacks of entangled, dried, thorny bushes at the top of the wall, for the same purpose as barbed wire. Women whose husbands were returning home from work in the city would pass by to pick small bundles of the fragrant plants from her small perfume garden, to place in their hair and between their breasts; Suleiman would pick a few stems and place them in the front pocket of his white dress before going to the Friday prayer sermon. She had stopped collecting eggs from her hens to eat, to allow them to become chicks and once they hatched she was delighted with their different colours and fluffy cuteness. The rabbits had grown and were heavy, Eve and the younger children doted on them, all fond of their cute pets. And all in between her preoccupations whenever there was a moment of inactivity, her thoughts immediately asked where would she be now if still at home, what progress would she have made, what successes would she have achieved—sometimes she comforted herself that she could still do it, she could still make it—if she ever got out, but sometimes it helped her to imagine she would have made bad choices had she remained in Britain; for instance, she would explore the possibility that she may have become a slut and would have caught a dangerous debilitating venereal disease—now that would have been worse than being kept captive here—or wouldn't it? She was not sure, so she imagined herself having stayed there and for whatever (unrealistic) reasons she had failed or neglected her studies (impossible, she was a genius) and never made it to university, but no matter how she tried to convince herself that there had been a possibility she could have gone down the wrong road in the UK and become unhappy, logic told her it would still have been the road of her choice, the consequences she would have borne of her own mistakes would have been a thousand times lighter than the torture of being kept against your will, your life left to languor by someone else's decree. And, had she been allowed to continue on the natural course of life she'd had in Wales, she would most definitely have been successful, and at this conclusion tears always stung in her eyes, but she didn't want to cry, nor think about it anymore so she turned to some chore or activity to take her mind off what could have been, and should have been.

*

Mornings were always a little glum if Suleiman's cheery presence was away, which was the case today as he had gone to The Dibt, to return after three days. Eve poured fresh tea she had made into the thermos flask and poured herself and Kareema a glass each, she placed Kareema's glass near her and took her own outside to sit on the ducka in the cool morning air. She took her first sip and noticed there was no movement in the rabbit pen; she got up to see if they had water, but to her distress the pen was empty. The door was closed, the metal mesh intact, but no rabbits. A knot turned in Eve's stomach and she ran inside.

"Aunt Kareema, have you seen my rabbits?" said Eve.

"No, aren't they in the pen?" Kareema replied, with a faint smile.

"No, they're not, somebody must have let them out! Come and see."

"I will," said Kareema "Just when I'm finished here." she turned her back to Eve and poured the yoghurt-like milk into the dry pumpkin for churning. Eve went back outside and joined the sleepy, puffy eyed children sitting on the ducka, each holding a glass or metal bowl of tea.

"Do you know what happened to the rabbits Dawood?" Eve asked.

"No." Dawood replied, looking at the ground. Something wasn't right, Bundar, looking guilty, avoided looking her straight in the eye.

"Will you help me look for them?" she asked, but no one answered. As she went looking under boulders and the firewood storage area the children watched her with guilty, knowing eyes. She searched for her pet rabbits in the area around the houses, but returned without them, distressed. Kareema had most probably opened the door for them and let them escape. As people passed underneath the house on their way to shepherd, Eve called out to them to let her know if they saw her escaped rabbits. Kareema, on seeing her sullen face gave a beaming smile and said: "Maybe the fox ate them!"

Eve said nothing, but had the scheming bitch-fox opened and closed the door to the pen too? There were no visitors that morning so Eve went to her room and bolted it from the inside for her usual morning nap, and when she emerged after hours of sleep she was renewed with optimism to search the land below the path, surely her cute pets would be there waiting for her to find them. She opened the door of her room and the waft of meat and broth filled her nostrils, the odour strong and unfamiliar. She passed through the Bawaba to find all her in-laws, including Dhalia and her daughters, sitting around a food spread, eating hastily. It didn't smell like chicken. She walked past them and out to the bathroom, insouciant to being excluded from good food when Suleiman wasn't around, especially if it was meat or vegetables, it no longer bothered her as it had when she was younger. She came up from the outhouse and sat on the ducka. One by one her in-laws came out to wash their hands, pouring for each other from the kettle. Mahmood belched and added: "Ya Salam! Rabbit meat is delicious!" Bundar punched him in the stomach before running off in the other direction away from the house, ashamed he had been part of killing and eating Eve's pet rabbits. A cry choked in Eve's throat and she confronted Kareema.

"Why did you kill my rabbits?" said Eve.

"They weren't your rabbits," Kareema replied, licking her greasy lips, "Your rabbits were eaten by a fox. The children found these rabbits so we slaughtered them, but they weren't yours—they were even a different colour!" Mahmood and Dhalia laughed, while Eve swallowed hard and suppressed her need to weep, the pressure building up in her throat, tearing at her vocal cords.

Early in the morning, she sat looking out to the east from her bedroom window, for many years she had looked out from here, she didn't know why she expected her rescue to come from that direction. Bored from the unchanging scene of motionless mountains, she slid down onto her back, lying on the bed. She was thinking of something and it happened for the first time: she couldn't see in her mind's eye what the letter 'p' looked like. She concentrated hard, but it wouldn't come to her. She tried to pronounce it and her throat and tongue were unable to produce its sound. She picked up a pen and book from the inner shelf next to her bed and tried to write it down, 'p' 'p' 'p', but her brain paralysed and panic raced through her mind. Try as she might, she could not imagine what the letter 'p' looked like. She commanded her hand to write it, but it froze because she didn't know where to begin its shape or what its shape was. Breathing hard, she started to recite the alphabet, she had only gotten to 'a' and her throat and brain clammed unable to imagine what 'b' looked like. 'c' was fine, but 'd' impossible. Going through the alphabet the letters k, q, r and u joined the others she was unable to pronounce or write or even see in her mind. She slapped her small hand onto her large forehead. How could she not remember? She knew these letters. Why couldn't she pronounce them or imagine their shape? Why did it hurt her throat when unable to pronounce them? What was happening to her? She knew all she had to do was open up her novel and there they would be, all the letters she knew, but were tormenting her unable to remember. No, she would remember them without assistance, there was no reason why her mind was finding great difficulty in seeing them, remembering them. Hours she spent trying to sing the alphabet, or write spontaneously, but these letters would not appear to her no matter how long she held her head in both hands or pulled them through her hair. Or stared out into the distance trying to recall them. Finally, she gave up, checked her book and instantly recognised and pronounced them. This unnerving experience would bother her many times, sometimes with whole words.

Time came to harvest the crops, done in two steps: first you go to cut off the tops with the seed pods, except if it was corn then you reap the whole stalks and remove the ears of corn at home. The other types of grain you had to cut off the panicles while it was still standing and return again to reap the crop with a sheared hand sickle. Many people cut their hands and fingers while reaping, bandaging the wound by cutting off a piece of their dress, head veil or shawl. Good grains were selected and stored for future grinding and sowing after they were beaten with sticks making the grain fall off its panicle, dried in the sun and stored in sacks or barrels. Eve helped reap the crop in one of the many pieces of land owned by Suleiman and Kareema, five of them had gone together. To everyone's surprise, Eve was able to do this task faster and better than the rest; harvested by each person squatting at the edge of the land, holding a handful of the lower part of stalks and cutting underneath your hand with the sickle, laying them down behind you; you progressed forward without getting up, moving forward in squatting position, a gruelling workout, and as each person progressed, they left paths of open space in the crop behind them. The others got up to drink tea poured from a thermos flask or kettle, but Eve continued non-stop until it was time to leave, her hands on fire, palms sore with blisters, but feeling good she had achieved something today, and had not thought about home. The corn was a treat while fresh, roasted on fire and eaten from the cob. The remaining ripened corn was removed from the cob by hand into sacks; the women and girls, including Eve, spent hours and days manually removing kernels from every single cob until their thumbs blistered. Both Aunt Kareema and Mother sent for Aunt Ethe to come and stay with them; they needed her help with clearing the husks and crusts from the seeds as she was more experienced in winnowing. Eve sat outside, watching the three women. Aunt Ethe licked her finger and held it up to ascertain which direction the wind blew; Kareema and Mother spread an extra-large palm frond tray on the ground below where Aunt Ethe stood high upon the ducka slowly pouring the grain from a smaller tray, shaking it gently side to side with her arms held high. Eve smiled watching the heavy grain flow down as a stream of husks and flakes drifted dreamily away with the wind. Away from them.

*

LIVING HERE WAS DIFFICULT IN DROUGHT AND GOOD SEASONS. EVE would ask women why they lived this hard life, why didn't they go live in the city or a different country.

"This is where we were born and this is where we will die. You can't run away from your origin. You can't leave your country." the majority replied. But what did it have to do with origin or running away from their own country? They could live an easier life in any of its cities, they didn't have to cut off or deny their roots; you are who you are, wherever you go in the world. With a small smile and shy flutter of eyelashes, some expressed they would like to live in Taiz, others in Saudi as they had seen the photos and heard the letters from a few women whom had been taken from nearby villages to live with their husbands whom worked there, and when they returned for a visit, the villagers heard how luxurious and easy life was in Saudi or Taiz; even the women's appearance changed dramatically: their skin became smooth and lighter in colour, their hair longer and thicker and, what the village women envied and liked most of all, these women became fat. Being extremely plump was the imagined standard of beauty in the village—imagined because unattainable too with the lack of fattening food and all the rigorous work and walking which kept them in phenomenally good physique. They liked to use the expressions 'she's beautifully fat' 'her butt is the size of a ducka'. Eve smiled at the difference in beauty standards between the cultures she had been exposed to. Here, the 'beautiful' ideal meant being white and fat (notwithstanding they always admired beautiful girls and women of all colours, features and sizes); back at home people watched what they ate and exercised to become slim and roasted themselves in sun until their skin peeled to become tanned. These cultures were so opposite and they wanted to be what the other culture did not want to be, but only in appearance because the women Eve had grown up around would never want to be the 'subservient', unquestioning, male dominated women here; and these beautiful village women would rather be dead than become the educated, 'immoral' city women. But with women from nearby villages going to live in different cities and countries, they knew city life was easier, but chose to believe living where you were born was necessary. Maybe it made this hard life easier to bear. Maybe Eve knowing what a different life she had back home made this life for her so much harder and tortuous although she didn't do any hard work.

*

THERE WAS ALWAYS LAUGHTER, STORIES OF ENCOUNTERS WITH dangerous snakes, scorpions; visitors were many in the morning and afternoon, all with their stories of past and present and gossip, but the monotony increased day by day. It had been years while Eve patiently waited for any of her brothers to return. The closest she came to a peak of hope would be when a villager was to return to work in Sana'a; she wrote to each of her brothers a letter telling them how much she missed them, some things that had happened, but mostly she described her pain and suffering by being kept in the mountains and begged them to come back and save her from the village. She cried while she wrote, reminding them of their promises and oaths, her tears smudging some of the words and, oddly, unsuperstitious Eve was overcome by a reassuring feeling the tears would mystically help her brothers feel and understand her pain. She massaged then clenched and unclenched her right hand, it hurt and cramped as soon as she had begun to write and she wondered if it was because she hadn't written in English, or at all, for so long. Her hope replenished handing the letters to Bundar to deliver, now all she had to do was wait; surely, she believed, they would come after reading her message.

Kareema was on a rant, beating her children from early morning. The girls took off without breakfast to fetch firewood and the boys to shepherd the sheep and goats, in hope she would be calm when they returned after noon, a safety mechanism they learnt to escape being beaten. Experience had taught them to notice if she was in a mood from the moment she awoke; there would be tension in the way she moved and spoke; the atmosphere thick with her menacing anger, you could feel it penetrate your chest. They tried to avoid the ogre, scampering quietly to collect their sickles, rope, flip flops and leave hungry to avoid being hit, sometimes they waited behind Eve's room and asked her to bring them tea and cold bread from the previous day to eat in hiding before they took off. After discreetly appropriating stale bread and a thermos flask Eve watched them with pity in her heart, and how painful it looked, the way they masticated at the hardened bread and gulped it down with tepid tea.

"Women know how to bake bread, fetch water, grind grains," Kareema shouted coming out of the house purposely not turning towards Eve seated on the ducka in front of the other house, "If you can't, you might as well not be alive!"

Why did they keep her from leaving if they were so upset about her not doing work beyond her physical ability? Eve had also noticed Kareema's mood always worsened when it was time for her menstruation. Kareema went in and out of the house on a non-stop fury she let out verbally. The children had reason to leave hungry when she was like this, she would look for absolutely next to nothing to take out the violent rage inside her by beating them mercilessly, both Eve and Dhalia had once tried to remove her iron grip from a battered Eman, still a toddler, but when Kareema was violent she showed unbelievable strength—they were unable to pull her away or even pry her fingers off the poor child. If you weren't her child or cattle she would release it onto you verbally. In the past, she had hurt the children, now married adults, to the extent Latifa still suffered physically from an injury caused by her mother. After breakfast she was calmer. Eve and Kareema were the only two moving around the house, for on days like this Dhalia stayed in her room with the doors bolted from the inside. Kareema sat next to Eve who with a smile handed her mother-in-law a glass of tea.

"Is it hard to learn to read and write?" Kareema asked with a broad smile.

"It's not hard." said Eve.

"So people who read and write are educated," said Kareema dropping the smile "And people like us women who can't read and write are like cattle? Cows?" She completely changed the direction of the conversation wanting to get into an argument.

"Of course not," said Eve refusing to be pulled in "Only cows are cattle and we are humans. It doesn't matter if we can read or not." Eve may as well have said 'yes, you are cows' because Kareema responded: "We're not cattle! We know how to bake, fetch water and grind grains! It doesn't matter that you can read or write, what good is it for anybody? If you can't bake bread and you can't grind grains then you are a COW!"

"If I wanted to learn how, I could," Eve said, unruffled, "But I don't want to, and do you know why? Because I can't live here and I'm going to get out of here one day."

"You're never leaving," said Kareema "We won't get money from Adam if you do. You say you can work if you want? Then I dare you to grind grains!"

"Okay, I'll do it," said Eve "Give me the grains."

"I'll soak them for you," Kareema smiled "And you grind them for lunch today. But it has to be ground very fine."

"Okay." said Eve.

Kareema soaked the grains and showed Eve how to move the almost cylindrical stone rolling pin with tapered ends, over the rectangular slab stone, these two dark rock pieces made up the grinder. "Don't let the pin roll and don't smack it down onto the grinder because it will break," said Kareema "I've had it since before my mother died…it was hers and she gave it to me. Anyway, you won't be able to get it right the first time, but if you always do it, you'll learn how."

The grains were to be sifted out of the water; the first time they went under the stone rolling pin, the grain would be cracked; the second time it was supposed to come out a semi-paste. On the third run, you were to spray a little water to make it easier before grinding it through to the other side where it should come out a fine paste. Eve moved the unbelievably heavy rolling pin back and forth, but the grains passed out whole and spilled around the sides of the slab onto the circular palm leaf tray underneath it. Kareema pushed her away to show her how. "Like this." she said, lifting the pin slightly going back and pounding it down with a turn of the wrist pressing forward. As Eve tried the same, Kareema shouted: "You're going to break my grinder! Be careful!"

At the end of Eve's long efforts, the grains were still mostly whole. Kareema laughed at the results.

"I'll do it today," she said, taking Eve's place in front of the raised platform, "And you can try again tomorrow." Eve was at the door leaving when Kareema said out loud: "She may as well be a cow." Eve turned to face Kareema, but she just carried on grinding.

During her attempt the next day, she used too much water on the second run, it had become so wet it was impossible to be ground by anybody, the soggy, cracked grains were put into the bucket for the cow. She continued trying to master grinding grain with the same tool the ancient Mayans had probably used, and everyday got better. With every day blisters burnt in her palms and Eve couldn't see how they felt it was worth the pain, surely they could buy a fuel-based machine, then all they would have to do was knead the flour instead of using this ancient tool? She considered it a workout, the repetitive movements she could feel pulling at her already taut arms, back and flat stomach muscles, no wonder all the women here had beautiful figures, plus there was nothing fatty to eat. Finally, by the end of two weeks, the grains appearing from under the stone rolling pin Eve pushed, came out a fine paste. Kareema rubbed a little between her index finger and thumb.

"It's finer than my daughters' dough!" Kareema said thoroughly impressed. She picked up the bowl and took it outside where Haleema sat enjoying her morning smoke with Dhalia. "Feel it," said Kareema "Eve ground it!"

"It's very finely ground. Eve can do this?" said Haleema "Oh yes, now she's a real woman!" Eve, standing in the arch of the Viking door with its metal bar and circular ring handle, rolled her eyes at the comment.

"I'm a woman because I am a woman," said Eve "If I never learn to work like you—I'm still a woman."

*

A CAR STOPPED AT BARH SALLIYA AT THREE A.M. EVE SAT UP IN BED, full of anticipation, believing Yusef and Sami had arrived to save her. She recognised Morad's voice, and it was the only new voice amongst those talking, he entered his room and she fell back asleep. At least Morad was here now, and she was leaving with him, no doubt about it. She had done time for no crime for far too long and there was no way she was staying any longer in these abysmal mountains.

CHAPTER ELEVEN

L IKE ALL VILLAGERS RETURNING HOME, MORAD BROUGHT letters with him from Sana'a. Surprised they had remained this long in Yemen, as a part of her had believed they had long returned to Britain, Eve received two letters from her brothers; she tore eagerly at the envelopes and her eyes dove hungrily into the words, only to be filled by dissatisfaction. Yusef only spoke about himself and how he was enjoying his new job as a tour guide. Sami asked her to be patient, he was working to save money to buy an air ticket and go back to Britain; that when he had money he would return for her. Neither brother mentioned contacting the embassy nor the police so they probably hadn't. Eve stared at the opposite whitewashed wall, all that time patiently enduring pain, believing they were coming for her, all the waiting and getting up when she heard a car stop, thinking it was them arriving to get her out, and they hadn't even been trying. She washed the exasperation from her face and entered Morad's room to find her parents and all her in-laws already there.

"Look what I brought with me," said Morad with a warm smile, knowing his sister would like what he presented, "They're from Yusef." He opened a suitcase showing her four books and stacks and stacks of *Newsweek*. Eve smiled gleefully as she read the back of the books, she wouldn't have chosen to read them, but years had passed and the only book she had was the one she carried from the airport to Yemen; just as hunger had the magical power to make a dry, unchewable piece of bread taste as sweet as honey, book deprivation had made any book an intriguing read. While everybody talked, Eve watched silently, waiting for them to leave towards their chores so she could speak to her brother. She was leaving with him, nothing would stop her, but she needed to talk to him alone, cognisant of others' meddling. She watched her big brother with eyes brimming with hope and belief, he was here and she was leaving with him. It was nice having him back, he was so different than the village people, well, he wasn't as open minded as she or his younger brothers, but he did understand her unlike everybody else whom surrounded her. Educated, good at heart, strong and trained in martial arts; he would laugh at their superstitions and joke about their way of thinking and beliefs; he would tilt his head backwards and laugh loudly from his heart when they made the most unusual and ridiculous statements or questions whether it was about city life or how things were made. Finally, the last person left the room, Dhalia picked up Suha, saying she would leave her with her grandmother and fetch water from the well; she never went to fetch water anymore, but this was her chance to show off her gold and how well dressed and pretty she was now her husband was here and she was in full adornment.

"So how are you?" said Morad "You're getting used to living here by now aren't you?"

"No," Eve replied "I'll never get used to living here—it's too hard and…strange."

"But you will." he said.

"I want to talk to you and it's important…Do you still love me?" she said.

"Of course I love you!" he said "You're my baby sister, you *know* I love you."

"You said you'd protect me," said Eve "And not let anybody hurt me. You said if I didn't want to get married you wouldn't allow it, but you didn't do anything to stop it…"

"You do know I spoke to Dad, but he was going to kill me?" said Morad "I told him in front of Adam and all his uncles that you're too young and don't want to get married and Dad threw a glass of tea in my face in front of everybody, it was so embarrassing! *He said he'd kill us both*, I wasn't worried about myself, but I was worried about *you*.

He said he'd slaughter you like a sheep, that's why I couldn't stop the marriage."

"So you let him sell me like a sheep?" said Eve. She remembered the horrid day and shuddered before continuing "Is it true Adam gave Dad money to marry me?"

"Yes." said Morad.

"You know it doesn't mean I was sold?" said Eve "I didn't agree to this so if Adam gave Pompous money it doesn't mean he bought me. I wasn't sold and I never will be."

"It's just a custom here," said Morad "They don't think like you do...to them getting money for marriage is something to be proud of. But it's not a sale."

"But they talk about it like sales 'I sold her for this much' 'she was sold for that much'?" said Eve "Do you know the bride wants to be paid for everything before she moves on her wedding day?"

"Yes," Morad said and laughed "Dhalia wouldn't take her trousers off until I paid her a lot of money!" his cheeks flushed while he continued to chuckle, knowing what it sounded like in comparison to the outside world, Eve smirked and shook her head.

"Morad, I can't live here anymore," said Eve earnestly "I'm going to leave with you—please don't say no, I *have* to go with you, I'm never going to like living here. I'm never going to get used to this way of life."

"They won't let me take you with me," said Morad "They'll say you'll run away to Britain and divorce your husband."

"I didn't ask to be forced into marriage," said Eve "I can't stand Adam, isn't it enough what he's done to me?" Guilt warped in Morad's face and she continued: "I'm your sister, do you want this life for me? Do you want me to be kept in captivity for the rest of my life or do you expect I'm suddenly going to be happy running after a cow with a twenty-litre container of water on my head?"

"I know you can't work like the village women, but they don't expect you to," said Morad "Adam's paying them a lot of money to serve you."

"Is it supposed to be a life?" said Eve, the pain of the years surfacing in her expression, "Do you think it makes a difference that

I don't do any work while I'm kept here? Morad *I'm dying...I can't stand it here!* You don't have to live here every day and go through all this..." she looked out through the door at the massive boulder opposite dwarfing the house, and continued "If Pompous wanted us to live here, why didn't he bring us when we were babies so we couldn't feel or know the difference? He should have brought us when we were little so we grow up running after goats and water with no ambition in life other than getting married and having babies and cows and we'd be content with it, like everybody else...But he didn't...we grew up in Britain, we lived in a city all our lives and then he brought us here to suffer. Yusef and Sami escaped, now I need you to help me get out of here."

"But...what can I say to them?" he said showing signs of agreeing.

"I'm your sister," said Eve "Do you remember how well I was doing in school? I was supposed to go to university and become a lawyer. Look at me! Look at these clothes I'm wearing, do you think this suits me? Think about all these years passing I was supposed to live, but instead I'm here in these mountains, suffering. I can still make it if you help me, maybe I won't be a lawyer, but I can still finish school, go to university and live my life. I'm still young and you know how intelligent I am—I can catch up with what I missed. I know you didn't want this to happen to me, Morad. I'm begging you, I'm *begging* you...help me."

Large tears rolled down from her eyes as she spoke, every word she said touched her brother's heart. Morad felt the pain he heard in her voice and saw in her face; he understood the logic in her words. He had been so proud of his sister, bragging about her extraordinary intelligence, school marks and reports in front of his colleagues and friends wherever he went, telling them what a genius she was and how hard she worked to increase her knowledge, and how proud she would make them by becoming someone big in the future. It pained his heart as he looked into her long-lashed brown eyes staring at him as if her life or death depended on his answer; looking up to him as her only hope to live a normal life. He had left her a child and now she was almost a woman, but years had been stolen from her. How happy and successful she would be had this not happened, had she stayed in Britain and continued a normal course of life. His chest heaved as he wept, he put his arms around her as she lay her head on his shoulder.

"I'll take you with me," he said "I'm your big brother and nobody can stop me. I'm sorry..."

He apologised over and over again as he cried in guilt, and she cried out of relief. Finally she was leaving the mountains. *Finally*, she was leaving the mountains! It took Morad longer to stop crying, feeling partially to blame because he hadn't stopped this from happening. Eve was beyond happy, giddy with hope turning into salvation she jumped up and down and twirled.

"You know I love you Morad," she said "Yusef and Sami let me down, but I knew you wouldn't! It's been so painful all these years, you're so lucky you didn't stay here all this time! I'm going to have my life back. Moo-raa-aad, I'm going to have *my life back!*"

She danced around the room to the pop music she could hear in her head. Morad watched his sister's display of happiness and tears streaked down his cheeks: Eve's beaming face full of pure innocence made her seem like a fourteen-year-old girl again, it stabbed him in the heart as he truly grasped how robbed she was of her childhood and how cruel it was of their parents to have done this to her. But he was going to give her, her life back. When she finished her gleeful dance, she sat next to him.

"When are we leaving?" she asked and smiled "Tomorrow?"

"No," said Morad "I have two weeks and then we'll leave." he paused then said "I'll talk to them tomorrow, don't say anything...not even to my wife."

"Why don't you tell them today?" said Eve "They can't stop you...right?"

"No, they can't, but they'll try," he said "Don't worry, next week you'll be packing your things and you'll be on your way to Britain. I'll send you money every month so you can study and not worry about a thing."

Eve clapped her hands in cheer, jumped off the bed and twirled singing: "I'm going home! I'm going home! I'm going home!"

Although Eve had always smiled and dealt with her ordeal in a much calmer way than had her brothers, sitting that black and orange evening on the ducka in the dark night lit only by a lantern, she felt lighter. A heavy load had been pulled out of her chest and cast away. Her in-laws' familiar faces who'd surrounded her for years, seemed once again like strangers. She smiled and laughed with them from the deepest of her heart, her smiles and laughter tasted of victory because soon, she would leave them behind and never see them again; everything bad and cruel they had done to her had become insignificant. She'd been lost for three years and soon she would be back home where she belonged, where she was free to do what she pleased with her life. More than anything, she wanted to resume her education; longed to be back in electricity and running water; to have a proper bathroom, an indoor bathroom; to walk on level pavements and in parks. She was hungry for books of her choice and not have to dig out the lone novel; the books Yusef sent were of no interest to her right now, no, she was going home and would be reading books and material which interested her. The others chatted and listened to Morad's funny stories about work and Sana'a while Eve's wistful eyes and thoughts wandered off to her childhood friends and neighbours. Where would they be? Would she find Samantha and Sarah? Trudy, Becky? Aunt Phyl would be the first person she visit, she doubted Aunt Phyl would have changed her residence. That night she fell into sleep a warm, full, content baby.

The next day she awaited Morad to tell everybody the good news, but he didn't bring the matter up. The third day when he broached the subject, the heated reaction was terrible: Suleiman, Kareema, Mother and Father, all angered, shouted at him, arguing loudly. Nonetheless, he kept a constant, strong tone.

"She can't live here anymore!" said Morad "She's not accustomed to live this hard life! Enough what we've done to her. She's coming with me and I'm sending her back to Britain so she can catch up with her education and re-compensate for everything she lost, God Willing!"

The response came from all four at the same time. A swamp of crocodiles bore their many teeth, shredding his words, his opinions to pieces. Imbroglioed in the quagmire of Eve's life and rights all were yelling, it was hard for Eve and the others watching to understand what anyone said to the end, but they objected fiercely.

"You're prohibited from taking my son's wife anywhere!"

"You have no right!"

"We won't let her leave."

"You're bringing disgrace to the family."

"She's not leaving until the day she leaves to her grave."

The argument continued until Morad stormed off with Eve following him into his room. She sat on a cushion on the floor looking up at her agitated brother seated on his bed.

"They are so closed minded!" he said "Their thinking is as thick and unmovable as these mountains!" he tapped his forehead with his fingers and swiped the air with his arm like a karate chop. Morad explained they'd need to go to the British Embassy to apply for a new passport as pernicious and pertinacious Suleiman refused to give him her current one, and it might take a while if she couldn't even show them a copy of the old one. He wanted her to stay in Sana'a for a short time until he organised her trip back to Wales. Eve smiled as they spoke, it was such a relief, all these years of hope were to be fulfilled. In spite of using litres of water warmed by the sun or a cooker, pouring from a kettle over her head to shower every day, she always longed for a long hot bath and real shower. She longed for all things routine and mundane back home: bread and cheese, milk, fruit, books, parks, which seemed unreachable luxuries in these harsh mountains. What excited her most, she would resume her education, and her intelligence wouldn't be for nothing; maybe her genius would still be high if she applied herself, and she might skip a year of education as she had done in the past and come closer to going to university.

All her in-laws stopped talking to her or even replying when she spoke to them; instantaneously shunning her because she was leaving. Yes she was going to leave the mountains behind, leave them behind, but it wasn't her parting they were upset about, or the insult of leaving an unwanted husband.

"You know Adam won't send them money if you aren't here. You have to stay!" Dhalia broke the silence only after everyone had left the house.

"Of course he will," said Eve "He's their son and they can ask him to send them money as usual."

"He's only sending money since you came," said Dhalia "He was in Saudi for years and he never sent one Rial no matter how many letters we sent and how many phone calls people made. You don't know how many times my father went to Taiz just to call him to send money and he never did. You're the only reason he's sending money. If you go, how will they live?"

"It's not my fault," said Eve irked by the fact they were trying to guilt her over something she was faultless in "I can't do anything and I can't stay here. They'll live, just like they lived before."

"No, it was different," said Dhalia shaking her head "Before, your father was in Britain and he always sent my father money to look after his house and land," Dhalia forgot to mention Father had been sending money to Suleiman to buy land and build houses which he chose to spend on himself instead of fulfil "And my uncles Yahya and Salem were in Saudi, they'd send him money sometimes, but now your father's here to look after his own land and our uncles too, if Adam stops sending money, they'll suffer!"

"What do they do with the money anyway?" said Eve "It's not like your father buys them proper food or makes their life better with it."

"Because he only cares about qat," said Dhalia "The truth is—if Adam doesn't send money my father will stop buying white flour, sugar, rice and gas. He'll just leave my brothers to starve and whatever little money he makes he'll buy qat with."

"It's not my fault! I have to leave," said Eve "I can't live here." Eve looked on, how unreasonable their justification for keeping her in the mountains all this time; deprived of her life to be this family's meal ticket. A hostage. Wasn't it enough she had been taken as a child to become wife to a stranger? Taken away from the middle of her family to be placed with strangers whom mistreated her merely for existing? A girl expected to be instantly a woman and wife. Kept prisoner for years where she was subject not only to harsh living conditions, but also to the cruelness of her in-laws whom viewed her as a strange outsider and a burden, no matter how much she came to love them. Now that she was finally leaving, they were upset and protested to her freedom. All she was, a guarantee ensuring *their son*, whom *she did not want*, send them a monthly allowance. Her tribulations, and the wasted years of her life, weighed nothing on their conscience; as long as her captivity meant money flowed to them, they ensured there was no way she could escape. Any attempt convincing anyone to take her out of the mountains was attacked aggressively and quashed. But not this time.

In the days following, intense discussions were held between Morad, his parents, Suleiman and Kareema; if Eve went outside, voices were lowered. They were discussing her. She heard it. Felt it. Knew it. She passed by them and they stopped talking, resuming only when she was well in front of the Second House; if she joined them, they dropped the subject abruptly, a tense, stiff-bodied silence followed before they changed topic. Suleiman glowered at her with sideway glances, his face no longer cheery; if they passed each other on the path or in rooms, he looked down or away from her, for she was doing him a great wrong and no longer deserved kindness. The intense hate and disapproval towards her, the darkness of his face, hurt her, for he had replaced her father when Father became unpaternal and she loved him; she had never been bad or rude to him, or anyone. Was it so wrong to want to live? To return home? And poor Morad, he always looked frustrated caught between doing the right thing, freeing his sister, and the wrath of both sets of parents whom by tradition he was supposed to obey—although he hadn't broken from tradition nor religion by trying to do the right thing even if it was against their unfair desires.

Eve woke up early, made tea and read the Quran. Serenely, she watched the dawn turn into morning. Running her hand through her hair she smiled for she had watched the sun come up from behind the mountains almost every single day for years and knew exactly where the orange ball would appear after the sky had blushed, between the peaks of two far away mountains. She had absorbed their colour from granite grey to chalky white and yellow, the shrubs, paths, every detail which she had seen from her east windows and from in front of her room over these three years. Now that she was leaving them, she could once again see their awesome beauty, carved by weather, glaciers and God. How happy and surprised her brothers would be to see her in Sana'a! It would only be a few days and they could tell her why they hadn't come back for her. She was no longer upset with them, she was leaving this dreadful place and had no hard-felt feelings towards them. How blessed she was to be finally leaving the harshness and tragedy behind, and to start running after the future ahead.

At breakfast, Eve sensed the tension from her in-laws had ebbed as everyone talked and laughed, they'd come to accept her departure because it was the right thing, she thought, but detected something in the children's eyes as they smiled at her, their eyes said 'there's something you don't know!'; Eve had learnt over the years adults spoke in front of children about everything, children were always aware of what went on, whether it was out in the open or supposedly a secret. They ate and Eve wondered if they'd heard their parents would be making more arguments before she left, but dismissed the thought for her big brother Morad was taking her with him and nothing was going to stop them.

A hawk shrilled, soaring through the air over them. Suleiman and Kareema stood up making ear-piercing: "Srrrrr! Srrrrr!" sounds, waving their arms in the air, hoping to frighten the hawk away from their egg-laying hens, as it whistled going back and forth over them in the sky.

*

EVE STOOD IN FRONT OF THE BED WITH THE BLANKET PULLED UP revealing the metal trunks containing her clothes. She pulled out a trunk and uplifted the neatly folded clothes and took out the novel, it no longer had the dust jacket with the demon, she just didn't find it one day. Many years ago when Eve had arrived in the mountains and Mirsaam and Aziza (Uncle Salem's daughters) and Huda had sat next to Eve and wanted to talk, Mirsaam was about a year older than Eve; Aziza and Huda were maybe two years younger, Eve spoke to them in English and they spoke to her in Arabic, from the looks on their faces, none of them understood what the other was saying. Eve tried explaining what she said using her hands while Morad sat on the floor next to the bed, translating for them sometimes, smiling at the interaction between his little sister and the girls trying to find something they could all talk about, even though they were worlds apart. Huda crawled over the bed, picked up Eve's book from the window sill and squeezed between Eve and Mirsaam. The dust jacket of the book illustrated a clock, clawing to the clock was a grinning horned demon. Huda said something pointing at the cover.

"It's a demon." said Eve, Morad translated. The girls became serious, muttering something, all repeating the same words.

"They're afraid of it and asking for God's protection." said Morad.

Eve laughed and showed them there was nothing to fear from the glossy cover by removing it and putting it back, touching the picture of the demon. The girls smiled. She picked up the book and growled as she put it in front of their faces, and laughing they retreated further onto the bed. One girl after the other held the book close to her face studying the drawing. Finally it was back in Eve's lap, but Aziza wanted to dare the demon a final time and lowered her head until her face was on the cover, as she lifted her head her nose bled. The three cousins said something excitedly to Eve, repeating the same invocation and pointing at the book in her lap. Morad rollicked laughing loudly and said: "They say the demon in your book bit her!"

"We're going home," presently she said to the book, now coatless—maybe one of the three young cousins had dealt with its dastardly demon—and placed it on the bed. Shortly, the 'things to take' besides the book were her toothbrush, toothpaste, soap, shampoo, deodorant and hairbrush.

"Clothes…" She placed her hands on her hips and looked down at the lilac coloured dress she wore, covered in tiny silvery patterns, it was light and fitted perfectly. She pulled out a dark green dress with black and white leaf prints. She smiled, how embarrassing if people back home saw her dressed like this, but she wasn't worried—she was to buy proper clothes in Sana'a. Morad entered her room and sat on the bed. She stretched white trousers with black triangular patterns at the bottom of the leg in front of him.

"No more elephant-ass trousers!" she laughed. Morad laughed too, but she could tell something was bothering him. She folded two small headscarves and looked at Morad. "Do I have to wear a sharshaf?" she asked.

"Of course," he said "You have to be covered when we leave here and in Sana'a. Once you're at the airport you don't have to wear it." He looked at the small amount of items Eve intended to take with her "Is that all?" he asked, surprised.

"Yes."

"When it's time just put them in my suitcase." he said.

"Three more days and I'm out of here," she beamed "It's been too long, I can't wait to get back home!" Eve's excitement did not infect Morad, instead he looked worried, his Adam's-apple bobbed up and down as he swallowed at nothing. He seemed to want to say something, but didn't.

"I'm so happy." said Eve.

"You are?" said Morad fidgeting in the same way he had years ago, when Father broke the news they weren't going back home, getting slightly up and sitting back down.

"You know what's most important?" Eve continued "I need to catch up with my education. So I'll be behind everybody my age, but I'm sure I'll catch up with my life and I'll still go to university. You know I don't care about food, but sleeping and living in a house without worrying about snakes and scorpions is going to be *heaven*!" her eyes rolled upwards and she smiled "I'm not going to let what happened stop me from living. So I have to make up for the years lost, but I'll make it and I'll have a normal life again."

Morad sat silently while Eve went on and on, chattering, excited to be going back home. Back to Wales, where she had longed to be for years, in daffodil-yellow brightness.

"I never lost hope," she said "I knew I'd get out of here. Even when things were really difficult and dark, *even* when I used to cry non-stop I always felt from the bottom of my heart and deepest of my soul that I'm getting out of here. *I knew it*—and see—it's happening!"

Morad looked at his young sister as she spoke non-stop. He listened to her excitement, the faith in her words; he saw the happiness and relief in her eyes. He watched her through his own worried eyes, with graveness he tried to conceal by smiling.

"Wait here," he said getting up "Don't go outside, just wait here and I'll come back and talk to you."

She watched him leave the room, giving him a radiant smile. She opened the outer door, unlocked during the day and locked during the night by her uncle and for a brief moment the insult returned, how humiliating it was to be treated like a prisoner. She stood at the edge of the path in front of her room looking down at the cliff, it had always worried her because children frequently played there and ran heedless if they went too far, a fatal fall would follow. She looked down and followed the path as far as she could, visually. She looked across the gorge to the east, to the relentless mountains. To the north far below them she saw people leaving with their cattle, women and girls on their way to fetch firewood and water, she knew who most of them were by the colour of their dress. She took a deep breath and closed her eyes, smiled, as she recognised the difference in atmosphere as she had felt it the first day she arrived, and opened her eyes smiling at the sky, pleased that soon she would be inhaling air and looking up from the tarmacked, level streets of Wales. She looked left and right, slowly scanning the view below her, soon, she would leave this scenery behind, and it would only be a memory.

"Eve?" Morad interrupted her from the inner door.

"I'm out here." she said standing at the door, smiling, her long locks dancing in the cool breeze.

"Come in," he said grimly "I need to talk with you." Eve walked in and closed the outer door as he stood silently.

"Come, sit down." said Morad leading her by her hand and they both sat on the bed. He stared at her without saying anything so she smiled and nodded to encourage him to say something.

"Eve, I can't take you with me." he said rapidly. The smile fell from her face, and a nervous smile repeatedly appeared as she said: "What do you mean? Of course you can…"

"No, I can't," said Morad his face elongated with sorrow "Uncle Suleiman has spoken to the car owners that you can't leave with me."

"It doesn't mean *I can't* go with you," said Eve "You're my brother, they can't stop us."

"You don't understand," said Morad "Because you're married to his son, he's your guardian and on top of that—Father has supported him." Eve began to cry as something twisted in her stomach, pulling at her heart, a painful feeling flowed downwards from her chest to her stomach and sideways across her chest.

"You're my brother," she said "They're lying to you, they can't stop me from leaving with you, they can't! It doesn't make sense….so I'm going with you!"

"I can't take you," said Morad "I've been talking with them for days, but they refused. I'm sorry Eve…I'm so sorry."

"No Morad, *no-oo*! I'm going with you!"

Morad got up to leave. He looked at her, his face full of regret. "I can't take you with me."

She held his hand tightly in both of hers. "I'm your sister…help me…*help me*. Don't leave me here…I'm going with you." she nodded. He walked away and she followed him.

"I'll die Morad, I'll die!" she said, her voice frantic, "I can't stand it here…don't leave me here to die…"

Morad stared towards her, his eyes brimming with tears. "You'll be okay." he said.

"No-o, no I won't be okay," she said shaking her head "I'm not okay," her voice rose "You don't have to buy me clothes or anything, just take me with you."

"It's not about money." said Morad.

"You don't have to send money while I study," said Eve "Just get me out of here and I can make it on my own! Don't leave me here! Please Morad, I'm *begging* you!" She could tell from the expression on his face, he wanted to. *She knew he could.*

"I can't Eve," he said "You're staying here." and he walked away as she stood at the door of her room, tears pouring down her cheeks, watching him walk away as she fell from a high distance, soul-crushed. Why couldn't he see, if he left her behind she would die. *She would die.* He reached the outside doorstep of the Bawaba, while she stood at the inner door of her room watching in disbelief, this could not have transpired.

"Morad," she shouted, he turned around, "I'll get myself out." A look of terror appeared on Morad's face as she turned running to the exterior door and lunged the bolt open. She heard him shouting her name, coming closer. She ran towards the cliff, the thought of not living here another day a mercy, no matter how painful death against hard and sharp rocks would be.

CHAPTER TWELVE

H E GRABBED HER AS SHE HESITATED LOOKING DOWN FROM behind the boulders at the edge of the cliff, his strong arms came around her, lifted her, and carried her back into the room as she fought to get back out, but he was stronger. He laid her on the floor as she continued to scream she would kill herself and begged him to take her with him. All he could do to refrain her while causing her the least possible pain, for God knew she'd known enough pain, was to sit on her stomach and hold her fisted, swiping hands.

"I can't take you with me! I can't!" he said, his eyes expressing his contrition, and guilt for not standing up more to the parents. He called out to somebody to fetch the padlock's key from Suleiman when Aunt Khatima appeared at the door.

"What happened?" asked Aunt Khatima.

"She was going to jump off the cliff." said Morad. Aunt Khatima knelt beside Eve now crying frenziedly, shaking and foaming at the corners of her mouth. She had been so happy and relieved to be leaving the village after all these years, now hysterical from the brutal impact of not being allowed, compounded by the fact he believed she would end her life yet still would leave her behind. Khatima wiped away the tears with the palm of her hand, but more flowed, she used the inside hem of her dress to wipe Eve's mouth and tried to console her, but left while Morad still sat on her. None of it made sense, she wasn't supposed to be living this still life, this unprogressive and vegetating state of non-existence, and she couldn't bear to think he would leave without her, but it was his intention. Her crying had ceased, with pensive eyes on the ceiling her chest and back heaved upwards in choppy gasps from the hard cry. Morad still sat upon her, saying something to her, she could hear him, but wasn't looking at him.

"I'm not going to get up until you calm down." he said, but she didn't respond, lost in despair; lost in these mountains where nobody cared about her, or what would happen to her. Suleiman sang joyfully, bolting the outer door from outside and a slow jolt of immense sadness went through her heart as she heard the padlock click.

"I'm going to get up now," said Morad "If you try to hurt yourself we'll have to tie you."

"We'll put her in chains!" said Suleiman jovially, who had come around and entered the room from the other side. Suleiman bolted the outer door from the inside and left the room singing the same song. Morad got up slowly.

"I'm sorry…" he said, breaking into a sob.

She remained on her back, while her eyes stared at the ceiling, no longer sobbing, but tears flowed and though her eyes stared at whitewashed timber she was immersed in childhood memories of home, nursery, school, streets, parks. She snapped out of the random memories and bit her lips together and could feel the sting of tears trickling between her hair and scalp. Nobody was going to help her get out: trapped in these mountains where Father had lured them. Her brothers had abandoned her. Big brother Morad, capable enough to get her out, had lifted her to heaven and dropped her into a freefall back into the hard, cold mountains. She lay on her back not moving for hours, drifting between happy childhood memories and the painful reality of where she lay, and back into childhood memories.

"Eve?" Morad said softly. She tilted her head slightly to see him at the door.

"Are you okay?" he asked, his voice gruff from crying.

"I will be if you get me out of here." she said softly and despondently.

"They won't let me," he said "I'm sorry."

She rolled onto her side, her back towards him and said: "You don't care Morad, if you stopped me killing myself today, you know you're not here to stop me tomorrow…" and heard him walk away and close the door of his room behind him. The hurt, immense. The hope of leaving, dead. She wouldn't cry anymore and didn't want to cry, but how meaningless her life had become. How purposeless all her intelligence, her success in school; her hard work—it meant nothing here. How pointless was life, youth, energy while trapped between four walls, not allowed to do anything. The only thing in front of her was wall, its uneven whitewashed surface lined by the brown rim of mud. Further down stood the legs of the chair on which she placed the water jug, a red urn made of clay, the water poured into it came out as cold as refrigerated water after a while. She extended her right arm and ran her palm over the plastic covered floor, feeling the uneven bumps of the mud clad ground beneath it; touched the nearest leg of the chair, colder than the plastic floor; her fingers followed the leg up, feeling the splintery rim of the wooden seat. She sighed and sat up, looking around her. There was a funny feeling in her chest and sense of orientation, it felt she had lain on the linoleumed floor forever, as if years had passed during those hours. Something she couldn't explain, but she felt older than she was and there was a deep feeling of peace. Peace. She wasn't leaving today, "I will one day." she said to herself and onto her bed she climbed and fell asleep.

*

EVE TOOK EVERY OPPORTUNITY TO ASK PEOPLE WHOM PASSED BY and sat in front of the house to tell her about life in the past here in the mountains. They told her their stories, and of how much more forestry and different animals were abundant; how scarce it had become from too much firewood collection and drought. You could live from the fortune of the fecund land, eating from its sorghum, barley, millet and corn; butter and ghee were in excess, as was drinking milk; honey was available, many families kept bees, even her paternal grandfather. They would smile, their sun creased faces turning sad in disbelief at how it was now in the village. They never used to eat white flour, they had no need for it, but now with constant drought and the land not producing as it used to, they had to eat this white bread which they all agreed was like chewing plastic. In their opinion, women and men of the olden days were stronger and healthier than the younger generations and they blamed this on the white flour, tins of tomato purée and all the artificial juices introduced to the village after people went to work in Saudi, Taiz and other cities: "It's not natural, that's why everybody gets sick these days." they said, "No one ever used to get sick.", "We could lift a huge bundle of wood onto our heads without any help and now they all need help and carry smaller bundles", "Now they are 'this hurts, this burns, this aches...' all these inflammations from the tomato puree and white flour ruining their health" they said, mimicking the younger ladies 'inferiority'.

They spoke of how fatter and healthier cattle was, how their milk and meat tasted better. You could collect milk from goats not just cows; cheese was made. A few of the much older people remembered how much Eve's maternal grandfather owned the majority of the land and its mountain sides; how good natured, but naive he was and how much he loved his motherless daughters. When famine came, he sold large areas of land in exchange for grains measured by handfuls and when he died, how his brothers inherited lots of his land because he didn't have a male heir, and how badly his young orphaned daughters were treated, like slaves, by Suleiman's father who was a relative and became their guardian, and how he took some of the daughters as wives for his sons and had stolen their land by forging deeds of sales which hadn't taken place. Some told stories, of stories told to them, of people whom remembered when the Turks came, they had invaded Yemen in the past, they reached the level landed villages far away and wanted to access these mountainous villages; fortunately for the villagers, the car route didn't exist back then so the Turks were unable to reach them because of the harsh terrain. Others told stories of the Imam's soldiers, a dictator who kept Yemen isolated from the world, coming and raiding the communal grain stores, kept for the hard years, leaving the villagers in famine when drought arrived, and kidnapping women from the village, they said the Imam had a sweet tooth and predilection for the women of this region (did they tell you it was seven inches long, Eve?). Every opportunity Eve asked how they travelled in the past when there had been no cars and what different routes led to the cities, from the information she gathered, it turned out to be the same route followed by cars currently, except it was more treacherous and not as 'smooth' as it had been made now; donkeys and camels were used by some to ride part of the way, but walking took weeks with many stops along the way before a path was cut out for vehicles and decades before anyone from the village owned a car (presently the number of automobiles in these mountains made the grand total of two); you had to stop at villages to ask for hospitality, to eat and drink and then carry enough food and water to make it to a flat land called Makbana which was only an hour or so away from Taiz, and there were cars in Makbana because it was such level land and close to the city. The other route led to a city called Hais, which was not yet really a city and always had the danger of epidemics, and you would be further away from Taiz and Sana'a and need more time to get to those cities by car. Some told stories of men and women in love, trying to run away to get married against their families' will, being caught up with and beaten and punished for their disgraceful act; the only couple to have successfully eloped had a car and driver from a different region waiting for them, but they were never forgiven and lived in exile from the mountains, never allowed to visit no matter what the occasion. The most painful memory they could not reconcile with, was how green and covered in forests the mountains were, how much it used to rain.

"We never needed to hide behind boulders or walls or build hamams," they said "Day or night, you could step into the trees, take your clothes off and still be covered from people's vision to wash and do whatever you needed to do. Now it's all gone…how can all those trees and plants be gone?" It rained in abundance and rain brought the fortune of the land. Now all these mountains produced were meagre crops, never enough to feed family and cattle until the next rainfall. After talking with a lot of chuckling and enthusiasm, each old face would scrunch and stare into a different direction, blinking slowly as if trying to relive and return back in time, when times were good. Or were they trying to figure out what had gone wrong, wondered Eve as she saw the misery in their quiet, kind faces over the desolation of what used to be a very green and productive land.

*

"I'D LIKE TO GO OUT, UNCLE." SAID EVE.

"You can't," said Suleiman "You'll try to run away and you might die trying."

"Uncle, I'm not going to run away," said Eve "Do you think I'm stupid? You'd catch up with me, anyway. When I leave everybody will know because it'll be by car."

"You're not leaving ever…do you know that?"

"One day I will leave Uncle and I'll never come back. You can't keep me here forever."

"Yes we can!" replied Suleiman, laughing.

"Let me go with Huda to fetch firewood." said Eve

"Your hands are too soft," he said "You won't be able to cut it."

"Let me try. Can I go with her tomorrow?" she asked sincerely and deferentially. Huda frequently went to land at far distances where firewood was comparatively abundant than the nearby areas, leaving early while still dark and returning in the scorching noon sun. Eve watched her as she appeared, a speck of colour in the east on a narrow, rocky path underneath a great yellow mountain, sometimes accompanied by her cousins. For Eve, this was an opportunity to see for herself if it was possible to find a route she could escape through. Suleiman said he would think about it and later in the day gave his permission. Next morning Eve followed Huda carrying the equipment: nylon rope to tie the firewood, a small axe and small sickle. They both headed to Barh Salliya, but instead of going upwards towards the south, Huda went down the steep.

"Wait, where are you going?" said Eve "You always go that way to get to the Shalallat."

"We're not going there today," said Huda, her dark brown hair faded at the tips framing her diamond shaped face, her slender fingers rubbing her small, sharp nose, "It's too far away and difficult for you, you'd never get there."

"Come on Huda," said Eve "Let's go there—I'll show you how to do cartwheels!"

Huda stopped to say her father had refused, but if she were to take Eve there next time would she show her new games too? Of course she would. Would she teach her new verses from the Quran? Yes, our eager explorer would do anything she asked of her. An agreement reached, Eve followed Huda down the steep, then down a slope leading to the land below the houses where they lived.

"Where are we going today?" Eve asked.

"We've arrived." replied Huda dropping the rope and axe and heading up the sloping hillside above the land to start shearing off shrubs.

"But we're just under the path." said Eve "We're under the house!"

"Yes." said Huda.

"This isn't our land," said Eve "We can't cut off their bushes!"

"My father took permission from Ahmed," said Huda "To let us take shrubs and he'll give him dry crop to feed his cows so you don't need to go far away." Eve looked up to see Suleiman, Kareema and Dhalia standing in front of the boulders next to the Second House, drinking tea and watching them.

"Go on Eve," Suleiman hollered "Start wood-gathering so we can watch you. Just be careful you don't cut your fingers off!" he laughed out loudly. "Evil bastard." Eve whispered under her breath, exasperated by her Uncle's arrangement. "Go on, start," Suleiman called out from high above "Before the sun gets hotter."

Young but experienced Huda instructed Eve, but as soon as Eve tried to feel for a branch to cut, the thorns dug into her skin, the pain, an electric shock. She pulled her hands out and the skin tore on the backs and palms.

"Let me do this one," said Huda "I'll find a less thorny bush for you."

Eve waited, her hands stinging as Huda cut off the barbed bush piece by piece until only a stub remained, grimacing as thorns pricked her. Eve walked down the slope and took a look at everything around her, she looked up constantly. Suleiman never moved, perched on a rock, vigilant and vulturine, squatted drinking glass after glass of tea, at least down here she couldn't hear the irritating smacking and slurping sounds he made.

While Eve's hands healed Huda sought permission from her father to let Eve go with her to the distant land.

"Why?" said Suleiman "She can't cut firewood, she definitely can't carry anything on her head. Why do you want her to go with you?"

"So, we can talk," said Huda "So she can leave the house, she's fed up always inside cooped up like a hen!"

"What if she runs away?" said Suleiman. Huda laughed.

"She can't run away," said Huda smiling at the needless worry "She can't even walk most of the way without help. A four-legged cow with overgrown nails has more chance of crossing the narrow difficult areas than Eve." they both laughed.

"What if she falls and hits her head on a sharp rock and dies?" said Suleiman with a little more concern "What if she falls off a cliff? What will we tell your brother then? He won't send us money if she's dead."

"I'll take my cousins with me," said Huda "And we'll take turns guiding her."

Eve delighted with the upcoming trip, hoped the view of the route from behind the mountains seen from behind the houses would show a path out of her captivity. She would be going past the mountains across the canyon to the east which she could see from her window, sitting on the bed. It would take Huda nearly two hours to appear on the route under that mountain. Eve would watch the specks of colour on the route, when they stopped she ran outside and waved, hoping they could see her, before resuming and disappearing behind a mountain on another route as they went down. Excited, the girls awoke early.

"You're going to perish today," Dhalia laughed and warned "Stay at home—better for you!"

"Huda, you listen to me," said Kareema with her steely face "If she can't walk back, leave her there for the hyenas! If she can't walk back—just leave her, do you hear?"

"You demon!" Suleiman shouted at his wife "May you not wake up the next morning! You want her to abandon her far away like an

153

unwanted cat? May the demons eat you for dinner!" He turned to Huda "Listen to me, ignore your mother. I don't care if you don't bring back one branch, you have to bring our Eve back."

Eve smiled, amused by the whole conversation, knowing to her Uncle Suleiman she was just a source of money; he did love her as did most of her in-laws, but his mourning would not solely be over the loss of her life. Four more girls were joining them on this trip: Mirsaam, Aziza, Naseema—Huda's cousin from her mother's side, and Higga—a daughter of Kareema's cousin. The girls talked and laughed and in the difficult terrain they held her hand and bridged her into the safer areas. When they passed in front or below a house, women came out to kiss hands with Eve. Some would say: "Poor creature, she can't live in this harsh country."

The girls were slower than usual because of Eve, making sure her foot was correctly placed, dithering whether to carry on or turn back before crossing difficult areas, after a lot of encouragement and help from her friends. Every time she faced a sheer drop where there was barely space on a lip of rock to place your foot, she put her foot forward then back, too scared of the rocky plunge a small slip would ensure. She held onto rocks and boulders, slowly making her way across mountain face where the other girls passed nimbly with the agility of ibex. They reached the path below the mountains Eve could see from her room.

"Look, that's our house." said Huda.

Eve stopped to look across the gorge at the houses so tiny from here, she was sure she could see two specks in the colour of Dhalia and Kareema's dresses. She looked around, mountainside cascading downwards, and they were still to cross the path taking them behind the mountain. Around the bend Eve expected to see path and land leading down in a joyous crescendo towards the valley of freedom, but the breathtaking view she saw also killed all hope: mountains rose and continued as far as the eye could see. There was no apparent way out, only chains of never ending mountain range.

"Where's the land?" asked Eve.

"We have to walk over that mountain," Mirsaam said pointing ahead "And the trees are on its other side."

They reached a difficult part of the route where a wide fissure separated the mountain face, Eve hesitated, there was only enough space to place the side of your foot against a crevice in the rock face to jump to the other side and a long drop down, with only death to meet at the bottom, the girls had to urge her a lot before she took the risk of crossing. They made the rest of the way with Eve stumbling along. She sat on a boulder and watched them cut at the trees, which were more abundant than where they lived, having survived due to the remoteness of the area, but if they carried on cutting the branches and bushes in large amounts as the girls were doing, it would eventually be depleted. The girls talked as they worked, Eve laughed with them, but only on the outside, upset there was no way out from this direction. Her only consolation, she still had the path and possibility to explore by going to the land towards the north. The girls tied their bundles of firewood and helped each other place it on their heads, the last one kicking it up and landing it roughly onto her own head.

*

EVE'S IMPATIENCE FUELLED HER FRUSTRATION OUT OF NEED TO SEE the routes leading north. Huda always went to the same place to fetch wood; nowadays Kareema only went to the well and back and had no land towards the north so there was no way she could ask to be taken there without raising suspicion. There was so much she wanted to see of the area, not just to scout for ways out, but she was genuinely interested and intrigued to explore these mountains; especially where an ancient building called The Fortress existed, many of the elder folk claimed it was full of hidden treasures, guarded by demons: during their younger days, a man had entered the building by being lowered on ropes, and shouted to his companions of a great treasure inside, only to hurtle to his death. In the more recent years, two attempts had been made to access the site and claim its treasures, but on both occasions the men had died, thrown a distance to their deaths by an invisible force. From the descriptions of where the building was situated, jutting out of a mountain face, Eve speculated the treacherous terrain was more likely responsible for the men's demise. She believed it could be the remains of one of the many ancient kingdoms that once existed in Yemen thousands of years ago, which she'd read about in Bundar's history schoolbook; and she didn't want to try to scale its impenetrable topography, just get as close as she could and see its majestical magnificence with her own eyes. She wanted to climb the highest mountain to the south west, just to see how high up they were, see the view on the other side and explore, for the thrill of it. But she was never allowed to go anywhere new. Until an argument broke out between Dhalia and Kareema.

"You do no work all day!" shouted Kareema "Your sister and brothers are all over the place fetching firewood, water and you just sit here and eat!" Kareema was relentless, going at Dhalia for hours, the latter ended up in tears from the argument.

"Why don't you fetch firewood from my mother's land?" suggested Eve "I'll go with you to help."

"Yes," said Dhalia "My aunt will let me, I'll take permission and get firewood to shut my mother up."

"I'll go with you to help." Eve repeated with a sunny smile.

"You?! Help?" Dhalia laughed "You'll break a leg and I'll have to carry you home instead of the wood!"

After breakfast, Eve and Dhalia headed north, passing through a nearby village, then downwards.

"Careful, careful," said Dhalia "Take your time or you'll fall."

As they descended Eve looked around, they were nearer to the hill where the car went up heading for Taiz. They departed the path and continued going around mountains and zigzagging diagonally down mountainside, Eve slipping on rocks and boulders which slid and moved under her feet, landing backwards as Dhalia laughed. Finally they reached two large pieces of land bordered by low rocky walls. Mother's land. Eve turned slowly in a circle, around them steps of land went up then down and the view was bordered by towering mountains near and far, surveying the huge bowl made of dark rock. Her trip to this area was of no value, except it answered her curiosity of the possibility of a way out—there was none. Eve sitting on the edge of the wall while Dhalia cut at shrubs and branches of skinny trees, watched women in print dresses of different colours appear behind their cows. How content they seemed following their cattle, waking up early to carry heavy loads from the wells and land, every day they did the same thing; their conversations were stories retold so often you'd know them off by heart. From living with Suleiman's family, she knew they were not happy with the hard work, they were used to it but it wasn't easy, but they did it to survive. Eve's eyes followed the red dressed lady and her slow cow into the distance until they reached a descending point to the south.

"Dhalia, where's she going?"

"They have land in that direction. Why?" said Dhalia.

"Nothing, just is it the same as here or does it look different over there?" said Eve.

"It's the same everywhere." answered Dhalia.

"How can cows walk over those narrow rocky routes? Is there a car route in that direction?"

"The car route had to be made for the cars," said Dhalia "All the men worked for months putting flat rock and filling gaps so the car could pass. I remember when the route was made for donkeys and camels, long before they laid slabs for the car, I was still a little girl and would go and watch. But there's no car route in that direction, the cows can't walk everywhere we can walk either—you've seen how they scuffle and get stuck when they run off in the wrong direction. Abdulhadi and Abdulhameed's cows died when they fell off a narrow path, the whole family was mourning, remember? Without the sour buttermilk their children had nothing to eat on. It's true it's diluted with too much water, but at least they could drink and dunk to soak the dry bread and swallow." She looked at Eve "Why are you asking? Do you want to buy a cow?"

Eve laughed loudly and said: "Why would I want to buy a cow?"

"To have a cow is to have a fortune," said Dhalia matter of factly "If you have a cow you're wealthy and don't need anything."

"To have a cow is a nuisance," said Eve "You have to take it out to graze, bring food and water back home for it and worst of all—you have to clean its stable."

"Are you sure you don't want a cow?" said Dhalia "I do…when I have a house of my own, I'll tell Morad to buy me one. Your mother loves cows, how come you're not like her?"

"My mother wasn't like this before," said Eve sighing "I don't understand why she kills herself running after the cow like this. You know, she doesn't even talk to me anymore, I go to sit with her and she's 'I have to take the cow to graze'. I come back when she's back and she gets up and 'I have to go give the cow to drink'. I come back later 'I have to clean the stable'. I go later in the afternoon and she's 'I have to salt the cow'—I mean what is this? I think she went crazy when she came to this country. I think she has Mad Cow Disease!" Eve chuckled before continuing "Dhalia, have you heard of Mad Cow Disease? Cows in Britain became sick with it. I think my mother has a different form of Mad Cow Disease!"

"Cows don't go crazy—Eve you're crazy!" Dhalia laughed. Eve explained Mad Cow Disease to her sceptical sister-in-law.

"I still want a cow," said Dhalia "You should want one too. Tell my father to buy you one."

"According to your mother," said Eve, smiling, "I am one."

Dhalia laughed "My mother's evil." she said.

They talked and laughed while Eve stood in front of Dhalia as the latter bundled logs, branches and bushes together, and Eve told her of all the wonderful things that existed in the outside world, which were ordinary to Eve, but to Dhalia and the rest were mind awing and probably fiction. They always had trouble wrapping their minds around things Eve talked about. It was time to leave, a perspiring Dhalia had made a large bundle of wood for herself and a small one for Eve.

"I'll put them on the wall," said Dhalia "Help you load yours and then I'll load mine." By 'load' Dhalia meant place on the head, she rolled the bundle off the wall and lifted it onto Eve's head. Eve held it with both hands to keep its balance, but it immediately fell off to one side. Dhalia lifted it again, kicking it to raise it higher and onto Eve's head, this time it fell forward. Dhalia lifted it for the third time and Eve held onto it as best she could, but it rocked forward, backwards and fell off forwards. Despite the laughter, it was strenuous, by the seventh attempt they were no longer laughing: the bundle of wood either fell off sideways, to the front, or backwards.

"There's something wrong with your head," said Dhalia wiping the sweat off her forehead with her arm, eyeing Eve's head, "It's like an egg."

"My head is not like an egg!" Eve replied, laughing, "Would you like me to have Frankenstein's head?"

"Who's Faraa-kish-nine?" said Dhalia.

"Frankenstein," said Eve "The film with a monster created from different dead people's limbs."

"You're crazy," said Dhalia "You can't create someone from the dead—it's forbidden. *Do they do that in Britain*?!"

"I said it was a film," said Eve "A story. Forget about Frankenstein, let's go home."

"You're not leaving the wood," said Dhalia "I'll put it on your head and you hold it." She lifted it onto Eve's head "Don't turn your head. Keep your neck straight. I'll walk in front because you're so slow, and you follow me. Step carefully!"

Eve held onto the bundle on her head, already tired, the knobbly branches dug as hard as rocks into her scalp, the logs as heavy as an anvil, and the ligaments of her neck objected to the weight. How did they manage doing this every day? Eve had always been struck by the size of loads women and girls carried, standing when they met each other on a path, chatting and laughing while the heavy load balanced on their heads. Necessity. Survival. It wasn't like the life of the city dwellers where you could make life easier for yourself. You did this hard work or you starved, it wasn't an option. Bodies and mindsets adapted for survival. Strong, skinny bodies capable of carrying heavy loads which would probably compress the spine of the 'children of the city'. Women always did the hardest work in the village, but wasn't that the case in the past even in the developed countries, women served men and worked laboriously; even until the recent past wasn't housework viewed as a female duty before women revolutionised the social perception of gender role? Dhalia walked in front, her slim body dwarfed by the huge bundle of firewood she carried on her head. Eve followed, resituating her grip on the bundle as it rocked back and forth and fell forwards, snagging and tipping the bundle off Dhalia's head.

"Eve!" she shouted "When are we going to get home if you keep making the bundles fall?" She placed the bundle onto Eve's head and lifted her own heavy bundle. But now on the ground with no wall to raise it on, it was much more difficult trying to load it. Several attempts, Dhalia panting would raise the bundle, step backwards bending her knees and heavily land it on her head, and as she tried to situate it, it would fall backwards.

"See what you've done?" said Dhalia, her mood soured, *"You've jinxed me!"*

Eve wanted to reply, but was too busy keeping her head motionless as her neck strained under the heavy load. Finally Dhalia had balance of her bundle and started upwards, Eve behind her. They had only ascended a few yards up a precipitous path when Eve's wood fell sideways onto another narrow path below them.

"Dhalia, it's fallen." said Eve.

Dhalia glanced at it, then at Eve as if she wanted to throw her after it, there was no way to get to it without spending a lot of time ascending a different path, before zig-zagging back down to get to the lower path.

"Leave it," she replied, now angered, "You're a nuisance, not a blessing! I wanted those logs for smoking the kooz."

They made their way back up, Eve looked behind every time they reached a higher level to ascertain no easy route could be seen. They passed through the Gayra village, the women shouting out: "Why isn't she carrying anything?"

"She has to learn to carry wood and water or how will she live?"

Were they being serious, thought Eve, struggling just to walk and get up the path? They arrived at the point where the car had stopped for Sami, they were so near the house, yet it seemed to be the most gruelling distance to cross. Eve had to stop, she bent down and held her knees to catch her breath before walking, swaying to be exact, back to the Second House where Uncle Suleiman stood waiting by the yard's doorframe.

"Empty?! You came back *empty?"* he said struggling to keep his smile concealed, feigning disbelief.

"Uncle Suleiman," said Eve "I'm never going again…anywhere."

She collapsed onto the ducka next to an exhausted supine Dhalia. Suleiman poured them tea singing: "My son has married the daughter of the city, city women don't work, city women just sit and do nothing, they can't carry heavy wood, they can't fetch water and eat with only the tips of their fingers…My son married the daughter of the city."

He wobbled his head and smiled as he handed them tea. While Suleiman elaborated on his made-up song Eve fell deep into thought, she could not make it out of the mountains by foot: the car route—they'd catch up with her; the mountainous terrain—physically and geographically impossible for her; the only way out was by car, and she needed her in-laws or parents' consent. Always the only option available—she had to convince them to allow her to leave, and it would be harder than trying to cross the impossible terrain, a brief lapse of helplessness worried her. Looking up at the sunny sky she inhaled fresh air and closed her eyes, longing to smell the scent of pine trees in Belle Vue Park. She opened her eyes and a smile broke out as a surge of determination rejuvenated her spirit. Yes, here she was helpless, but not without hope. She still had hope telling her, cheering her, she would leave. She *would* convince them. They *would* listen to her. They *would* understand. They *will* let her go. There was no reason not to. How long could they keep her captive? (Oh Eve, you poor cow.)

CHAPTER THIRTEEN

E VE STOOD UP IN AWE WHILE A GOLDEN EAGLE SOARED HIGH above and below her. She watched it angle in the air and spread its wings, playful, powerful. Free. A wingspan of freedom the width of the skies, spanning continents. Yet here she stood with all her human intelligence, unable to escape the boundaries of illusionary borders drawn by tradition, unable to breach the confines of her Uncle's cage.

It had been a long, painful year. The stresses of her situation were driving her to despair and beyond, so Eve went to the First House armed with knowledge, seeking Father's support.

"I need you to help me get a divorce or tell Adam to divorce me." she said in a determined, but not angry, voice.

"Women can't divorce men," said Father "So if he doesn't want to divorce you, you can't get divorced."

"You lied to me when I was a little girl and you're lying to me now," said Eve "You couldn't kill me then, and you took advantage of our fear and unawareness of the law. You forced me to marry him—now you help divorce him." She stared at her father wanting acknowledgment and assistance; he seemed uninterested in, and undisturbed by, what she had to say. "I understand the Quran," she said "I've read the Hadeeth—women can divorce men. Why did you lie to me?"

"I'm not going to help you get divorced," said Father not looking up from his book of Hadeeth "It's shameful. God said He hates divorce."

"What the clerics say He meant by this, is it's a painful solution to some cases of marriage. God didn't prohibit divorce," she said "He allowed it. He knows how much people will suffer if they can't get a divorce. If God allowed it, who are you or anyone to stop me from getting it? Help me, this is your fault, you ruined my life, you stole my childhood and my future. Now help me fix what you made wrong!"

"You will not embarrass us!" Mother shouted "Stop saying it before someone hears you!"

Father snorted, finally lifting his head out of the book, and said: "Let her say it, let her shout and scream it—who will hear her? The police? The judge? There's no authority she can go to so she can talk all she wants, but she'll never get a divorce."

Eve grimaced as her heart and soul were being ground to a fleshy pulp at Father's satisfaction of her helplessness "I'm your daughter," said Eve, sullenness had crept into her voice, "Enough…don't do this to me anymore. I need your help…" She looked into her parents' faces searching for the paternal protection and maternal affection that had once existed, but couldn't find it in Father's cold expression. Or the red-faced glare of Mother. It seemed because she was married she was not a daughter to him anymore. Mother frowned at her with piercing eyes, Eve detected hate in the glower, her mouth and cheeks taut with disdain at her daughter's request; the way Mother looked back at her could have been no different had she announced she was thinking of becoming a prostitute. This always baffled Eve, how they made themselves deaf to common sense. What she requested could not cause the rage she saw in Mother's face, for Eve could understand the in-laws' inequitable 'logic' behind their unacceptable behaviour: Suleiman keeping her as a source of income, and the Uncles' indifference to her pleas as they were out of ignorance and living in an environment so closed from the real world, it was so backwards you could find similarities to the Dark Ages (in the popular sense). But she could not give the same excuse to her parents, they'd lived for decades in Britain, they were living a normal life and brought their children up in a modern way so why were they wearing the mask of ignorance? Eve knew them and had grown up listening to them brag about her education, and she had seen the pride in their eyes, on their lips, when her teachers praised her performance; their beaming faces when they came to watch her in school plays, concerts and netball matches. Did they now want her to believe they were as ignorant as these poor people whom had never stepped out of the mountains? She knew better than to believe this. For some reason they were trying to prove to everybody they shared their same principles, and the best way to prove it was to sacrifice their only daughter's life; it made no real sense to Eve, but it was the reality before her eyes—there was no other explanation. Except, Eve…maybe knew why: she had run away and the Social Services took her to a home because Father abused her, beating her terribly. It was uncomfortable, touching the scab of an ugly scar of fact that maybe her own action had resulted in her parents forcing her to get married. No, it wasn't justifiable—forcing a child to marry a man because she didn't want to be battered. Why had he begun to beat her anyway? She had never done anything wrong, no boyfriends, no problems in or out of school, a child genius, socially and academically adept; was it because she was growing, and too westernised for him to handle? Was his own conflict—happy, proud and boastful father of her extraordinary intellect conflicted with his Middle Eastern values, for she would reach a certain age and be independent and live how she wished? Had he ended her life and academic future for the sake of avoiding a speculated shame—a worry about honour? He had predetermined her a sin because she was born a girl, he had machinated her fate in fear one day she might date. Even in this dire situation where her parents' indifference to her pleas scorched her to the deepest of her soul, Eve could smile and laugh softly imagining Father having honour-based visions of Nostradamus apocalyptic proportions about her future—seeing her becoming a young woman, her lovers fervently undressing her, and Father shrieking then falling behind the sofa as he raised his arm to cover his sight from the unbearable prophecy.

Dhalia and Eve ran out and stood behind the house, curious to identify the loud flapping noise, too loud and close to be their neighbour dusting blankets. They both gasped then smiled, three vultures had landed on an outcrop of rock in throwing distance from where they stood. Such large birds, Eve felt intimidated. More were landing, their huge wings making the loud beating noise and they stared down their beaks, shoulder-hunched heavy-coated old men on rocks, at something. Eve and Dhalia scanned the land far below to see three men kneeling next to a fallen cow, it had been hurt badly and wouldn't get better so the men put a quick end to its pain. Eve watched the vultures waiting for the men to leave so they could descend on the carcass.

Getting nowhere with her parents and in-laws did not lessen her efforts and she yo-yoed back and forth between the First and Second House trying to get a divorce, or even release from the mountains, from parents and in-laws; discussing, emphasising all the many compelling reasons for being unable to remain here any longer and her right as a free person to leave.

"Uncle," said Eve "I've been here for almost four years and still I'm not used to living here. Every time I talk with you or my father you don't listen to me. I want you to listen and understand me—I can't live here anymore, the longer I stay the less likely I'll ever get into university, you have to let me go! Please Uncle Suleiman, please have mercy on me."

"You're my son's wife," said Suleiman "You're going to live here until the day you die." Talking to Suleiman over the past years she tempered smouldering exasperation with patience, but it was wearing thin and telling on her soul.

"Uncle, you know I don't love your son," she said "You know I was forced to marry him, and we'll never be happy together. Let me go, I can't live here, I can't and I won't work like you do so why keep me here when I'm a burden. Uncle, please let me go."

"You will have my son's children and you'll learn to work," he said "Anyway, he sends us money to serve you."

"You can't serve me forever," she said "Aunt Kareema and your sons and daughters aren't happy to serve me and they shouldn't have to. I don't belong here, I can't stand it here Uncle Suleiman, please, if you say it's okay then my brothers will come get me."

"Your Aunt and my children will serve you with their legs over their necks if they want their brother to take care of them," he said "Why do you tire yourself with the same request? You're staying here forever. You're never leaving, this is your country!"

"If you're worried about Adam sending money," she said "He will, even if I'm not here. He wouldn't leave his parents and brothers to starve just because I've left! Please Uncle, let us talk about it more…"

Suleiman got up and said: "You're only leaving here when we carry you to your grave."

Seldom over the years, and only when Eve unrelentingly importuned her Uncle day and night to allow her to leave, would he send for his brothers in The Dibt. When they arrived the next day, the brothers in the mountains, including Father, were requested to come meet at Uncle Suleiman's house. So Uncle Suleiman, Uncle Nageeb, Uncle Faris, Uncle Salem, Uncle Yahya, Uncle Arif and Father sat upstairs discussing her request. Nageeb and Faris were of the opinion she would change her mind and want to stay if she were to have a baby. The rest were of one dead end opinion, she would not be allowed to leave the mountains—no explanation needed. She would be left perplexed and vexed, after a long anxious wait, at how they came to such a conclusion.

"Why are they leaving?" said Eve "I haven't spoken to them yet, I want to discuss the matter with them."

"We told them your reasons—we know what they are," said Suleiman "You want to leave and we've talked and decided you shouldn't leave."

"But Uncle, this isn't fair," protested Eve "How can you discuss my life without me?"

Suleiman walked away singing a song about unhappy people. Every time the Uncles were sent for, Eve's hope peaked: this time they would understand. And every time they left, she was piqued and devastated, remaining three days in her room, crying painfully most of the time, before entering long sleep which sapped her energy rather than rejuvenating it. She'd emerge three days later, smiling, but deeply anguished on the inside.

They spoke, laughed, socialised, ate and drank together, but when she brought up leaving—her voice became unheard: Kareema and Dhalia would become silent and not respond, not even a single word; Suleiman would give a cold, negative reply, leaving Eve smouldering in frustration.

*

THOUGH HER PATIENCE KNEW NO END AND HER HOPE, THAT ONE day, she would leave these mountains behind remained, she had begun to change. No longer did she long to be back in Wales, it seemed too far away, and she had been left too far behind. All she wished for now was to live in the city of Taiz, but they said she couldn't live on her own in the city as it would be disgraceful and dangerous without a male guardian to protect and take care of her, so Sana'a with her brother Morad would be nice. What she dreamt and wished for now was to live in a real house, with real windows, electricity, running water and an inside bathroom (Eve, the house you live in is very real). How relaxing and safe it would be to sleep in a room and bed she didn't have to check for snakes and scorpions before falling asleep! How stress-free it would be to leave these strange people with their strange habits and malicious gossip behind. Though she didn't know it, this change in what she desired had come about by the constant captivity and rejections of her release translating into her hope and patience depleting. She couldn't see it because she still had faith in abundance to get out, but her hope to get back to Britain had abraded. Being content to live in a city in Yemen was a way of believing the closer the destination she wanted to leave towards—the sooner leaving the mountains was to be realised. She closed her eyes visualising what the living room would look like; how her bedroom would be; hot baths and showers. Even in her dreams she no longer dreamt of school, education, parks, of life. Living between the walls of a normal house in a city, eating fruit and vegetables, represented the ideal life now in her fantasies. The verve of who she used to be, was whittling away.

Sometimes she remembered her childhood friends or a friend and imagine what had become of them, which universities and specialisations they would be in. She contemplated if any of them remembered her. She studied the details of the tree trunks used as beams for the ceiling, and wondered how many young people were now studying law as she had aspired to, while years of her life had passed her by doing nothing…achieving nothing. This thought left her smarting. She, had become nothing. Momentarily, pangs of slight pain lived inside her chest and disappeared. She rolled onto her side and stared at the plastic covered floor, wondering when she would be allowed to leave so she could live in Sana'a, in the luxury of the city. She also talked less with her in-laws and visitors, she just sat quietly and listened or she'd be deep in thought, she could hear them, but didn't listen to what they were saying, they became a hum in the background of her mind.

*

MORAD RETURNED A YEAR AFTER HIS LAST VISIT, SINCE HE HAD LEFT Eve crushed. Naively, after that whole sorry saga of the previous year, she still had faith in him that he would help her this time (highly intelligent, our dear Eve had a sad flaw—she truly and whole heartedly believed being good would deliver her, was it because she was cut off from the real world too young and along with it realistic experiences where she would have seen sometimes you have to be aggressive to get a good result, or was it because most films she had watched the good guys always won in the end—who knows, but she remained angelical and believing right would present itself because she had never been bad and never would be thus missed many chances where, let us say, had she been a little mischievous she may have had a crack at escaping). Presently, she thought if their in-laws had convinced him last time to leave her, she would be more convincing and find out what they had told him to sway his decision and counter-attack it. Morad's presence brought confidence she would be leaving the mountains soon. Morad listened to his sister's argument and agreed with everything she mentioned as reasons to be allowed to live in the city with him.

Eve had too much faith, she saw everybody and expected everybody to be true to their words as she was and became as ecstatic, if not more than the last time. There were no reasons to stop him. Unfortunately, last year's event would repeat itself, except this time he couldn't bring himself to tell her he'd been browbeaten into changing his mind. People heard she was leaving and came to say goodbye on the last day. Morad had given her a small grainy grey suitcase the size of a briefcase to put her belongings in. Eve slept late, every time she closed her eyes they opened, longing and so eager to live in the city, exhausted from the drag of the years waiting to leave. Morad woke up at two thirty a.m. to get ready—Eve heard him, sitting on her bed, dressed and covered by the huge black skirt and hood, ready and waiting, half empty suitcase next to her and heart full of happiness, the moment had finally come. Every time Morad emerged from his room he looked towards her with a sullen face and doe-eyes. Eve's heart went out to him thinking his sadness out of having to leave his wife and three daughters after only a month of vacation. She heard the car coming down the route, it would stop at Barh Salliya and she wanted to be there before it stopped. Suitcase in hand, heart somersaulting for joy, she knocked on his door.

"Morad, come on the car's arrived." she said.

Morad got up, picked up his suitcase, a drowsy Dhalia shook her head. He stepped out of the room and looked down at the floor. "You're not coming with me." he said and dashed towards the Bawaba. Eve ran after him, the sound of the cloak making heavy swoosh-swoosh sounds with her stride.

"I am coming...you said...everybody knows...I've said goodbye," said Eve "I'm ready, I've been waiting..." she held his coat sleeve as she walked beside him.

"Stay here Eve." said Morad.

"Don't leave me here," she said "Don't do this to me again..."

Suleiman and Father waiting in front of the Second House, grabbed her as Morad walked away.

"Take me with you." Eve screamed after him "You said you'd take me! Don't leave me here...*you said you'd take me!*" He continued walking quickly without looking back.

"Morad! Morad..." she cried out after him "I can't live here anymore, I can't. I'll do anything, I'll be your servant just take me with you...I'm begging you help me! *Help me-e!* Don't leave..." She withered to the ground as the two men holding her by her arms, held her back from life. As the car passed below she got up, gripped the wall and screamed after it: "Morad come back! *Take me with you, I'm dying!*"

She thumped her fists on the stupid half empty suitcase, addressing God: "Why? Why can't I live? Why can't I be alive? Make them help me my God! Make them help me!"

Suleiman dragged her back inside where she knelt doubled over her knees, face to the ground, a black pile on the floor. The hood of the black cloak, spread in an arch over her, heaved as she wept, and the skirt of the cloak in a circle around her twitched. Completely covered, the in-laws looking in only saw the cloak and heard her sobs coming out from beneath it. The blackness had coated her insides too. What was wrong with her brothers? Why did they refuse to help her when they always claimed they would? There she knelt and wallowed under the darkness of the cloak, in the darkness of the early hours, in the darkness of her captors' nescience, crying until the sun dawned, breaking into and interrupting her misery. As the first light came in, Eve dreaded the day; she wasn't supposed to be here today, the sun was not supposed to shine on her in this room, it was supposed to meet her half way to Taiz. The new day was supposed to start on her way to a new life. She looked around the room, how insipid it suddenly looked, and how much she abhorred it. As daylight became stronger her dread of the day ahead increased. The ladies living nearby would pass, one by one they came to see her empty room, only to find her sitting on the bed and their surprised 'Good-mornings', 'You didn't leave?' and 'Why?' poked into her wounds. She asked God to help her. She asked Him to have mercy on her.

Something had changed, she no longer came out of her room, she lay on her bed day and night, or slumped on the floor weeping for hours every day. Suleiman looked in from the door, the sound of her pain finally pierced his heart, he opened his mouth wanting to say something comforting then closed it, what could he say? His face fell and skin crawled as he felt he couldn't trap an animal the way he'd caged her life; his eyes watered, she was being tortured. Caught between his great greed and creeping contrition, it almost felt he could free her. But he swallowed hard, his chest inflated as he prevented himself from crying, this is how it had to be. His face hardened as he convinced himself she had everything any woman could wish for, she just didn't appreciate it, and was behaving spoilt. He shook his head vigorously right to left as if he were saying no, as he attempted to physically shake away his conscience, and left without saying a word.

CHAPTER FOURTEEN

E VE READ WITH RAPACIOUS VORACITY THE STACKS OF *NEWSWEEK* magazines Morad had brought with him recently and over a year ago (which Dhalia had refused to give her last year under pressure from Kareema). A lot had happened and was happening in the world while she remained in the dark, unaware of what went on. Intrigued and longing to know, she went through years' worth of journalism like wildfire through dry bush, absorbing news, knowledge, feeding her hunger. All day and night she sat in her bed situating the pillows to make her as comfortable as possible, reading what was going on, or had gone on, in the world. So much had progressed in science that amazed her; atrocities to civilians caught between warring factions, shocked and horrified her; murderers whom got away with their crimes or were convicted, disgusted her. What humans could do to each other was disturbing. Articles which made her laugh and those that made her cry. The world had advanced in so many different ways, yet innocent cherub-faced children lay dead in a pool of blood on tiled floors from war; she found war the worst brutality that existed and the civilians caught in between were the most afflicted. Mankind had made the world a most beautiful place, yet it was man who could make it most horrific. Now she only left her room to make coffee, and Dhalia missed her company, she would poke her head through the door asking Eve to put down the magazine and come sit in her room, which she did, but with *Newsweek* in hand and as soon as visitors came to engage Dhalia, she would be reading while they gossiped. She couldn't get enough of what happened in the world, and these were the first professionally written materials she had since the novel. Anyone peaking in from the door would see her eyes focused on the article in her hand, the yellow glowing lantern next to her in bed, and when the kerosene ran out, she lit candles she'd ordered especially from Taiz, and read until her eyes were sore. When she finished them all, she turned to the four books he had brought, trite, but entertaining after a reading drought.

*

THEY STOOD IN FRONT OF THE MASSIVE BOULDERS GAZING AT THE landscape.

"Look, the hateen is coming!" said Dawood, pointing to the west where there seemed to be a white line, probably clouds, far away on the horizon.

"What's hateen?" asked Eve.

"It will be all white, and it'll rain and be cold for months." said Dhalia.

"Will we be able to grow crops?" asked Eve.

"We might." said Suleiman his eyes slitted, estimating how long it would take for the hateen to arrive.

Eve wondered what was so different about raining, isn't it what they wanted? She awoke shivering the next morning, it had become extremely cold. She opened the window above her bed, but all she could see was white, the panoramic mountain vista obscured from sight. She went through the Bawaba and stood at the door, nothing could be seen, not even the trees in front, surrounded by a dense fog. They told her it would become wet and Kareema and Mother brought in large amounts of firewood from the storage areas, to place inside the houses and huts to keep it dry. The cow was no longer taken out to graze as it started to drizzle non-stop for months. Vision was obscured, you couldn't see anybody coming until they were right in front of you. When the dry wood almost finished, people cooked pan-fried bread on kerosene cookers or small wood fires, Eve and the children loved it, so much tastier than the dense bread. Eve cuddled up in her bed with *Newsweek* and coffee to re-read the most interesting articles while they lived inside a cloud for three months. When the haze finally crept away, it unveiled the stark mountainside next to the house had dramatically come back to life: dried shrubs were now fully leafed; vibrant yellow, violet and white flowers had sprung up; green plants she had never seen before had pushed up wherever there was soil; grass had grown on the edges of the land and earthy and fragrant scents sweetened the air and invaded your nostrils. Eve could imagine what a beautiful, forested place this could have been in the past, before its inhabitants had desolated the trees and shrubs for firewood.

It had been a long time since she dug out her supernatural novel, she ran her palm over its hard, rough navy cover, looking down at it lovingly as if it could commune. This book was her only connection to home, it had been her companion over these four years since the day she departed dear Britain. Painfully bored, she thought she might find it interesting to read again, she had lost count of the numerous times she'd read it, but this had been the longest she'd buried it since last trying so surely it was readable. Arranging the pillows behind her she made herself comfortable, placed both palms on the cover, almost reverentially, and closed her eyes, then she opened the book. She began to read the first story, but it was pointless, she knew the following sentence before reading it. She went to the last story—the same. She tried the third and second, but the more she read, the more frustrated she became. She flipped through the pages as anger brewed inside her, annoyed she had been reading the same book for over four years, besides inserts of pharmaceuticals. Reading it now exasperated her. *It mocked her*, being there for years unable to leave no matter how hard she tried. She slammed it shut and threw it across the bed. What was once her companion, giving her a brief escape into the world and lives of its characters, had now become a painful reminder of how extremely long she had been here. It represented the slow days of long weeks of extended months of the wasted precious years of her life. The years she was supposed to go from child, to teenager, to adulthood; robbed of the experiences which would have moulded her character into the person she was meant to be. *Supposed to be*. Her literary companion was now a source of pain. She picked it up and jumped off the bed, hurriedly went to the First House, and marched up the stairs where she stood in front of the deep round oven. Weeping, she placed the book on a step and pulled at the dried branches and bushes set to one side above the steps leading to the roof. Eve placed the shrubs into the oven, poured a little kerosene over them and lit them with a matchstick. She picked up the book, looked at its cover and began to cry again. Her anger returned as she ripped out pages and threw them into the flames.

"I will get out of here!" she said to it.

She continued until there were no more pages, only the cover in her hand. She closed it, only a shell of what it used to be—so wrong without its core, feeling bad and guilty over what she had done, wishing she hadn't done it. She felt the texture of the cover one more time and tossed it after the rest of its body into the fire and watched as the flames leapt higher consuming the pages, and then itself. When the fire died, she bent over the oven to find some pages hadn't burnt completely, but blackened and curled—just how Morad had left her that early morning. Immense loneliness overcame her, the only thing connecting her to back home, had perished. She sat on the mud-covered stairs below the oven, staring ahead lost in thought.

*

SITTING OUTSIDE THE MOUNTAIN-GREY FIRST HOUSE IN THE COOL morning, her in-laws, all the Uncles and their wives and Grandmother Haleema deliberated why Eve wasn't pregnant. They came to a conclusion (through no medical knowledge, but guesswork would do just fine): something must be wrong with her. She herself had no desire to become pregnant, not wanting to have a baby from Adam and not wanting to go through childbirth like she had seen so many women go through, their screams travelling the distance from where they lived; women going back and forth, sometimes for days until the pregnant woman gave birth—or died. A few times a pregnant woman was taken by car, after two days of being unable to give birth; and each time the car returned from halfway, carrying a pregnant corpse: "She exploded." they would say; Eve mused probably because they waited so long before deciding to take the woman to Taiz, and consequentially would lose both mother and unborn child before reaching the city, where the nearest hospital was. What she hadn't witnessed with her own eyes and ears, she had heard from relatives whom spoke in great detail of the agonising pain and tearing of tissue and what it was like and what happened delivering each one of their children. Eve was absolutely sure she did not want to go through childbirth, in fact every time Dhalia went through the painful ordeal of delivering a baby, every time one of the aunts had a baby, Eve would be extending her arms upwards, palms open in prayer to God to make her infertile. Now the congregation of in-laws were addressing Eve's fertility with as much graveness as a politician trying to solve all the issues of the Middle East; to the in-laws, Uncles and Aunts there had to be something wrong with Eve, or she would have become pregnant. Again, the fact Adam was never there did not form part of the equation resulting in no pregnancy. They sat outside, passing around the kooz one evening, still discussing Eve's fertility as if it were a topic of major concern while the subject of their topic went in and out to smell fresh air as they discussed her, without her.

"Don't be afraid," said Grandmother Haleema, giving Eve a sympathetic look as the latter came up from the bathroom steps, "You will become pregnant one day."

"Never, God Willing!" Eve replied. Everybody gasped and she left them in their joint mortified state to learn the next day they had decided she was infertile, and needed to be treated by a doctor, to 'untie her knot' as Grandmother Haleema had put it.

"They're taking you to Taiz," said Huda "To the doctor who all women go to that can't get pregnant or have too many miscarriages."

"I don't want to have a baby." said Eve.

"You must have a baby," said Huda "If you don't—then you're not a proper woman."

Eve smiled, not only amused by the many reasons village people had for a woman not meeting the standards of being woman, but she saw an opportunity to escape as soon as she got to the city of Taiz for which she had to plan well.

"We're going Tuesday," said Suleiman, sipping loudly at his hot tea, "The doctor will examine you, then he'll give you medicine to make you pregnant when Adam comes." He sipped at the tea quietly in a more contemplative thought, "I want you to give my son a child—you have to give him a son." he added walking away.

Monday night, Eve took out the one handbag Adam had brought with him years ago from Saudi, she had wondered at the time why he'd even bought it, no women ever wore or had purses or handbags in the mountains, not even when they went to Taiz. Eve placed all her gold into it, she planned to run away, sell some gold and travel to Sana'a, to the British Embassy. Extremely excited and anxious she could hardly wait for her flight to freedom.

*

THE CAR STOPPED AT BARH SALLIYA. UNCLE SULEIMAN SHONE THE way with a torch so they could make their way in the dark. The only female on this trip, her Uncle would sit next to the driver and she next to the door.

"Oh, my son's wife is an American woman!" announced Suleiman as he noticed her handbag. He had never met an American and only heard about them from others or the word mentioned on his transistor radio.

"Uncle," said Eve "All women wear handbags, not just Americans."

"Shh!Shh!" said Suleiman.

"Why?" said Eve.

Suleiman lowered his voice: "Stop speaking, other men aren't supposed to hear your voice. It's rude."

"Uncle, that's nonsense." said Eve.

"Shh." he said, elbowing her.

"Ouch!" she glared at him from above the white scarf covering her face. Women spoke with men, Eve saw this happen all the time, but for some mystical reason they weren't supposed to hear their voices when they were in a car. She looked out through the window, nauseous from the smell of the vehicle, it had been years since she'd been inside one. Exhilarated to be finally heading out of the mountains, she hoped it would be easy losing Suleiman in the city. Wistfully gazing out into the darkness she saw the silhouette of a thin man coming down the path towards them. As he neared she frowned, recognising his saunter. Uncle Arif. With his rifle over his shoulder.

Suleiman smacked his lips as he spoke "Your Uncle Arif's coming to help me take you to the doctor."

Upset running away would be a little bit harder now angry, armed Uncle Arif would accompany them, Eve blurted out: "How many people need to take me to the doctor? I can walk on my own legs!"

"Shh!" said Suleiman and he elbowed her harder, and she elbowed him back this time. The car moved slowly and sleepily down the dark route, and in her mind she plotted how to sidle into streets and weave away unnoticed to get away from her captors.

CHAPTER FIFTEEN

T HEY REACHED THE DAYNA VILLAGE, A GROUP OF WAITING
men dressed in their finery for travel to Taiz got into the car,
squeezing into the back and middle, more than the car was
designed to fit. Along the way, more men waiting clung onto the
outside of the vehicle, some sat on the roof and bonnet, the car had
become a leaf overloaded with lithe ants. When they reached a steep,
rocky down way or upwards, the people outside climbed off and
walked ahead, without the car stopping, then waited to get on at the
safer parts of the route. For hours the car crawled over rocky,
winding paths; the men spoke and smoked cigarettes, making Eve
more nauseous, the layers of the face veil and scarf seemed to hold
onto the car-tabagie fumes. Four hours later they arrived at relatively
flat lands called Makbana, Eve noticed the women here didn't run
away from the sound or sight of a vehicle, some stopped to watch,
very different from the women in the faraway mountains. Nor did
they have to pull up water by hand to fill their containers, instead a
pump sent water gushing out of a pipe. She noted their sunburnt and
dry skin, a harshness in their gaunt faces so unlike the pretty
mountain women, they dressed differently too, though they still wore
the elephant-ass shaped trousers and covered the back half of their
head and hair, parted at the side or middle, but their dress was only
knee high—which the men on the car joked about and commented
how inappropriate it was to be so short. From the men's conversation
Eve came to learn, in Makbana women were allowed to get onto cars
and go to Taiz without a male companion; their dialect and even

some of their traditions were different. In the eyes of the mountain villagers the Makbani women were immoral. Eve knew the latter opinion was derived from the fact *they* did not approve of women having the freedom to go and come as they pleased. The car jammed with gossiping men provided Eve with confirmation of what she had read in the Quran and Hadeeth, women could separate from husbands, two women were named from Makbana, the men discussed how both, shamefully, divorced their husbands.

"I'd divorce her before she'd divorce me." said one of the passengers.

"I'd lock her in a room and never let her see the sunlight!" said another.

"Women like that should be beaten." said Uncle Arif. Known as being the strictest uncle in Suleiman's line of brothers, all he was interested in was keeping the ladies in the family oppressed (unsuccessfully), Eve had seen him tell off even the youngest of his nieces about things the other uncles did not find 'shameful': he didn't even want the girls to part their hair from the side, it was an immoral hairstyle in his book, they should only part it from the middle. Hypocritical and finding normal things immoral to tell off young neices, he had no problem in pursuing his adulterous affairs with married and unmarried ladies; it didn't matter to him to disseminate fabricated religious fervour while inseminating other men's wives and daughters.

Eve paid close attention to the flat roads, wishing she had been brought to this region instead of the mountains—it would have been easy to get out of Makbana: they were only an hour and a half away from entering the city and it was all level, dirt roads and Wadi Rushwan (by God she would have walked it leaving in the dead of night) and more importantly, women could get on a car without a guardian—no questions asked, no permission needed. Still on the outskirts of Makbana, one of the passengers lit a cigarette, it was more than Eve's stomach could bear confined in the car for hours, all the men wearing strong perfumes and smoking cigarettes, a sickening combination, and she started to gag.

"Stop the car, I'm going to throw up." said Eve.

"Shh!" said Suleiman.

"Stop the car!" she said to the driver. Eve jumped out and ran across the sand-like soil, she couldn't find anything to throw up behind. She lifted the veil and pulled down the scarf off her face.

Arif got out of the car shouting: "Cover your face!" stamping his foot "Put the scarf on your face!" although with her back towards the vehicle nobody could see her face (as if any man would find her stretched gagging face spewing her guts out attractive). Too queasy to care or respond to his tantrum, she held her head in her hands. Suleiman passed water to her and she rinsed her mouth.

"What's this?" said Arif prodding the handbag which Suleiman had picked up from the ground.

"It's Eve's," said Suleiman, passing it to Eve, "She's an American woman."

"Uncle *please* stop saying that," said Eve "It's silly."

"Throw it away," said Arif "It's shameful you carrying that. Why'd you let her take it? Throw it away or I will."

"This is mine," said Eve clutching her bag fearing they would discover the gold and know her plan, "You're not touching it! Is there anything in this world that isn't forbidden or improper by you?"

"Suleiman," said Arif "Why do you let her wear this as if she's not one of us? As if she's a city woman? Throw it away before the people start talking."

"Just get in the car and leave my son's wife alone," said an easily amused Suleiman "She's an American woman!"

"Cover your face." said Arif. Eve pulled the scarf back over her face and the veil down, they walked towards the car, Arif embarrassed she had exposed her face and was carrying a handbag, and Eve embarrassed by Suleiman calling her an American woman just because of the handbag. As she got into the car, Suleiman announced: "My son's wife is an American woman!" How annoying she found the amusement in his voice as she laid her head to the side of the car, still dizzy and green.

They arrived in bustling, crowded Taiz, people were a flowing, noisy river. Eve assessed it wouldn't be difficult losing Suleiman and Arif in this crowd. The pavements were covered with goods, forcing people to spill onto the road and vehicles to slow down to a crawl.

Some people pedalled carts with fruit, others with colourful plastic toys, nail clippers, razors, cigarette lighters, hairclips and ointments. It was so loud the din was inside her head not just around her, but even louder were the colourful shirts most men wore, making Hawaiian shirts seem soft pastels. Eve opened the door, Suleiman grabbed her by the arm, she looked at him and he let go, only to turn her head to find Arif standing in front of the door. As she came down, Arif held her by the arm and she could not help but feel under arrest, from hand to hand. Suleiman took her by the hand and they made their way down the crowded pavement while Eve scanned both sides of the street for a police station. The only signs in English were for hotels. They passed a café where men held ornate china teacups while drinking tea out of the saucers. She took a look behind her only to see Arif's stern face.

"Stop looking at everybody!" he snapped.

She was led into a hotel where Suleiman spoke to one of the two male receptionists and booked a room. Up the stairs, Suleiman in front of her and Arif right behind, they led her to the fourth floor. The room had an aroma she couldn't recognise, too strong on her sense of smell accustomed to fresh, unpolluted air. It had two wooden double sized beds. The bathroom though clean, also had the strange scent: air freshener. Suleiman went to fetch breakfast, Arif got up to lock the door, he pulled out the key and placed it in his pocket.

"Uncle Arif, where's the doctor's clinic?" asked Eve.

"It's far away." he replied abruptly.

"Where?" she asked.

"A taxi will take us." he said as he lay back on the bed, the rifle beside him. Suleiman returned carrying a big round metal plate full of smaller plates and bowls. Arif immediately locked the door, leaving the key in the keyhole.

"Eat Eve, eat." said Suleiman with his mouth full "Why do you peck like a hen? Eat."

For someone who had eaten only tea and dry bread for the majority of four years, Eve wasn't interested in the food. For travellers going to Taiz from the mountains, eating good food was looked forward to and part of the good side to the tiresome travel, but Eve had no real appetite this morning, the smell of cooked liver, eggs, spices and vegetables made her queasy, and the taste of strong flavour after all the years of blandness was strange on her tongue, she thought probably because of the nausea. She ate a little, washed her hands and picked up a glass and sat on one of the beds, sipping at the tea as she studied the door, deliberating if she ran out while they ate, would she be able to beat them down the stairs? And out of the hotel? She could disappear into the crowds. She looked at the rifle on the other bed, would Arif actually use it if she was beating them down the stairs? She turned around as Suleiman sat opposite to her. Arif was in the bathroom washing his hands. Eve got up, opened a door next to the window and the sounds of the street poured into the room from the balcony.

"It's so noisy here." she said watching people beneath her going in every direction.

"In the village we're blessed with peace." said Suleiman.

"I'd rather be blessed with noise if it means living in the city." she said smiling at her uncle.

"You're a daughter of the city," Suleiman laughed "You can't live without electricity or running water." he commented, despite the fact she had lived for years without in the mountains. They watched the streets, a hive of busy, happy people. Eve smiled as the kind sun and soft breeze played with her long, flowing tresses.

"Look!" said Suleiman "Look what the authorities are doing!" Eve followed his finger. Men in olive-green uniforms tipped a cart full of raisins, scattering the poor man's merchandise into the street as he raised his hands to the sky in despair. The 'uniforms' went on to a toy seller who had laid his goods on a scarf on the pavement, kicking the toys as the man protested loudly. Other pedlars hurriedly pushed their carts away, while those sitting on pavements picked up the corners of their mats or shawls, bundling the goods and running before the authorities ruined what they depended on earning a day's living with.

"Why are they doing this?" said Eve.

"It's not allowed," said Suleiman "Selling on pavements or blocking streets."

"Why don't they just tell them to leave if it's not allowed?" she said "They didn't have to ruin his goods."

"It's not allowed to block the streets." said Suleiman.

"The streets weren't blocked," said Eve "People and vehicles were still moving. It's unfair. These people must be really poor, Uncle…have you seen how they look and what they sell? They should have told them to leave, not ruin their goods, this is wrong."

"Now you're a politician?" said Suleiman, smiling, "Oh, my son's wife is President Ali Abdullah Saleh!"

Eve rolled her eyes "Uncle, you say the most stupid things! You make me embarrassed—stop saying silly things."

"Oh, my son's wife is an angry politician!" said Suleiman, laughing when Arif appeared at the door of the balcony, scowling as usual.

"Get inside," said Arif sternly "The people can see you."

"Nobody's looking up," said Eve "And even if they did…who cares? What does it matter? They don't care and neither do I."

"I'll throw you off the balcony if you don't come inside right now!" said Arif.

"You're not touching a hair on her head." said Suleiman standing in front of his daughter-in-law.

"If she doesn't come inside," said Arif "I'll shoot you both before you ruin this family's reputation."

"Go inside Eve," said Suleiman "Put your sharshaf on, strangers shouldn't see you." Eve did as ordered, although it made no sense—villagers didn't wear sharshafs in the mountains.

"Uncle Arif?" she said as she tied the skirt of the cloak around her waist "If it's a bad thing for people to see me, isn't killing me for it even worse?"

"She always asks questions nobody thinks of." Suleiman said and laughed from outside.

She tied the hood eyeing the door, listening to both men talking on the balcony. She picked up her purse, this was the perfect opportunity. As quietly as possible, she turned the key in the door once - it sounded thunderous in her cautious ears - then a second time and opened the door.

"Where are you going?" Arif shouted from the balcony door, striding towards her. She froze and he slammed the door shut and she held onto its handle.

"I want to go outside." she said.

"NO," said Arif "You're trying to run away!"

"Why'd you open the door Eve?" said Suleiman with concern and disappointment on his face.

"I want to go for a walk," said Eve still holding the handle "That's all."

"Do you think I came to Taiz for no reason?" said Arif "I came to guard you so you can't run away or be kidnapped. If you run away it's on our honour and pride—you're *our daughter* and I won't let you destroy our reputation by running away. The gossipers will say you ran away with a lover!"

"I'm not running away," said Eve "I want to see Taiz." But Suleiman pulled her away from the door.

"You can't go outside on your own," said Suleiman "You'll get lost or be kidnapped."

"Uncle, I'm eighteen," said Eve "I won't be lost and believe me nobody wants to kidnap me!" she frowned, *they* had already kidnapped her.

"Women are kidnapped all the time in the city," said Arif "If you're kidnapped, the whole family will be disgraced."

"Why and how would anybody kidnap a woman from the middle of a crowded street, in daylight?" she said.

"It's happened before," said Suleiman "It happens."

"Really?" said Eve "So you know people it's happened to?"

"Yes!" said both men simultaneously.

"Who?" she said "What's this woman's name? Is she from our village?"

"I don't know anybody that it's happened to," said Suleiman "But we hear stories about the city."

"So women being kidnapped in Taiz, is just another of your many superstitions." said Eve.

"You can't go outside," said Suleiman "I'll go later and call Adam to tell him we're in Taiz. I'll ask him to call to the hotel."

"Will you take me to call my brothers?" asked Eve as tears welled in her eyes, it had been years since they left on the promise to come back.

"Yes," said Suleiman "I have Morad's number. I'll tell him to tell Yusef and Sami to call here, there's no need for you to go out."

Eve's hope of returning home revived, it would be so much easier for her brothers to rescue her from Taiz. They were probably too afraid of going back to the mountains and not being allowed to leave, but now she was in the city, all she had to do was wait for them to pick her up, she thought with a smile.

Suleiman left to make the phone calls, Arif waited until Suleiman returned before leaving the room. There was a knock at the door. Suleiman answered and one of the receptionists carried in a telephone, plugged it into the wall, plonked the phone onto one of the beds and left without a word. Suleiman answered the phone, it was Sami. After talking for a while he handed the receiver to Eve.

"Why didn't you come back for me?" she asked after an awkward reply to his 'how are you' was she was not good and had been stuck four years in the mountains, this being the first she'd left.

"I'm sorry Eve, I wanted to, but I couldn't."

"Why couldn't you?"

"We couldn't."

"Anyway, we'll talk about it when we meet. I'm in Hani Zabeed Hotel, you know it—where all the people from the village stay, come for me today."

"Umm, Eve…I can't."

"What do you mean you can't? Please come or I'll have to run away on my own."

"You can't run away Evez, it's too dangerous!" he warned "There's a lot of sick people out there and you're a girl—you won't be able to get anywhere on your own!"

"Then come and take me, you're my brother, they can't stop you. All that nonsense that I can't leave with Morad isn't true, if I leave with my brother no one can stop us."

"It's more complicated than that Evez. You're Adam's wife, we can't take you against his will."

"Have you been brainwashed?" said Eve becoming exasperated her brother couldn't differentiate between law and concocted, customised customs "I'm telling you, if you're my brother I can go anywhere I like with you. They took advantage of us when we didn't understand the law, but now we know it's not true. Sami, *please*, you and Yusef come for me. I'm depending on you to save my life."

"Listen," said Sami "We're not in Britain, alright? We can't just take you—you're somebody's wife."

"Somebody I didn't agree to marry," she said frustrated "Now I'm living a life I didn't choose—I'm not even alive…I helped *you* get out of the mountains, *now you help me!*"

"I'm going to say this slowly," said Sami "I can only take you if Adam calls me and says it's okay."

"But he'll never say that," said Eve "They'll never let me out. Sami, this is my best chance, come and help me while I'm still in Taiz. My life…it's gone, I just want to live what's left in a city, I can't stand living there anymore. I have all my gold with me! We can sell it so we can go back home, but I need you to help me escape…Okay?"

"Don't try to run away," said Sami sternly "You'll be raped and murdered, I'm telling you! When I get a call from your husband, saying he gives permission for you to leave, I'll come and get you."

"Sami, please," she said "I helped you get out of there…I helped you and now it's your turn to help me."

"Goodbye Evez." he said, and hung up.

In disbelief, Eve kept the receiver to her ear as the tone went on. It would never happen. She gently returned the receiver to its cradle with both hands. Why she continued to believe they would come for her when she had read their uninterested letters is a mystery, the fact was, she just couldn't give up hope—it was all just a fantasy which only she believed and dreamt of because they had never actually lifted a finger to do anything to help her leave the place they themselves were all too keen to escape, but she had kept alive and smiling based on false hope, but at least it was hope. She sat with her face buried in her knees, alone in her captivity, alone in her efforts to escape. Suleiman tried to soothe her, but when she lifted her head, the same disoriented feeling came over her of many years passing by in moments and the wave of calmness and peace rushed through her being. But she felt, her body—hollow. Her mind, heavy.

After lunch, with seriousness more than the event called for, Suleiman and Arif got ready to go buy qat, putting on their ornate belts and curved dagger Jambias, Uncle Suleiman folding and wrapping his head shawl on correctly.

"When are we going to the doctor?" said Eve, she wanted to get out of the hotel to make a run for it, the hope of her brothers saving her, painfully dead.

"The clinic will open at three in the afternoon." replied Suleiman as he pulled out the key from the keyhole, Eve looked on thinking to be extraordinarily lucky they were leaving the door unlocked, but, to her horror, he locked the door from the outside.

"Uncle Suleiman! Uncle Suleiman?" she shouted, banging her fists against the wood.

"What?" he answered, his voice slightly muffled from behind the door.

"Why are you taking the key?" said Eve "I'll lock the door from inside."

"You'll open the door and run away." he said.

"I won't Uncle Suleiman, I won't run away."

"We'll buy qat and come back quickly."

"What if there's a fire?"

"You'll die." said Suleiman and she heard both men laughing as they descended the stairs, amused by the joke. She rushed to the balcony and waited until they appeared, and watched them as they disappeared into the crowd down the street. With all her might she pulled and shook the door, but it was pointless. "Help me!" she shouted, slamming her palms against the door, "Open the door! Open the door!"

The two hotel receptionists stood outside the door, called on by the occupants in the next room on hearing the racket.

"What's wrong?" said the receptionist.

"Please open the door," said Eve "I don't have the key."

"We can't open the door," he said "You already have the key and your guardians have just gone outside."

"They forgot I was in here," she said "They thought I'm ahead of them and locked the door. Please open it so I can catch up with them."

The two receptionists conferred with each other, then one replied: "I'm sorry, we can't. If you're inside and we open the door, we can get into trouble. You have to wait until they return."

"No, listen," said Eve "I'm supposed to be with them. I was in the bathroom and they thought I'm waiting outside, that's why they locked it. They're probably looking for me right now in the streets!"

"I can't open the door," said the receptionist "They'll cause us a problem because you're 'a family'. I'm sorry." By 'a family' he meant female. Eve threw herself onto the bed, she would have to wait until they took her to the doctor.

*

EVE PICKED UP THE DISCARDED SOFT RED STEMS OF THE QAT, MOIST and cold to the touch, methodically breaking them at their joints between her fingers until a heap of broken stems piled in front of her. The vapidity had turned into a vampire gnawing at her brain, stuck in this insipid room, two uncles tediously stuffing their cheeks with green leaves, hardly saying a word to each other. It was time to leave, Suleiman broke off good juicy stems from the dry leaves and put them into a plastic bag to take with him.

"Come on," he said "We'll take you to a doctor, he'll fix you and you'll have a baby to play with."

Eve did not want to be *fixed* (skip the garage, just take her to the airport), she wanted to be *freed*. It was as if they had agreed to keep her sandwiched between them, Suleiman held her hand tightly and pulled her behind him, if she tried to walk next to him Arif tugged at her pulling her behind Suleiman. They went down narrow, crowded streets. A taxi stopped and they got in then drove for almost half an hour before stopping next to a narrow pavement. Many signs were affixed to the exterior of the building, one above the other, most in Arabic and a few in English with many spelling mistakes. They led her up to a gynaecologist clinic. White plastic chairs were lined against the walls, one side of the waiting room for men and one side for women. A white-veiled nurse sequentially called out the name of the patient whose turn it was to see the doctor.

"It's crowded." said Arif.

"I'll see the nurse." said Suleiman.

Arif pointed towards the women's side, Eve obediently sat. She looked around, the way in was the way out. The nurse appeared, looking at her clipboard to call out the name of the next patient, it wasn't the female's name she called out, but her male guardian's. Suleiman got up, Eve watched as he whispered something into the nurse's ear, they moved to one side of the door of her office where they couldn't be seen from the men's side. Suleiman pressed money into the nurse's hand, Eve didn't know what she had witnessed, but it was corruption, quite common in Yemen, he had just bribed the nurse to jump queue. When the patient in the doctor's office came out, the nurse looked at her clipboard and called out Suleiman's name, who waved at Eve to get up while Arif remained seated. The doctor seated behind a wooden desk, his office neat and orderly, was in his forties, and slightly overweight, his black hair balding, no beard, no moustache, wearing western trousers and shirt—he looked very different than the strikingly handsome village men. On one side of the room, an examination bed with a monitor above it. The doctor greeted them.

"My son's wife does not become pregnant," said Suleiman speaking slower and louder than usual and enunciating his words as if he were speaking with someone who did not fully understand the language or was slightly deaf "And we want her to give him a son."

"What's your name?" the doctor asked Eve.

"My name is Eve."

"How old are you?" (Both hearing and language fine.)

"I'm eighteen."

"How long have you been married?"

"Four years, I think."

"You were married at fourteen?" the doctor said, his eyebrows rising high above the frame of his spectacles.

"Yes." said Eve, as her ashamed eyes lowered to gaze at the desk. He pursued to ask her a series of questions regarding menstruation.

"Your daughter-in-law speaks broken Arabic," said the doctor turning to Suleiman "Her speech is like a foreigner who's learnt to speak our language?"

"She was born in Britain," said Suleiman "She came four years ago and married my son. She learnt Arabic herself and now she can speak like a bulbul sings!"

"Do you speak English?" The doctor asked her in Arabic.

"Yes Doctor, I do." she replied in English.

"She can speak English!" said Suleiman, laughing loudly as if it were a novelty.

"You married very young." the Doctor continued in English.

"Yes." said Eve.

"I need to examine you," he said "Please lie over there." Eve got up and the doctor pulled the sheet over her.

"Uncover your abdomen." he said. Eve expected to hear Suleiman object as she uncovered her stomach, but he just looked away. The doctor pulled the elastic waist of the trousers and folded it below her hips so he could examine her properly. "This is going to feel a little cold," he squeezed gel onto her lower abdomen and ran a handheld gadget over it, pressing so hard it hurt as he watched the monitor. "Everything looks normal," he looked at Eve "Where are you from?"

"Wales."

"Your English is very good. Are you sure you're eighteen? You look sixteen."

"I'm definitely eighteen."

"So you live in a village?"

"Yes," she paused then "Doctor, I was forced into marriage, can you call the police to come here? I have to get back to Britain and they can help me." The Doctor gave her a smile and wrinkled his forehead.

"Even if I call the police and they come," he said "They won't help you unless you have someone from your side of the family to confirm what you say, and still there's not much they could do. Not even the authorities dare get involved in family matters, the police aren't much help, and to be honest, you should be afraid of the police—it's not like the UK here—they abuse their powers and take advantage of vulnerable girls and women, so be careful! Besides that—your uncle might kill me if I interfere with his family." He looked at Suleiman then back at Eve. "Do you have someone from your side of the family here in Taiz I can call?" he said.

"No…no." she said. The doctor made an apologetic facial expression that there was nothing he could do then pulled two tissues and wiped the gel off Eve. She got up and sat next to Suleiman in front of the doctor's desk.

"What's wrong with her?" said Suleiman "Can you fix her?"

"There's nothing wrong with her," said the doctor "Your son just needs to be patient until it happens."

"But it's been more than four years and she's not pregnant."

"Where is your son?" said the doctor "Is he waiting outside? Has he had a medical investigation?"

"No," said Suleiman looking offended "There's nothing wrong with my son! He's in Saudi."

"How long has he been in Saudi?"

"Two years since he left last time."

"How long have they been together?"

"Four years."

"What I mean is, how much time has your son been in Yemen with his wife," said the doctor "You say they've been married for four years, but he's been away two, how long has he actually spent with her?"

"Ah," said Suleiman giving it some thought "When they were married I think he stayed for two or three months and when he came back the second time...I think two months and then he went back to Saudi."

The doctor laughed and said: "Now I know why there has been no pregnancy—there is no husband! If he's been with her for only five months over many years, what are the chances of getting her pregnant? Your son needs to stay longer with his wife, there's nothing wrong with her and she's very young."

"So she doesn't need medicine?" said Suleiman.

"No, she has no medical problems."

Suleiman's face was troubled, from his perspective, if there was nothing wrong with Eve, then there must be something wrong with his son. Eve wanted to run out of the door and to the street towards her freedom while Suleiman fretted over his wished-for progeny. They were leaving the office and the doctor said in English: "I hope you can make it back home, God Willing."

"God Willing." Eve replied smiling brightly underneath her veil, she stepped out of the door and Suleiman asked: "What did he say?"

"He said he hopes I have a baby." said Eve.

"God Willing! God Willing!" said Suleiman throwing a sun of a smile at the doctor before closing the door.

Eve looked around the waiting area, Arif was nowhere in sight. With Suleiman's back to her while he spoke to the nurse of his concerns, Eve ran towards the door and down the stairs, she heard him shout her name; she made it down the last flight of steps and saw the sunlight coming in from the street. Heart thudding in her chest, she dashed towards the aura. Arif blocked the light, standing in the doorframe, he'd been waiting outside.

"Where are you going?" said Arif "Why are you running?" he ran his thumb under the rifle strap. Eve was lost for words.

"Eve! Eve!" shouted Suleiman running down the stairs.

"Why were you running?" said Arif.

"I need to go to the bathroom." she said.

"If you want to go to the bathroom tell me, and I'll show you where it is in the clinic," said Suleiman "Don't run off without me."

"She ran away from you?" asked Arif.

"There's nothing wrong with me, the doctor said I'm fine." said Eve in an attempt to change the subject. It worked. Suleiman became silent and apprehension filled his expression.

"If there's nothing wrong with her," said Arif "Then why didn't she become pregnant?"

"It's from God! They'll have a baby when God wants them to," said Suleiman with a touch of chagrin in his voice "I'm taking Eve back to the hotel then I'm calling Adam to tell him what the doctor said."

They held her by both arms, flagged down a taxi and back to the hotel room where they left her interned and went to make phone calls, and to buy a long list of things in a rush before the car would leave for the mountains at ten in the evening.

Alone, Eve sat in the room as it got darker. Although night was nearing, the streets of Taiz were as gaudy as they had been in the morning; there was something about this city and its people, they were extremely energetic and gave off a happy, bustled vibe, but it only amplified her despondency. Her whole being wanted to be out there in the world. She was young, full of energy, and her soul, body and mind wanted to live. Not be confined by walls. Rules. Tradition. Marriage. Eve pulled at the locked door before standing in the balcony watching men and women walk in every direction going around their lives, envying their freedom. She watched women wearing sharshafs like hers, made up of skirts and hoods and a few women covered in black cloaks like long coats, most of whom carried handbags.

"*Are they all Americans?*" she said to herself and laughed.

The light faded from the sky and so did her belief in the opportunity of running away.

Suleiman returned, carrying a heavy box filled with fruit and vegetables. He pulled out a packet and opened it offering sweetmeat to Eve.

"It's sweet, you'll like it." he said. Eve broke off a little, her sad eyes studying Suleiman.

"Uncle Suleiman," she said "Why won't you let me live my life?"

"You are alive my daughter," Suleiman said with his mouth full "You're not dead."

"Uncle, I'm as good as dead. You don't let me leave the mountains so I can live a normal life. Let me go Uncle Suleiman, *please let me go*. I can still catch up with what I've missed."

"You eat, you sleep—you're alive. You'll have a baby! I've called Adam and told him you're fine, nothing is wrong with you," he paused and swallowed the sweet "I've told him to see a doctor." he added gravely. It was pointless, she went back to the balcony and watched lights and people moving around.

When it was time to leave the streets were less crowded. Arif walked in front of her and Suleiman followed carrying the box on his shoulder. Sometimes, too many times, she walked too fast, stepping on Arif's leather sandal, snagging it off his foot. He would stop to put it on, irritation drawn on his face, his expression—priceless, she stifled her giggles, but it kept on happening. As he tried to get it back onto his foot Eve walked on.

"Stop!" he shouted "When I stop—you stop. Don't walk away on your own." he said catching up with her.

She constantly looked left and right for an opportunity of flight, but all she saw were dark alleys with groups of men loitering and leaning against the walls at the furthest end with an air of something dubious going on, it seemed unwise to run into a dangerous situation, especially that Uncle Arif was such a good shot. They waited long in the car until all the passengers arrived and did not leave at ten. The journey back was more tiresome than the morning's, the car much heavier and slower with everybody's boxed purchases and sacks of sugar and flour. The car broke down before they reached Makbana so they all got down and sat on the ground while the driver worked to fix it. Eve was sleepy, upset to be heading back to the mountains; over four years in the rocky prison, and she'd spent less than twenty-four hours in the city before being taken back to captivity. The men talked with fatigued voices, the morning travel, long day and journey back had taken its toll on everybody. Arif snatched the bag from Eve's lap.

"What's this for?" he said "Why do you wear it?"

"I thought they'd give me medicine," she said "And I'd put it into it."

"You can carry your medicine in a plastic bag, like everybody else." said Arif.

"Leave her alone." said Suleiman, he took the bag and handed it to Eve.

"Why do you let her be different?" said Arif with rage in his eyes "Make her like all our women! She's disgracing us carrying a bag! Only the Disbelievers carry bags!"

"Are all the women in Taiz 'Disbelievers'?" said Eve tired of his tirades "And what do bags have to do with religion? Why are you always angry?"

"Why are you always different?" said Arif.

"Because she is different," said Suleiman "Now leave her alone!"

Eve didn't fear Arif's scowling face, but today she feared his menacing rifle. She looked around her in the still night, hoping the car couldn't be fixed and they would head back to Taiz, it was still closer than the mountains, and maybe this time she would escape. She looked up at the night sky, not many stars were out and dimmed at that. Although she had two uncles with her, and was surrounded by many male villagers, she felt alone, and alienated, as if she were not part of the throng; was it because she was the only woman? No, it was different—she felt like an outsider who hadn't been fully accepted, they viewed her as an outsider. A nightingale whistled a melody, Eve's heart smiled as if it sang only to keep her company and turned looking towards the trees hoping to see it.

"It's a bulbul," said Uncle Suleiman smiling "Do you like its sound? They say when a bulbul sings it's to forget all its problems, because when it sings the sound fills its head with beautiful thoughts so there's no room left for its worries, but its song can also make people forget their problems too."

The moonlit pebbles and trees were coated with one blueish-grey colour, she quietly recited a poem about the 'silvery moon' and its 'silver shoon' she had learnt many years ago when she was free. The car was fixed, Eve endured uncomfortably the long journey back. The winding up the rocky mountains took forever, it didn't feel adventurous as it had the day she and her brothers enjoyed the thrill when they first took the road to the village. She hated the music playing, especially what she recognised as being played during her forced wedding. By the time they reached the houses she was knackered and groggy, as was every passenger. A sleepy Kareema opened the door for them, even early in the morning she wanted to know about Eve's fertility.

"What did the doctor tell you? Can you have babies?" she asked, handing them glasses of tea from overnight, sour and lukewarm.

"Yes." said Eve.

"Did he give you medicine?" said Kareema.

"No." said Eve.

Suleiman told Kareema what the doctor said. Eve took a lantern and went to wash up, before laying her aching body on the bed. How different it felt than when she and her brothers came here: filled with awe and excitement, they hadn't felt tired on arrival. As her heavy eyelids closed, her last thought was waking up at 7 Melin Walk to find this had all been a dream, and she would still be fourteen years old.

She awoke to the sound of her nieces giggling outside her door. She opened it and the little girls ran into their aunt's open arms. She picked them up one after the other and sat them on her bed then sang with them rhymes she had taught them, reaching into the square hole behind her bed, she pulled out a plastic bag and handed each of her nieces a bar of chocolate and packet of crisps. When they were done eating, she gave them their toys, colourful hairclips and bobbles, they kissed their aunt, and after she lowered them off the bed they ran off to show their mother the treasures brought from Taiz. Eve remained seated on her bed staring at the whitewashed wall, melancholy crept over her that she would live the same repetitive days over and over again. She shook her head, unable to fully accept in her mind it had been four years even though she knew it as a fact. Though she had not lost faith one day she would leave these mountains, she knew better than to hope help would come, and her belief it would be someday soon, was gone. The uncertainness of when she would be able to leave turned her stomach inside-out. She closed the door and embarked on a two-day period of crying and misery dwelling and simmering in her dolours, before descending into a darker place, musing which way was the least painful to end one's own life but every time the fear of pain put her off as none of the options available would be painless, before emerging from her room again, fresh with optimism she would leave.

*

DAYS WENT SLOWLY BY AS MONTHS BLENDED INTO EACH OTHER. EVE became glum and dejected while everybody fussed about Adam returning soon, but it wouldn't take her long to come out of the depression by viewing his home-coming as an opportunity to convince him to let her go. When Adam arrived, carrying gifts of material, gold, perfume, incense and much more, he also brought his medicine in the form of injections and tablets. Unlike Eve, he was not amused when she had read the ingredients of his medicine to find it included the extract from urine of menopausal women; it hurt him women's pee was to cure his male problem.

"I went to a doctor after you called me, and he said my chances of impregnating are low," said Adam "He gave me medicine which will help and I have to see a doctor in two weeks' time to check me."

"There's something wrong with your water?" asked Suleiman, all the more perturbed for his progeny.

"Yes." replied Adam. Eve sitting behind them looked up and said silently: "Praise to God!"

After having wild and rambunctious sex one night, she had the strangest gut feeling, an unsettling instinct she would become pregnant from this very night, but dismissed it as being worried, after all she'd heard it from the 'horse's mouth' a doctor said he'd probably never impregnate her so there was no way what she felt in her bones could be true.

After a few weeks of being pleasant and nice while she tried convincing him to divorce her, or at least allow her to live in the city with her brothers, which all ended in vain, she stopped having sexual intercourse with him. He would say he bought her and could keep her where he wanted; his mind was closed; he did not, and would not, think about her reasons and explanations as to why she could not live here; he didn't believe she had a right to live her life the way she wanted, or where she wanted. To him, she was something he owned and made decisions for, whether she liked what he decided or not. Adam complained to his parents and in-laws she refused to have sex with him: she had grown and become too strong in knowledge for him to overwhelm her with force without causing him embarrassment in front of the whole family: where morality wouldn't stop him from raping her, shame from the community and worrying what other people would say about him could. Haleema and the aunts embarrassed her, lecturing her how wives should give their husbands 'the pleasure' and to let Adam feel that enjoyment while he was still in Yemen. Other female relatives also 'advised' Eve while they spent afternoons in Dhalia's room, according to religion it was a sin not allowing your husband to have sex whenever he wanted, but still many ladies here had fortuitous headaches when husbands had upset them (No, the panacea in your stiff syringe will not alleviate the pressure, replied the wife.).

"You know the angels curse you all night until morning if you don't let your husband sleep with you!" said Grandmother Haleema.

"It's a big sin." said Aunt Fulla.

"The angels must know I was forced into this marriage," said Eve "And they'll be cursing everybody who took part in forcing me into this life."

Eve was agitated by this conversation, and her agitation wasn't from its inappropriateness alone for she could feel something different in her body, it was as if her brain, her insides, everything inside her were changing from within: a lining creeping underneath her skin and innards, she sensed her cells changing in tiny movements. Something she felt was not right, and she worried she might be pregnant, but it was too early to tell.

A beautiful morning, she enjoyed the cool breeze blowing against her skin as she stood on the doorstep of the Bawaba watching the whole family talk as they sat outside taking pleasure in banter under the blue-carpeted grinning sun. Purple Dress Lady passed by, on her way to visit someone. She kissed hands with Eve at the doorstep, then held a lock of Eve's hair in one hand and used it to point at the latter.

"I hear you don't let Adam sleep with you," said Purple Dress "You have to, he's your husband. The angels will curse you! Let your husband be happy while he's here."

"Mind your own business." said Eve brushing her hair out of the woman's hand with one stroke of her arm.

The woman turned towards the female in-laws and made a most revolting suggestion: "You all go inside with him and hold her down—let him sleep with his wife with your help."

Kareema, Dhalia, Huda, Haleema and the little girls got up, embarrassed by the vulgarity, leaving only the men sitting outside as Eve raised her voice, angered and embarrassed. "You're so rude," said Eve "Don't you have any common sense?"

The woman walked away, looking at the men as she said: "You haven't tamed her yet, she's still as wild as when she came from Britain."

Adam was to go to Taiz for a follow up, Eve watched silently as the family recommended he find the best doctor to help him. Adam returned a few days later, in the early morning he cried in grief while Eve's heart hosannaed with silent joy so loud angels must have danced in heaven. His father patted his back and his mother, squatting on the ground, looked at the floor in shame.

"The doctor said my water can *never* make my wife pregnant," said Adam "The doctor in Saudi had said there is a possibility, but this one...he said it's *impossible*."

Eve seated in the background on the bed, soul brimming with relief and happiness which she didn't let show, watched on with a blank face, but mentally she was doing the energetic Prisyadka her feet hardly touching the ground. One worry she could put behind her.

As women chatted and laughed in Dhalia's room, Dhalia closed her eyes and moaned. "My back's killing me," she said placing a hand on her back "My period's flowing too heavy this time," she turned to Eve "You look well—isn't your period bothering you? You're usually lying on your back with your legs up the wall when it comes."

"It's messed up this time," said Eve "Just three drops a few days ago and it stopped."

Haleema stopped smoking. Fulla and Khatima laughed, eyes wide with happiness. Dhalia smiled at Eve.

"My daughter, you're pregnant!" said Haleema with joy, getting up towards a bewildered looking Eve.

"I'm not pregnant," said Eve shaking her head "Blood came down. It's a period. It's just messed up."

"Those drops are what we call a dusty confirmation," said Haleema, her arm around Eve, "Some women get a few drops of blood the first time the menstruation is due when they're pregnant, some even have a proper menstruation during the first month. You see, I told you God would untie your knot!"

The women congratulated Eve, and she cried in fear it could be true for she didn't want God to untie *this* knot, this was a knot she wanted to be tight, tangled and never undone (have a crack at the knot of marriage, why not?). Dhalia raced to the Bawaba to tell her mother whom ran outside shouting to Suleiman and Adam to come out. They stared down at Kareema and she informed them, grinning from ear to ear: "Eve is pregnant! Eve is *pregnant*!"

Both men came running down to join the smiling, jovial family, except the young, nineteen-year-old at the centre of the excitement worried and scared, still not wanting to believe she could be pregnant. They were mistaken.

"You're going to give my boy a son and me a grandson!" said Suleiman with a look of joyous gratitude, and he kissed Eve's forehead, "Why are you crying?"

"I don't want to be pregnant, I can't be pregnant," said Eve "The doctor said he can't make me pregnant. It's impossible!"

"God can make anything happen," said Suleiman "The Saudi doctor's medicine has worked."

"God can make the impossible, possible!" said Haleema.

"I'll go back to the doctor in Taiz and throw his results in his face." said Adam smugly.

The next two weeks passed with everybody praying Eve's period would not come. Eve spent most of the time alone, facing the direction to Mecca, hands cupped upwards, arms raised to the sky, tears streaking down her cheeks, begging God to make her infertile, to not allow her to be pregnant. Regardless of her pleas and supplications emanating from the essence of her soul, she was with child.

Rain had been scarce over the past year, it would become cloudy over them then it would go rain somewhere else. Thunder and lightning seemed more abundant than the light rain drops that fell and in many houses lightning had struck, a few people had died or were injured in separate incidents. Kareema's family had a strange history of being struck by lightning: her father, grandfather, two of her uncles, one of her aunts and a number of cousins had all died, by thunderbolt (family tradition to be upkept by her brother in the near future). She had vivid memories of how her mother became a widow and told the story many times of her father falling across the doorstep, her mother holding her dead husband in her arms as she wailed and cried and it had turned into a phobia, for Kareema became tense and fearful as the sky clouded. Eve liked to sit alone in her room while it rained and rumbled, watching the sky and landscape change from her eastern window, but Kareema cried intensely as she wanted everybody in the house around her when it started to rain all way through until it ended. Was it because she felt reassured by a crowd or that she wanted to lessen her own odds of being struck by lightning, Eve couldn't tell, but Kareema's fear intensified when lightning started to strike houses more often during the year. Paranoid, she would cry and cover herself with a blanket curled into a ball, covering her ears with her hands and wailing she would be struck and die. Nothing Eve, Dhalia and the other adults tried could soothe her, calming only when the thunder stopped completely. To make an intolerable situation worse, Aunt Hasna, a near neighbour, would come with all her eight children when the sky darkened, seeking comfort in numbers (lessening Kareema's odds of striking the jackbolt). The Bawaba darkened by the clouds and rain became more dismal, crowded with women and children full of fear. They squeezed together, sitting in one side of the room, some of the infants smelt bad, of urine and diarrhoea; Hasna's baby cried most of the time if he wasn't asleep as did his siblings. The atmosphere full of imminent death by lightning induced by the adults, made it unbearably grim. Bright lightning lit up the Bawaba, striking all over the area, thunder did not clap, but applauded, the steel doors, windows and bolts rattled and so did your lungs. Neither Eve, Mother, Dhalia nor Huda felt afraid, but there were days when lightning struck so near the house you could feel a vibration in the ground; they flinched from the long-lasting brightness of light then startled from the loudness and long roll of thunder. Usually, Eve liked the rain, it had been a long time since it last rained heavily, but being crammed into a human accordion to one side of the Bawaba with twenty-three women and children every afternoon was an uncomfortable ordeal, especially while the majority waited with impending doom to be struck by lightning.

It's funny when you wait with certainty for a specific thing to happen and it never does, but when something is to happen it's when you least expect it. After lunch, Eve put on a sequinned dress in shades of metallic green; she didn't like sequins at all, preferring velvet, lace, silk, the more comfortable fabrics, but sequinned were the most fashionable dresses in the opinion of the villagers and Dhalia begged her to wear it. Dhalia hung the many necklaces of different sizes around Eve's neck and pinned the rest to her chest. Dhalia admired the bracelet Adam had gifted Eve this time, but said it was such a shame it always came undone because its clasp was loose. The afternoon was sunny, Haleema came to pass the day with them. Fardoos, Akram and Eman were extremely sick with measles so when the sky clouded Eve helped Kareema carry the febrile children to Dhalia's room and lay them on the big bed, and sat next to them, to one corner. Busma, Dhalia's youngest, slept in the closed hammock hung on the small single bed. Haleema, Mother and Dhalia sat side by side, atop rectangular cuboid cushions on the floor, smoking the kooz.

"I'm going home before it starts to rain." said Haleema surveying the sky and getting up.

"It doesn't look like it's going to rain today," said Kareema, sitting in her place, "It's just cloudy."

Minutes passed and it started to rain lightly, Dhalia set the kooz to one side, another superstition that you shouldn't talk, read, write, comb your hair, smoke, look into a mirror or do anything while it rained. They sat serenely and quietly as it drizzled, suddenly all Eve saw were brown pieces of wall flying from over her head as a tremendous sound deafened them. She thought the kooz had exploded, but realised lightning had struck. She jumped off the bed and turned to look at the wall behind her, two holes had been blasted into it, the mud and whitewash blown off. Eve turned to look at Dhalia, Kareema and Mother still sitting in their places as if no time had passed.

"We've been struck by lightning!" Eve said, but couldn't hear her own voice, her ears rang, a fog clogged the inside of her head. She looked at the three women whom just stared straight ahead then she shook them by the shoulders, one after the other, shouting in their faces: "We've been struck by lightning!" but still couldn't hear her own voice. It was eerie as she put her face in front of Dhalia's, then Mother's, Kareema's—their eyes open wider than usual, it seemed they were staring right through her. Eve stepped back and upright, like watching a film in slow motion their faces moved from blank to confused, to scared then slowly their mouths opened in a scream, but all Eve heard was a slow, low noise coming from their mouths, a tape recorder playing on exhausted batteries. The men upstairs must have heard it as a scream because they immediately ran down. Suleiman and Adam asked Eve if she was alright, she pushed them away and checked her three little in-laws who had been on the bed next to her; they were unconscious and feverishly unaware of what happened. Dhalia screamed on opening the hammock and not finding little Busma inside—her uncle Bundar had picked her up. Dhalia thanked God. "I thought the lightning had taken her!" she said, then she started to shout "I've been struck by lightning, my back's burnt!" Two men told her it was impossible as she would have been in terrible pain. "I'm burned…Oh my God!" cried Dhalia "I've been disfigured, I'm going to die!"

Adam put his arms around Eve while Suleiman splashed cold water onto her chest.

"You don't have to do that Uncle, I'm fine. I'm not scared." said Eve.

"No," said Suleiman, splashing another cold cup of water over her, "We have to so you don't develop a chest disease or lose the baby from fright."

Kareema and Mother cried, still sitting on the cushions. Adam, Suleiman and a dripping Eve turned to Dhalia.

"I've been struck by lightning! My body's burning!" said Dhalia, and she semi-fainted into her father's arms.

"You haven't been struck by lightning," said Suleiman "Eve reassure her, take a look at her back." Eve lifted the dress and examined Dhalia for any marks.

"There's nothing Dhalia," said Eve "You're okay."

Dhalia stood upright and said: "Thank God I'm not disfigured."

They examined the room, dry pieces of wall, brown and white, were on the floor. Eve didn't know why she had thought it was pieces of the kooz flying around as it was intact. The wall above the bed had two big gaping holes baring stone. On the blanket just below where Eve's hand had been resting a burn mark and across the bed parallel to the burn another hole on the wall, behind the bed.

"God is Most Kind, Most Merciful," said Dhalia "It just missed Eve and the children by a little!"

"It looks like it zigzagged between them." said a neighbour.

Dawood crouched on the floor in front of the wall opposite the bed. "Whose is this?" he said and lifted up Eve's bracelet.

"That's Eve's," said Dhalia "It was on her hand when the lightning struck!"

Eve turned her wrist, there was no mark. She put the bracelet on and noticed it needed a firmer press to snap shut, she shook her wrist, to her surprise the buckle didn't open up as it always did. She removed it and examined the buckle closely and couldn't believe how close she'd come to being struck by lightning: the buckle looked as if it had melted and solidified by the lightning. She passed it to Dhalia who was also surprised at the marks of where the ripple of molten, hardened gold appeared in place of the previous smooth finish. The lightning had thrown the bracelet off Eve's wrist and unintentionally fixed the clasp.

"Thanks to God it didn't melt on your wrist!" exclaimed Dhalia.

All the women who had been in the room would have the ringing sound in their ears until the next day. It wasn't long after the light rain had stopped, Haleema and close neighbours came to check everybody was alright on hearing lightning had struck at Suleiman's house. They still sat in Dhalia's room.

"I told you to take this dress off when it's raining," said Haleema, pointing at Eve and eyeing the dress which she had sewn for her, "It's because of *this* dress lightning struck in the room."

"Why is it the dress' fault?" asked Eve, it was the most absurd thing she had heard yet.

"Because this dress has sequins made from the stars," said Haleema with much conviction "Look how they sparkle and shine. The lightning comes from the sky and followed the shiny sequins because they're made from the stars."

The sight of Dhalia laughing and slapping the wall, then her hand slapping the floor as she let herself crumble on the ground in titters at the idea, while Eve twisted left then right trying to ease the pain in her sides induced by gales of thunderous laughter issuing from her small mouth was enough to make anyone who looked in join in the hysterics ('twas a knee-slapper)—Grandmother Haleema remained stony-faced throughout staring at the rollicking riot. Recovering, but still chuckling, the mirthful duo asked her how she thought people could reach the stars, let alone make fabric out of them, but the old woman would have none of it and warned her never to wear it while it rained. Eve sat in her room, alone, she could hear everybody talking excitedly about the lightning from in front of the Bawaba, each person telling their version of the story. Eve had heard of pregnant women having miscarriages when being startled or frightened and stared down at her flat stomach and *hoped*, she would have a miscarriage: the sound of the lightning had been deafening and had shocked her. Adam popped his head into the room.

"Come outside, sit with us." he said.

"No, I'm cold."

He walked to her, hugged and kissed her and returned outside. She wasn't that cold. Taking a cautious look towards the door she squeezed at her stomach and pressed hard and downwards from below her navel, eager to assist the wished-for misfortune.

*

ADAM LEFT FOR SAUDI, SHE HAD COMPLETE THE SECOND MONTH OF pregnancy. It was a strange feeling being pregnant, she never vomited, but was always nauseous, hated the scent of *Camay* soap and some types of perfume and incense. She could feel the changes happening inside her, but it was the constant queasiness she hated most. She couldn't get enough red tea—craved it and no longer preferred it with milk.

She sat on the bed, head tilted downwards, looking sideways at the room where she'd been kept for almost five years. Left alone, and now pregnant. She looked down at her stomach. Why was she pregnant? God, she didn't want this. She had to get rid of it before it progressed. Would God punish her if she got it out of herself? How could she be punished if it wasn't a baby yet? Eve wished a hospital be near or even a pharmacy available so she could have an abortion, she'd heard so many stories in the village of the 'immoral city women' becoming pregnant from adultery and getting the babies removed at a clinic, or buying a miscarriage inducing pill from pharmacies. She debated in her own mind if it was wrong to cause a purposeful miscarriage and when she decided it wasn't, she closed the door, stood on the high bed and jumped, landing heavily on her feet. She jumped off the bed time and time again. When she tired, she waited for pain, for blood to flow, but nothing happened. The next day she picked up a heavy metal trunk packed full of clothes and things and walked around her room, straining her body in hope the weight would bring about the miscarriage. She continued the jump and carry method day after day, wanting, *wishing,* the pregnancy to die; she didn't want a baby from this man and she didn't want to go through childbirth. She had to leave and return to normal life, *her life.* Sometimes Suleiman banged on the door, curious from the sound of Eve landing on the floor. "What are you doing?" he asked "What is that thudding noise?"

"I'm just dusting the blankets, Uncle." she replied.

Eve's attempts to cause her miscarriage continued, as did the pregnancy. But as her stomach grew so did her motherly instincts, guilt poking her conscience every time she jumped off the bed, the burden of guilt increasing every time she added to the trunk's weight. As she washed, she stroked the wet bump. Could it feel? Did it know what she was trying to do? She looked down at her belly holding it with both palms. What if they were wrong—and it had a soul before four months?

*

EVE SAT ON HER BED LEANING ON A PILLOW TO HER SIDE, LOOKING out of the east window. Getting out of the mountains seemed far away and less likely to happen after all those years of failed efforts. She rested her head as nausea intensified, and took a deep breath when it resumed to its normal tone then gasped, startled by a movement in her stomach. And there it was again: the motion of a butterfly wing flapping then it became slightly stronger like the twitch of an eyelid. Eve held her stomach, tilting her head downwards, mouth open, eyes softened and awed. Her baby moved inside her. She closed and opened her eyes concentrating on the baby's tiny movement, only a small flickering feeling.

"I'm sorry…I won't make you fall out," she said "It's not your fault."

*

GRANDMOTHER HALEEMA, DHALIA AND KAREEMA PASSED THE kooz between them in the serene morning. Kareema cocked her head sideways and laughed, she looked at Dhalia and said: "I prefer it when she recites Quran."

"My father doesn't," said Dhalia chuckling "He wishes she would wait until mid-morning."

"Why?" asked Grandmother Haleema "You're lucky you have someone reciting Quran in the house. Now our sons are away working, there's no reciting."

"I like it," said Kareema "It drives demons away." (Not enough to repel you, Kareema)

Dhalia smiled, her gold teeth glinting, and said: "My father would rather drive her away when she does it at the top of her voice hours before the sun comes up!" All the women laughed. "He asked her once to stop reciting before dawn," Dhalia continued "But she said

207

'Uncle Suleiman the Quran and Hadeeth say the angels bear witness to the person who recites during these hours.' and he couldn't object anymore because she stumped him with religion!" The older women cackled and Dhalia laughed.

"Eve's the only girl I know who can use religious sayings to prove a point against what a man says." said Dhalia.

"And your father blames your husband for giving her all those religious books—so he curses Morad for his sleeplessness!" said Kareema.

Grandmother Haleema chuckled and picked up the kooz, setting it nearer to the door of the Bawaba so she could hear Eve, in her room, better.

"I don't understand a word she's saying," said Grandmother Haleema "Can you?"

"Only when she sings in Arabic." replied Kareema.

"She sings like a bulbul," said Dhalia "She can go on for hours!"

"The men who worked in Saudi know about where she was born and brought up," said Grandmother Haleema in a contemplative voice "They say living in Britain is like living in paradise and can't understand why her father returned to the village...Maybe it's still difficult for her to live here, maybe she longs to go home so she sings like a bulbul to forget...forget where she is, forget where she used to be. Forget her pain."

The women said nothing more, making only a soft kurrkurr noise as they lightly drew smoke from the kooz and listened to the sound coming from Eve's room. Inside her room, Eve couldn't see the walls: immersed in memories and places where she frequently heard the songs she now sung; or she was surrounded by her friends and classmates while performing in a concert or play in front of an audience, or she was running over hills and besides streams with her friends, exploring woods and parks, walking past Himalayan magnolias and kicking through piles of golden leaves. She smiled as she sang and swung around her room in dance, but this happiness only lasted for as long as she could sing. Once she had stopped singing, her eyes once again saw the four whitewashed walls of her room, she stood still as if expecting some magical force to transport her back home. When this didn't happen, all she could feel was a wrongness eating at her soul: the wrongness of an innocent man jailed for a crime he didn't commit; the wrongness of a bird born to fly and be free, caged for the pleasure of its owners, its captors. She hastily went to her bed and threw herself onto her stomach, snatched a folded cotton sheet and covered her head. After lying motionless for a while she turned onto her back, uncovered her face and looked at the furthest wall. Was Britain real? Had she ever lived there? Or was she mad and imagined Wales? No, all the memories of people and places and things that had happened, a life with all its fullness of senses and surroundings could not have been a figment of craziness. Then why was she here, unable to leave? Why had her intelligence, her kindness and goodness all amounted to nothing and did nothing to change her immured circumstances? Could it be possible that she was mad, had she lived her whole life here?

CHAPTER SIXTEEN

F ROM IN FRONT OF THE BAWABA EVE AND DHALIA WATCHED
the fulvous sun contaminate the clouds with its rusty-orange
tint as it went down, into the Red Sea, it disappeared beyond
the horizon where Eve's eyes constantly and fervently searched for
her evasive life and future. Suleiman went back and forth fixing
something on the yard door. Eve went inside to get ready for prayer.
During afternoons the girls played house on the ducka outside Eve's
room, pretending the ducka and windows of her room were their
imaginary house; they used leftover ribbons and rags collected from
Haleema's house, tying it to the mesh and steel bars of the windows,
decorating their pretend house, there were often long ribbons
dancing in the wind outside the window, long after the children had
finished playing and went off to their chores. Eve's room was dark,
she lifted herself onto the bed and looked down at her seven-month
stomach, removed her watch placing it onto the pillow when she
noticed a long dark ribbon next to her wrist which she had sat exactly
next to. She followed the ribbon upwards towards the window,
wondering how they'd managed to get it on the inside, had they
pierced the mesh? When she reached the top of the ribbon she saw
its snake-head knocking into the metal mesh of the window
desperately trying to get out. Pregnant Eve, light as a feather with
fright, leapt to the floor and ran screaming to the door: "Uncle
Suleiman a snake!"

Suleiman came running, axe in hand, and swiped the snake to the
floor, hammering it with the back of the axe until it stopped moving.

Dhalia and Kareema splashed Eve with cold water asking God to give her the baby and not let it fall—worried the fright might cause a miscarriage. It was enough being constantly worried about snakes and scorpions, sleeping in terror, but now one had actually been on her bed disturbed her sleep and she startled, imagining something crawling over her.

Whenever a snake was killed, if there was a pregnant woman in the house they brought the dead snake and asked her to stand up: whoever held the snake said the woman's name, and asked the question, does she have a boy or a girl and threw the snake into the air. If the snake landed on its stomach, the pregnancy was believed to be a boy; if it landed on its back with its stomach upwards, it was considered she was carrying a girl. Dawood, followed by a group of children, came running into Dhalia's room with a dead snake, long and black with a white belly, hanging from a stick.

"Eve, come outside," said Dawood "Let's see if you have a boy or a girl!" The women poured out of the room to see the result.

"Dawood, don't let it touch me." said Eve (a dead snake was as deadly as a live one to her), she screamed as Dawood teased her, chasing her with the snake extended on the stick.

"Stand straight." said the women.

"Omen, omen, give us a sign, does Eve have a boy or a girl?" Dawood said loudly, and he threw the snake high up into the air. It twirled like a baton then landed, stomach downwards.

"A boy! A boy!" shouted Dawood, with a big grin of glee on his face.

Dhalia's amused expression turned into anger, she became jealous whenever someone else had a newborn boy and now she became unreasonably irked by this meaningless game. Frowning and upset, she shouted at her little daughters, ordering them to go inside then grabbed a sweeping palm-brush and chased off Dawood and his friends.

*

MOTHER STILL SPENT MOST OF HER TIME RUNNING AFTER THE COW, it had become her whole life.

"When I'm having the baby you're going to be with me…right?" Eve asked Mother one morning.

"Of course, what a question to ask!"

"You're always out, shouldn't you stay at home just in case I go into labour?"

"I won't go far. I'll be here, don't worry."

Eve watched her Mother follow the heavy cow down the path. Ironically, Mother's cow was due to calf around the same time Eve was due.

The regular afternoon visitors were passing time with Eve and Dhalia at the latter's room when Haleema arrived after a long day of delivering a baby, she informed them the woman had screamed so much and taken so long, but would be fine now. This prompted Aunt Fulla to ask if Eve would be a 'screamer' or a 'muffler' (some women were able to suppress their screams during childbearing), to which Grandmother Haleema replied Eve would scream so much she would drive them up a wall. Eve wanted to know why this conclusion.

"Because I've seen you when you get a thorn in your hand," said Haleema "I've seen you run away screaming from insects. I've seen and heard you when you had an earache—you were like a child!"

"I *was* a child when I had the ear infection," said Eve "I was only fourteen."

"You were married by then so you were a woman—not a child." said Haleema "May God help us when you have the baby…you'll drive our souls out of our bodies."

"What do you mean?" said Eve.

"You'll scream and scream like crazy, I can tell," said Haleema "You won't scream calmly or withhold screaming."

"I won't scream," said Eve "*I won't scream at all!*"

"We'll see." said Haleema.

"You'll see." said Eve determined not to scream during labour, or only scream in moderation if she had to. Why did they look for the worst? That she would die (Kareema's regular reassuring prediction)? That she would scream abnormally?

When the time came, Grandmother Haleema was sent for, the old lady sat puffing at the kooz while watching Eve seated on the bed her heart trembling in her mouth waiting for something to happen. The pains began in her lower back, nerves were being plucked and the pain spread as lightning branches far away in the sky, painful but it didn't make her scream. Eve walked around the room, stopping only when pain increased. She looked down as something wet her trousers and inner thighs. "Grandmother Haleema, I think my water broke." she said, disgusted.

The pain increased, Eve stifled moans as she walked in circles or lay on the bed. Haleema watched her silently, smoking the kooz.

"Ooooh, oooh…Grandmother Haleema…do you think this will be over in an hour?" asked optimistic Eve—a fellow villager had literally dropped a baby into her pantaloon (a vending machine dispensing a gumball) while cleaning the stables, the birth was so quick it was over before she could even think to let go of the brush.

"Only God knows when the baby will come out," said Haleema with a faint smile at Eve's naivety "You just have to be patient."

"Ow! Owww! Owww!" Eve bent towards the bed holding her back "Aaah…oooh." she stood upright "You see," said Eve sitting on the bed, smiling at Haleema "I'm not screaming. I can handle the pain and not scream."

Haleema puffed smoke out of her mouth and said with a sly smile: "My dear, you have only seen one side of love yet."

Eve smiled back then scrunched her face as she groaned from the pain in her back, but if this was what pain would be like, she could handle it—no screaming, no drama. She looked at her watch then let out a groan.

"See?" said Eve looking at Haleema triumphantly "I'm not screaming. I won't drive you up a wall!"

Two hours later, the serene blue sky and quiet village startled to the sound of Eve's long shrill shrieks tearing through the peace. Mother, Kareema, Haleema, Dhalia, Fulla, Khatima and Hiba (a neighbour) were all in her room, holding her and trying to calm her as she screamed. And screamed. And screamed. Abdulrazaq, a nearby neighbour, was so disturbed he sent a message to the women asking them to tell her to stop.

"Help me! Get the baby out of me!" she begged "Why isn't it coming out? I can't stand this pain…oooh…I can't stand this paiiiiin!"

A wooden bed was brought in, the bed she slept on was too high and they decided she couldn't have the baby kneeling. Hasna arrived, she kissed Eve on the head and said a prayer for her quick delivery.

"Bring buckets of soil and spread it underneath her," said Hasna "We'll tie a chain or a head veil onto the beam that holds the lantern wire, and she can hold onto it and push the baby out, just like I do." Eve's eyes widened; soil? Chains in the ceiling? It sounded like some setting for torture.

"No," said Haleema "Her skin's too soft and will tear from kneeling and her body's too small, she won't have enough strength in that position. We'll put her on the bed when it's time."

"It's time!" Eve cried "It's time…aaah."

Poor Eve, nobody had educated her about childbirth, only stories of pain and pushing, tears and tearing. She got onto the bed and started to push, thinking she could make it happen of her own accord, but nothing moved.

"Why isn't it coming out?" she asked "Why can't I push hard like the women?"

"It's not time yet," said Haleema "When it's time you will push."

She screamed and wailed in pain for hours. Women from nearby villages came to check on her. Everyone tried to calm her down as she screamed from pain she could never have imagined had she seen and heard a thousand and one women go through labour, she could never have guessed how it felt for them, no matter how detailed they told their stories. They wanted her to quieten down, but the only reason they gave her to do so was because it was improper and shameful, these ridiculous comments *'that the men would hear her'* grated on her already pained nerves. She screamed and cried all through the night and calmed a little the next morning.

"We have to hold you from behind," said a tired Haleema, sitting beside her, "So the baby doesn't come out from behind."

Eve, breathing hard as Khatima wiped sweat away from her forehead, asked: "What do you mean the baby doesn't come out from behind?"

"Some women who nobody holds for," said Haleema "The baby comes out from the anus and the women are injured down there."

"Babies can't come out of the anus…can they?!" said Eve alarmed looking around at everybody.

"*Oh yes!*" said Haleema "If nobody holds them properly."

"Hold me properly," Eve said edging forward, bewildered by the horrible thought, "Don't let it come out from behind!"

A push overcame her and she understood it came naturally even if you didn't want to push, it was involuntary. Sitting on the rim of the bed she pushed at Haleema's instructions, Kareema holding her from behind. But how strong your body was did make a difference, to be able to push the baby out, Eve could not put out of her mind the twelve-year-old child-wife who had recently spent three days in difficult labour and had 'burst'—her body first violated by sex with an adult had been overburdened with a pregnancy her small frame could hardly uphold then died in pain as the baby stuck inside her cervix. Eve pushed and pushed as Haleema waited underneath the skirt of her dress. Eve begged the women to get the baby out of her, to help her, but Grandmother Haleema told her only God could help her now then reassured her that soon the baby would be out and the pain over (Eve would have preferred instant death than to feel a second of this pain); Eve didn't believe it: since the other day when she screamed louder, they said the baby would come out because she was screaming louder. When she calmed down as the pain lessened, they said the calming meant the baby would come out. But no baby came out. Screaming and pushing, there was nothing except icky warm fluids gushing out of her, topping pain with disgust. The ladies picked her up and moved her back to the rim of the bed, hoping the change in position would make her stronger. Eve longed for her mother's presence, to comfort her at least. Feet on the floor, she screamed and pushed.

"Why aren't you here with your daughter?" some women asked when Mother appeared at the door.

"I've been here since yesterday," said Mother "The cow's calfing, I have to go check on her."

"The cow's giving birth today," Eve, limp and angry, managed a sarcastic laugh, "When I'm having a baby? Mama, leave the cow and stay with me—she's not your daughter, I am one of your kine....Aaaaah..."

After the last bout of pushing, sleep overcame her and she withered into Fulla and Dhalia's arms, supporting her on either side.

"She's sleepy," said Haleema "The baby's coming out soon!"

Eve not completely asleep, but exhausted, drifting in and out of consciousness, heard the visitors repeating what Haleema had said. Her eyes were only closed for moments and she wished to slip into death while in this peaceful state. Only moments, and the ripping pain and pressure pushing down sent her on a round of screaming. When she calmed, prune-like Obeida suggested something to Haleema to which the latter agreed and asked for a mat to be brought in. They helped Eve lie down on the mat placed on the floor whom thought they believed she could push better on solid ground to help the baby come out quicker, but it wasn't what the ladies were intent on. Supine Eve was surprised when all the ladies in the room circled her and grabbed the mat, lifting it, and her, shaking her vigorously, side to side, to and fro, as she screamed: "Put me down! What are you doing?"

Haleema was saying: "Galgilooha! Galgilooha!" which explained why they were shaking her, as it meant sorting and cleaning a small amount of rice or grains by putting it in a flat metal or palm leaf tray, shaking it side to side with a circular motion, tossing it slightly, this resulted in flakes and crusts rising to the top which they removed by blowing, while heavier stones gathered at the bottom, making it easier to separate grains from flakes and stones. By shaking her, they thought they were helping the baby come out. Eve screamed as the pain increased, they put her down and lifted her to the bed. She pushed with all her might and looked eagerly at Haleema reappearing from under her dress, but Haleema shook her head and said Eve's vagina wasn't opening wide like other women. Again, they made Eve sit on the rim of the bed hoping it was the best position. Mother returned to the room.

"Can you hold her from behind," said Kareema "So I can rest my hand for a while?"

"Mama, stay with me…it hurts," said Eve in tears "I can't…I can't."

She pushed and screamed as Kareema and Mother switched places. But Mother wasn't holding her correctly, Kareema had been holding tight, keeping Eve's buttocks squeezed together, and Eve was petrified by the news a baby could come out of the posterior, but Mother hardly touched her.

"You're not holding me right," said Eve "Hold me properly like Aunt Kareema—with strength." Mother got onto the bed and put her knees against Eve's back, pushing Eve forward, she placed her hands on Eve's waist and squeezed with all her might.

"Stop, Mama," said Eve "Why are you squeezing me? I'm not toothpaste!"

Dhalia laughed, took Eve's toothpaste from the shelf and showed the women who'd never seen toothpaste before how it was squeezed out of the tube, and the room filled with laughter.

Not long after, crying replaced the laughter, Eve had pushed and pushed but not delivered, and now lay as limp as a ragdoll. Suleiman several times came knocking on the door, his eyes full of tears, asking if he should go get the car to take her to Taiz, but Haleema said it was too late. The only sign of life when pain made her scream, and even her screams were becoming fainter and shorter. Dhalia held her in her arms, weeping. Haleema wiped the tears away from her old eyes. Eve lifted her head and saw Kareema who had always expressed hate towards her, who had constantly predicted pregnant Eve would die during childbirth, crying too, gently then hard.

"Why are you crying Kareema?" said Haleema.

"She's going to die," said Kareema "She'll suffer more pain and then she'll die. Look at all the pain she's gone through…it's too much."

Eve was touched to see Kareema crying over her, maybe somewhere deep in the monster there was human compassion, maybe she loved her after all. Twenty-four hours after she began she had delivered a baby boy. Eve was in so much pain she no longer cared what they did to her when the women lifted her and sat her on the slimy warm placenta, for they believed during childbirth a woman's vision weakened and sitting her on the afterbirth restored it. Kareema and Mother lay her on the bed of which the mattress had been folded in half for the top half of her body to rest on, the bed ropes covered with faded rags. Kareema covered her with a blanket. Blood flowing heavily out of her body could be heard splattering on the ground underneath the bed, something rolled painfully in her abdomen. Haleema carried the baby to Eve and held it beneath her so she could see it properly and her breath was taken away: God had given her the most beautiful baby in the world. She looked without blinking at those beautiful brown eyes with long lashes, the perfect tiny mouth, the cutest cheeks ever created and the long dark hair covering his head. Momentarily mesmerised by her son's face, she could not feel pain.

*

WHEN ADAM RETURNED HE WAS THRILLED WITH HIS SON, IT SEEMED he was happy as any father would be with a child. Eve had long discussions with Adam regarding their son's future, her reasons for moving to the city were clear and the weight she put on their son having a proper education made sense to him so he agreed that upon his departure Eve and son would go live in Sana'a with her brothers Morad and Yusef, Sami had already left Yemen and was back in Britain. A month and a half after Adam's return to Yemen and everything seemed to be going well, with the exception—she was pregnant again with a pregnancy she did not want, again. She had requested at Adam's arrival they abstain from sex until he provided her with contraceptives from Taiz, but her request caused such a commotion: Kareema accused her of wanting to use the pills so she could have an affair—another well believed village-story that the 'daughters of the city', as they called city women, all used pills to avoid becoming pregnant because the only thing girls and women did in the city was have adulterous affairs; but concupiscence overrode the fear of pain and she continued to please Adam as an obedient wife, in hope of making it out of the village and everything was fine until his parents dissuaded him, it was not a good idea, reminding him of how she was forced into marriage and how much she wanted divorce; they asked him if he was stupid enough to believe she now loved him and warned him not to come back crying when she divorced him and ran off with another man to Britain. Eve and Adam quarrelled over the change of his decision, but without result, he no longer agreed they go live in Sana'a.

During his last and third month of vacation, Adam and his father frequently argued about money. Suleiman wanted more money and a large amount in order to buy land for Adams' future, but Adam wasn't interested. Eve was enjoying cardamom tea with Dhalia, Mother and Kareema on the outside ducka while Layth played inside with his father. Suleiman entered to see Adam and left the room angry after a while. The shrill sound of her baby crying made her jump, she ran through the Bawaba, her stomach was being cut with a knife at the thought of her son being scalded by a thermos flask of hot tea tipping over him—she had done such a great job of making sure thermos flasks, hot pots of water, knives were always out of Layth's reach all throughout a year and it was constant diligence as devious Dhalia purposefully put them back in front of him and within his reach. Adam admitted to slapping Layth out of rage because Suleiman harangued him for money.

"You want to be with another man, don't you?" Adam replied to Eve's demand for a divorce.

"Adam," Eve said, then paused to calm down, "Let us live in peace. Together we'll never be in peace, this isn't a life. You keep me here by force, you obviously don't care about your son, so just let us go. I don't want another man. I don't want you."

"You're mine," said Adam rage rippling through his face like a current "I bought you with my money."

Whenever he said he owned her, bought her, a cold column went down her spine, red-hot anger filled her chest: to be told you were owned, purchased with money, inflicted grave insult, ignited extreme rage; it defied logic and her soul objected through every fibre of body and essence of spirit silently screaming it is not true, *I cannot be owned, I am not a possession.* But the captive circumstances nailed her down in her captor's domain, the years she had spent against her will living a life imposed by the person who paid for her prison, the futility of her fight for freedom welled up an exasperation deeper and more bitter than anger, tears stung in her eyes.

"Stop saying that, I wasn't bought."

"*I do—you are mine.*" The insult never lost its sting no matter how many times it had been repeated, the words were blades which never dulled, coated in stinging, pungent poison.

"I am not a piece of furniture," screamed Eve becoming livid "I'm not a house—you cannot own me! You *do not* own me!"

Eve asked her little sister-in-law to take Layth from her mother's house to play at Barh Salliya. She watched the young aunt carry her son from in front of the Bawaba and when they disappeared down the path, she marched into the house and sat on the bed next to where Father sat on another bed.

"Abbah, I want a divorce," said Eve her eyes desperately seeking agreement from Father "Adam won't let me leave, he's a bad father. *He just slapped my baby*…and he won't divorce me."

"You can't have a divorce. You're his wife." Father replied, as cold as a stone.

"Abbah," said Eve "When are you going to make right what you did wrong? There's a man who says he paid you money in exchange for me, do you agree with that? Doesn't it make you ashamed? You put me in this mess, now you get me out of it!"

"Paying parents money is tradition, a dowry, it doesn't mean I sold you," said Father "He only says that because he knows it upsets you."

"This is ridiculous," said Eve "If they're ignorant and this is the way they live, that's their problem, but you know better. I didn't agree to marry so you go lie in that bed—you belong there, not me!" She argued for almost an hour trying to get her parents to see the light, to even slightly understand her pain, but their ears and hearts were not listening and Adam would leave without her gaining freedom.

*

LEANING AGAINST THE WALL, EVE LOOKED TOWARDS HER SON sleeping next to her on Dhalia's bed, while Dhalia lay in her usual place on the smaller bed on her side, neck outstretched, smoking the kooz as Aunt Fulla recounted the story of a crime which had recently happened in Taiz, of which the horrific nature, and conclusion, shook the village and spread like fire across the hamlets.

"They said her beauty was extraordinary," said Fulla "But while her husband went to work every day, she opened the door for her lover and they made love in her husband's bed. Her husband must have noticed something, some say maybe a shopkeeper who saw the comings and goings hinted to him that she was having an affair so he waited round the corner until he saw the man go into his house and he surprised them," Fulla paused to suck at the small ball of qat in her cheek, then went on "So the other man was hiding behind the wall, waiting for the husband to come in and when he came in he shot the husband!"

"But I thought you said it was the husband who startled them?" interrupted Eve.

"Yes." replied Fulla.

"Then how can the other man be waiting for him, if it was the husband who snuck up on them?" asked Eve.

"Well, your Uncle Yahya said this shows how devious this woman was: she and her lover had already planned to kill the husband so they could be together freely, they had made a plan that when he entered the house the other man, hiding behind the door, would shoot him, so when she heard her husband open the door she stood in the hall and he said to her 'Where is he? I know your lover's in here!' and she told him he must be mistaken that he must have seen the man enter the neighbour's and she told him to search the whole house, then she purposely led him into the diwan (Eve wanted to know if the wife entranced him into the diwan with a belly dance (Eve was ignored)). When the husband was in the diwan the lover came out from behind the door and shot him, filling the husband's chest with bullets and they cut his body into pieces to dispose of him!"

Eve shook her head, the story had more holes than the supposed husband's chest.

"What happened then?" asked Dhalia, stretching her arm to hand the pipe to Grandmother Haleema without either of them taking their eyes off Fulla.

"The neighbours called the police and they arrested both the wife and lover and took them to court. The lover told them everything and they executed them both."

"Do you think they flogged them for adultery?" wondered Dhalia, it didn't seem to occur to her death was a more extreme punishment.

"I don't know," said Fulla "But they executed the man in the usual way with a bullet, but the wife had to pay for her horrendous crime so the authorities put her in this massive blender, like the ones they make lime juice with in Taiz, but bigger and she was blended to death!"

Eve burst into peals of laughter at the idea of such a contraption for capital punishment, it was as ridiculous as the story, both meant to instil a fear of such a demise into the village women: a warning to keep away from adultery while their husbands were away for months, or years, working.

"I think it would be against human rights for such a method of execution, there is no such device and it would never be allowed." said Eve.

But Dhalia had sat up and all the other women in the room wore concerned looks, horrified by both the crime and way of execution of the female culprit, while Eve still laughed at the idea, amused at her relatives' willingness to believe it.

"Bad women are the firewood of hell," said Grandmother Haleema "They lead men into destruction."

"Why is it always the woman's fault?" said Eve.

"Because it's women who fill men's heads with bad ideas." said Grandmother Haleema.

"How? On one hand you say men are superior to women and on the other you say women can easily trick men. Which one is it?"

"When men listen to women it leads them to their downfall," replied Grandmother Haleema "Because of this woman both the husband and the lover are dead."

"If this story's true," said Eve "Then both the wife and the male lover are to blame, they both sinned in adultery and they both took part in the murder. Why is it only the woman's fault?"

"Oh Eve, don't you know women are the cause?" said Grandmother Haleema with a stern look "A man is like a dog—if a woman pats her lap he will come panting, but if she raises her arm and shoos him he'll run away. So if a woman wants a man she can lure him, and if she's chaste she will chase him away and he won't dare come back."

"It's always a woman's fault," said Eve "Don't you think men made this up long ago so they can do what they like and be blameless? If a man and woman are having an affair it takes two sides to be willing to commit the adultery, they're both to blame in equal measure. It's not fair to always blame women: if a son becomes bad towards his parents—it's the daughter-in-law who turned him against them; if all offspring are female, the husband remarries—because it's the wife unable to bear a son; you even blame a woman for humankind having to live on earth instead of immortality in heaven—you all say if it wasn't for Eve who tempted Adam to eat from the Tree of Immortality we'd all be living in paradise now, but why is it Eve's fault? The Quran doesn't say Eve encouraged Adam to eat from the tree, it says the devil tempted and tricked them *both* to eat the forbidden fruit, but does anybody remember that? No, because it is Eve's fault, a woman's fault so women are to blame for everything: *pain, crime, hatred, inferiority* anything you can think of it's always the woman's fault. In the Quran it says they both sinned and both repented to God so why can't you understand it was both of them that sinned not just Eve? Men like to repeat Adam and Eve's story just to keep reminding us we're always at fault, we're always wrong, but we don't have to blindly accept it. Each person is responsible for their own actions—*male or female.*"

It was pointless, since an early age it had been drummed into the women: the female sex was the stem of all sin and pain. Eve couldn't understand how they could ignore what was so plainly stated in the Quran, which they revered, what was so clear in everyday life, which they lived, that woman was no more or less a sinner than man, and each had to carry their own weight of good and bad deeds; that God would judge every single person individually, not according to their skin colour, gender, wealth, position but against what they did. But living in an environment where men dominated and were thought to be superior, by selecting what suited them in religious sayings, while ignoring statements which equalised gender, it would go unquestioned that Eve and her daughters were always to blame.

*

WITHOUT DOCTOR, NURSE OR ANY MEDICALLY TRAINED MIDWIFE Eve spent again twenty-four hours in labour before giving birth to her second child, but at least this time she knew from the start there was nothing they could do to help her. She was overjoyed to have a girl, but beautiful baby Nadine was born at a very dangerous time while a terrible cough was spreading all over the villages; and once this disease took hold of a child it rampaged their little bodies for months, only lasting less, if it claimed its victim's life.

The whole family broached a subject they knew Eve would refuse, they wanted Nadine circumcised.

"You've made up circumcision for girls," said Eve "It's not mentioned in religion."

"You have to circumcise my son's daughter," said Kareema "You can't leave those things hanging out of her vagina."

"They're not hanging out," said Eve "They're part of the body God gave her."

"They'll grow and *will* hang out!" said Kareema and she scolded Dahlia when the latter mentioned that even when Eve was naked you couldn't tell she wasn't circumcised.

"She has to be circumcised," said Haleema "Or she'll be hot and have lovers and bring disgrace to the family."

"That's nonsense," said Eve "It's because of your character, your upbringing, your control, not parts of your body." The women frowned, their stern faces unaccepting.

"If circumcision made girls and women chaste," said Eve "How do you explain the behaviour of women here? They're all circumcised, but many of them lose their virginity or commit adultery, you're always gossiping about affairs and bastards of past and present. You see—it has nothing to do with it. My daughter won't be mutilated."

Day after day they tried convincing her and she refused.

It was a clear, cool morning, sheep bleated from nearby land. Eve finished breastfeeding Nadine while Kareema watched. Kareema carried Eve's water into the bathroom, and Eve gently placed Nadine into her crib and kissed her. Eve was grateful Suleiman had built her an outhouse outside her room where she could wash and listen to her children while either Kareema or Mother babysat Layth and Nadine.

"You didn't take the cow to graze?" said Eve to Mother whom entered and sat on a trunk.

"No," replied Mother "I gave her dried leaves. I want to grind sorghum today, just thought I'd chat with Kareema for a while before I start."

Kareema returned to help Eve walk slowly to the bathroom. Eve poured water over her head and heard the outer door of her room close, maybe there was a draught and they didn't want Nadine to get cold. Through the cracks of the door she saw Fardoos carrying Layth on her hip, coming around the corner.

"Fardoos!" Eve called out, Fardoos came nearer to the door, "Why is Layth with you?"

"My mother told me to take him to play at Barh Salliya," Fardoos replied, stealing glances through the gaps, curious to see Eve's naked body, "I came to tell you he's with me…there."

Eve reached for the soap and froze to the shrill cry of her baby, a cry so sharp and full of pain, Eve was momentarily immobilised. Something was wrong with her baby. Throwing on only the dress, she walked as fast as she could, tendering her stomach. She pushed at the door, but found it bolted from the inside.

"Open the door," she said "What's wrong with Nadine?" She could hear Kareema, Mother and a third person talking as the baby's squeaky shrieks rose.

"Open the door!" she shouted banging her fists on the sharp petals of flowers wrought of metal patterned on the door, blood streaked down her arms from the gashes. She got onto the ducka and peered through the window. "No-ooo! Leave her alone!" she shouted "Stop!"

Kareema's dress was pulled over her shoulder and she had Nadine in her lap. Mother held Nadine's tiny legs apart, and Purple Dress Lady who circumcised Dhalia's girls was doing something around Nadine's crotch as the baby screamed in pain. Eve ran around the house to get in through the Bawaba, pain jolting up her cervix, blood pouring to the ground and splashing over her legs and feet. She reached the internal door of her room, but it was bolted from the inside too. Now the baby no longer cried, but made faint whimpering sounds.

"Open the door!" Eve shouted, banging and pushing at it, "You dogs open the door! Stop it, I'll kill you all, you're killing my baby!" her voice hoarse, face red with anger, she banged and rammed at the door, the pain increasing in her lower abdomen. The door finally opened, and Purple Dress Lady and Eve grappled. Eve held the woman who hurt her daughter by the throat and throttled her. Mother pulled her off and the woman left, rubbing her throat, muttering: "She's wild, you haven't tamed her!"

Eve, stiff with pain and horror, turned towards her child lying motionless in Kareema's arms, a small puddle of water mixed with a little blood ran below Kareema on the plastic floor. Shaking, Eve knelt next to her unconscious baby whose lips were thinner than usual in her pale face, her chest heaved every few seconds. She wasn't asleep, but had fainted from the pain. Eve gently picked her up and sat on the bed, rocking back and forth.

"What did you do to my baby?" she said, looking at Kareema "How could you?"

They had performed female genital mutilation on the two-week-old baby, removing her clitoris and labia minor with a razor blade, and tied a rag with a piece of onion around her crotch in lieu of a bandage from which a little blood oozed.

"If you'd have let us do it on the seventh day, she would have felt less pain." Kareema retaliated.

Eve sat distraught, a circle of blood appeared on the mattress below her as she began to haemorrhage severely from throwing herself against the door. They had mutilated her daughter under a made-up belief which had nothing to do with religion or facts. Eve held her whimpering baby, looking through helpless eyes, all she could see in their future was darkness living in these mountains.

CHAPTER SEVENTEEN

S ULEIMAN GAVE INSTRUCTIONS TO HIS CHILDREN TO KEEP AWAY from the sick, worried they would bring the disease to Eve and Dhalia's children. Dhalia, accompanied by her daughters, visited sick families, objecting that her children were old enough not to be hurt by the malady.

Upon returning, Dhalia always came directly to Eve's room, kissing and hugging Layth with sudden unfamiliar affection, before picking up baby Nadine. When Eve, Haleema and Kareema asked her to wash and change before touching them, she laughed and said: "Don't worry, my girls don't have the disease and they were there." then lowered baby Nadine so her sneezing, coughing daughters could kiss her, sometimes their snot sticking to her cheek. But Dhalia did bring the sickness: only one month old and Nadine was coughing and coughing, then a gasp that never seemed to end. She started to vomit and diarrhoea violently, her tiny body rapidly lost weight. Layth had the cough too, but it wasn't as severe as Nadine's condition; though he coughed and made gasping sounds, he was not brought down by it, he still ate and played whereas Nadine vomited all the breast milk she fed. Eve never left her side; changing, washing, feeding and praying.

"We have to take her to a doctor." said Eve.

"No," said Suleiman "After a month she'll be better."

"She's too sick," said Eve "Other children have been taken to Taiz and the doctor has given them medicine…it helps them."

Suleiman walked away, leaving Eve in tears over her sick baby. She couldn't understand why he wouldn't take her to Taiz for treatment, especially that her father sent him large amounts of money every month. She did everything she could to make Layth and Nadine comfortable, but it killed her she couldn't ease her baby's pain. Poor Nadine, too young: the coughing, gasping, vomiting and diarrhoea devastated her, weeks into the sickness and Eve's agony over her daughter's suffering was torture. Nadine's breathing wasn't normal, her eyes rolled upwards, she didn't respond to her mother's voice. Eve begged her uncle to take Nadine to the city for treatment with such passion and emotion, everybody witnessing the request was brought to tears: Kareema, her sons and daughters, Dhalia, Haleema, Salem, Hasna, but Suleiman refused to do so answering: "God will cure her."

Eve writhed in agony as her daughter withered in front of her eyes, and over her father-in-law's callousness towards her daughter's pain. Terrified, since before Nadine's sickness babies and infants were dying all around them, and cemeteries began to fill with new graves of young lives taken early.

Goats bleated outside in someone's land near the house in the peaceful, calm morning; the shepherdess responded with sounds and throwing stones ahead of them keeping them from straying out of the land. Eve sat on the bed playing with Nadine's hair, she was almost unconscious, but looked calm. Haleema and Dhalia returned from visiting a mourning mother whose baby had died from the disease that very morning. Haleema kissed Nadine's cheek, Nadine's eyes opened, she gazed into her mother's worried face, Eve smiled down at her little angel. Nadine's mouth stretched in an ugly gape and her eyes rolled into her head.

"Nadine?" said Eve raising her baby to her face "Haleema—*my baby*!"

"God, give her her child," said Haleema "My daughter calm down…they are given by God and taken by God."

"Don't take my baby!" said Eve, Nadine gasped and her irises reappeared, but her breathing was abnormal, her chest heaved and her little mouth was still in a terrible, open yawn.

"Why is she breathing like this?" said Eve.

Haleema hesitated then solemnly said: "Eve you have to be strong. Her soul is struggling right now, she's entered her deathbed. May God be kind with you my daughter." Eve cried as if death had already claimed her.

"God I'm begging You, cure my daughter, don't take her from me, I can't live without my baby. God don't take her, take me."

"You're squeezing her too tight," said Haleema "Here, put her down, let her rest and try to breathe." Eve placed a half-lifeless Nadine onto the bed and leaned forward over her, thighs parted, her face hovering over the little weak baby's face; noticing every slight movement, she couldn't lie next to her, it was too far away with death in the air. She stroked her daughter's light hair gently. "Eve don't sit like this," said Haleema "Lie down next to her. You can't stop death from coming by sitting like this!"

Eve's tears fell in abundance from her eyes and onto her baby's face and neck.

"My baby isn't going to die. She's not dying...she is not dying... she is not dying. Don't say that!"

Eve could see, Nadine was dying. When visiting the sick and the dying she had seen the expression on adults and children's faces as they took their last breaths, that near-death expression, the movement of chest finding difficulty breathing was now all over Nadine. She knew she was dying, but denied it—God would keep her alive. He would—He always made miracles and He would help her baby live. She would not accept she was passing, but the agony tearing her up inside told her, she was. Anguish and pain shredded her body and soul, but it didn't help her baby, it didn't make a difference. She always felt God, right now she could feel Him even stronger as she felt her prayers and supplications cleave her chest open, exposing inflating red lungs and beating heart as her soul directly communicated with God to make her baby better, *let her live. Let her live.* She wished she had died before ever having a baby, but if she died now who would look after Layth? Her beautiful baby Nadine could not die. Why was she dying? Suleiman emerged from the outer door, he stood with his right hand extended to it and stared at Eve crouching over her baby bewildered death would claim her. With an expression both sad and angry he watched baby Nadine, her life being smothered and sucked away by a disease which could be treated. He watched the pained face of a defenceless baby fighting a losing battle for her life as the pained face of the helpless mother cried above it, begging God to take her life and let her baby's carry on.

"Suleiman, my son," Haleema said as she wiped her tears away "Why are you being so unreasonable? Take Eve with her baby to Taiz, let the doctors see her. You should have taken them before, at least give Eve the satisfaction of the doctors trying to save her baby…Suleiman, don't let your greed cost Eve her daughter's life. She carried her for nine months inside her, she went through a lot of pain and saw death to bring her into this world and now you're just going to let her slip away when you can do something about it?"

"If it's her destiny to die we can't fight God." said Suleiman.

"Uncle Suleiman," Eve said, crying, "He gave us science and medicine so doctors can heal the sick. Uncle please…I'm begging you take my daughter Taiz…they can help her."

Suleiman snorted and left the room saying, almost cheerfully, "When she dies, the cemetery is ahead of us. We'll bury her and come home to eat lunch!"

Eve froze in shock, the tears abruptly stopped, bitter anger welled in her stomach and consumed her, she reached for a bowl and threw it after him. How dare he talk about her daughter as if her life meant nothing? How dare he trivialise her death? To Eve, her daughter was life itself. Haleema and Dhalia ran after Suleiman voicing their anger: "If it was one of your children you would have taken them a long time ago!"

"How many times have you taken Fardoos and Akram to Taiz when they were ill and in pain? And they weren't dying, just in pain? But they are *your children*. You monster, *fear God*!"

Eve cried bitterly, a burning sensation throughout her body swept over the pain as her soul caught fire and evaporated her tears. Eve watched her little daughter, sleeping now and gently kissed her cheek. Fardoos followed Layth into the room. She picked up her son and hugged him hard, kissing him repeatedly on the cheeks.

"You stay here with Aunt Fardoos," said Eve "Fardoos, you hold Layth and look after him and Nadine. Don't let him come out of this room."

Eve knew what she had to do, she knew how she had to be, to be heard. Being agreeable and respectful wasn't enough. Being patient, reasonable and convincing meant nothing to them. For all her patience and rectitude—good had not won in the end—her whole life had been wasted believing wrong would be remedied because she was in the right; because she turned the other cheek she hadn't been slapped, but brutally battered—for being logical and kind she had become invisible: in films the good guys always won; in religion, truth and goodness saved you and evil was ended and wrong—rectified, but her life had been withering all this time and nothing turned out right. She had to become a menace, cause them disruption to be heeded. Who were they, to decide her daughter should not be given a chance to live? She pulled the inner door of the room, closing it behind her as she stepped out, and walked out of the Bawaba to see Suleiman, Kareema, Salem, Faris, Father, Mother and Dhalia sitting on the ducka in front of the First House, talking and, *laughing*. The dried tears stung the corners of her eyes and cheeks, she was angry at how normal the day seemed outside her room: the sun was shining, the mountains stood as menacing and intimidating as ever, and the rest of the family chattered carefree, while her daughter's life slipped away inside. In the cold. In the dark. They were not affected by her daughter's fading life; only she and her daughter were bound together in despair.

"Suleiman," she shouted from in front of the Bawaba "You're going to take me and my children to Taiz to see a doctor. My daughter is sick, she's dying. We're not going to wait until Tuesday for the cars to leave, you're going to reserve the whole car and take us today!"

"Oooh...we're not going anywhere," said Suleiman, mocking, "God will cure her or He will take her!"

"You're going to take us to Taiz," said Eve "If you don't—come watch what I'll do. You're not going to eat or drink *until* my daughter is treated by a doctor!" and with that said she walked back through the Bawaba, Suleiman shouting after her: "What are you going to do?"

She went straight to the pantry, picked up a twenty-litre container of kerosene and poured it all over the food and utensils in the Bawaba. She returned to the pantry and started splashing kerosene from a larger container over the sacks of rice, grains, sugar and flour.

"She's pouring gas over our food!" Kareema screamed, and attacked Eve, punching her in the head and back, pulling at her, but today the manic strength was Eve's, she would not be pushed or pulled away. She continued to pour gas over all the food stocked as Kareema punched, pulled and screamed: "Eve is beating me up! Eve is killing me!"

Eve smiled, despite with every punch received in her back and shoulders the impact vibrated through her lungs. She had heard from Faris and others how Kareema, many times in the past, falsely accused them of assaulting her, by shouting and screaming she was being attacked by them and now she understood the story (Uncle Faris had only been saved from dishonour and punishment because her own mother testified against her falsity). Kareema was still punching at Eve's back when Salem, Faris and Suleiman raced in and pulled Kareema off.

"What have you done?!" shouted Suleiman "You've ruined our food!"

"You care about your food? You care about *your* children?!" said Eve "Well I care about *my* children. *My daughter is dying and you refuse to take her to see a doctor.* If you want to be able to *eat*, you take us to Taiz. If you want to be able *to live*, you throw us out of your life, *make* your son divorce me!"

"I'll take you to Taiz," Suleiman said, angrier than he had ever been, "I'll take your daughter to a doctor and I'll *make sure my son divorces you!*"

"Good!" said Eve and went to wash her hands so she could prepare Layth and Nadine for travel. As she walked out of the Bawaba, Kareema pretended to faint.

"Eve beat me up," said Kareema, shaking violently, "She punched and kicked me in my stomach..." Eve laughed loudly, this woman was a real piece of work.

"You're a great actress Aunt Kareema, you'd win an Oscar!" said Eve, although only she understood the joke.

All the Uncles were outraged by Eve's actions, they sent for Nageeb to come up from The Dibt, he had to be there by the next day, when Eve, her children and Suleiman would be back from Taiz. The car arrived within an hour and by afternoon they were in the city. The doctor explained to Eve there was no cure, the disease would take its course over the months and disappear, but there was medicine to help Nadine fight it and medicine to replace the minerals lost from dehydration. The doctor severely scolded them and questioned why they hadn't brought her earlier; that Nadine could have and *would have died* due to dehydration caused by the severe vomiting and diarrhoea, he administered medicine for her through a drip. He requested Nadine stay overnight in hospital where Eve and Layth spent the night on one bed with her while Suleiman prowled and brooded in the halls of the hospital. Eve was satisfied, the menacing act of sabotage had saved her daughter's life. On the way back to the mountains, Suleiman refused to help her hold one of the children so Eve carried them both all the way, but she didn't care—it was worth it, knowing baby Nadine would be alright. Another silver lining to the cloud-fume—the 'gas-watering' made her in-laws request she be divorced from Adam. Eve gave Nadine the medicine as per the doctor's instructions, full of belief her condition would improve.

Over the following weeks her in-laws borrowed utensils and food, and cooked at Eve's parents' home because the kerosene had ruined all the grain and flour; its properties infiltrated into everything. The walls and floor needed to be buried and new coats of mud-dung would need to be cemented all over it, until gas could no longer be detected before storing food in there again. If only Eve could as easily smooth over the damage they had done to her life, but it was irreparable. The Uncles sat outside discussing the situation, a frowning Dhalia stood to one side watching them.

"He has to divorce her," said Kareema "I don't want her in my house!"

"He will divorce her," said Suleiman "I'm sending Mahmood to Taiz tomorrow to call him again and confirm what I've already told him of what happened—he wouldn't believe me!"

"She beat me up," said Kareema "I'm still injured from her attack!" Eve chortled with laughter, Kareema was really playing the role.

"But we saw you holding her with one hand and punching her back with the other?" said Faris "Eve had both hands on the container pouring gas over the sacks with her back towards you."

"Kareema's lying, she didn't beat her," said Suleiman exasperated "But what she did to the food is unacceptable!" he concluded shaking his finger at Eve.

"I'll continue to ruin your food *until* you get me a divorce from your son." said Eve.

"You will not!" said Suleiman.

"I will," said Eve "I've had enough. I've been patient for seven years. *Seven years!* I've been patient, kind, reasonable. I've talked and I've talked and you never listen. Whenever I convince someone I should leave, you turn them against the decision," Suleiman frowned and became silent.

"Whenever I reason with you, with valid reasons why I should leave, and you know I'm right, you send for your brothers and you all sit upstairs and make a decision about my life without me," Faris nodded and Nageeb looked at her with sombre, knowing eyes.

"And your decision is always that I'm not allowed to leave. Are you happy now? Are you happy? My life is gone…Because of you *all*, my life has been wasted…I'm supposed to have finished university by now, but instead seven years of my life have been stolen."

Empathy glimmered in Salem's expression, his glinting teeth hidden beneath his clasped, concerned lips. Her words hit home with the three turbaned uncles, their eyes admitted worry, concern and guilt for their part. All except Uncle Suleiman: his face creased and eyes gleamed with the same angry expression of the woven roaring tigers Eve had once seen on a blanket first arriving at this village. His gaze directed anger and blame at her, for he would need to spend money on new supplies of food which she had ruined, instead of qat to stuff his cheeks with.

"You kept me here all this time, just so you get money from your son—I'm not some kind of hostage held for ransom…enough! Your son should send you money whether I'm here or not, it has nothing to do with me. You were happy to let my daughter die because of your greed for qat and money—you heard what the doctor said," Suleiman just silently held her gaze.

"I don't want your son. I'm going to get a divorce and leave these mountains!"

"We don't *want you anymore*!" said Suleiman angered, veins surfacing in his forehead.

"Good, about time!" she said, overwhelmed by a sense of relief.

Finally, it was happening. Divorce. Leaving the mountains. The Uncles went upstairs with Mother and Kareema. Eve played with her son in sheer delight, then watched both her children sleep, knowing they would get a chance to live in the city.

"Take your things and your children," said Nageeb as everybody came down into Eve's room. "You'll stay in your father's house until Adam divorces you."

"With absolute pleasure!" said Eve "And when will the divorce be finished?"

"Suleiman will send his son to call Adam and explain to him what needs to be done," said Nageeb "You're really happy, aren't you?"

"Yes I'm happy," said Eve "I've been talking to you all for years, but you never listened. And now what do you see? I *am* getting a divorce. I *am* leaving."

"She's so happy," said Faris "When women get divorced they want to die, but she's happy!"

"You always were different," said Nageeb "We all thought you'd change and be like us and accept our ways, but you'll never be like us will you?"

"I'm one of you," said Eve "You won't accept me the way I am just because I was born somewhere else, you want me to believe in everything you believe, and do everything you do, but I can't. I'm not asking *you* to change, just let me go—you love this life, these mountains, I've seen a different life, a different world, I can only be myself."

Eve could only be herself, but the past seven years had brought changes in her character and thinking, she was aware of these changes and knew why and how they had occurred, but no matter how hard she would try to correct them in the future, they would stay with her forever. Father carried Layth and Mother took Nadine, while Eve quickly packed a trunk of things which Nageeb and Faris carried to the First House, glad to be no longer welcome at Suleiman's. Suleiman became emotional, tears welled in his eyes as a smiling Eve walked past him, and Dhalia cried too. Kareema shouted insults at Eve whom turned around, now elevated on the ducka in front of the First House, to face Kareema.

"Kareema, you're an evil person and the whole village knows what you are," said Eve "You can shout insults at me all day, I really don't care…you've been shouting insults at me for the majority of seven years and you have noticed it seems I can't hear you. I can reply to your insults with bigger insults, but I don't want to be a lowlife like you. The only thing you'll get by shouting is a sore throat."

Kareema immediately quietened. It was liberating to be able to tell Kareema what she really thought of her (if only you'd jackal-and-hyenaide from a long time ago Eve, and been ejected sooner).

It wasn't difficult adjusting to her parents' house after living in the same room for all those years. Happy, her patience had seen her through. Mother was outraged by Eve's joy to be finally getting the long-awaited divorce. To Eve's appalled disbelief Father seemed indifferent.

"You see how many years you've wasted from my life?" said Eve "All for nothing. I'm going to get a divorce now and I'm going to leave—can you now tell me why you ruined my life?"

"We thought it was good for you to be married," said Father "We believed by coming here you would grow up a proper Muslim." Eve snorted at the comment.

"Good for me—how?" she said "I was always well behaved in Britain, then you threw me into the arms of strangers while I was still a child, I could have easily become promiscuous here. You didn't teach me Islam, all what I know about my religion is from books, which if I didn't have—I still wouldn't know about properly, but what I know for sure, Islam forbids what you did to me. You didn't do this to Yusef or Sami, you didn't force them to marry—you only did this to me because I'm a girl as if being a girl meant I would sin and bring shame to our family. I didn't deserve the prison you condemned me to just for being a girl."

"Well you're getting what you want now!" said Father.

"How can you sit there and say I wanted seven years stolen from my life?" said Eve.

"The past is the past." said Father.

"The past *you changed* and ruined for me is going to affect my future," said Eve "My life is going to be so hard because of what you did to me." she added with solemnity, knowing it would be true.

Mahmood returned from Taiz informing them Adam would be arriving soon. Eve waited restlessly, desiring the divorce, she already felt restrictions lifting, but in actuality they were not. A sense that before long, she would be divorced and allowed to leave, she could already feel the freedom just around the corner. She sat on the ducka outside Father's house, in the morning under yellow sun, playing with her children. She looked towards the west and felt she was still fourteen years old, her neck jerked, as she snapped out of the feeling.

She kissed her children, her heart dancing and soul eager that her little ones would begin a good life, be in a better situation with all the opportunities they would have in the city. She looked down at Nadine, still sick, but not dying—something as simple as treating dehydration had meant life or death and she had almost been denied the chance to live.

*

ADAM ARRIVED, THOUGH EAGER TO SEE EVE HE WASN'T ALLOWED to enter Father's house, an instruction from his parents. Eve waited impatiently to receive the divorce papers, but the next day Eve's trunk was taken back to the room.

"Why are you taking it?" said Eve.

"You're still his wife," said Nageeb "And he wants you to stay there until everything is final."

"Why do you complicate things?" said Eve refusing to move "Give me my divorce papers and that's it. Hey! Where are you going?" Father and Mother carried Layth and Nadine off to the Bawaba and into 'Eve's' room. Eve raced after them, taking baby Nadine into her arms.

"Have you got the divorce papers?" Eve said glancing at Adam whom looked nervously to his Uncles.

"Adam doesn't want to divorce you." said Suleiman.

"But he will." said Eve.

"I'm not divorcing you," said Adam "I love you."

"What love?" Eve asked incredulously "You are divorcing me." she turned to Mother "Take Nadine and Layth to your house, I don't want them to see us arguing." Mother left the room, carrying Nadine on one arm and holding Layth by his hand.

"If he loves you and wants to keep you—that's it," said Nageeb "You stay."

"*I am not staying here!*" said Eve, she turned to Adam "You have to divorce me. Do you understand?"

"You're my wife, you're staying" said Adam.

Eve explained why he had to divorce her and why she had to leave. She had been forced into marriage, didn't love him. *Hated him.* She had to go and live and give her children a chance at a normal life with an education. She couldn't stay here any longer, she *wouldn't* stay here any longer. He could get married to someone else and live a happy life. She could bring up her children properly. *But she just couldn't live this life anymore.*

"I'm not divorcing her." said Adam.

"You will." said Eve.

"Let's sit outside and talk." said Nageeb.

They sat in a circle, some on the ducka, some squatting on the ground, while Eve stood. Nageeb and Faris tried persuading Adam to allow her to leave, but he kept repeating he loved her and would not divorce her. Eve tried to reason with them, but it was pointless: she seemed to be the only person who heard her voice. As the conversation progressed, Eve's opinions were cast aside. Eventually, everybody who, at the beginning, was of the view Eve get the divorce, were now all against it; they agreed she had to stay in the mountains as Adam's wife. She couldn't understand the disjointed events unfolding before her eyes: the day had started joyously, with her to be divorced and allowed to leave this prison, and now it turned into a dark dead-end. Her important reasons, common sense and facts were not valid in the eyes of the uncles, in-laws and parents; she was a woman being treated like a toddler, and they decided what was to happen to her. What she said was heard, but not important enough to be regarded; she was there, but they could not see her; she existed, but not allowed to fully live. It was eerily like being in an episode of the *Twilight Zone* (a very prolonged episode), which she had loved to watch as a child, never had she imagined to be living a real limbo. Immeasurable anger gushed through her being as they dismissed her as if she was an object. Owned. Taken. Used. Picked up and placed.

Scream after scream surged through her throat and burst through her lips, startling herself and those present, her eyes widened.

"Let me lee-eave," she shouted "Let me lee-eave!" She continued to scream and shout as four head-shawled men swirled around her. She pushed and kicked, screaming as they lifted her. She looked up at the sky, her fists swiped at the air.

"What did I do?" she shouted, her face incensed, demanding an answer, "What did I do God, what did I do?! What crime? What sin? What did I do?"

She had been good her whole life, enduring, waiting for good to prevail, waiting for God, her brothers, her uncles, the police to save her and let her leave. She screamed and shouted as they carried her into the room. That horrible room. Eve was no longer herself, she had gone from the quiet, patient, pain enduring angel to a crazed, screeching banshee demanding an answer from God, and she could not stop screaming. They placed her on the bed and stood facing her, confused about what to do for never had a woman in the family caused such a commotion.

"Where are you Adam?" said Nageeb, exasperated, "GET INSIDE!"

Adam walked in meekly and got onto the bed next to Eve who still shouted: "LET ME OUT OF HERE! LET ME OUT OF HERE!"

"Look Adam," said Nageeb "She's really angry. She's had enough! She's *never going to be calm*, let her go...divorce her."

"But I love her." said Adam, with the most put-on affectionate tone.

Eve turned to him like a crazed bull and said: "*You love me?*! *You don't love me*! *YOU THINK YOU OWN ME*! WELL YOU DON'T! Divorce me!" With great force and anger she slapped him with her left hand "Divorce me!" she screamed in his face. He looked down at the floor, all the men were stunned—women didn't slap men.

"Be a man!" she screamed in his face, and got down off the bed and pushed him, "Divorce me!" and she slapped him again "You bastard your mother got you by accident! You pervert—divorce me! Aren't you a man? Divorce me!"

Every time she slapped him a bloating expression appeared on his face and he looked down at the floor.

"Divorce her!" Faris and Nageeb simultaneously shouted at him.

Everyone in the room ordered him to divorce her. All he had to do was say 'you are divorced' and this hellish seven-year confinement would be over. Everybody watched him, but none as intensely as Eve. Crazed, furious, ferocious Eve.

"I love her," said Adam "I will not divorce her!"

She slapped him with a full swing of her right arm and pounded the bed with her fists.

"You bastard divorce me," she yelled "Your sisters are sluts! Dhalia has been screwed by Adel, Ali and Kayid! Latifa has been screwed by Kayid, Idrees and Nishwan and everybody knows where and when! Huda has lost her virginity to Ramsey! Divorce me you bastard before I tell you all of your sisters' love stories. Divorce me! Divorce me!"

Eve's voice was unrecognisable, hoarse and thick; her eyes bulged as she screamed obscenities about Adam and his sisters which affected all the uncles whom all watched open mouthed, their faces stretched in shock, their eyebrows raised so high it seemed their foreheads began at the middle of their scalps at how such disgusting words could come out of their sweetest, kindest, genteel niece. Eve didn't plan this, she wasn't even thinking: every time she paused, she realised what she had just said. Her body shook and her skull felt abnormally hollow. Unable to control herself, she burst into screams followed by insults against Adam's sisters and hollered to be allowed to leave. All the men, including Suleiman and Father, ordered Adam to divorce her, but he shook his head and whimpered a faint: "I love her."

Eve screamed shaking her head, still angrily pounding the mattress, her long hair flailing. Then she let out a long, painful sob, tilting her head upwards and shaking her head in a 'no' gesture towards the ceiling. Men started arriving to spend the afternoon, as usual, chewing qat in Suleiman's upstairs room and one by one, the men around her went upstairs while she still screamed and shouted to be allowed to leave. Nageeb came down at one point with Salem, their cheeks stuffed with green qat, they spoke to her in soothing voices.

"Eve my daughter, please stop shouting and screaming," said Nageeb to his once seraphic (now demonic) niece "The men upstairs can hear everything."

"They're saying we haven't heard her voice in almost eight years," said Salem "And now she's screaming like this? You must have done something terrible to her!"

"Please my daughter, hush up," said Nageeb "Calm down."

Eve, her hand shaking, held the collar of his dress and stuttered: "Will you let…let me…let me, let me leave…I…I…I want…aaiiee… leave…let me leave…"

"Shhh, shhh—I'll talk with them," said Nageeb "I'll talk with Adam and Suleiman." Sobbing, Eve placed her teary, snotty face on Nageeb's chest then abruptly sat up.

"I WANT TO LEAAAAVE! I WANT TO LEEEEAAAVE!" her voice rose again and her throat hurt.

Never had she felt so bewildered, words no longer formed in her mouth, just howls, and she didn't know how to stop. She didn't want to, but couldn't prevent it from coming out, scream after scream escaped her lips as if they were taking flight from her body with a life of their own. She had no control over it as her neck shook her abnormally light feeling head; wails where no words could describe the feeling of injustice, an emotion and feeling so extreme it vocalised into sound.

By the middle of the afternoon she lay still on the bed, exhausted. Her eyes stared at the floor, but she didn't see its pattern;

she saw the green grass in Wales, faces of childhood friends, memories of play and study, an oriental red dragon made of cardboard and crepe with two dozen children's legs instead of its own slaying a white dragon in battle. She looked towards the door, Layth appeared with Mother behind him carrying Nadine. Mother placed the baby girl behind her young mother on the bed, picked up Layth and placed him next to his sister.

"You've disgraced us." said Mother, her voice so riddled with shame she could die.

"You disgraced yourself the day you sold your fourteen-year-old daughter." said Eve, with a husky voice worn out from shrieking.

Mother left the room with her head bowed. Eve turned onto her other side and took a deep breath of her daughter's scent, she reached out to touch Layth's cheek and noticed her chest hurt, probably from screaming. She placed Nadine nearer to her and Layth lay next to his sister, facing his mother who put her arm across them. She watched their eyes grow smaller into sleep, and did not notice when she herself followed. She awoke in the morning, attended to her children thinking, today she would finish everything and get out of this place for they had reached the point of no return, but with every movement a soreness stiffened her joints. After breakfast they were to discuss the matter further so Mother took Eve's children with Fardoos, to Barh Salliya.

"Now we have to decide what's best for everybody," said Nageeb "I say we let Eve go. Adam has to divorce her." Salem and Faris agreed.

"I don't want my son to divorce Eve," said Suleiman "But she doesn't want him. Adam, you have to give her, her papers."

"I will not divorce her," said Adam "She's mine!"

They argued back and forth, everybody was with Eve being divorced, but Adam wouldn't have it; and they came to the same conclusion as the previous day—Eve was to stay. It sent her into an even worse screaming fit which entailed Eve being carried to her room, and her screams ended in the evening where she lay like a limb on the bed. Adam left for Taiz the next day, to wait until the next flight to Saudi. The Uncles requested Morad and Yusef come to the village to sort things out, the reply returned Yusef would arrive after three weeks, but Morad couldn't.

Eve had changed. She was back to her quiet self, but tension could be detected in her eyes. She woke up the next morning to find it extremely difficult to move, her whole body sore, so much more than the previous day, unable to move her feet more than an inch at a time no matter how hard she tried. All the energy in her body had been sucked out, leaving her drained. For two days she moved by inches, it took forever to get to the bathroom. With an amused expression Kareema watched her as she inched across the yard, towards the outhouse.

"Do you think pretending you're so ill you can't walk will get you out of here?" said Kareema goading her and with a smile.

"Pretence is your thing Aunt Kareema, not mine," said Eve calmly "I'm not ill, I don't know why my whole body is sore and I can only move like this."

In a few days' time Eve could move normally, but still there was something wrong, she didn't know what it was, but she felt different—jumpy. If a door slammed or a metal plate fell she startled, her brain froze in terror and her heart pounded in her ears, her whole body and mind immobilised by an immense fear, it would take her a few moments to understand what had happened, and longer for her brain and heart to calm down. While drinking tea with Dhalia, Kareema and Mother on the ducka in front of the Bawaba, Eve noticed a bright green leaf fall from the Thorn of Christ, twirling down until it reached the ground and she burst into gales of hysterical laughter.

"What's funny?" asked Dhalia.

"Did you see the leaf?" said Eve "That one...on the ground, it just fell!" and she resumed her side-splitting laughter.

The others looked at the leaf then at Eve, holding her sides in pain from laughter which would not stop.

"I know...I know it's not funny," said Eve, still laughing, "But it just fell! It just...it just...it just fell!"

Eve laughed raucously and uncontrollably as if she had seen a scene of extreme hilarity, and every effort she made to withhold her laughter or muffle it, made her guffaw harder. Eventually she did calm and looked at the leaf and a tear rolled down her cheek, knowing it wasn't funny at all, but for whatever reason had seemed hilarious. Later, she would look back at how hard she had been laughing and was convinced she was losing her mind; she could feel herself only a hair's breadth away from insanity. As the whole house slept, she awoke from her sleep feeling something wrong with her face: her mouth felt taut to one side, it felt her mouth was where her cheek was meant to be. Shaking, she placed her hand on her cheek expecting to feel her lips there, but they weren't. She placed her hand under her nose and sighed as she felt her mouth where it was supposed to be. She closed her eyes into sleep and awoke again to the feeling of her mouth pulled near to her ear. She did the whole hand on cheek, hand under nose check, but this time wasn't sure, maybe her hand was feeling wrong because she definitely felt her mouth pulled tightly to one side. She got up to look into the mirror, but was too afraid of what she might see to look into it immediately so first she edged into the reflection of the mirror, showing the corner of her face and one eye, then slowly, her whole face. She took a deep breath, her mouth was where it should be. She touched one cheek then held both cheeks with her hands, pressed her hand against her mouth.

"I'm going crazy." she whispered.

She looked at her children sleeping peacefully in their cribs and kissed them gently, went back to sleep to awake again to the feeling of her mouth being pulled to the left side of her face, doing the whole face feel, mirror check before returning to sleep.

Layth played with Dhalia's daughters in the quiet morning while the mothers chatted.

"Dhalia, is my mouth pulled to one side?" said Eve.

"No, why?" said Dhalia.

"I had this feeling all night that my mouth is in my cheek."

"May God protect us all!" said Dhalia, genuinely afraid, "When a mouth is pulled to the cheek, it's when a demon slaps a human!"

"I think it's my nerves," said Eve "Can you take a good look, is it…maybe just a little to one side?" Dhalia looked closely and seriously.

"No, it's where it has been all these years." said Dhalia.

It was still ten in the morning when Eve heard the call to prayer, but it was way too early for the noon prayer.

"Why are they calling to prayer this early?" said Eve.

"What call to prayer?" said Dhalia.

"They're calling to prayer." said Eve.

"I can't hear anything." said Dhalia.

"Of course you can," said Eve "Listen." Dhalia listened, her eyes moving sideways then up.

"There's no athan," said Dhalia "It's too early."

"Do you mean—you can't hear it?" Eve laughed and got up. She could definitely hear it, word by word. Dhalia got up and stood next to Eve by the door. No call to prayer could be heard.

"Maybe a boy shepherding was practising." said Dhalia.

"Maybe." Eve smiled, but it wasn't a boy's voice that she heard.

Layth played with his cousins in Dhalia's room. Eve finished feeding Nadine then sat on the chair beside the bed. She looked to her left and saw a single ant running across the floor, her eyes followed it, the corners of her mouth turned into a smile and the smile erupted into frenzied laughter. The sight of the animated ant in a rush to get where it needed to go was hilarious in her eyes, she laughed until she felt she was going to die because her sides hurt so much from the pain of violent laughter. She slid off the chair and lay on the floor laughing softer. Soon she wasn't laughing, but face down looking at the patterns on the floor, it hurt her nose, but she didn't care, it felt calm down there while she analysed why the ant seemed so ridiculously funny, certain she was on the brink of insanity. She rolled onto her back and heard Nadine on the bed making baby noises, and Layth and her nieces in the next room playing.

"God," she said softly "Who's going to take care of my babies if I go crazy?"

And there it was again: the call to prayer in a most beautiful voice. Eve glanced at the clock on the wall. She opened the door and walked along the path, the sound did not near, nor become distant. Nor did it end like the normal call to prayer, but it went on and on.

She tilted her head towards different directions, but couldn't make out where it came from, it seemed to emanate from everywhere and she stood staring, listening, at the cool blue sky.

Eve seemed normal, until she gazed at nothing and burst into fits of sudden unruly laughter for no reason. It was difficult, for she knew she was losing her mind, but there was nothing she could do about it, except ask for God's grace.

In the balmy morning she played with her children on the bed, when they did something cute which made her laugh. Kareema placed her foot on the doorstep, knee bent, as low as possible she slowly poked her head through the door, a tortoise head warily emerging out of its shell, to see if her daughter-in-law was having a laughing fit. When Eve saw her, she stopped laughing abruptly and Kareema retracted slowly the same way as she had entered, leaving Eve in normal mirth at her comical appearance. They often came to peer in at her, to check if she had gone crazy, even when she laughed out of amusement.

CHAPTER EIGHTEEN

OVER SEVEN YEARS SINCE LEAVING THESE MOUNTAINS, YUSEF finally returned, begrudgingly at that—forced by Morad whom could no longer bring himself to see what his sister had suffered and become, now suspected to be a madwoman. So many years older than when they last talked, Yusef was taller, muscular and handsome, Eve, though she had grown, still seemed so much younger than her real age, but there was a strange gleam in her eyes where once an intelligent spark had lived. She described to her brother the suffering of those years, Suleiman's happiness to let ailing Nadine die and she told him how she felt she was on the brink of madness. Genuinely worried for his sister he told her to come live with Mother and Father while he sorted her husband out, he would go to Taiz and return with the outcome, and Eve did not raise her hopes that he would ever return, but was grateful when he did. Adam was still being stubborn and refused to divorce her, he wanted her to come live with him in Saudi. But Eve wanted a divorce, her brother advised her how better life for her and the children would be in Saudi in comparison to life in Yemen.

"I can't live with him Yusef," said Eve pleaing for her life "I want a divorce."

"Listen," said Yusef "It was difficult convincing Adam you can't stay in the mountains anymore. Your only chance to get out of here is to go to Saudi. *Think* of the good life your children will have there!"

"What about my life?" she said, the thought of living with Adam reducing her to tears, "Don't I deserve a life?"

"To go to Saudi is your only chance to get out of these mountains," said Yusef sombrely "Or you'll stay here for the rest of your life." And with that he left the mountains never to grace them again with his presence.

Having had enough time to chew the whole thing over, Suleiman had a change of mind and objected, he wanted her to remain with them in the village, he would go to call his son, but returned from Taiz crestfallen, this time Suleiman's objections to Eve leaving were ignored by Adam and they were to go to Sana'a to start the visa application process (of which the actual papers she would never see) handled by Latifa's husband Hammed Abdo.

So she returned to the room which she now deeply detested.

*

IT WAS A TIRING FIVE-HOUR JOURNEY FROM THE MOUNTAINS TO Taiz directly followed by being packed with twelve people in a shared taxi called a 'Bigo' on the seven-hour serpentine trip to Sana'a over the Sumara Pass with its two-way winding path bordered only by thousand metre plunges where it seemed to be the law in Yemen to drive recklessly and dangerously (but it did offer a breathtaking scenic view). The first trip she was escorted by scheming Suleiman resolute on preventing her departure, but then it was Father who always accompanied her.

Adam returned from Saudi and arrived at the hotel unexpectedly where he amorously, and unwisely, tried to approach Eve. They had just recently been through the worst case of rejection between husband and wife in the mountains, and now he wanted to make love? Needless to say, Eve was vicious towards him, she made it clear how much she hated him and wanted a divorce. Adam responded by stealing all of Eve's gold, only returning it when she held Hammed Abdo accountable with one hour to find his cousin whom he'd witnessed taking the jewellery, but not raised the alarm, and return the gold or she would go to the police—it was all she had of monetary value if she were to escape. Father took Layth out so Eve and Adam could discuss things, instead they argued fiercely—Adam found his little soft sex kitten had turned into a sabretooth tiger when not in absolute captivity, the arguments continued until one day it became such an ugly screaming and shouting chaos heard by the whole hotel, as she pushed him to divorce her, he ended up having some kind of fit at the bottom of the hotel stairs where his muscles convulsed and he had to be carried away and hospitalised. Adam was brought back from the hospital and carried up the hotel stairs into a different room as Eve refused to allow him to enter the room she, her children and Father occupied. Yusef went back and forth between the two rooms, trying to mediate a peaceful solution.

"He said he'll make you happy if you go to Saudi to live with him." said Yusef.

"He can't make me happy. He'll make my children unhappy." said Eve.

"Let me bring him here so you can hear for yourself how well he'll take care of you." said Yusef. Adam followed Yusef into the room.

"I swear by God I'll be a good husband," said Adam "I'll let you live the best life and I'll never hurt you. I'll give you everything and make up for everything you've suffered. I swear by God or may He strike me with lightning if I'm lying." (Careful—you have family history)

Eve agonised, why couldn't he just divorce her and let her live her life with her beautiful young children? She didn't want a luxurious life, she wanted her freedom. She wanted to take her babies to a safe city where she could take care of them.

"Why don't you just divorce me and let me bring my babies up properly?" said Eve in a semi-whisper.

"I'll take good care of you all," said Adam "I'll give you everything, I'll be a good husband." Eve's eyes followed Layth running across the room, back and forth.

"Will you be a good father?" she said.

"Yes!" said Adam "I swear by God I will, I'll give them everything."

"You used to say Layth doesn't need an education," said Eve "That he just needs to work in a restaurant or shop…do you commit you'll give Layth and Nadine an education?"

"Yes, with God as a witness! I'll give them an education and bring them up as best as possible."

Eve looked away, tears brimming in her eyes all she wanted was to run away, leave him, take her children where nobody would disturb them. But she couldn't bear the thought of depriving them of their father and all the importance he should have in their lives. She knew if they stayed in the mountains he would never have been around anyway, but now he was promising to be responsible so what right did she have of depriving them of such a vital person? Would they feel something missing if she did leave with them, never to see him again? It was too overwhelming and she wanted the best for her children; she longed to have had this chance to get away when she was still alone, but she could not think about what was best for her, not now, there were two innocent children whom she had to think about and not endanger, they and their well-being had to be first and foremost when she made a decision. No, she couldn't do it. If he was going to take care of his children and allow them to live in the city, she might as well sacrifice what remained of her own so they could live in an environment where they could flourish, too much had already gone from her life, but their's was just beginning so she agreed to go Saudi. Unhappy with her decision, she fully understood it meant putting up with being wife to a man she absolutely abhorred. She sighed, then that is what she would do for her children's sake, for them to grow up with a fatherly figure. But maybe the worst was over, and now they would embark on a new life. Normality.

Adam left for Saudi. Eve, her children and Father went back and forth between the village and Sana'a for two weeks at a time. Every trip to and from Sana'a was a burden, one Eve endured with patience, knowing she would finally leave the mountains forever and her children would have a life. Yet, the weeks spent in Sana'a were like being in heaven: running water, electricity, good food, TV, and TV wasn't limited as in the past with the abundance of channels and things to watch with the satellite dish. How much people's dress and hairstyles had changed! Music was so different too. More importantly, she could take Nadine to see doctors as she still suffered from vomit and diarrhoea, but she was lively—not limp and dying; Eve could not forget the way Nadine looked when death had approached her, and Suleiman's steely readiness to let her die without remorse. Yusef's heart softened over weeks of talking with his sister face to face, he offered to let her live with him so she wouldn't need to go to the terrible man known as her husband and be able to start a new life. However, this short-lived dream ended when Yusef's fiancé telephoned Eve, by the time Eve put the handset down her dream to stay with her brother had been put to an end.

*

A SILENT SADNESS FILLED EVE'S HEART IN THE TAXI, ON HER WAY TO the British Embassy she had longed to reach. Now, well into the eighth year since her abduction, she had an appointment, but she wasn't going there asking for help, but to get a passport renewed, to continue an unwanted way of life with an unwanted person. Why had the British Embassy been as far as the moon when she needed its help? Why hadn't she been able to get there eight years ago? She looked down at the cancelled black, child's passport she had carried with her coming to this country, it seemed so long ago and a past so difficult to think about, now replaced with a red, adult passport allowing her free movement between multiple countries, but still she couldn't even leave towards a lone local city without male permission and escort. As she left the embassy carrying Nadine, Father carrying Layth, she fought an overwhelming impulse to take her children and bolt to where they could never be found—not by anyone. The thought and desire not to go to Saudi so strong, she would rather stay in Sana'a or go anywhere, but to him. They got back to the hotel and she mulled it over, a seed that had been in her thoughts since first arriving at Sana'a was now fully stalked and ready to produce panicles. Merely thinking of returning to Britain left her feeling intimidated, it seemed lost in her past, she would be unable to fit in. So she intended to stay in Sana'a, sell her gold to rent a small flat and have money to sustain them while she looked for work; she had befriended the cleaning lady, Fatima, employed by the hotel, Fatima's salary for cleaning the hotel with its five floors was next to nothing, Eve would be able to pay her the same if she were to babysit for her while she searched for work and then worked and Fatima had happily agreed at the thought of the same money for less work. But when she informed Father of her decisions he scuppered her plans, she was still in a delicate situation—freedom had not yet been gained.

"It's too dangerous for you and your children to live on your own in Sana'a," said Father "You don't hear of what happens to women here?"

"Don't worry, I'll be careful," said Eve "Abbah, please let me go, let's go search for a flat today."

"No," said Father "Sana'a is too dangerous. You can't live on your own here…without a man to protect and take care of you. It would be shameful! If Yusef's fiancé hadn't changed his mind about letting you live with him, you could live with him, but not on your own. It's just unacceptable."

"That's it then," she said "If you won't help me set myself up here—I'll have to leave the country."

"You're not going anywhere other than to your husband or back to the village." said Father, and he meant it.

"Abbah, listen to me," said Eve "I can't live there—I can never work like them. My children will have no education and no health services. Think about my children. Why can't you see how much I've suffered because of what you did to me? My whole life is ruined, the future I had—gone. Don't do this to my children, I'll do everything and anything I can to give them a normal life."

"You think about your children and the great life they'll have in Saudi," said Father reproachfully "The education, the hospitals there, food in abundance, the life—everything! If you waste this chance your children will suffer in the mountains forever. You might as well live with their father for their sake."

Eve explained to her father what was good for her children: to keep them away from arguments and living with an unbearable person, but he refused to understand. Eve's instinct told her to get on the plane and off to the UK. She tried to turn her mind, to defeat her diffidence, she should return to Britain no matter how scared she was of going back there, but every time a tidal wave of fear swelled in her stomach as if what was once her home was now a scary country with no place for her after so many years.

They were to return to the mountains one more time before going back to Sana'a to book their flight.

*

THE ROOM SHE HAD LIVED IN FOR EIGHT YEARS LOOKED DARKER. Smaller. Eve felt out of place and restless waiting for the week to pass, knowing they could change their mind at any point and she might never leave the mountains. Sitting on the bed as she pensively stared out the window, she felt the drain of eight years wasted from her life, the room so drab in her eyes now, and the view to the east no longer awe inspiring. She thought of the school and university years lost, experiences she had missed, and a future that would never be.

The last day women came to bid Eve farewell, spending the afternoon in her room. Eve engaged in most of the conversations, but anxiety welled in her stomach and apprehension weighed around her. As the evening drew closer her worry she would not be allowed to leave grew stronger. Her distraction was interrupted by an argument between an old lady and Dhalia.

"They will not kidnap her because she'll be with her father the whole way!" said Dhalia.

"Yes they will," said the old lady "It's happened. They will watch and wait and when her father is unaware they'll snatch her!"

"Eve, listen to what she's saying." said Fulla.

"What is it?" said Eve.

The old lady got up to give Eve the warning, opening her palms and stretching her arms towards Eve, convinced what she was saying was true. "You be careful in the plane on your way to Saudi," said the old lady "The criminals might kidnap you!"

Eve smiled and said: "They can't kidnap me with the plane in air—how will they get away?" and the room filled with laughter.

"They can," said the old lady "They will snatch you when your father's unaware!"

"Maybe these criminals have wings and can fly!" said Fulla, and the room filled with laughter again before the women moved on to a different subject. The old lady got up, placed a hand on Mother's shoulder and bent towards her.

"Tell her father to keep his eyes open," said the old lady "And not let go of her hand."

Instead of feeling relieved, early in the dark morning, she felt nervous to the degree of agitation, the memory of the times she had packed her belongings only for Morad and the vehicle to leave without her, playing over in her mind. The anger and anguish of being left behind, multiplied with every passing second. She was supposed to be leaving this morning from the mountains and she knew in the deepest of her mind, they could decide to not allow her to board the car and this dreadful thought made minutes drag like hours. She would take her children to wait in Father's house, nearer to Barh Salliya. As she walked through the Bawaba, Suleiman and his children sat up from their sleep. Eve kissed and hugged the younger children goodbye, while Suleiman kissed and hugged Layth and Nadine. Her in-laws cried, but she had no more tears. In front of the Bawaba Suleiman kissed hands with Eve and kissed her forehead repeatedly.

"You know you'll come back here to live eventually," he said, giving her a sly look, "Maybe in a year, or less even."

"No Uncle Suleiman, I won't. I'm never coming back." said Eve looking back at the man she had loved dearly as a father for many years, even when he had done her grave wrong, and no longer did she feel any affection towards him, nor did she feel animosity, her whole being only resonated with the loss of her life.

"This is your country," Suleiman said louder, a sob making his voice croaky and thick, "Your origin…You'll come back with your leg over your neck!"

Eve looked him straight in the eye "I swear by God Almighty I will not take one step towards returning here." she said, and left him standing—watching his prisoner go free, carrying baby Nadine as Father carried Layth.

They only sat for a few minutes in the First House where Aunt Ethe and Mother cried inconsolably. The car could be heard coming down the steep and up to Barh Salliya. Eve, heart pounding in her ears, hugged Mother and then Aunt Ethe both still crying. As she stepped out of the door, and with every step until she reached the car, she expected to hear Suleiman shout 'Stop! She cannot leave! I forbid you to allow my son's wife onto the car!' and Father to grab and drag her back to the gloomy room. Mercifully, it didn't happen. Eve was eager to get to Sana'a. As the car moved slowly forwards, she felt a sad relief; the sadness was not out of leaving her eight-year rocky prison, but about the years wasted, *the life wasted*, when the result was, she did eventually leave. But only after her childhood, teenage years had ended and she was now an adult who hadn't experienced the norms of life. Eve could feel her heavy heart and soul in tatters, someone had taken them, put them on a boulder and hammered them with a rock until their ends frayed then put them back into her chest, but they were no longer whole. Eve did not look back, not once. She just stared straight ahead, the towering mountains both threatening and suffocating her as she passed beneath them.

CHAPTER NINETEEN

A T THE AIRPORT, ON THE PLANE, ALL SHE FELT WAS A HEAVINESS inside her chest, going to Saudi was not what she wanted and bitterness was welling in her heart after her last attempt at convincing Father to allow her to stay in Sana'a had failed: she had decided there was no point in going back to Britain—what would it be like after all these years she'd been buried alive, no completion of education, what would she do for a living? At least in Sana'a the English language would allow her to find a decent job. She wanted Father to accompany her to sell the gold and help her find a flat so she could find work. But Father had replied Sana'a was too dangerous a city for a woman to live alone, and went on to threaten he would drag her back to the village even if he had to tie her up and pay people to help him get her back there, he ended the discussion saying he was going to telephone her husband that he was returning her to the mountains. Eve didn't know and would never know if Father had ever called Adam about her plans, but a few days later Adam phoned requesting she sell all her gold and transfer him the money for he needed expenses and to pay for their air tickets, having spent all his money on furnishing the flat, and when she refused stating these were his responsibilities he gave her an ultimatum: sell the gold, give his cousin the money to transfer or go back to the village immediately. Now on the plane, the only comfort, the thought of Layth and Nadine having a good life and the relief of electricity and water, schools and hospitals, food and proper bathrooms, recreation and safety all being available.

He appeared among the airport crowd awaiting their loved ones, her skin crawled underneath her cloak at the sight of him. It was extremely hot in Jeddah and quiet for a city in the daytime. Arriving at their destination, Adam opened a metal door which revealed metal mezzanine steps going steeply upwards. Eve told him to hold Layth, feeling the frailness of the steps moving under her feet. He opened another door at the top of the stairs and led them into an open area bordered by four walls with nothing but a solitary sink. He unlocked yet another door and led them to a room with three bare mattresses on the floor. Eve placed Nadine on a mattress.

"Is this where we're going to live?" asked Eve looking around at the starkness.

"Yes, it's very nice." said Adam.

Eve got up to look around the flat.

"There's no kitchen?" said Eve.

"Yes there is." said Adam.

"Well I can't find it." she said.

"Follow me." he said so they followed him out of the room.

"Here it is!" he said smiling, standing in the middle of the open area with the sink.

"This isn't a kitchen..." said Eve

"Yes, it is." said Adam.

"There aren't any counters, cupboards," said Eve "Where's the fridge and the cooker? There isn't even a roof!"

"I haven't bought them," he said "We don't need them."

"We don't need them?" said Eve "How do I cook?"

"I'll buy a hot plate today." he said. Eve looked at Father as the sun came scorching down.

"Adam, there's no ceiling," she said "It's really hot out here, nobody can stand this sun. Can you look for a better flat?"

"No, this is good," said Adam "You can cook and when you finish, go inside from the sun."

Eve examined the rest of the flat: two empty rooms, the only sign of furniture, the inner room with the three mattresses on the floor and a used cupboard shoddily covered with wall paper. The bathroom was clean, it had an Asian toilet, no bathtub, but there was a shower and a bucket (ah, the amenities of modern life). Wanting to wash the children, she unpacked clean clothes, towels, and their soap and shampoo. She turned the latch of the shower to allow water to flow from the tap into the bucket, she waited, but nothing came out. She turned the latch back up and stepped back, expecting water to pour out of the shower head, and still no water.

"There's something wrong with the water." Eve said to Adam.

"Um…there's no tap water," said Adam "You see, this flat was built in violation…and they couldn't get the plumbing connected with the rest of the building, but every Tuesday when the water comes, there's a tap in the middle of the wall in the kitchen, you have to stand there and one of the guys who lives in the building will turn the switch on and water can flow through the tap and you can fill containers."

"I don't believe this," said Eve "I'm in the middle of the city— and still no running water? The kitchen is roofless—it's a yard and there's no furniture—what kind of flat is this? Could you find a proper one please?"

"No," said Adam "You just have to fill up the water containers."

"Father say something!" Eve said, looking towards Father, "Didn't he say I should sell my gold because he's furnished the flat with his money? Well where's the furniture? This isn't a flat!"

Father remained silent, he didn't like what he saw, but kept his lips shut tightly together as if words were trying to escape against his will.

"I'll buy a hot plate so you can cook food," said Adam "I'll go buy lunch now…I'm hungry."

"You see," said Eve looking at Father, her eyes watering, "He wanted my gold sold so I'll have no money if I'm to start my life on my own. What is this? How can we live without water and on the floor? Abbah, I told you he can't be trusted…my children are going to suffer, I know it…"

"He'll probably buy things in the near future and move you to a better place," said Father, visibly unhappy, "He won't let you live like this…he can't let you live like this…you just have to be patient. If you don't like it here, you can come back to Yemen with me and I'll take you back to the village."

Eve felt the burn of being deceived, certain Adam had done this on purpose, even if she returned to Sana'a now, she had nothing to live on. On his return Adam confirmed he had no intention of purchasing anything or moving at all. The building was made up of flats and its occupants were all men, from foreign Arab regions, working in Saudi; no women, no children which troubled Father more and he asked him to consider moving them into a block occupied by families, but Adam insisted it was safe and there was nothing to worry about. Adam kept fixing Eve with lustful contemplations, she looked away disgusted and dreaded the nearing night. The children fell asleep and Father took a mattress and went to the other room to sleep. And now Adam wanted to make love.

"No, I'm tired." she said, pushing him away.

"Come on," said Adam "I want you…"

"No, I'm tired." she said and lay next to her children.

The next night Adam tried harder, but she told him she wasn't feeling well, intent on never having sex with him until he proved he would take care of his children, and even then she wouldn't want it, but endure it. Almost a week she successfully avoided him, but he knew how to play on her fear. You see, in the past when she was younger, although she loathed herself after making love with him, she enjoyed the physical pleasure and couldn't get enough of it, but now the mere thought of him touching her with his hands made her skin crawl, the thought of having sex with him, repulsive. She could no longer tolerate him, but she had to suppress her feelings as much as her life had been repressed in the village. Nothing felt right here.

"If you don't sleep with me tonight, I swear by God I'll send you back to Yemen with your father next week, and you'll go back to the mountains," he threatened holding her arms above her head by her wrists and pushing her against the wall, rubbing the Roman figurehead at the stern of his eager ship against her "I can make you leave…you don't have a residency permit. Your children will go back to the village and never have an education."

"It's not that I don't want to," she said, really not wanting him to dock into her harbour of his ardour, "But my father will hear us…it's too embarrassing."

"We'll be quiet," he said "I mean it…let's sleep together tonight or I'll send you back. I'm giving you what you've always wanted—to live in the city, your children to live well, I'll make it even better for all of you."

Hesitantly, and regretfully on her part, they made love. Every day he swore by God to move them to a better flat and promised to give his children an education when they reached nursery age. The last night before Father would return to Yemen, Eve went to make tea in the roofless kitchen when confronted by a large scuttling cockroach between the rooms which had stopped in front of her and raised its front questioningly (who the hell are you?). She screamed and Father and Adam came, Adam noted the threat and stomped the insect.

"Are there cockroaches in this building?" Eve asked, this was the first time she had seen one since they arrived.

"No." said Adam, swiftly scooping it up in a dustpan.

Father left the next morning. The electric hot plate exploded while she made tea, Adam bought a new one which exploded too. During Father's stay, Adam left in the morning before work to buy bread, eggs and cheese for breakfast; during the day he returned with snacks and delicacies; before noon he was back, carrying a small bag of vegetables and a chicken. Eve stood in the searing-hot noon Saudi sun cooking in the roofless 'kitchen', her brain melting from the heat. The day Father left, Adam went to work as usual, but locked them inside taking away the key. The middle of the day arrived, but he didn't bring anything with him for her to cook and didn't return until after lunch time had well passed.

"Where's the food?" said Eve "The children are hungry."

"I already ate out," said Adam "You can wait until dinner."

"Dinner?" she said "You bring dinner after midnight when you close up?! The kids are hungry, they've been crying."

He went to sleep in the air-conditioned room which he kept locked while he was out, leaving them in the unbearable heat. The next morning he didn't bring eggs or bread, or anything for her to make breakfast. He didn't even bring drinking water. By noon, the children were dizzy and irritated, thirsty and hungry.

He had stopped bringing food for breakfast and lunch. Instead, he ate out while his children and wife starved at home, only bringing food after midnight, and when Eve split a little to leave for breakfast and lunch on the hope it wouldn't spoil in the searing heat, Adam would throw it outside or stamp on it. Eve tried to keep her children occupied, playing with them, telling them stories, singing songs, but the young children couldn't stand the pangs of hunger and thirst, Layth and Nadine cried, twisted and turned, rolling on their backs, crying and kicking until they turned in circles on the floor, tiny animals caught in a trap writhing in pain. No matter how Eve coaxed and held them, they only calmed for a few moments before crying more until they fell asleep, hungry. Only when her children were fast asleep would Eve cry bitterly, not in pain for herself, but for her children's suffering. Why was he punishing their children? What kind of a father would leave his children starving and thirsty? Why did he want them to come to Saudi? Prior to coming here, she worried if they rowed and argued as they did in Yemen, it would upset and have a negative effect on her children, but she never could have guessed he would starve them or make them suffer this way. She kissed her innocent children's sleeping faces with their long thick eyelashes, such beautiful young children and such harshness inflicted on them for no reason at all, and such a terrible father. Day after day he left in the morning and came back at the call of prayer, finishing a sandwich as his children watched with hungry eyes; if they came closer to get a bite, he ordered or pushed them away and she could see Kareema's traits in him, but even execrable Kareema could be excused for being greedy in the remote mountains where eggs, meat and cheese were scarce, but what excuse did he have for his behaviour? He ate lunch at restaurants; at midnight he returned carrying take away: he didn't want them to starve to death, but to starve every day. Eve fed her children after midnight, as she ate the tasteless food, made bland by anguish, she looked ahead, swallowing morsel after morsel, hoping her pain would go away; not the pain of hunger—the torment she and her children were in; the regret of not running away to where they could never be found. Her fault.

In the heat of a blistering Friday morning, Eve tried convincing Adam not to starve his children.

"Just buy two eggs and a piece of bread," said Eve "I won't eat any of it, but for Layth and Nadine to have breakfast. I'll feed them all of it in front of you. When it's lunch time just buy a piece of cheese and bread for them. Bring water for them to drink…it's so hot here. It doesn't cost a thing."

"Do you think it's because of money?" said Adam, he owned a store, falsely registered under the name of a Saudi person, he hadn't been able to find a partner when the rules changed regarding foreigners and business ownership and had to make an illegal mock sale or sell it legally for a fraction of its worth—he chose the former. "I can buy them the best of everything if I want to, but I don't. *I want you to suffer.*"

"Why?"

"Why?" said Adam "You don't want me, you don't love me and now I have you where I want you!"

"But what about our children?" said Eve "Adam you have to feed them, they're suffering too much! This apartment has no water, most Tuesdays nobody switches on the water and when it does come it isn't even clean. If you don't want us, let us leave."

"You're staying here forever," said Adam hell-bent on forcing her to totally and absolutely love and adore him of her own free will (say fella, you give a whole new depth to oxymoron), when her heart would as passionately want him as her flesh when in avid, ardent ardour so he could enjoy palpitating her body while populating her heart (he really was both ox and moron) "If you want to leave—remember what I told you about the prison Saudis put illegal residents in? The shit and piss in there is ankle high! They'll keep you and your children in there for months before they deport you. You'll get diseased wallowing in other people's waste and your children will die before you leave just like many other children have died in there."

"Is that why you brought us here on a pilgrimage visa, instead of a residency application?" said Eve "So you can do this to us? If we go to the police willingly and tell them we want to leave, surely they'll let us—it hasn't been that long, why would they throw us into prison?"

"That's not how it works here," said Adam "You came under the Omrah visa, but you stayed in Jeddah. They'll pack you with others in a cell to soak in everybody's shit, then you'll see how your children will suffer."

"Then let us live a normal life," said Eve "Just feed your kids and let us live in a small flat with running water."

"Never." said Adam.

"Then why'd you bring us here?" she said "I don't understand."

"With all the problems you were causing," said Adam "They would have let you leave the village and you'd go to the city and work. You'd divorce me, I know you would," he frowned, paused to think then continued "And you'd fall in love with another man and get married. I'll never let it happen! Here I can make you drink from a cup more bitter than myrrh."

"If you want to punish me—punish *me*!" said Eve "But don't punish our children, they're just babies... you're supposed to be protecting and taking care of them. They have nothing to do with this, none of it is their fault."

"They're not my responsibility." he said. Eve couldn't believe her ears.

"Not your responsibility?" she said, glaring at him "You're their father!"

"I don't care," said Adam "They're not my responsibility."

"Why did you go to a doctor?" said Eve "Your sperm couldn't impregnate me, but you had to go and get treated—those two babies are your children—you can't do this to them!"

Adam's face contorted with anger at being reminded of his medical problem which had marred his reputation as a man. "I'll make you suffer." he said and stormed out, locking them inside as he did every single day.

He continued leaving them without food and water until midnight. Every time noon prayer called, he returned eating and drinking as Layth looked up at him from his lap. Layth watched his father wash down the last morsel of a sandwich with a mouthful of pop, then innocently reached for the can. It spilled over his father's shirt who in turn slapped him with such force little Layth's body jerked towards the wall, banging his head against it. Eve screamed and held her crying child in her arms, his face covered in blood, but Adam refused to take him to the hospital. She no longer allowed him to plough her field from that day and forever, but it was too late—he had already sown his seed into her fecund womb.

*

SITTING WITH HER BACK FLAT AGAINST THE MIMOSA WALL SO ITS cooler surface might cool her down a little from the unbearable heat in the room, she felt the minuteness they made as part of the world. A spiralling upwards feeling as if she could see herself from high above, then the flat, then the whole building, then Saudi and the whole world spiralling in space, and how tiny and lost they were in this huge world and vastness going on without them. Her pregnancy made no difference to Adam, who continued to leave them starving, which wasn't surprising, if he didn't care about his children suffering in front of his eyes, of course he would not care about the health of his unborn child (Oh Eve, Father would have done right by you if he'd paused to think about Adam never sending his family an allowance before he forced you to marry—all the indications of an irresponsible person were there long before).

Eve awoke to the feeling of something crawling over her stomach, under her nightgown. She jumped up pulling and shaking at the gown, an insect fell out and she screamed. Something entangled in her hair, she whacked at it and another many-legged creature fell out. Flicking on the lights she looked around the room and to her alarm they were being invaded by many cockroaches, scuttling over the carpet and mattresses. She picked up a sandal flicking them to the ground before killing them, but as soon as she finished, more came out. No sooner had she returned to sleep, she awoke to their legs entangling in her hair and running over her body so she remained awake guarding her children until Adam returned.

"There are cockroaches all over the place," said Eve "I don't know where they're coming from, we need insect killer."

"The flat's full of them." said Adam flatly.

"I thought you said there weren't any?"

"I lied," he said "I sprayed insect killer several times so your father wouldn't know."

"This is disgusting," Eve said looking around at the newcomers "They'll give us a disease!"

Adam shrugged. He had sprayed the house before they arrived from Yemen, the effect had worn off and now the vermin were back. With the days Eve, scared of the tiniest and most harmless of spiders, would be living with a swarm of cockroaches. She watched, in horror and revulsion, as a line of them came out of a crack in the wall and made their way across it. As the days passed, the line branched into lines of differing size cockroaches. Nights were hellish for as they slept, the odious insects crawled over them and she startled from sleep, whacking and shaking them off. Drowsy, sitting on the mattress watching them, squashing them with a shoe when they got closer, it made her sick; it was pointless - they were infinite. All through her pregnancy she made sure Layth and Nadine stayed well away from them, and it was just as well there was no food to cook or they would have caused them a serious illness (more hepatitis A anyone?). In exacerbated lamentation, using a shoe she crushed the cockroaches against the wall, taking out her frustrations from life against them, intent on killing them all: both time consuming and futile: as soon as she finished killing a swarm, a new line appeared from the crack.

All day, the silence was only broken by her own and children's voices. It wasn't like the silence of the mountains: serenity punctuated by wildlife, breeze and the beautiful backdrop all around, people to talk with; but it was a maddening hum of electricity and air conditioners. Eve slid open the one window in the room and shook at the metal bars, trying to loosen them. All she could see, standing on the tips of her toes, were rooftops and sides of taller buildings; the awful smell coming from the pipe ventilation of bathrooms forced her to hurriedly shut it again.

As she stood filling up water containers, the flow of which was no broader than the diameter of a pencil, in the sweltering, hot Saudi sun, Eve reflected on all that was happening. It would have been so easy for un-paternal Adam to just let them leave, to live their own life, and he would not be responsible for any expenses or matters. She could find no reason to justify what he did to them: no proper food, no water, no family, no one to talk to other than her children, also suffering; locked inside a cockroach infested flat. It had been much better living in the village, not that she wanted to go back there ever, but their living conditions had been better in the village. He constantly nagged her for sex and she always refused as she had found a way of stopping him raping her: whenever he tried to force himself upon her, she screamed and shouted for anyone to call the police; afraid people in the building would hear, he immediately withdrew, for he would be in trouble too if the police came. Plus, many people in the building knew him, they were his friends and acquaintances, some were from the mountain community near his village, he didn't want to be shamed, that ever-present concern of 'what will the people say' she had constantly heard in the village was finally put to good use. She endured the suffocating captivity with patience, knowing just like she had made it out of the mountains, she would make it out of here too. Someday. Of course she always tried to reason with him to allow them to leave, to find a way so they wouldn't be thrown into prison (which he called Abu Za'bal) for months as he warned her was inevitable, but he ignored her reasoning; echoing the same ignorance of his uncles when they would not take her pleas into account. She explained to him all she wanted was he let her and the children live a normal life, and she would be an obedient wife; or to divorce her and marry another woman who could love him and he would be happy with; she assured him he need not be jealous she would be with another man, as she had no intention of getting married (God knows her experience with him was enough to put her off marriage for life), all she wanted was to raise her children in a normal lifestyle. Most of the time they argued and he always said: "You're never leaving these walls!" In an effort to get her to sleep with him he would sometimes say: "After you have the baby we'll move to a different flat." Eve could not understand why it had to be after she had the baby; or he would promise to buy her clothes, as he had thrown all her clothes into the rubbish and left her only slips and nightgowns to wear, on condition she slept with him, would she like some new clothes? She would prefer to wear a flour sack.

He left them living in inhumane conditions, but Eve tried to see the bright side, at least there were no snakes and scorpions to worry about, at least he promised to move them into a better place to live and give Layth and Nadine an education promising to have them added to his residency permit after the baby was born, and it would allow them to go to school. Eve knew he could, he always flashed his money to show her he could treat his children better *if he wanted to*, but he never did, and she wasn't sure he ever would. He wasn't a miser, but a tormentor: he chose to make them suffer, while he spent only on himself. What she knew for sure, she would never love him for since their arrival in Saudi and with every day passing, her hate for him intensified. She could not stand the sight, sound or even scent of him—repulsion had become a chemical reaction. He neither looked nor smelt bad: he was handsome, smartly dressed and clean, wore the best perfumes, but his detestable character made him ugly in her eyes. She loathed him, and all she could see when she looked at him was his ugliness oozing out of him. Her very soul grimaced at his sight, his being; a hatred so intense it wanted to burst out of her and be blatantly expressed and as she did not allow this to happen, it weighed heavy inside her chest, stifling her breathing. She could accept him being a bad husband, but he had no excuse for being a terrible father to their beautiful, innocent children. Even when he locked them inside and left, it felt a little bit better because he wasn't there.

She gave birth to their third child, beautiful Munwa, the first time in a hospital, albeit Adam refused to pay for an epidural, still it was comforting to know you were in safe medical hands just in case something went wrong, although the pain was the same. But still he did not move them to a proper flat, nor did he add them to his residency permit—he had her exactly where he wanted her: an illegal immigrant under his mercy, though she was being incredibly stubborn as he sighed and fantasised about making love to her, feasting his eyes on her body even if he couldn't sink into and slide over her tantalising silky skin nor delve to his deepest into her sweet warm grip. He piled his dirty clothes in front of her instead of taking them to the launderette as was usual, he wanted her to handwash his clothes. But there was not enough water, how would they brush their teeth or wash if she used it on the clothes, she objected. He replied she should wash his clothes and he would bring drinking water and lunch every day for the children. She immediately agreed. Eve waited until her children fell asleep then went to the roofless kitchen, carrying two water containers. She squatted legs apart over the wash basin and picked up his shirt and trousers. Checking the pockets to remove any tissues, she pulled out a One Rial note and stared at it, wondering how long it would take to save money to get to the British Embassy.

*

NOW TALK ABOUT THE STRAW THAT BROKE THE CAMEL'S BACK, sometimes it's the smallest thing that can cause a huge irritation which changes things drastically. She was surprised when Adam told her their neighbour in the mountains had been given a mobile phone by his son, for it to be used they had to stand in a specific area to be able to receive or make calls. Eve was astounded, she didn't even know what mobile phones were, could it be possible to have been introduced to the village? Would she be able to call Father and tell him how she and her children were being treated? Adam constantly denied her requests to call her brothers. Eid came and Adam returned from outside informing her he had called his family. She wanted to speak to her family, but he refused and it turned into a huge row at the end of which he picked up baby Munwa wrapped up in her white baby shawl and callously tossed her like a rag-doll, her mother screaming as her daughter rolled out of the blanket and across the mattress. Now there was no calming Eve, screaming for the police until Adam shoved her against the wall, his hand covering her mouth, she wide-eyed and alarmed, he promising to move her to a better flat, his face swollen with anger and shocked she would shout so loud and get him into trouble, not caring about being thrown into the filthy jail he always threatened her with; but all she wanted right now was to be taken to call her brother. Asking her to lower her voice he promised to do so.

At the telecommunications centre, she sobbed, explaining to her brother the torment they had been subdued to since arriving in Saudi.

"Don't come back here," said Yusef "Because you'll go back to the mountains."

"Why can't I live in Sana'a like you?" said Eve.

"Because you're a girl—I mean a woman," said Yusef "You can't live on your own, it's dangerous, against tradition and not right."

"Then I'll live next door to you—they can't say anything then." she said.

"It's the same as living on your own," he said "And you can't live with me."

Eve was hurt by her brother's remark, she never intended to live with him since he had agreed while she was in Sana'a, and his then fiancé, now his wife, had asked her not to before she left for Saudi, and even more hurt he really didn't care after everything she had explained to him.

"Give me Adam," he said "I'll make him treat you right."

*

"YOU'RE NOT GOING ANYWHERE," SAID ADAM "YOUR BROTHER SAID I should put you in a proper apartment and next year it's time for Layth to start nursery, but first we'll move into a different apartment."

"If you divorce me, I can live my life and you can live yours." said Eve.

In a week's time they moved into a rooftop flat. There were no cockroaches, to Eve's relief. There was running water and the kitchen, though empty of counters, cupboards, food and appliances, was indoors. Adam still did not furnish anything and continued to lock them inside when he left.

*

EVE LAY MOTIONLESS ON HER SIDE WHILE HER CHILDREN PLAYED in front of her, she had begun to get headaches which left her unable to move. The children would play next to her, crawl over her and she couldn't even speak. More symptoms bothered her: she felt pain in her left armpit, and when she examined herself she found a swelling in her skin. Soon there was a swelling in her forehead and right shin accompanied with pain up to half the thigh and down to the toes.

She would be overcome by such fatigue and need to sleep, except she wouldn't sleep, she lay motionless and lethargic as her children played around her, and when they tired, they snuggled as close as they could get to her body and fell asleep. Pain extended from her neck to between her shoulders. Extreme dizziness threw her off balance. The pain in her armpit sometimes jolted into her breast. She noticed the reflex in her hands was not as it should be, and she struggled doing nimble things with her fingers. Sometimes when she talked, her tongue became heavy and her words slurred.

"Take me to a doctor." she pleaded with Adam, but he always told her there was no need.

Adam finally bought a TV and satellite dish. Eve watched a documentary about wildlife, the Komodo dragons were said to sometimes dig out freshly buried corpses, she smiled remembering the villagers' description of how it moved, realising *this* was the demon they believed took away their dead according to their star sign, truth mixed with fear. True it ate the dead, but because they couldn't fathom an animal digging up a grave, the only other explanation they had was it must be a demon and from there the myth continued. In the heat of a sweltering Saudi morning, she flicked through the channels and stopped at a doctor describing the symptoms she was feeling. The morning programme was about cancer, breast cancer, the symptoms she felt were exactly what they were describing. Adam refusing to take her to a doctor made every disease described on TV programmes sound like what she was suffering from. This self-diagnosis tortured her, she jumped from disease to disease, from cancer to sclerosis to dystrophy and back to cancer, as she flicked from channel to channel, but breast cancer seemed the closest to her symptoms. She spiralled into fear that she would die of it; death would be a mercy to her, but she could not die, her children's lives would be lost without her, their father would send them back to the village. She observed her children playing and thought about what would happen to her children if she passed: Layth would be abused by his grandmother Kareema, instead of going to school he would be running after sheep and goats, and when he'd be a teenager he would be sent to work in a restaurant or shop, blocking any chance to have a better life; Nadine and Munwa would be abused by cruel Kareema too: they'd be carrying heavy water and firewood from the age of eight, they'd probably be married before they reached eighteen and have baby after baby. Eve shuddered at the thought of her children's probable future if she were to die.

"I think I might have cancer." said Eve.

"You don't have cancer." said Adam.

"How would you know?" said Eve "I have all these symptoms and the doctors on TV mentioned the same symptoms. I need to see a doctor."

"You don't have anything." said Adam.

"When I find the swelling or when I have a headache and can't move—take me," she said "At least a doctor can tell us what I do or don't have. Please…?"

"No."

Eve continued to collect the change she found in his pockets when washing his clothes. September drew closer and Eve was keen on Layth starting nursery. Adam promised to get their legal status sorted out, until now they were still illegal residents in Saudi, which meant no education for the children. She opened the subject many times with him, but he kept avoiding the matter or setting back processing them onto his residency permit. They always argued about it.

"You're my wife," said Adam in exasperation "I have a right to make love to you."

"You kept me a prisoner in the mountains and you're keeping me a prisoner here," said Eve "You have no rights with me."

"You know the angels curse the woman who refuses to come to her husband's bed until she does." he said.

"Then let them curse," she said "Anyway, you don't even pray so they're probably praising me." He tried to touch her and she snatched away.

"Don't touch me!" she said, disgust drawn on her face, "I told you it makes me sick. Don't even think of it."

"I will have you!" he shouted and grabbed her by her arms and wrestled her to the floor, Eve let out three screams, scaring him off. He got up furious, yes he badly wanted sex with her, but he didn't want the risk of being exposed to the police. Layth called for his mother from the other room where she always slept with them, bolting the door from the inside, worried if she did not, Adam would sneak into the room overpowering her while she slept.

*

"DON'T LOCK US INSIDE," SHE PERSISTED IN HER REQUEST WHICH he'd always declined "Leave the doors unlocked or give me a copy of the keys."

"Impossible," said Adam "You'll run away."

"Don't you hear about fires in the news all the time?" said Eve "If a fire breaks out in this building, my children and I will burn to death."

"Good." he said.

"You don't mind if we burn to death?" she said "Then let us leave…why should you care?"

"Because you'll go to someone else," said Adam "But I'll never let it happen. You're *my wife. Mine!*"

"Don't change the subject," she said "It's dangerous to leave us locked in. Every time a door slams or I hear a loud bang I think a gas canister has exploded."

"No, no keys." he said. Eve shouted for anyone whom heard to call the police.

"Don't forget the prison you and your children will be thrown in if the police come!" he warned.

"I don't care! Somebody call the police!" she shouted.

"Stop it," said Adam "Be quiet before somebody hears you! I'll cut you a copy of the keys…be quiet!"

He left the house, Eve's heart beat quicker with a small triumph. She was intent on getting to the British Embassy and asking them to help her get back to Britain, to return without being thrown into the dreadful prison Adam kept threatening her with every time she told him she wanted to leave. Adam returned with the keys, one for the flat door and one for the door at the top of the stairs leading down from the roof. He held them out to Eve, she reached out to accept them, but he raised them higher.

"First you swear by God you won't run away," he said "You won't leave the house, you'll only keep the keys in case there's a fire."

"I don't have to swear about anything," she said "You can give me the keys so if there's a fire we don't die, or you can keep the keys and I can shout until the police come."

Reluctantly, he handed her the keys, suspicion painted all over his face. He took the elder children out, leaving Eve and baby Munwa alone. She placed the keys in her bag with the change she had collected, aware enough not to leave the apartment while he was around. She would wait until his vacation ended, he was probably waiting outside on the street corner anyway. Waiting for her to come out—to give him reason to confiscate the keys.

*

THOSE TWO YEARS LIVING WITH ADAM UNDER ONE ROOF WERE HELL on earth. She remembered how people in the village described life for those whom had gone to Saudi as living in paradise, she too had seen the photos and heard from the relatives, while she was in the mountains, of how luxurious a life they lived—if only they could see the torment she was in. Adam returned from work with news of Yusef's in-laws coming to do Omrah and on their way back they would come to Jeddah wanting him to take them around to good places. She asked if they would pass by here, he replied they might. Eve prepared a letter for Yusef from that day; telling him she feared she might have cancer and about her symptoms, Adam refusing to take her to a doctor. She wrote him Adam would leave them as illegal residents and not have them added to his residency permit or get them one of their own; that Adam had made it clear he would not provide his children with an education. She wanted to come back to Yemen, but Adam would not let her and now she was determined to escape to the UK.

*

FINALLY EVE MADE UP HER MIND, HER RESOLVE STRENGTHENING as she washed her children and dressed them. She put on her cloak and face veil and left. It had been a long time since she had seen the stairs of the building, she actually felt dizzy.

"Can you take me to the British Embassy?" she said to the taxi driver.

"The British Embassy is not in Jeddah, it's in Riyadh," he replied and Eve's heart sank into her stomach, "Would you like me to take you to the British Consulate?"

"Yes please."

CHAPTER TWENTY

EVE OBSERVED THE EMPTY STREETS, SHE HAD NOTICED DURING the day you hardly heard any movement, but during the night the streets came to life and assumed this lifestyle was due to the extreme, hot weather. They passed a mega toy store and Eve smiled as childhood memories flashed into her mind, she came back to the present as Layth fidgeted beside her. She hoped she and her children would soon be on their way to Britain, where they would create happy childhood memories between them. The Consulate was far away, it took a while to get there. The car stopped under high walls with flowers and bushes towering above them and the taxi driver pointed her in the direction of the consulate.

"How may I help you?" said the employee, black hair impeccably groomed wearing white dress and i'qal.

"I have a problem," said Eve "I need to leave Saudi, but my husband won't let me. I have a British passport, but I don't have a visa or permit to live in Saudi. My first two children are included in my passport, but my youngest was born here so she isn't on my passport. Can you help me go back to Britain because my husband won't allow it?"

"Have a seat," said the clerk, looking a bit confused, "I'll ask someone more senior to look into your situation."

A few minutes later he reappeared and directed Eve to a smaller office with a glass screen between the chair she sat in and the empty seat on the other side of the glass. An employee named Rick with long wavy blonde hair, moustache and beard appeared and occupied the seat. He asked Eve to explain everything so she did and told him she wanted to return to Britain. First he told her it was amazing after all these years she hadn't lost her Welsh accent, then informed her if she returned to the UK she would probably live in poverty as she had no right to benefits after all the years spent abroad—she said she would find work—he said unemployment was high and she would probably not scrape by with what she would earn with three young children to care for; he went on to ask if she had any relatives in Yemen so she could return there and from there, if she wished, she could return to the UK. Then he asked her which she would prefer to return to Yemen or UK? To UK, but was worried about the disease infested prison she and her children would be thrown into. Why did she think she would be thrown into prison? Because they were illegal immigrants she replied. He believed they would not be thrown into prison, but would have to check so he disappeared again into the bowels of the consulate.

Eve felt tears welling up and swallowed hard to avoid crying, her hope of going to Britain seemed grim for her children, it was not what she had wanted to hear, her bubble of confidence and happiness which had flowered from the escape had been rudely burst and she felt overwhelmed, she had even foolishly entertained the idea the embassy would immediately help her out of this situation whisking them to safety and she and her children would never return to Adam. Everything she wanted to do seemed intimidating and frightful. She took a good look at all three children, and thought hard. Should she take them to Britain and give them a life of poverty? Should she go back to Yemen and find work and provide them with a life which she could afford, which could also be poverty? Of course in Yemen she could find work: she had seen people she knew in the village find work in companies, travel offices with the help of her brothers and they didn't have a fraction of her intelligence. She racked her brain not knowing anymore what was best for her children: to go to Britain or Yemen? The man had said she wouldn't be granted any support so what would she do in the meantime? Dick, or Rick, whatever his name, caused her to remember how high unemployment was and the long queues she had seen (as a child) in the news of people looking for work so she knew she would not find work easily or quickly especially with no education or vocation. If she couldn't find a job, how would she feed them? Or even provide a roof over their heads? Surely the Social Services would claim she was unable to take care of her children and take them away. This thought she could not bear, it convinced her not to go to Britain. She would start her life in Yemen, where nobody could take her children away from her. Rick returned informing her she could apply for an exit visa, she could apply for a temporary passport for her daughter, and there's no prison or detention cells for immigrants whom volunteer to leave the country.

Eve left the Consulate feeling uneasy, she had expected to be relieved. At every opportunity to get away from the situation she was in, she always ended up diffident, daunted by the outside world from all the years of confinement. She wanted to leave *this* situation, but in which direction to go she found her options immensely formidable. Why was she so scared to go back to Britain? Why did she have to worry and think and overthink it? Maybe she should run away in vast Saudi with her children, but with no residency permit and the constant inspections for illegal immigrants she knew it wouldn't work. She was grateful to see the taxi driver waiting and as the taxi pulled out, she was alarmed to hear the call to noon prayer: Adam would go back to the apartment and find they were not there.

The taxi pulled up to the pavement. Eve reached into her purse and counted the small notes and coins to pay the taxi driver, the idiom 'save a white coin for a black day' had proven to be correct for her. Nervousness churned in Eve's stomach, the flat was as empty as they had left it, no sign of Adam so they were lucky he hadn't returned while they were out. It didn't change a thing, she would have to tell him in order they process a passport for Munwa. Less than half an hour passed and she heard Adam unlock the outer door. She took her children into the bedroom.

"Layth, play with your sisters and don't come out of this room until I say it's okay. Understand?" she said.

"Yes Mama." he said and smiled at her.

As she shut the bedroom door Adam opened the flat door and startled at Eve's sight, from his reaction she knew he'd been back and not found them.

"Where did you go?" he demanded, his eyes bulging, face red, and he'd evidently been crying—his posture slouching as if he'd been punched in the gut.

"Don't shout and scare the children—let's talk." she said.

"Where did you go? I came home and the house was empty! I was shouting your name! My heart was going to stop I thought you ran away! I even looked under the mattress! I went looking for you in the streets! Where did you go?" Tears streamed down his angered face, Eve had never seen such huge tears (she couldn't see her own face while she cried), he was afraid of something—afraid he was no longer in control of her.

"I went to the British Consulate," she said "We're going back to Yemen."

"You're not going anywhere! How dare you leave the house without my permission?" he said "You're my wife and you're staying here—I decide. You will never see the sun again!"

"The British Consulate has all your details," said Eve "They know how to find you."

"You're my wife, you do as I order! How dare you leave the house without asking my permission? This is a scandal!"

"I don't need your permission to do anything, I'm a free person. You kept me captive in Yemen, you kept me captive here, but I'm still free and soon I'll never have to see your face again!"

"You're *mine, I own you!*" said Adam "You will go to hell for leaving the house without my permission! You're not a good person!"

"I'm a better person than you'll ever be!" said Eve.

"If you were good you would obey me—your husband," said Adam "Didn't you hear the real story about the woman whose husband was working abroad a lot?" Eve rolled her eyes, knowing a woman-control story was about to be told. "This woman was living on the ground floor," he continued "Her family were living on the second floor. Her father was dying and her sister came down to tell her to come see her father before he dies, but she said 'no, I don't have my husband's permission to leave the house', her sister said 'but your father's dying' and the woman refused because she didn't have her husband's permission. Her father died without her saying

279

goodbye to him. He was buried without her attending his mourning. Then her husband came back and knew what had happened and was happy. This woman goes straight to heaven (assisted by Adam's finger jabbing the air upwards)!"

Eve shook her head at the end of the story she'd heard hundreds of times over the eight years she had lived in the village.

"We have to get Munwa's birth certificate so we can apply for her passport." said Eve.

"*Listen to what I'm saying and what you're talking about?*" he said "You left the house without my permission! That woman didn't see her dying father who lived in the same building because her husband didn't give her permission!"

"That woman is stupid!" said Eve, now glaring, "I—am—not—that—woman!" She was fed up of being lectured into submission. They argued intensely. Adam didn't want them to leave, but Eve made it clear they would come looking for her and find him.

"What about the prison?" said Adam "You'll be thrown in people's piss and shit and your children will die of disease!"

"There's no prison," said Eve "You were lying to me, but if you try to harm us or make it difficult for us to leave—*you'll* be thrown into prison."

"Don't believe what they tell you," he said "They're lying. You have to stay with me, I'm your husband and I say you stay. You stay!"

"I have a brain—I know what to ask and who to believe. We *are* leaving and you have no say over me."

Adam pushed her hard and she fell to the floor next to the television, and somehow this act of aggression seemed more insulting and injurious to her emotionally than when he had raped her, due to the hateful vehemence on his face towards her and it was the first time he had done something where the sole intention was to hurt her physically. She snatched a pair of scissors out from the small trolley the TV was on, and held them towards him, and got up with them pointed towards his chest, walking backwards until she reached the bedroom door. As she turned towards her children, concealing the scissors, she bolted the door from the inside. Munwa and Nadine were playing, Layth sat next to them also playing, but Eve could tell from his posture, he was tense from the arguments he heard. Layth looked up at his mother whom smiled down at him, she kissed his head and joined them in their play, hating that her children were being exposed to the aggression between them. She hated Adam for not letting her children have a normal existence and wasting two more years of precious life. If there was one thing she was determined on, it was not wasting any more of her and her children's lives.

Eve's escape to the consulate coincided with Yusef receiving the letter, concerned over his sister's situation he continually called Adam demanding he let Eve and her children return to Yemen; requesting to talk to her. A puffy eyed Adam stood at the door.

"Yusef wants you to call him. We'll go in the afternoon."

He watched her with his soured expression, still angry she had found a way out and would soon be free of his prison. Through almond sized opalescent tears he begged her to stay and promised to furnish the flat immediately, put Layth in nursery and correct their legal status. It was too late, she replied, they were leaving.

*

ON THE PLANE, ON THEIR WAY BACK TO YEMEN EVE WAS FULL OF mixed feelings: going to Saudi had been a great mistake; she should have run off two years ago when she still had gold to sell and gone back home to Britain. But she had gone to Saudi ready to sacrifice her life so her children could have a normal one, a life with a father, but instead they had been subdued to unnecessary suffering and witnessed the cruel, cold irresponsibility of a selfish man whom placed getting back at their mother before their welfare. She now wished she'd chosen to go back to Britain, but knew she couldn't risk her children's wellbeing by exposing them to homelessness and the possibility of them being taken from her custody, as the only person in their young lives whom actually cared about them and thought about their future. Every decision Eve made would be based on what was best for her children. She had to find a job in Sana'a; Yusef would have found a house for her to rent by now; and she would need to find a day care centre; she had to enrol into computer and business courses, her head ached full of worries and plans, things she had to do, to make sure her children would be okay. Eve smiled down at her children, she didn't care how hard she had to work, she would give them everything they needed to start a proper life, to be prepared for life. All she desired was never to see Adam again (whom Yusef had deposited at the side of a busy road, leaving him chest-heaving and distressed watching the car roll off with Eve) and divorce would ensure it.

Disappointed to learn Yusef had not looked for a place for her to rent, they arrived at Yusef's house; Noora, his wife, greeted them, pregnant with their first child. They were shown their room which consisted of a double bed in the middle and a single bed against the wall. The children went to sleep immediately. Eve, Yusef and Noora sat in the living room and Eve spoke about everything they had been through.

"We'll divorce you from him, the bastard!" said Yusef.

"I want him to leave me alone so I can bring up my children in peace." When Eve mentioned the children, Noora's expression changed and she looked at Yusef from over her vulturine-beak nose inclining her chin to her chest.

"You're young," said Noora "You'll get married to someone you love, you don't want *his* children."

"Noora, they're my children!" said Eve, surprised by the comment, "And I have no intention of getting married."

"Don't worry," said Yusef "Everything's going to be okay."

Eve entered the bedroom to check on her sleeping children, tired from travel. She shivered as she passed the living room heading for the kitchen, Sana'a was freezing cold in contrast to blistering Jeddah. She wanted a hot cup of tea to warm her. Noora didn't notice her pass by and continued to say: "She's not keeping the children. She won't let go of them easy or we'd send them to their father tomorrow. We'll give them back to their father…she can get married and before she gets married she has to…"

Eve couldn't bear to hear more and went off to the kitchen. A dense cold warped inside her body matching the temperature of the room, she made tea, but no longer desired it. Everything darkened in her eyes: the walls, furniture, the atmosphere. Cold and dark and again in a situation where people wanted to decide her life without including her.

"Don't worry about anything," said a smiling Noora entering the kitchen followed by Yusef "Listen, I know before, when you wanted to stay in Sana'a with Yusef instead of going to Saudi…I told you I didn't want you to live with your brother because we were getting married…and I know it hurt you, but you know…I was still a fiancé and wanted to start living with my husband alone after marriage…"

"Don't worry about it, it's in the past." replied Eve, smiling back as her chest ached knowing how easier life would be now had she stayed in Sana'a instead of going to Saudi. "Thanks for letting me stay with you now," continued Eve "I'd like to pay half the rent while we're here. I can look for something much smaller, but I hope to move out at the soonest."

"You're living with me," said Yusef "I'm your brother and I'm taking care of you—you're not living on your own."

"I need to get a divorce," said Eve "I have to take care of my children."

"We'll help you," said Yusef "Meantime, you just stay at home and relax."

"So I can get a job I need to take some courses." said Eve.

"What kind of courses do you want to take?" said Noora.

"Computer and business courses." said Eve.

"How will you be able to when you have children?" said Noora, still driving at her own personal point, "You can only take courses and work if you don't have children to worry about. You can send them to their father, you know…and start your life."

"I'll find a day care centre for while I'm taking courses," said Eve "And when I have a job, I'll get a babysitter." Noora glanced at Yusef, with a look of discontent.

"You have plans," said Noora "That's good."

"Yes," said Eve "With most of my life wasted I need to catch up with a lot, for my children's sake. I want my life to start over again."

"It will," said Noora "And we'll help you. But you know the most important thing you need a lot of to start your life, is money...you need a lot of money!" she looked at Yusef sitting quietly.

Eve couldn't sleep easy, the bed was comfortable and she was tired, but something was eating at her. From what she had overheard, her brother and sister-in-law had a hidden agenda for her. It worried her, but tomorrow would be a new day, everything would be fine, especially the sooner she found a house to rent.

*

"I'VE SPOKEN TO ADAM," SAID YUSEF "I'VE TOLD HIM HE HAS TO divorce you or you'll divorce him. He did say he's prepared to be a good father and give his children all their needs if you stay with him."

"No," said Noora "She wants a divorce." Eve looked at Noora who seemed eager to get her divorced, if only there'd been an advocate like her ten years ago.

"He said he'll pay for all your expenses every month," continued Yusef "He had a condition that you don't live alone—I told him you're living with me. Tell me, do you still want a divorce? Oh, and he said he'll pay for Layth's kindergarten upfront, he knows you care about their education. So what do you say?"

"I want a divorce," said Eve "I hate him. He made us go through hell, but it doesn't mean he can't see his children and he still has the responsibility of paying for their education and expenses."

"So you want a divorce?" said Yusef.

"Yes she wants a divorce." said Noora.

"Yes." said Eve.

Yusef spoke with Adam and arranged for a meeting with family members so the divorce would be immediate with no need for court, but Adam refused to part with her and demanded to see her. Yusef told Eve how Adam broke down shaking and weeping, getting down on his knees and leaning forward with his head bowed, a crumbling mountain of couscous, begging for her clemency in front of everybody; that he wanted to speak to her, he would be a good father and husband and provide everything for them in Sana'a.

"Well it's too late," said Eve "He should've done that the two years we spent in Saudi."

"After the kids go to sleep, we want to talk with you." said Noora.

"Okay." Eve smiled. After putting the children to bed, she joined them in the living room.

"So now you're going to be divorced?" said Noora.

"Yes, finally." said Eve.

"Your brother and I are going to support you," said Noora "But we want something in return…"

"As soon as I work I'll pay you back for all the legal fees." said Eve.

"No, not that," said Noora and she looked at Yusef whose face was clouded, he looked at the floor and said nothing. Noora continued "You have to give us your passports."

"Why?" said Eve puzzled "So I can't run away to Britain? Noora, I'm free to leave if I want."

"Not because of that," continued Noora glancing at silent Yusef, "That's not why you have to give us your passports."

"Then why?" said Eve.

"Don't worry about it now," said Noora, sensing Eve wasn't going to be that easy to manipulate, "Now we just concentrate on your divorce." Eve looked to her brother and he looked away.

"Yusef, do you hear what she's saying?" said Eve "Are you agreeing with it?"

"No I don't," said Yusef "Don't listen to her, *I* don't want your passports or anything."

"We'll talk about this again," said Noora "Anyway, there's something else you have to know—when you begin the divorce, you're going to give him his children back. *Throw them at him* so you can live your life!"

"My children are my life," said Eve "What is this nonsense?! Noora you're pregnant, can you imagine giving your child away?"

"Eve, you're young," said Noora "You have to get married…Do you think he'll pay for their expenses if you divorce him? He won't—

you throw them at him, make them his problem and you go and live your life! Get married!"

"They're *my* children," said Eve "I'm not getting married. I won't send my children away."

"Okay, enough of this discussion," said Yusef "That's it, you don't have to give him your children."

"If you're keeping your children then you have to give us your passports." Noora demanded.

"Enough already!" said Yusef.

They talked about different subjects, but Noora's requests troubled Eve, she couldn't shake off how easily her sister-in-law suggested she abandon her children, as if they meant nothing. Eve left the room and Yusef and Noora quarrelled in hushed voices. The children were fast asleep. Thirsty, she found the water was empty and on heading for the kitchen to fetch a bottle she heard them still quarrelling.

"We can't force her." said Yusef.

"Yes we can," said Noora "We'll wait until she begins the divorce and then we'll send the children to him. She has no money, she won't be able to do a thing, *then* she'll give us her passports! *Then she'll do as we say*! She isn't like you at all—she's got strong character and so stubborn!"

"Hush, she'll hear you," said Yusef "She's been through enough shit already."

Eve closed the bedroom door behind her, pressing her back against it to allow its cold surface to shock her out of the daze and slid to the floor. She felt herself become dizzy with the dilemma—again people had plans for her. Again she was facing people trying to control her life, it seemed since her Father's first entrapment her life had fallen into a pattern, but this time she wouldn't allow to it happen. She got up and sat on the corner of bed watching her sleeping children, she delved deeper in thought as to how to get out of this quandary. What to do? It was one thing when her parents changed her life and took advantage of her young age and vulnerability, putting her in an environment and circumstances where strangers kept her prisoner, in a remote area where no authority or understanding existed, with no chance of escape. It was another matter being an illegal immigrant on Saudi ground, alone, kept under lock and key. Now it was a completely different feeling, striving so close to her freedom and her children's welfare. Here and now, she was aware of what she could do to be free, but the only reason which could keep her from achieving her freedom and living a peaceful life was the bad intentions of, again, strangers trying to take hold of her life for their own personal gain. Another hindrance towards getting out of this predicament was her financial situation—it didn't exist, she had no money and nothing to sell.

Eve wanted the divorce more than anything, it rang like an alarm bell constantly in her mind that it had to happen, but having no income to pay for her children's expenses and living in her brother's house, whose wife had the intention to throw her children out as soon as she was divorced, she had to accept, no matter how hard and unpleasant the fact, currently divorce was not an option. The whole night she spent weighing it up in her mind. During breakfast it ate at her heart, what she had to do.

"Yusef, I've been thinking about what you said," said Eve "If Adam's prepared to be a good father, I don't think a divorce is good for the kids."

"Alright," said Yusef "I'll arrange a meeting between you, and you can discuss your terms with him."

Eve sat silently watching her children eat, her plate of food seemed as appetising as a rubber tyre.

*

"I'M SO GLAD YOU'VE COME TO TALK," SAID ADAM TEARS ABUNDANTLY welling in his eyes and streams of regret running down his face, "I'll do anything, tell your brother not to divorce you from me."

Eve was repulsed and wanted to throw up, literally, and swallowed hard to keep the bilious surge down. A strange force always brought them together, from crossing the world from Britain to be entered into the forced marriage, to escaping the mountains only to live with him under one roof and now, after she had left the hellhole she cohabited with him in Saudi, she was again pushed into being with him, negotiating her children's future. They always ended up under one roof, opposite sides of the magnet being pulled together, while the closer the proximity they shared had the opposite effect and they repelled each other. Her skin crawled and stomach lurched, her eyes wanted to look away, for he disgusted her and she despised him. The contrast of the last few days of being so close to getting rid of him and now sitting near him, discussing future life with him, exasperated her to tears which she struggled to keep down. If anyone was to blame, it was her father who had turned her life upside down ten years ago. It was agreed he send money for Layth to enter an international school and monthly allowance for their expenses, which Adam would transfer to Yusef. Both Adam and Yusef rejected the idea of Eve renting a house on her own; to live on her own was too dangerous and unacceptable so she had to stay with Yusef, but she made it clear to her brother she wanted to move out. Yusef and Noora explained it was both dangerous and taboo for a young lady to live on her own with only her young children in the city, but Eve wanted this so badly. The situation was intensified by fear arising from the arrest of the 'Sudanese Serial Killer' on the news, this murderer had killed many young women in university, disposing of their bodies in an acid bath. According to Yusef and Noora, he was the only murderer to catch the media attention (and probably a scapegoat), while many murderers and rapists went around unhindered. Backing out of the divorce was the only way she could keep her children safe and close to her; to keep her sister-in-law's plans at bay, and she backed out of the divorce with the intent it would be until she got out of her brother's house. Eve insisted on paying half the rent until she found a place of her own, but Noora and Yusef refused to accept so she only used the money to buy food and necessities for her children and herself, and when she wanted to search for a house to rent, Yusef and Noora reassured her that Yusef was already doing so.

At the kitchen table Eve discussed her plans with her brother: she wanted to enrol into computer studies, later into business studies; to take her children out. She wanted to go to the British Embassy to see how they could guide her or direct her to support because she wanted to finish her education. Most of all, she insisted on searching for a house so she could move out sooner and not intrude on them any further. Yusef agreed to everything, he even gave her advice about the best places and times for her plans. The next week when Eve had settled in and was ready to embark on the first steps to start her life, Noora and Yusef asked her to sit with them. To talk.

"This is my house and you have to live by my rules," said Noora in an authoritative tone, affecting superiority, "You can't enrol into any institute while you live here. You cannot go in and out of the house as you please. There will be no taking your children out for walks, I won't allow it, I don't want you going in and out of the house. When I go to the supermarket or when I go out, you can come with me, if you want. There will be no going to the Embassy while you live here. You can't sit in the living room or watch TV. Stay in the bedroom and kitchen. When guests come, if I tell you not to come out of the bedroom do not come out and don't let them hear that you or your children are inside. You're not allowed to use or answer the phone, only if you see my mobile or Yusef's mobile number then you can answer. Never use the phone, not even to call your parents. Do not open the door of the house, not even if your parents were to arrive."

Noora droned on with her draconian rules like a sentencing as Eve listened with equanimity—occasionally Eve glanced at her brother whom just sat there quietly at the kitchen table not objecting to any of it, not stirring a muscle.

"You do know I want to move out of here?" said Eve "It's been weeks and you won't let me search for a house. How can I find a house if I'm not allowed to leave?"

"We're searching for a house for you." said Noora, but they were not searching for a house at all.

"But I need to see a doctor to find out what this lump is and why I'm in pain," said Eve "I want to know if I have cancer or not. I want to know what's wrong with me."

"Yes," said Yusef, he hadn't turned into a stone statue after all, "Tomorrow you can go."

"You can go with me," said Noora "I need a check-up, you can see my doctor."

At the shiny tiled hospital, whose cleaners wiped the floor with dirty grey headed mops leaving both floor and air smelling a mix of bacteria and disinfectant, the doctor checked Eve by doing a physical exam of where she felt a lump in her breast and armpit.

"There's nothing. You're fine." said the doctor.

"For sure?!" said Eve immensely relieved and unable to believe, "Is there any kind of instrument I should be tested by, or a blood test or any kind of test so we can be sure I have nothing?"

"No need." said the doctor straightening her hijab.

"Then what was causing my symptoms?" said Eve.

"It's not anything physical." said the doctor.

"I'll call Yusef and tell him the good news." said Noora as they left the hospital.

Light-hearted, Eve returned to her brother's home happy, one worry she could put behind her. Yusef returned from work, throwing dark glances at her with his frowning face every time he passed her. Not long after the children slept, Noora and Yusef said they wanted to talk to her—it was never a good sign.

"The doctor said you don't have cancer." said Yusef rather flatly.

"Yes, thank God," Eve smiled "It's such a relief! If Adam had taken me to a doctor, he would have saved me so much worry and tears."

"You don't have cancer?!" said Yusef, suddenly irate, "How can you not have cancer when you had all those symptoms?" Eve was taken aback at her brother's discontent.

"It's a good thing that I don't, Yusef." said Eve feeling punched in the stomach at her brother's disappointment.

"You were lying," said Noora "You lied to us…You told us you had cancer. You don't have cancer!"

"I told you I think I have cancer and he won't take me to a doctor." said Eve.

"You lied to us just so we would help you." said Yusef.

"You lied to us." said Noora.

"I didn't lie to anybody about anything," said Eve "What has the illness got to do with you helping me? Anyway…you should be happy I don't have cancer, not upset!" Now she was upset, perplexed at their bizarre reaction because she didn't have a terminal disease. "I'm happy the doctor said I don't have cancer." said Eve.

They continued to berate and make her feel bad about not having a serious illness, before leaving her alone in the kitchen. She tried to figure out how good news like this could upset them, but all she could feel was terribly hurt.

All during her stay at her brother's house Noora and her truculent mother enjoyed launching malicious verbal attacks at Eve, shouting at her, insulting her; both seemed to suffer from an inferiority complex, through trying to project they were superior they exhibited their own feelings of mediocrity, where they could only feel better about themselves by attempting to belittle others. Eve always felt she was walking on, sleeping on and breathing in sharp thorns; intensely uncomfortable, she and her children out of place and unwelcome. She looked back at them with her penetrating eyes, through their virulent tirades and saw how small they must feel if this was their only way of release. Her patience became stronger with the increasing suffering as she remained composed in the face of their contumelious bombardment, while on the inside she was hurt (a tremulous soft-bodied rabbit looking up at the giant hand reaching out to pick it up for slaughter) having done nothing to call forth such treatment.

Three different places throughout a decade of her life, three different schools of abuse, all similar in one way—they were a prison. Her life was being imprisoned, she was still living the life of a caged bird, except here in her brother's house she could not sing; the air was so thick with tension towards her, song didn't even occur to her nor did it come to her tongue unwittingly; no song could make her remember a past life full of happiness and freedom, no music could make her forget the barriers surrounding her. She was not allowed to leave the house to do what would let and empower her to become independent. One thing she was sure of, it would only be a short matter of time and she would find a house and leave.

*

WHILE HER BROTHER AND SISTER-IN-LAW WERE AT WORK, EVE TOOK advantage of the few days Noora's maid was around, asking her to keep an eye on the children and she left searching for a place of her own to rent, and institutes running courses she wanted to take. The day care centre she found was alarming: the all-female employees seemed nice and were ready to answer all questions, but they just sat together drinking tea, chatting cheerfully, leaving the children in the rooms unattended to. Eve found toddlers in two rooms playing, some crying. There were stains on the floor and the stench of the urine saturated carpet filled the air, the canteen room unused and covered with dust. Eve took the application form with her, knowing it would be better to employ a maid to babysit while she took courses than to leave her daughters in a place like this. Now she needed to find a house to rent, she knocked on so many doors and didn't find any so she stopped at the nearby grocery shop and asked them if they were aware of any houses or flats for rent. The shopkeeper said he would ask around and let her know.

One afternoon during her maternity leave, Noora needed something and couldn't wait until Yusef returned from work so she asked Eve to go on an errand. Eve paid and asked: "You didn't find a house?"

"I did," said the shopkeeper "And I spoke to Yusef, he said there's no need for it. He told us to stop searching."

"You found a house?" said Eve "Where? Can you show me?"

"It's been taken," he said "I *did* tell Yusef and he said no so I showed it to someone else! That one over there, with the broken window."

Eve was dismayed, a house had been available and in an area easy to live in, Yusef had let it go. "Why didn't you tell me about the house the shopkeeper found for me?" she said to Yusef when he returned home.

"You're not living on your own," he said "You're staying with me and I'm going to take care of you."

"Yusef, it's like living in a prison here." said Eve.

*

ON A COLD, CLEAR AND SANA'A SUNNY-BRIGHT MORNING FATHER arrived at Yusef's house.

"See—I've come back to live in Sana'a." were Eve's first words to him.

"We all thought you'd have a good life there," said Father "Like everybody else that goes to live in Saudi. How did we know he would do all that to you?"

"Why did *you* do this to me?" said Eve "Why did *you* force me to marry him in the first place? Why'd you bring us to Yemen even? My life's a mess—I had a normal life and you ruined it for me. You ruined my whole life."

"It'll be okay now." said Father.

"How is it going to be okay?" Eve's voice rose annoyed Father was treating her forced marriage as a mere hiccup in her life, when it had been the unchewable morsel that had choked her to near-death and now she was living the post-brain-damage parallel life as opposed to the normal one she was supposed to have had, "Do you realise my three children have been through hell with me? Do you realise ten years of my life are gone? Do you understand I will never be the person I was meant to be? Do you know what I've been through? No—you don't, because I was the only one suffering all this time, me and my children."

"I didn't know this would happen…" he whimpered, reduced to tears.

The next morning as Eve and Noora sat drinking tea, Father walked into the kitchen and sat at the head of the table, opposite Eve.

"Listen Eve," said Father as if about to impart important news "I caused you great injustice…and I'm sorry. I'm truly sorry and I want to make it up to you. Tell me, what do you want?"

"Make me fourteen again," she said as tears stung in her eyes, "Give me back the ten years taken away from me. Return me to the point before we came to Yemen so I can live my life the way it was supposed to be. Can you do that?"

Father remained silent, guilt covered his face; his eyes said he would do anything to be able to turn back time, to right his wrong-doing.

"Of course you can't," said Eve "There's nothing you can do to make my pain disappear. You can never make it up to me." She shook her head in dismay, how it weighed on her soul and ate at her spirit, knowing what she could have been and never fulfilled. Her sad, accusing eyes dug into Father's conscience and he wept, full of regret.

"Uncle," said Noora who had been listening quietly "Eve has been through a lot and you know…she has three young children, she needs your help." Noora didn't mean what she said, but eagerly wanted to find out what was in Father's head for he had said he would give Eve whatever she wanted so Noora wanted to know what he was prepared to give, and more importantly, how it would affect what she and Yusef had been expecting to get from him.

"I'll give her anything she wants to make her happy." said Father, looking towards Noora.

"Like what?" said Noora, curious and serious, "What do you want to give her? She won't ask for anything so you tell her what you'll give her."

"I'll buy a house for you and your children," Father said and smiled at Eve "I'll buy you gold…I'll cover you from your head to your foot in gold! I'll give you money so you won't need anything."

Noora shifted in her seat, aggravated, what Father said disturbed her. Eve wondered where this affection and willingness to help had been while she was trapped in the mountains, and prior to leaving for Saudi.

"I don't want any gold," said Eve "If you buy me a house that'll be great. It would be the best thing for me and my kids so I can have a start, not worrying about rent and if I find a job, whatever I make will be enough to feed and clothe them."

Father smiled while Noora frowned, unable to conceal her displeasure.

"Soon I'll receive a large amount of money," said Father "And I'll buy you a house, I promise." Father finished breakfast and got ready to leave.

"Say goodbye to Yusef for me," he said to Noora "I'll be back soon."

*

Yusef came home early, barging into Eve's room, his face incensed, his posture menacing as he clenched his fists, towering over Eve as if he wanted to fight.

"What did Dad say to you?" he demanded.

"What?" said Eve.

"He said he'd give you something," said Yusef "He told you about the money he's getting soon." Eve was surprised Noora had called to his work, to tell him about the conversation.

"He said he'd buy me a house." said Eve.

"What else?" said Yusef.

"He said he'd buy me gold, but I told him I don't want gold, just the house is enough."

"Did he tell you when?" said Yusef, looking angrier.

"No," said Eve "Why?" He left without answering, a storm of dark clouds agitating in his face.

Two days before the fourth month ended since arriving, Yusef came into the bedroom shouting at Eve to pack her bags.

"I found a house for you," said Yusef "And after you leave I never want to see you again!"

Eve was hurt by his words, but excited about the house, she would finally live on her own. "Where is it?" said Eve.

"You don't need to know," he said "And I never want to see you again!"

"Yusef what's wrong? Why are you shouting? Why are you being like this?"

Yusef raised his voice, saying cruel things as if Eve had been the nefarious, sinister sister who'd done him grievous injury. The workers arrived to disassemble Eve's wardrobe and carry her things out so she and her children sat in the living room. Yusef entered shouting at Eve: "You never come back here! Ever! Do you understand? Don't you dare call Father or contact him in any way or something bad will happen to you! I swear by God if you call him even once something terrible will happen to you!"

"Never call us!" Noora joined in "Cross out our numbers from your notebook and erase them from your memory! And don't you dare call your father!" and she walked out of the living room.

"Yusef, tell me," said Eve standing up to talk to him calmly "What did I do wrong? What's happened? Why are you talking to me like this?"

Yusef raised his voice and pushed her until she almost fell back into the sofa, in front of her children sitting next to her, and left the room. Eve stopped the tears welling up in her eyes, turned and smiled at her children and spoke to them softly, reassuring them everything was okay. Things were not okay, she didn't know where they were heading and for whatever reason Yusef was threatening her not to contact Father (don't you know, Eve? Money is thicker than blood). Yusef and Noora asked her where her money was, to give it to them. She pulled it out of her purse and handed it to Yusef who counted it then went to shout at the workers to disassemble quicker, and returned.

"This money I'm giving to your landlord for three months' rent." said Yusef.

"Give him two months' rent," said Eve "And give me the rest so I can buy food and things."

"I don't care." said Yusef, and he took away the money.

As the workers finished loading the parts of the wardrobe into the pickup truck, Eve and her children waited in the living room silently, the children watching TV hardly moving when Noora returned to blow her last blast of venom.

"Don't think because you're leaving you're going to ruin my furniture!" said Noora.

"When did we ever ruin your furniture," Eve replied calmly, with a laugh, "Or anything in the house? We've always kept the house clean, tidy and in one piece."

"I know you're jealous of me because you don't have *anything*," said Noora "So you'll probably try to ruin my furniture before you leave!"

Eve was both insulted and amused a person at such a mature age could think like this, mostly amused because it was a reflection of what Noora herself would probably do. Eve was happy to be leaving a place where people resented her not allowing them to dictate her life, where their only response was to constantly hurt her and try to bring her spirit down. Father's promise of a house had obviously upset them because they wanted the money, *all of it*, to themselves and would end up ripping off Father of all his fortune. She could understand how people came to hate for reasons of great injustice, but could never understand why people became abnormal and irrational over money. She sensed Noora felt threatened by her, for no reason Eve could know; Noora felt like a lesser person around her, even though Eve had nothing material or monetary, there were aspects in Eve's calm, kind, composed character which made Noora feel this way. She was happy to finally be heading off to live in peace with her kids, but deeply hurt by the way it was done.

They arrived at the apartment which was in an area, at the time, remote and Eve had no idea where she was. If you needed anything you had to travel for hours along dirt roads. Their bags were put down and the wardrobe assembled. Yusef went around in circles, waiting for the workers to finish assembling, many times he came into the room where Eve and her children sat on the floor, and said horrible things to her and kept on repeating: "Don't ever come to my house again. Don't ever call to my home, mobile or office. Don't you dare call dad or you'll regret it!"

He was about to leave, Eve got up towards him. "Yusef wait," she said "Can you give me the rest of the money so I can buy food?"

"I've given it all to the landlord." he said.

"But I told you to pay for two months only so I'll have the rest for food," she said "You can see we don't have anything."

"I don't care, it's not my problem." said Yusef and he left them without money, without food, without even a mattress to lie or sit on. Without a blanket to cover the kids from the freezing cold. There were no telephone lines in the house (in fact there were none in the whole area) so there was no way to call anyone she knew who could help them and he had threatened her not to contact Father. It was the month of Ramadan, where good deeds are fortified and multiplied for its doers by the holy month, people fasted all day to feel for those so poor and go without food throughout the year, to become more pious and sympathetic towards them. Her brother had abandoned her without a penny, no food or drink and made sure he'd taken her to the outskirts of the city to make it difficult to contact Father. He'd gone from one extreme to another: from not allowing her to live on her own because it wasn't safe, to throwing her into a remote area where she didn't know her way around. For a month where people raced to do more good, her brother had done her wrong. In Yemen it was fundamental, culturally and religiously, male members of the family, whether the father or brother, uncles or nephews, stood by and assisted female relatives no matter how rich or independent the female was. The brothers protected and helped their sisters, fathers their daughters. To abandon a daughter or sister meant you were not a real man. It was disgraceful. But Eve was left alone, scared of the unknown.

CHAPTER TWENTY-ONE

THE FLAT HAD FOUR BEDROOMS, THREE BATHROOMS, A KITCHEN and a Diwan (large living room). The rooms were spacious, cornice and pastel coloured frieze mouldings topped all the walls, and extravagant chandeliers hung from rose mouldings in the centre of the foyer at the entrance and the salon between the bedrooms. As night drew closer, the changing light threw a kaleidoscopic array of patterns against the walls through the colourful semi-circles of stained glass above the windows and the children played in the empty rooms while Eve sat kneeling in the middle of the house, weeping a torrent of grief. Never had she felt so alone and vulnerable, a big gaping hole flowing with hurt was where her abdomen and chest were supposed to be. She heard people, ladies, going up and down the stairs talking, then quieten down. Someone clattered on steel stair banisters. Long after the sun had set, the children were hungry and asking to eat, Eve knew there was nothing she could do for them tonight, the next morning she would have to find a telecommunications centre and see if the employees would allow her to place a call to Saudi and pay later so she could ask Adam to send money immediately to buy food and things, but tonight the children would sleep hungry, on a cold floor. There was a knock at the door, Eve opened it to find a woman standing there wearing a sharshaf, her face covered by a black veil.

"My name's Shareefa," said the woman, pulling down the scarf off her face "People call me Om Yaqub. I'm your neighbour, I'm renting the basement floor." Eve allowed her in and introduced herself.

"I heard you crying," said Shareefa "My dear, your eyes are so red, what is the matter?"

Eve briefly explained to her the situation. Shareefa got up, kissed Eve on the head and gave her a hug.

"Don't worry," said Shareefa "I'll lend you money to catch a bus tomorrow and to call your husband. He'll send you money and you'll be alright," she gazed around at the empty room, "How could your brother leave you here like this? This is a sign of the Day of Judgement nearing! It's dangerous for you to be here on your own, women here are raped and killed all the time, *you really shouldn't be living alone*...call your parents—they'll come and live with you. Don't worry, you don't know this area, I'll show you around. The nearest telecommunications is about a three hours' walk from here, but much quicker by bus." She left, returning with a large metal plate filled with bowls full of food.

"Those poor children are hungry," she said "And you, fasting without breaking your fast. What has the world come to? Brothers throwing out their sisters and nephews without anything to eat!"

After they finished eating there was insistent rapping at the door. Shareefa opened it to two middle-aged women, four teenage girls and many young children. Some were Shareefa's children, and the landlord's two wives with their sons and daughters. Shareefa explained to them what had happened and they were sympathetic.

"How could your brother throw you like this without food or money?" said the landlord's first wife.

Eve shrugged and tears rolled down from her eyes, the question brought a wave of emotion she could not withhold.

"Is he your real brother or your half-brother?" said the landlord's second wife "Even stepbrothers don't do this! Is he only your brother because you breastfed from the same woman?"

"He's my brother from both parents," Eve said, swallowing down, trying to stop the tears.

"How cruel and cold he is," said Shareefa "If he has no sympathy for you, what about the children? How could his heart allow him to leave them without food?"

Eve wiped her cheeks with her palm, though they were trying to comfort her, their many questions and emphasis on Yusef's abnormal cruelty were fingers probing into her freshly-opened wound, making her unable to conceal her distress. Although she put on a brave face and tried to convince herself she would be fine, she was deeply hurt by her brother's actions. All the ladies expressed their upset over Yusef's conduct: "How unmanly."

"How cruel."

"How forbidden what he has done."

"It's shameful, what kind of a man is he? His wife must be behind this!"

"Most brothers are good until he marries a bad woman and they play with their minds. She must be behind this."

"Men don't do this to their dependents! Brothers don't do this! This is unheard of."

"He left you with no food," said the second wife "But did he offer to bring you food?"

Eve clamped her lips together and shook her head, trying to keep the sobbing in, embarrassed to be crying in front of strangers.

"He didn't say he'll come back to bring you money to buy food?" said the first wife.

"No." Eve let out like a gasp.

"He just left her here," said Shareefa "With nobody, without anything, in the evening. She doesn't even know this area. He just left her with her babies like an orphan, like a branch cut off from a tree!" The frowning women and teenage girls shook their heads.

"Why don't we fetch my husband's mobile and you call your brother," said the second wife "And tell him you need his help."

"Yes," said the first wife "His heart might loosen-up and he *will* help you. Call him!"

"He told me never to call him," said Eve "Never to go to his house…he told me many times never to call to his mobile…never call my home or office."

She tried to suppress her emotion and tears, but her chest had been straining like a bottle full of compressed air and their questions made her burst, crying and feeling raw, a feeling of nakedness more exposed than a body without clothes, she felt they could see her soul inside-out. All the hurt expanded in her chest and a great pressure began the overspill, a volcano of dolefulness and distress erupted and flowed never-ending tears. Eve was overtaken by the sobs and couldn't believe how hard she was crying, as her jaw and face ached from stretching and opening so wide, and how much she really hurt as she covered her face with both hands, wanting to disappear from sight and existence, and her body shook. The women sitting on the opposite side of the room felt her pain, and they cried with her. Empathy. For the first time in a long time, people felt for her. The strong sentiment had surprised her, coming over like a flood, yes she had always wanted to live on her own, dreamt about it, wished for it, but the sudden abruptness of how Yusef had kicked her out and cut his relations with her, his reasons for doing so, left her feeling vulnerable and unprepared. His cruelness and callousness towards her shocked her for he was her brother whom she'd been close to until they came to this country, and she loved him.

Eve's children fell asleep. She took off her head veil and cloak and spread it next to her on the floor, picking them up one after the other she laid them next to each other on the cloak, then covered them with three towels. On seeing the makeshift blankets, the women asked: "Why don't you put them on a mattress and cover them with blankets? It's freezing cold, they'll become sick."

"She doesn't have any," said Shareefa "My daughter checked the other rooms…her brother's heartless."

The women and teenage daughters cried again and as they wiped away their tears, they fussed over Yusef's cruelty, disturbed at how anti-man, anti-tradition he was being. Both landlord's wives and three daughters went upstairs and returned carrying pillows, two mattresses, two blankets and thermos flasks of tea, coffee and water. They touched Eve's heart with their genuine sympathy and acts of kindness, but at the same time she was extremely embarrassed and wanted to die because she had bothered these people and was being given charity. Embarrassed because they were not needy, but her wealthy brother and affluent Adam had put her in this situation.

The next morning, Shareefa lent Eve money to catch a bus and make a phone call. Shareefa accompanied Eve and her children. Looking around as they walked Eve noted there were only five houses dispersed in the area, most of the land was empty, its moist dark brown soil looked like it had been farmland. Shareefa confirmed that until recently the whole area had been used for agriculture. The dirt roads loose soil covered their shoes, no matter how many times Eve wiped it away with a tissue. When they finally reached the main road to wait for a bus, Shareefa pointed to the left and said there was a small grocery store, it had some things, but most things were in the market, about two hours away by bus.

Adam seemed to savour the situation she and her children were in, Eve detected the satisfaction in his voice, but could not suppress weeping as she asked him to send money for their urgent needs, but he refused, making them go back and forth to the telecommunications centre to call him while both upstairs and downstairs neighbours provided them with breakfast and supper; enjoying Eve's difficult situation, he made her make several more calls before finally sending money. He said there was no need to buy furniture, a fridge, TV, he would send these from Saudi. When he did transfer money, Eve paid back her neighbour. She left her children in the flat with the second wife to babysit them, and went to a bustling, overcrowded market with Shareefa to buy food, water, mattresses, blankets, a gas stove, gas canister, kitchen and hygiene utensils. It was all they would have for a long time as Adam did not keep his word and never sent any furniture, he wouldn't send money every month either, choosing to send one month and leave them without the second, and the month he did send would be an amount insufficient for one month's needs.

They were difficult days, but tranquillity filled Eve's mind and soul, and serenity filled their home. They were happy, much more than they had ever been when she was in the village, Saudi and Yusef's house. She had peace and freedom. Neighbours constantly warned Eve about the dangers of living alone, a young lady with three young children, she was warned not to open the door to any strangers and to install extra bolts on the doors. After receiving money from Adam the first time, she purchased necessities and awoke with renewed resilience: no matter how hard it was, no matter how long it would take, she would find her independence. She knew what she had to do: she needed qualifications and this would help her get a job. Her children were healthy and she would make sure they were well in every way.

*

ALTHOUGH SHE WAS BLISSFULLY HAPPY WITH HER NEW SEMI-independence, enjoying life alone with her children, she was no longer the Eve of a happy childhood in Britain, but a changed, different person; traumatised by a forced marriage, changed by ten years of being buried alive, flawed mentally by the constant criticism of her captors whom had persistently pointed out how everything in her character and behaviour was so shamefully wrong; moulded by a persevering belief that one day she would find her freedom, though it had taken her a decade to break free, and still she was not truly free. Her captivity had left her naïve without the experience of how people are in the real world so she found out the hard way, not all people are honest; appearance and conduct could deceive; how people presented themselves wasn't always how they really were, and it varied, how long it took and what it would take to see the real person underneath. With time, she gained the awareness which gave her a shield; she became a good judge of character and what she presumed about others she met and interacted with often proved true. But the naivety she had once been fully fledged in had turned into a different streak of singularity—if a person was her friend and somewhere down the line took advantage of her, she would continue allowing them to take advantage be it monetary (when she would have it) or assistance fully knowing she was being taken advantage of, but she would choose when to close the tap and usually she would let it flow for a long time; she would not be wary of anyone, with the exception of those she perceived as foul or dangerous. She had disappeared from Wales into the mysterious mountains of Yemen a genius teenager with a shining, bright future ahead, and reappeared a decade later in the capital of Yemen, a young woman without any qualifications, and mother of three young children. Her mind always reverted to being fourteen years old, and she knew it was wrong—not that she behaved childish, for she conducted herself more maturely than those older than her age, but when her mind wandered about all the things she wanted to do, when she was inside her thoughts, she thought like a fourteen-year-old as if she still had time and the potential to do it all. She would snap out of it suddenly, as if becoming aware then and there she was twenty-four, not fourteen. There is no describing how she managed to get through those difficult days and months, how she and her young children made it through trying and dangerous situations, harsh conditions, but what a struggle it was. When late at night one of them was so ill and fevered she would have to take all three of them to hospital, walking down the uninhabited roads in the dark night, it was God's grace nothing bad happened to them, if any evil soul had caught sight of them they would have been easy prey.

When the father is irresponsible and cares not for his children's well-being, and when the mother is caring and rational, burdened alone with the responsibility of providing for her young, but is still wholly dependent on the irresponsible father, she becomes very economical, planning everything out to fit the pattern of when he would send money, so she calculated and made a list of all things needed which could be bought cheaper in bulk, the items which could not be purchased in bulk she organised the needed amounts into labelled envelopes and she rationed food. This way, everything was either purchased or set aside for. This way she was able to make insufficient funds for one month, last almost for two. As the fear of Yusef's threats diminished, she went tens of times to the telecommunications centre, asking her parents to come live with her, even if only her mother came, life would be a little bit easier as she could look for work and enrol into studies. Her parents always met her requests with rejection, *just as always*. They weren't prepared to leave the village just so she could sort her life out (her life which they had thoroughly messed up). It was bitter irony, during the long years in the village they had always objected to allowing her live in the city on her own, according to them it was 'shameful and dangerous for a female to live by herself in the city'—there had to be a male member of the family to 'take care of her', but now they showed no care nor worry towards the fact she lived alone in the city, and she had informed them of what had transpired and where she was and how direly she was in need of at least one of them to stay with her to babysit the children. She needed their help, their support—which they were unwilling to give, leaving her smarting from the caustic bite of their paradoxical nature.

*

EVE VISITED DIFFERENT INSTITUTES UNTIL SHE FOUND ONE THAT RAN computer and secretarial courses, after making a few enquiries she decided on a five month Secretarial Diploma, the problem was it cost seventeen thousand Yemeni Rials, it wasn't a lot of money, but to Eve it may as well have equated a million pounds—it was out of her reach with Adam sending hardly a month's allowance every two months which would not be enough even for their basic needs had she not been so frugal in their home economics so she was back at the telecommunications centre explaining to a refusing Adam how the course fees were inconsequential to him and she would be able to find work, he sophistricated that she didn't need to work with him sending money; she countered with he knew what he sent was not enough and every second month they went without and if she worked they could start saving for their children's future (Oh Eve, don't you ever learn? He cares not for their present or future), but he refused: he didn't want her to study, he didn't want her to find a job, his aversion—she would attain her autonomy (and he lose access to her anatomy).

The next day she called her brother Morad, in hope he would lend her money to take the courses. He was doing well and had been working for a long time in a prominent company; during her time in the mountains she had watched him be generous to his in-laws to the degree of extravagance, and was certain he would help his little sister in a time of need like this.

"So how are things now?" said Morad over the phone, after apologising for neither visiting nor even contacting her since her return to Yemen.

"Well, Adam doesn't send enough money for his kids," said Eve "He sends only for one month and the second month he doesn't send at all. When I call he says he doesn't care if we don't have anything."

"That's bad."

"Morad, I need your help…"

"Anything, tell me and I'll help you." (Lip service, a phrase merely parroted as it was the thing to say.)

"Thanks, I need to take a Secretarial Diploma course, it lasts for five months and at the end, if I pass, I get a certificate. When I get the certificate I can find a job. It costs seventeen thousand Rials, but Adam refused to pay for it. Can you lend me seventeen thousand Rials and as soon as I get a job I'll pay you back?"

Morad became quiet then said: "I can't."

"Why not?" said Eve.

"I just can't." said Morad "but if you do take the course, when you get the certificate let me know and I'll help you search for a job." His voice wavered with indecision and contrition.

"Morad please, I know you can," said Eve smiling down the receiver "If you're worried I won't pay you back I'll write and sign a document that states how much I owe you. Please Morad, it's really important, you know what happened to my life…this course will be a starting point for me to get up again."

"I can't," said Morad, he needed to check if it was allowed through Dhalia and Suleiman, "It's very difficult to find a job in Yemen, *you* won't be able to get a job. Ummm…you know what, I'll think about it. Call me…the same time tomorrow."

She called him the next day and his reply was, no, and she knew fully well it wasn't the amount—it wasn't about the money—but her brother's heart had hardened from years of poison dispensed through the ear administered by his in-laws, he was under the thumb and she was no longer his favourite and most loved person. She returned from the telecommunications centre, a bird with broken wings, a funny feeling in her chest, a small hole emitting melancholy into the rest of her body. If she couldn't pay for the course, she would not get a certificate. If she didn't have a certificate, she would never be able to find work with decent pay. The next morning she awoke full of hope Father would give her the money to get into the course, he had recently offered to buy her a house, which she was still expecting to happen: this amount she was asking for was nothing in comparison. She spoke to both her parents and by the end of the conversation she was in tears, he refused to give her the needed money; they both refused her alternative request Mother come live with her for a while so she could find a part time job to pay for the course. Betrayed again, unable to understand why her parents were so removed, a sense she was not their daughter at all. Father had obviously gotten over himself and had no regret towards how he had ruined her life—the whole 'remorse-forgiveness' act he had shown at Yusef's house was nowhere to be detected.

*

THE CHILDREN SLEPT, SHE WATCHED THEM FOR A WHILE BEFORE going to the room where her wardrobe stood. She took out the childhood photos and her school reports which she had found in Father's house in the village, and spread them around her on the floor. She looked into each one, reminiscing, smiling. She came upon the autobiography she had written as a project given to them by Mrs. Price in second year of secondary school and read it; it had a lot of happy memories and photos, full of hope and projected success for a jocular Eve at that age, in vast contrast to what and how she was now. The reports, photos and autobiography reminded her, how happy she was then and free of responsibility; how bright, intelligent and full of life she had been, on the path to success and a great future. Now, she sat crying on the cold floor, a woman whose life had been stolen, whose life had been changed by someone else's decision. A mother of three with no means to support them: no money, no certificate. A woman in desperate need of a job and no way to find it. A daughter with no parents. A sister with no brothers. A wife with no husband. Everybody in her life who was supposed to aid and protect her, love and shelter her, had effectively abandoned her. Paradoxically, everyone who had prevented her natural course of life, everybody who had kept her cocooned between walls, hidden from the real world, not allowing her to develop and grow into an adult able to take care of herself, had now left her to fend for herself. Alone in her solicitude. She was not prepared to let the weakness of her position affect her children, she wasn't going to let them feel lost or abandoned. She would be their everything. In utter helplessness and fragility she looked up to God, tears streaked down her face, she grit her teeth until her jaw hurt.

"God, help me, I know You will. Help me find a way to protect and provide for my babies. God I'm begging You, I have nobody but You, keep my children safe. Help us need nobody…help us need nobody." She collapsed on the floor after her prayer, shaking, in tears, palms down on the photos of a happier younger Eve who beamed with life and success.

A few weeks later there was a knock at the door, someone returning from the village who worked in Sana'a. He brought a letter for Eve, from Mother. Intrigued what news Mother was sending Eve opened the envelope, and to her surprise Mother had sent her twenty thousand Rials so she could take the course, and there was enough money for transport too. This was the first gesture of support from Mother since they had first arrived in Yemen ten years ago. She immediately enrolled into the five-month course for a Secretarial Diploma, a six days a week study from Saturday to Thursday. She would make breakfast, get Layth ready for school and take him and the girls downstairs to the neighbours to babysit them while she went and returned from the institute. She would catch two buses to get there and walk the rest of the route, happiness in every step, she was on the way to a better future.

She called Morad to let him know she'd started on a Diploma believing he was actually interested because he said he'd help her search for work when the time came (here we go again), and again he told her he'd help her find a job as soon as she got the certificate. She called Mother to let her know how she was progressing. Eve found juggling studies, taking care of the children and the house chores difficult at the beginning, but she managed, and came to enjoy everything she did. To be able to live her life with nobody disturbing her was a blessing and to do this while she watched her children live happy made everything she did so rewarding, she even came to enjoy getting through the hard, gruelling experiences and the feeling of relief at the end. She made friends with fellow female students and was good friends with the neighbours, daughters and mothers. They all kept saying it was impossible to find a job without a bribe or 'medium' or a connection, which meant you had to know someone influential in the company or government, or someone who knew this type of person to get a job or pay them a bribe to get the job. But ever optimistic (not to mention quixotic) Eve refused to believe it was true and would prove it by finding a job at the end of the five-month study.

There were so many similarities and differences between the people in Sana'a and the people in her village: their lives and ways were full of tradition, some had beliefs which didn't make sense fixed on superstitions, divorce was looked down at, but it happened. Men and women were disgusted to hear about forced marriages, especially of young girls, stating with much passion how they would never do such a thing to their daughters, oblivious their remarks made her hurt from Father cut deeper. Many had lived their whole lives in Sana'a, but the majority were originally from different cities and also villages, settled now in Sana'a. There were the highly educated and the completely illiterate; the decorously civilised and the boorishly belligerent—and being educated or unschooled did not determine the former or latter characteristics. Though it was a Third World Country, they lived and wanted the same things as any person wanted in a First World Country, a good education for themselves or their children, to go to university, a house, work, to travel and see the world, to found families of their own, to have independence. They loved western music along with Arabic music, they read Quran then watched whichever popular American series was running. Eve could not see much difference between these people's lives than those in Britain, except for religion. The Muslim majority, small percentage of Yemeni Jews and minorities of foreigner Christians lived in harmony and followed their own religions.

*

TO HER DISMAY, ADAM ARRIVED TO DISRUPT HER BRIGHTLY coloured peaceful world before she was to take the exam of the fourth month, bringing greyish-black auras with him. She still couldn't stand the sight of him, for while he was away, she managed to forget about him and now he was here, a painful reminder of a forced past. He brought clothes for the children as gifts and he brought her a set of gold and he wanted to make love, but she told him she was on her period for living with him had caused her to be turned off from him forever (where did the voracious fire go, Eve?). Turning the key in the door of the room, she laid the mat and prayed so he would not see her, during menstruation women didn't pray. He suspected she was lying to avoid him and as they sat talking he suddenly grabbed her by the crotch to feel for a pad, she screamed out of surprise and invasion of privacy.

"Why are you lying? You're not on a period." he said, still fondling her contours above her clothes.

Through conversations she initiated, it was evident he still had no inclination of providing them with a normal life, for he would initially agree when she suggested that once she had a job they both start to save for their children's future and provide for them better, but it became evident from what he said later, he had no intention of buying furniture for the house, he would not send enough money for his children to live reasonably, nor did he care about saving or doing anything to better their lives.

"I thought you said you'd be a good father?" said Eve.

"That was a deal I made with your brother so he wouldn't help you get a divorce," he said "Now your brother isn't in the picture anymore, I'm not obligated by the agreement."

"I can't believe you just said that," she said "What has Yusef got to do with this? They're our children, your children. You're their father and you're responsible to take care of them. Don't make them live beyond your means, just give them enough to live properly. At least give them beds to sleep in, furnish a house or buy a house for them, send enough money for them to eat well."

"I don't have to do anything," he said "You can't force me."

Unable to break through the walls of her erected bastion, nor break through the double doors with his throbbing battering ram, nor tempt her to lower her snatching drawbridge so he could dig into her delicious grip with his engorged passion, Adam probed her with indirect questions, jealous over reasons existent only in his suspicions. Jealous Eve had a different man in her life. If only he knew how hard it was for her leaving the children with the neighbours, studying, cooking, cleaning and worrying if he would send money or not in two months' time and he was jealous she had time for 'another man'? Was her teacher a man? No, a woman. What was his name? *Her* name was Ahlam. Were they all girls? Who? Her classmates. Men and women.

"Men?" he said, angered his face bloated with rage, "You sit with men?!"

"Each student has their own desk and computer," said Eve "What's wrong with you? You know, society and the whole world is made up of men and women."

"I want you to drop this class and join a women's only class!" he said.

"I won't do that."

"Are there curtains," said Adam "Or screens between you and the men?"

"No," Eve laughed and touched her hair, "Why don't you buy me a cubicle on wheels? Then I can walk all around Sana'a surrounded by mobile curtains!" she continued to laugh finding his closed-minded desire she have absolute no communication with men, amusing. How did he expect it to be possible? Even if there were places for study and recreation for women only, how did he think they got around normal everyday life? To travel by taxi or bus, to go for medical treatment, merely going to a shop or grocery store would entail interaction between both sexes. Did he really believe the country should be segregated by gender? Not all arguments were entertaining, most of the time they were horrendous and loud, by the end of which her throat would be sore. He turned the peaceful house into a realm of torment and suffering, he had brought hell with him. He started to show disturbing behaviour, following her instead of staying with his children. She would spot him standing across the street, watching her while she talked and laughed with her friends outside the building, waiting for her taxi to arrive, only crossing over to her when he saw she noticed him.

The constant quarrelling affected her, she sat on the chair in front of the monitor and tried to calm herself before embarking on the exam; unable to move her stiff neck, the headache so blindingly intense she could hardly open her eyes. Despite her condition, she still passed with flying colours.

The quarrelling began early in the evening and became so severe Adam stormed out of the house with Eve screaming after him not to come back. He'd stay in a hotel. She turned the key in the lock and sighed, at last he was no longer in the house and, hopefully, soon not be in the country. The next morning was the weekend, a Friday, so there was no institute. The children slept while she prepared breakfast and swept the carpet with a sweeping brush. As she scooped the sweepings into the dustpan, a movement in the foyer caught the corner of her eye, she turned and screamed on seeing a man in a dark striped kaftan walking through the middle of the house.

"It's me!" said Adam and laughed, holding up his hands placating Eve who, with hand on chest, breathed hard out of fright.

"You scared me!" she said "How did you get in?"

"I made a copy of the keys while you were at the institute," said Adam, laughing, "I slept in the diwan last night!" As you can imagine, the tension filled the house again.

*

"I DON'T THINK YOU SHOULD LIVE HERE ALONE." SAID ADAM morosely.

"It doesn't matter what you think, this is the reality," said Eve "I live here on my own."

"I'll ask my uncle to send my aunty to live with you." he said.

"She won't," said Eve with a laugh "I've been trying to convince them all this time and they refuse."

Adam called Eve's parents and, much to her surprise, they instantaneously agreed. So Mother came to Sana'a to live with Eve at Adam's request. He complained to Mother that Eve refused to sleep with him or allow him to touch her. Eve explained to Mother how he tortured them in Saudi, how he refuses even now to give his children a normal life or be a good father. Mother always sided with Adam so now Eve was not only subject to Adam's demonic presence, but also

Mother's constant dour disdain. If her Mother and Adam continued to tell her the cursing angel story, she was positive her brain would explode, it was as if they actually believed she would be intimate with him because of the story, regardless of its religious authenticity; she understood religion and was familiar with its teachings and hadeeth, and she was also fully and painfully aware of the soul-cringing, body-shuddering effect he had on her for she could not bear to be in the same room as he in the presence of others, let alone be with him intimately. Mother was furious and always showed contempt because Eve was 'disobeying' her husband, but as for the subject of her derision—well, if Eve had to choose, they could send her straight to Hades rather than to bed with him. Getting no gratification from Eve, Adam didn't stay long and left to Saudi, and Eve returned to a peaceful home. Adam left unhappy, she hoped by now he understood they had no future together and would divorce her. He would have to eventually, for why would he want to keep a woman as a wife if they had no friendly relationship and not had sex for years, and never got along? If he didn't divorce her, once she found a job she would hire a lawyer to get her divorced as soon as she could afford it.

Eve complete the courses and was ready for work, happy with her success, she went home with her Diploma set on finding a job soon, confident she would. She purchased several self-training books which gave insight about business and the corporate environment and learnt how to write memos, reports and business letters, she learnt about marketing and sales strategies. First, she called her big brother asking him to help and guide her in a job search, he replied he could not (were you really that surprised Eve?). She sat at home, pen and legal pad in hand, and began to write her CV. It was pitiful and practically empty, the only information, her personal details, last secondary school certificate and the Diploma. Glaringly blank, the A4 sheet highlighted the absence of any work experience and the lack of a full education. She wished she was still on good terms with Yusef, if he would let her use his computer maybe it would look a little bit better typed up, but it wasn't an option so she was happy with her handwritten resumé.

The *Yemen Times* and *Yemen Observer* newspapers she now purchased weekly, answering every suitable advertised job vacancy; sending the CV and a cover letter, and following up with a call. She answered every ad, but no result. It had been six months since she received the Diploma, answering ads of job vacancies which never resulted in an interview or even a phone call, she began to feel it was pointless. Maybe they were right—you couldn't find a job in a good company or any company without a middleman and a bribe. So she gave up on the ads because if that was the case—she had nobody, and even if she were to have money one day, she would not use it to bribe. She put out the word she was looking for work in hotels, even as a cleaner if a secretarial position wasn't available. Mother, friends and neighbours opposed and objected she work in a hotel, apparently there was consensus in society that working in a hotel was the same as working in a brothel—but as long as what she would do was achieved legally and not immoral, she would work wherever the opportunity would come. She had to work, to ensure her children's well-being and future; to be independent. Their father was showing no stability or responsibility towards them, by far the most irresponsible person she had ever known.

*

HAVING FAILED TO FIND WORK IN A HOTEL, SHE RETURNED TO searching the newspapers. At first there had been an eager anticipation and delicious delectation in searching through the newspaper ads, circling the printed announcement thus creating with ink her oasis of hope, but it now seemed to mark a border, a fringe she was not allowed to cross further than writing a letter to, and these advertised roles and companies would remain as mythical creatures in mystical lands whose doors disappeared to the poverty-stricken mum-of-three and only appeared to those with enchanted keys or genies. One month had passed since she answered the last advertised job vacancy and given up, disappointed, exasperated she would possibly never get a job if it was true what they said about mediums and bribes. Simmering in her aggravation of unemployment Eve answered the ringing phone. Her smile mirrored the immeasurable happiness filling her heart being poured through her ear, for it was the last ad she had answered, her faith in perseverance replenished. It would give her a new, good start in life, it didn't mean her pain and suffering would end, but a certain type of suffering would. She was called for an interview in reply to her application to an advertised position of a secretary of a local company, it would be her first interview ever and while nervously waiting for her turn with other nervous candidates (whom were silent and seemingly much more composed than she (whom she correctly suspected of having university degrees)), she trembled going over her memorised responses and was very well prepared, having made great use of the business study manuals during the seven months after completing the Diploma. Instead of finding three old hags looking back at her through one shared glass-eye she was interviewed by two down-to-earth ladies, and she was frank with them about having not gone to university and no work experience, but she convinced them she would be able to do the work of a secretary very well and answered their questions, exuberating confidence. They told her the reason she was shortlisted was due to her cover letter, very well done and convincing (understandably, her CV did not merit a mention). On returning from the supermarket one afternoon, and just as she arrived home and walked through the door, the telephone rang. It was the Human Resources Manager, officially offering her the job; the working days were six days a week from Saturday to Wednesday, eight to five, and Thursdays half a day until one p.m. Her salary would be one hundred and fifty dollars per month which was not much, but to Eve it was much better than nothing. She had mixed feelings, excited and nervous to be starting work which she had always wanted, but the most difficult emotion which wrangled between her heart and mind was parting with her children for most of the day, it filled her already saddened soul with guilt, though it was for their interest she had to work.

So she started work with her first ever employer, and it was nerve racking. She was not just the secretary, but also the switchboard operator. It was difficult at the beginning, as it would be for anybody starting work for the first time, only the difficulty tripled, nay quadrupled, with being the operator and secretary: you cannot learn step by step with twelve lines ringing, fifty internal extensions requesting calls to be transferred and a rabble of several different employees from three different companies requesting typing, translation, sending, receiving and distributing faxes all without taking into consideration this was her first job ever, each one of them believing their's was the most urgent, most important work to be attended to first. They had no understanding of what the job actually entailed, just huffing impatience and eye-rolling irritated comments. Only management upstairs showed patience while she tried to get to grips with her many-tentacled work. In her inexperienced eyes the work was overwhelming and difficult, she thought she would never get a grasp of it, even her antecedent, the good witch whom was said to have been *excellent at it*, whom was supposed to have provided Eve with training, had suddenly become ill overnight prior to Eve's first day and the evil forces seemed to have sensed her absence (if not cursed her with the illness) and had released the kraken so by the second week Eve seriously considered quitting, but the immense need of an income banished the idea from her mind and she carried on, no matter how impossible it seemed to get used to or take control of her work. The fax was situated on the first floor, her desk on the ground floor, she was responsible for sending and receiving all faxes and mail, keeping a register of everything sent and received and distributing them, she would be running up and down the stairs of both three-storey buildings (situated in separate yards), receiving and transferring the phone calls from whichever office she was in. By the time working hours ended she dragged her legs out of the office, not walked. Gradually, Eve was able to perform her work by conducting it not as she was shown, after her predecessor returned in good health, but as her confidence grew she organised and went around it in a way which saved time and made more sense. As a secretary for three companies and management situated over two buildings, it was hectic so organising, being punctual, fast and reliable was a must. Two months' time and she was controlling her work smoothly and efficiently, she commanded the many-buttoned switchboard and the simultaneous ringing lines with such fluidity (a sorcerer merely waving his slender fingers in the air) as if born with an *Alcatel* know-how manual in lieu of an umbilical cord, she remembered how she would screw up transferring calls, transferring to wrong people and how overwhelmed she was, and thinking of quitting and she laughed in reminisce as it was all so easy now, it just needed time. Finally her brain and energy could be put to use and she enjoyed her work and learnt so much from it.

Earning her own income brought an abundant peace and happiness to being independent, it no longer meant going without food and necessities when Adam didn't send money. It was still tough because her salary wasn't much, but she made use of what she earned and could not be happier and content with life. She would not worry about it too much, though—it always hurt, him not caring about his sweet children enough to take care of their expenses, nor show them love at all. When he called, she reminded him of his responsibilities as a father, nonetheless he began to send less money and it wasn't long before he ceased to send money at all.

She received a raise for her performance on completion of the trial period, plus transport expenses. Everybody in work respected her, all her female colleagues became her good friends. Everyone she worked with were unique characters, there was work and laughter, seriousness and practical jokes.

Work was great. Life was peaceful. Eve was free and happy for the first time in a very long time. Best of all, with Adam always abroad, she lived and felt divorced and single. She relished delightfully bringing up her children the way she wanted, despite her neighbours constantly reminding her that with a low salary, the responsibility of three children with a wealthy, irresponsible father, living on her own, even though Mother was there, without a male family member, in Sana'a, this was a hard life. Eve looked at it as a blessing to be able to make ends meet, to have peace of mind, and to be able to make her children happy and safe. She was content to have the opportunity to work, allowing her to take care of her children, she counted, *felt* every blessing. She had anticipated a bleak future ahead for her children, viewed from a very dark place, the places she had been kept in. With God's grace she had saved them from that dire path.

Having so much ambition and indefatigable productivity, which had lain dormant for a decade, she poured it all into work and only a few months into her first year of employment a Sales Manager of one of the companies noticed her skills in correcting and modifying letters and faxes she typed for them; bringing to their attention serious, not to mention costly, mistakes they would have made had she not spotted them, and her willingness to accept more work. He taught her about the activities of the company he worked for and gave her work to do for him, and she completed the assignments outstandingly. He was so impressed he spoke to his manager, and told her if she continued to perform like this, she would be promoted to their company. She wanted it so much: to belong to only one company, not be divided between many—where all work you produce as the secretary is considered somebody else's result. To be able to stand behind a finished piece of work was what she wanted. Surely, by the end of the first year she was promoted. It felt great achieving and reaching set goals, to go on towards her other goals in life.

Day by day her contentment with life grew, she had enrolled into college, was acquiring skills and know-how in work, gaining qualifications all while being with her children; she was starting foundations for her life and for her children's future.

Bellicose Adam refused to pay Layth's school fees, and absolutely objected to Nadine and Munwa having an education, his explanation, well, they were girls so they didn't need an education. Eve had to take Layth out of his current school and find a private school with tuition she could afford for all three. With Adam not being in Yemen, it was like he didn't exist at all, she would forget completely and absolutely about him until his rare phone call and all she could feel towards him ranged in shades of dull greys grading into black between indifference and absolute disgust. He refused completely to take any responsibility for his children or pay for any of their needs, he only wanted to talk about how much he 'loved' her. After many efforts trying to make him understand love was not just words but actions, and part of the action would be to take care of his children and show responsibility towards them, she ended up frustrated knowing he would never be a responsible father. She spoke to one of her female friends at work about wanting a divorce and asked if she knew of a good lawyer.

"No, no!" responded Nada "You have three children, don't get divorced! Anyway, when men find out you're divorced they'll try to take advantage of you! And you know even if you do get a lawyer and go to court, the judge will probably rule in favour of your husband that you stay his wife and it won't be quick, you'll be in court forever. Judges and lawyers can be bribed by your husband and you'll lose in all situations. Don't do that, don't get a divorce, think about your children."

Eve knew it could be impossible for someone else to understand why she had to get the divorce, but their understanding didn't matter, but she was quite surprised at her female colleague's reaction and opinion, especially because she was an architect, an educated woman. Eve was offended by the suggestion, which was a common belief among some women in the city, that a divorced woman was an easily accessible pre-perforated route to pleasure, her virginity being no longer a barrier—didn't they know a woman's chastity was her defence whether the blushing virgin or the experienced divorcee? It was her honour which would protect her from men's advances (no camel would be passing through her carmine needle-eye). But she had heard from many people getting a divorce initiated by a woman was deemed unsavoury by judges, and women languished in courts for years and years without achieving it, this concerned her greatly. Maybe it would be better to wait until Adam got tired of her constant rejections and eventually divorced her of his own accord.

CHAPTER TWENTY-TWO

I T WAS THE LAST DAY IN RAMADAN, TRANQUILLITY AND PIETY
emulsified with the air, it penetrated your skin and filled your soul
and flowed out into the atmosphere, you could feel the holiness.
The next day would be Eid and the public holiday had already begun.
Eve enjoyed the days off with her children and their excitement
towards Eid, for her the month of Ramadan had the same flavour as
her childhood Christmas seasons, the same peace, jollity and goodwill
all around. The whistles of a joyful bird filled the apartment, it was
the doorbell ringing, Eve answered and the smile fell off her face. To
her dismay and resentment, the last day of Ramadan arrived with a
smiling Adam at the door. She closed it, Adam came closer, putting
his hands around her waist he tried to kiss her, but she turned her
cheek and arched her back, pushing him away with both hands and
walked off, leaving him where he stood in the foyer.

"See your daughter," Adam complained to Mother "I haven't
seen her in a long time and still she won't greet me!"

Mother was now fully aware of who he was, she had witnessed
her daughter's constant pleas to him to send money for his children's
expenses, and watched her daughter and grandchildren go without
food and necessities before she earned enough, she had seen his
outright irresponsibility as a father and husband, and it was enough
for her to stay silent and no longer take sides with him.

Her phone rang several times, colleagues wishing Eve a happy
Eid. Adam's face clouded with jealousy, even when her female friends

called. Eve had made it clear to him they were not to argue in front of the children, but Adam would neglect Eve's precaution not to disrupt her children's peace, raising his voice and picking fights in front of them.

"Adam—in the diwan, not in front of the children." Eve said, her face was so tense he understood if he mentioned one more word in front of them, no good would come of it. He left the room and headed to the diwan. She found him sitting in the window sill, smoking a cigarette, looking out of the window oblivious to the leafed branches of peach and fig trees in the garden shaking their fingers in the breeze. The diwan was sunlit, the red, green, yellow and blue tainted glass qamariyas sent a colourful sense of fresh brightness throughout the room which clashed with the tension and grimness under the roof. He put out the cigarette.

"We have to put an end to this," said Eve not sitting down "And it has to be civilised and peaceful. Adam, divorce me."

"I will never divorce you," said Adam "You're mine."

Eve was sick of hearing this phrase, she had heard it a lot throughout her life.

"I'm not yours," she said "I never was. According to our religion forced marriages are invalid."

"You love me," he said "You want me. *You have to obey me*. You will treat me like a husband!"

"We can't live together," said Eve "We will never *be* together. It's almost been thirteen years, we have this conversation over and over again. There's nothing in this world that will change how we feel— please leave me to bring my children up in peace."

"You're mine!" said Adam, becoming more exasperated by each second passing "You love me! *You love me!*"

"You know I can't stand you," said Eve "We haven't had sex in five years—if I loved you, do you think we'd be like this?"

"I want to, but you refuse," he said his chest heaving with a sigh, his body tingling and aching all over remembering her sultry, insatiable, indefatigable concupiscence when she had been his playful princess high upon a mountain top whose eyes had always searched westwards after something obscure by the Red Sea, "I want you."

"*I don't want you.*" she said.

"I can take you now by force," he threatened "I'm your husband and you're my wife!"

"And I can kill you, defending myself from being raped." she said.

His eyes widened from the seriousness of her tone and face. "Who's tricking you?" said Adam "Who's changing you?"

"No one," said Eve "I've never wanted you—you simply chose not to listen to me the whole time. I've always been your prisoner, but now you have to hear me because I'm not in captivity—I'm a free woman. Divorce me."

"Oh my God, somebody's put a black magic spell on you!" he said pressing the top of his hair and his forehead with one hand "It's why you're like this—you're under a spell!"

Eve grinned in pain at his absurdity. "There's no magic, no spell," she said, sighing, "Please listen and be reasonable, don't start talking nonsense and imagining a past that never existed. Let's agree to talk about three things, you and me, our children and divorce."

"I'm listening." he said, but his impatient face expressed he wanted her side of the conversation to be over already.

"I was forced to marry you as a child," she said "I've grown up and know I don't have to be your wife. I have never loved you. You obviously don't love me…"

"I do love you," Adam interrupted, bursting into tears "I love you more than anything on this earth!"

"You don't love me," said Eve "Love is more than just words, *this isn't an Egyptian movie.* You kept me a prisoner in the mountains for eight years, you didn't allow me to finish my education or even live in the comfort of the city. By an act of God I was allowed to leave the mountains to live in Saudi, but even there you tortured us. I will never forgive you for what you did to my children…You told me you'd make me drink from a cup more bitter than myrrh and it's the only promise you ever kept. I wanted to divorce you more than anything in the world, but because I put my children's lives before mine I believed you understood the seriousness of how being a father is important for them, and I believed you would take good care of them and be part of their lives, but you didn't. When you call you don't want to talk to them, you only want to talk to me and you don't want to discuss anything serious and real. You're *not* a father, you don't behave like a father. You're just like your mother…she has no motherly instincts and feelings for her children and you have no paternal feelings for yours. You're not even up to your responsibilities, if you don't love them at least be responsible for them financially—after all, you did bring them into this world. Make sure they have food to eat, clothes to wear, give them an education, but no—you even refused to pay Layth's school fees and you said the girls don't need an education. You know, I would've put up with you forever in Saudi if you'd been good to your children…"

Adam blinked and lowered his head, as if he could suddenly see where he could have made things right, where it would have been wise to stop obdurate revenge.

"Anyway, it's over," Eve continued "You have to divorce me. *Divorce me, marry another woman who will love you.* Think about it Adam… divorce me and marry a woman who will make you happy and love you." she willed and wished so hard to get this message into his brain, it almost felt she could psychokinetically will him into doing so.

"I don't want another woman," said Adam "I want *you!*"

"You will never have me." she said

"We've been married for thirteen years!" he said

"On paper, a date on a document," said Eve "Only two years consecutively under one roof Adam and it was like living in hell. Adam, I don't want you in my life, let's divorce like normal people."

"You're mine. You are mine." said Adam, he seemed unable to say anything else, "I will never give you a divorce."

"You will eventually divorce me," said Eve "You have to. When you see that you'll never touch me, I will never give myself to you— why would any man stay married to a woman who doesn't want him?" She waited for a response, he just stared at her grinding his jaws in anger.

"Now, our children," said Eve "You've made them suffer a lot and you refuse to pay for their education or any of their expenses.

They should be receiving the best education you could give them, not an education I can only afford, which just isn't good enough."

"I don't care," said Adam "They're not my responsibility." This got underneath Eve's skin, how easily he forgot the trouble he went to in order to have offspring. She took a deep breath.

"You're their father," she said "Of course you have a responsibility towards them."

"They're not my responsibility—I will not give a Rial!" He made such a face that said a childish 'so there' it clashed with his mature age, she just wanted to slap it, but she restrained herself. At least physically.

"You were as fertile as an impotent man without testicles," she said "*But you went and got medical treatment*—you should have thought about responsibility before going to the doctor!"

"I will never divorce you!" he said his chest heaving harder. He glowered then a forced grin appeared on his face, "I know important people," he said, and took out of his wallet a business card of a VIP in Yemen and handed it to Eve who looked at it indifferently and returned it. "They can help me make you kneel at my feet." he continued.

Eve snorted a laugh, did he think flashing someone's name would intimidate her? "You might have someone's business card," she said "But I have God. He will protect me and my children from you…But tell me, does it make you proud or insult you, to say you'll ask men to help you intimidate me? What kind of a man are you?"

"I'm your husband!" he shouted, aggravated she showed no fear, no submission, "You cannot talk to me like this! I forbid you to work! I order you to obey me! I can go to the police and they can force you to obey me!"

"Do you think I'm stupid?" said Eve losing her composure "Do you think I don't understand the law and rights? Do you think I believe your lies? I'm not stuck in the mountains where I can't tell the truth from the lies!"

Adam looked at her, despise and hate surfacing on his face "That's the problem," he said "You're educated. That's the problem—you understand, you think, you analyse, you want to make your own decisions. If you weren't educated, if you were illiterate like the other women, I wouldn't have this problem!"

"Educated? Hah!" said Eve, how it burned, "Problem?! Easy— divorce me, end of problem! Marry illiterate woman—be happy!" and their voices rose as they shouted and argued fiercely.

That evening Adam eyed Eve while the latter focused on TV, how deliciously she dressed in her dusky-rose fishtail evening gown, her beautiful impeccable dark curls cascading down her back, the slender neck he loved to kiss and bite, her small smooth shoulders he would embrace pressing her swelling bosoms against his bare chest while with lip, tongue and nose he would suck up the honey of her mouth and inhale every one of her sweet exhalations. Having worked himself into a frenzy he could no longer think of anything but the throb being supplied from every vein in his body, it had swollen for too long with frustrated desire for this mermaid and it demanded to swim in her depths, but instead Eve watched, with her children and Mother, a re-run of a film about releasing an oversized black and white mammal from captivity—why couldn't she show the same empathy for him? Alas all he could do was observe her and absorb every detail of her nubile body and recall the same imagery when, alone, his hand would assuage his whale of accumulated ache.

The morning of Eid, Eve put on a happy face, not wanting to spoil the celebration for her children, but there was no diffusing the tension in the air. She was stressed and distressed with Adam's perturbing presence. The children went upstairs with the neighbours to enjoy the Eid related customs of greeting everybody and getting candy. Eve and Adam rowed. Mother tried to calm them down, but they both ignored her. He was still insisting on having sex as if all the years between them, all the bad things he had done and she had said to him, as if yesterday's conversation hadn't occurred.

"I want you to come to my bed right now," shouted Adam "Obey me!"

"Get out of this house!" shouted Eve.

"I want to make love to you," he said "Obey me!"

The shouting became louder.

"I can't stand the sight of you," said Eve "The smell of you makes me want to throw up, the sound of your voice makes me *hate you*! I'm telling you I hate you, you disgust me and listen to yourself!"

"You will obey me, you're my wife!"

"I'm not your wife," she said "Get out! Leave!"

"You're my wife, I bought you with my money!"

"Go get a refund, I didn't agree to the sale!" (Should've been labelled *caveat emptor*)

"You're mine! Mine!"

"Go to hell—you're not a man! I'm telling you I don't want you, I hate you. Do you have any respect for yourself? Do you have any dignity?"

"I'll send you to the House of Obedience!" he shouted.

Mother tried to quieten them all during the argument, following them from room to room as they quarrelled, waving her hands—a sea lion giving landing instructions to a plane—telling them to lower their voices that the neighbours could hear them, but neither cared and continued to argue so violently Adam left the house, stuffing what clothes he could into a suitcase, blinded by anger leaving half of them. Eve gathered the rest in her arms, not wanting a reason for him to return.

"You forgot these!" she shouted, throwing them out from the door, the clothes covered the steps, she slammed the door shut, not caring if he returned or not to pick them up. The relief she felt after closing the door was immense, she was still agitated by the experience, but at least he was out of the house.

Eve returned home from work one evening to find a government employee waiting to serve her a subpoena: to attend court under a request made by Adam to be forced to 'obey him' as his wife. Eve panicked, never did she think she would have to go to court, she had always believed no matter how long it would take, Adam would come to his senses and divorce her, which would entail writing out the divorce document and only going to court to get it stamped and legalised. She remembered what Nada the architect and other people told her, how long, hard and terrible getting a divorce through court is for women because judges were always on the husband's side; how women were humiliated in court just because they are female. Eve also remembered what she was told in the village and also here in Sana'a, something called 'the House of Obedience', Adam had threatened her with it many times: it was said that women whom didn't obey or want their husbands were sent to this prison called 'the House of Obedience' where they were beaten and tortured until their spirit broke and they agreed to be an obedient wife; most women left humiliated and tormented, broken spirited women, back to their husbands' houses. Eve didn't know if this was true, if such a place existed and was exercised or was just a myth to scare women, but the document the government employee showed her had the words of marital obedience, and it was enough to alarm her. Overwhelmed and scared by the possibility of being sent to such a place she searched for Yusef's number whom she hadn't called in years. She looked down at the name, her thumb on the dial button hesitating, she lowered her arm and looked down the street, many people had offered their assistance if she needed it and given her their numbers, they had told her to consider them her brothers and would be more than happy to help her out at any time of need, Yusef had asked her never to call him. It seemed too much to call a friend and bother them with such a personal issue, she just wanted the name and number of a good lawyer. The person who answered was a friend of his: Yusef was in Oman and would not be back for weeks, he called every night to check everything was alright, he would tell Yusef to call her.

Yusef received the message and called, having given her the contact details of a lawyer, he told her to wait until he returned in a few week's time so they could meet the lawyer together. Yusef's return coincided with Father coming to Sana'a. The three of them went to the lawyer's office. Eve sat between her father and brother on a leather sofa, the safest she had felt in years, but it was only temporary and false as neither would ever protect her. As they waited, she noticed the titles of the different business lawyers on the doors of the offices.

She sat in front of the lawyer's desk, informing him of the whole situation. She answered his questions. He was dark skinned, dark haired and wearing black framed glasses. He wore a modern business suit, but its colour was not right, a dull turquoise which could only have been popular in the sixties, but there was something about him, as if he'd been sucked through a time warp centuries ago and ended up here.

"I have to be honest with you," said the lawyer "You're in Yemen. Here, women are oppressed and judges are always on the husband's side because we're dealing with a closed mentality."

"Why?" said Eve.

"They believe if they allow many women to divorce their husbands," said the lawyer "It will be bad for society because many more women will follow suit."

"Don't the judges look into each case individually and decide what's right?" said Eve.

"You're in Yemen," said the lawyer "The judge will always be on the husband's side. I want you to be prepared we'll probably lose the case, you will remain his wife and the child expenses the judge will rule will be negligible."

"I'll lose the case?" said Eve "I've been done wrong and I can prove it. And how can the child support be trivial? The Quran says each person is to support his children according to his income—he's wealthy and he should support his children."

"Well, here in Yemen the court doesn't care if a child eats well," said the lawyer "They don't care if a child wears only a sack on his back and if they never go to school—the judge will see how much a quarter sack of flour and rice costs and order only that amount in payment is made, which is probably next to nothing compared to how much your children need and you spend. I'm telling you this so you be prepared. The judge will rule in favour of your husband so don't be surprised, and then we'll appeal. The judge will shout at you, humiliate you, he'll call you a liar, he will be very mean and rude to you, be prepared to hear a lot."

"How long could the case last in court if we're going to win?" she asked feeling a dark cloud choking her from the chest upwards.

"It could last forever," said the lawyer "They tend to allow things to drag on so it could last many, many years depending on the Judge and how he allows the trials to proceed, but we won't win."

Eve sat staring at the lawyer for ten seconds without saying a word, his attitude was grimmer than his clothes. She turned to look at her brother sitting silently and detached at the corner of the desk. Troubled and confused, she frowned as they went down the stairs—instead of reassuring, the lawyer had distressed her.

"Are you sure he's good?" said Eve "I mean you heard what he said, he doesn't sound good."

"He told me I could lie to your sister," said Yusef "And tell her yes we're going to win, but it's better she knows the truth so she doesn't get a shock later. He's being honest."

"But he hasn't looked into cases similar to mine," said Eve "So how can he have an answer so soon? He's already saying that I'll lose."

"He's probably done cases like this before." said Yusef.

"And evidently he's lost them all!" said Eve, they both laughed in the rain under grey sky.

"Did you hear what he said about judges and how they treat women?!" said Eve "Come on, they can't all be like that?"

"You're in Yemen," said Yusef "Expect anything." And he got into his car and headed off without offering them a lift. Eve and Father stood in the rain waiting for a taxi to stop. From the right window of the stuffy inside of the taxi Eve watched the rain and people going about their seemingly carefree lives, a thousand worries whirling through her heart and mind. Her father looked out of the left side, his mouth upturned, regrets surfacing on his face, how terrible this had all turned out. The voiceless emotions could be heard, she felt his remorse and he could feel her despair. They remained silent until half way home.

"This is all your fault," Eve said to Father calmly "The injustice you've caused me goes on and on…" They were silent the rest of the way.

*

"FATHER STAY," EVE SAID AS FATHER PACKED HIS BAG "COME TO court with me…"

"No, I have to go home." he said.

"Why?" she said "You don't have cows anymore."

"The house and land are alone." said Father.

"No dad, I'm alone," she said, and the tremor in her voice came from the cold shivering fear and worry she was filled with by having to go to a male-biased court where the balance of her life would be determined, where distortion had made man stand for more than a woman, and she needed her father and brothers to be with her, now envying the support her divorced friends and colleagues received whose fathers and brothers hadn't allowed them to even step into court and had represented them instead, sparing them the uncouth exposure and tribulations of trial, "I have no one to stand by me in court. Stay and support me, even if it's just sitting next to me."

"The house is alone and the land." he said.

"You didn't mind leaving the house and land for forty years when you went to live your life in Britain," said Eve "Dad, you owe this to me, I'm scared…"

Father dove into a solemn silence and left Sana'a the same day.

The lawyer's pessimism disturbed her. His dark prediction, his helplessness towards what he believed would happen made Eve feel he didn't know what he was doing. He gave her no strategy or plan of action as to how to win the case. He didn't tell her if he had prepared a reply against the claim made by Adam. Whenever she called, all he said was not to worry; he repeated the same gloomy conversation he had given her at his office. She told him she would not live with Adam even if the court ruled in his favour, and she wanted custody of her children and this was a must, but he replied that she would probably lose custody if she didn't live with her husband. By the time Eve put the mobile down on the desk, she was certain she didn't want this lawyer representing her. It was the only thing on her mind that evening, to terminate the authorisation and find a good lawyer so she arrived at his office the next day and informed him (lied that is) that her husband and she were sorting things out outside of court, then tore up the authorisation going down the stairs of the building, wondering if she had time to find an apt lawyer and be prepared before the hearing.

Through her contacts she met with a lawyer the same day and explained everything to him while the two lawyers working with him took notes, Eve was reassured, these people were obviously professionals. Ismael, the senior lawyer and head of the firm, reassured her she would win the case and custody of her children, he told her about a similar case he had represented, a girl also married as a minor and he had won the case for her; he even showed her the documents. He, No'man and Rasheed were appalled at what she had been through. They requested copies of documents, of the marriage contract, old and new passports, children's birth certificates, which she immediately pulled out of her handbag.

"You're very prepared for this." said Ismael surprised at her efficiency.

"Since the day I was married."

When Eve asked him about the fees, Ismael replied he was so touched by her story, he would do it for free. Though appreciating his kind gesture, Eve insisted on paying, but he refused saying as she was taking care of three children alone he would do the work for the Face of God so she called her friend, telling him she had to pay or she wouldn't be able to use their services, and a sum was agreed upon. The lawyers constantly contacted her to clarify information, Ismael called her and read excerpts from the response and claim for her to agree to or comment on. When both the response and claim for divorce were prepared he sent her copies. She read them and was pleased with what she saw, and called him to thank him. When the court date neared, they met at his office, he gave her some advice of what to expect, he didn't say anything bad about judges and more reassuringly he was confident and believed strongly in a positive outcome.

"There's just one thing…" said Ismael, "I think you should wear a face veil like all the other women who'll be in court."

"But I don't wear a face veil, I'd be a hypocrite to wear it to court."

"I appreciate your honesty, and that's why I believe in your case because you're an honest person. Honesty…" he said dwelling on the word "That's good, but all the women in court…their faces will be covered, we wouldn't want the judge to think….You know, you think about it. I strongly recommend you wear a niqab."

The request disturbed Eve. Why was it important to cover her face? Would the judge think she was immoral if she appeared in court with her face showing? She covered her body with a cloak and hair completely with a head veil, wasn't it modesty enough? If she wore a face veil only to court, then she would both look and feel pretentious, she would be uncomfortable portraying a lie. No, she would not cover her face.

CHAPTER TWENTY-THREE

T HE WIDE DIRT ROAD WAS SURROUNDED ON EITHER SIDE BY bleak looking residential buildings. The surrounding area looked haunted, as if people no longer lived there, despite the fact they did. The taxi stopped below a giant arch door, opened inwards and manned by two soldiers. The yard lead to a number of buildings around a courtyard. The main building for hearings was three-storey and rectangular, its outer walls the colour of sand and dust, the windows small. Its design was the same architecture of traditional buildings, but dreary as if it belonged to a yellowed photo from the past and upon entering the courtyard Eve felt she too had stepped into the past and become the same dusty sand yellow and in here her life became monochrome. She made her way through the crowd in the yard, the stairs were packed with men, the few women whom arrived were accompanied by male relatives and the men in the stairs parted for them to pass as the sea had for Moses. Eve had to go up the stairs, but the men did not move.

"Excuse me, I need to pass." she said again, still they didn't move. The corridors of the court were loud and grim: people arguing, some shouting insults at each other. It seemed all the people entering the premises had the same fatigued, worried expression of years spent in court on a matter which could have been easily resolved; a sense of hopelessness filled the air, it may never be resolved, pained, but unable to give up and having to see it through to the end. The employees were comfortably part of the furniture, sitting behind desks piled high with folders gathering dust while new dust particles chased each other in the sunbeam coming through a pokey window. Eve found the waiting room; the courtroom would remain closed until the Judge was ready to enter. When an employee stapled a handwritten table to the door she got up to see the list: her name and Adam's the fifth in turn—finally divorce was to become a reality. She sat back on the bench, noticing the men opposite staring at her, she looked to the other side of the room to break the intruding curiosity with movement only to find those on the other side staring at her too, uncomfortable from the unblinking gazes she got up to look for her lawyer and found him arriving. He reassured her again, not to worry. The clerk unlocked the courtroom door, Eve sat in the front row with her lawyers. The Judge entered as the clerk announced him, and everybody stood up, a short, but lean man in his forties, his dark moustache and goatee impeccably groomed, he wore a traditional long brown coat over a white dress, his silvered head neatly wrapped in a cream and purple patterned head shawl. The clerk called out the names of both sides for each case, both parties approached the bench and stood at opposite sides. Eve thought everyone would leave when her turn came, leaving only she and her lawyers, Mahmood, now working in Sana'a (his shock of unruly hair now tamed into a suave haircut), and Adam's lawyer (both authorised to represent Adam in his absence) as she had requested from her lawyers a private session, but as her name was called and she approached the bench she turned to see everybody still sitting and watching. Mortified she would be explaining private details of her life in front of strangers, she felt her chest tighten.

"My client, Adam Suleiman, is a religious man," said Adam's lawyer "A good person and hardworking. He gave everything to make his wife and children happy. He provided them with everything they needed and more, but his wife, Eve Zakaria, chose to stray. She chose to throw away the blessings which he provided them with and leave her children unattended to and spend all day in work, a job she does not need, morning and evening. Her children are lost. They do not have a mother to take care of them! My client demands you obligate his wife to leave the employment, employment she sought without his approval, and enforce she stays at home to attend to her children. He also requests her mother be removed from their home as she is the cause of all problems between the daughter and my client,"

If only Mother could hear this, how offended she would be, Eve toyed with the idea of telling her just to show her how wrong she had been all this time, but decided not to mention this accusation to avoid hurting her feelings, though she had always supported Adam, fiercely attacking Eve's requests since she was fourteen years old.

"Our Yemeni law," Adam's lawyer continued "Is taken from our Sharia'a and Holy Quran which condemns the irresponsible actions of women whom stray from their homes. Islam prohibits the breaking and dissolvement of marriage; especially a marriage which has resulted in three children. Sir Judge, I demand my client's wife be compelled to leave her job, stay at home, take care of her children and obey her husband and satisfy his needs at his request."

"What do you or your client have to say?" said The Judge giving Eve a quick and penetrating look with his wisened eyes.

"Sir Judge," said Ismael "I implore you and the opposing attorney to read again our response to their *false claim*. I also urge you and the opposing attorney to read the request of my client for a dissolution of marriage, a divorce which is not prohibited by religion as the other party mentioned, but a divorce which our Prophet, may prayers and peace be upon him, declared permissible and the best solution to a failed marriage. A marriage which my client refused and was led to like a lamb to its slaughter, when her brutal father forced her into an unwanted marriage, a child not fit for sexual activity at the hands of a grown man twice her age. In fact, it would have been more merciful of her father to have picked up a knife and cut open her throat instead of the suffering and pain she had to endure!" Ismael went on to paint Agnus' suffering of thirteen years: being kept against her will in the village, the suffering in Saudi. He pointed out she had been underage making the marriage invalid, and her father and in-law's forgery and deceit falsifying her as seventeen years of age on the marriage contract when actually she was just a young girl, wanting to play and study; how the plaintiff had taken advantage of her young age and raped her; her lawyer emphasised on how she had been raped although she was still a little girl, not a fully grown woman who would desire sexual activity; he went on explaining because of the culture of tradition, misleading concepts and false beliefs practised in villages they led his client to believe females were not allowed to request or apply for divorce; his client at that young age was a prisoner of unjust, captive circumstances which led her into a type of nervous breakdown which was more like a case of madness; how the plaintiff took her to Saudi but purposely made her suffer more resulting in her hate for him intensifying. Ismael pointed out how Adam had broken the law by putting her into unliveable living conditions. He stated how his client had vowed and not allowed the plaintiff to be intimate with her since 1998, comparing her abstinence to Mahatma Ghandi's and a mystical Rabia'a Aladawiyah (although a silent, but thoroughly embarrassed, modest Eve could not see the similarities). Ismael pointed out Eve had three legal reasons to dissolve the marriage, and each reason alone was enough for its dissolvement: first her young age at marriage, during which the legal marriage age was fifteen years of age (fifteen?!), but she was still fourteen; and he added the argument that although this law had been amended in 1999 to lower the age of marriage (lower it! Can you believe?!) her marriage happened during its effectivity and even after amendment it stated 'the guardian of a young girl may enter the marriage contract on her behalf, but the male partner cannot have sexual intercourse with her, she cannot be sent to his house for marriage until she has reached the age to be prepared for sexual intercourse even if older than fifteen years of age'; secondly the long years of absence of husband allows the wife to dissolve the marriage; and finally the hate his client feels for the plaintiff makes it impossible for her to stay and live with him under one roof, which makes it imperative to dissolve the marriage to enforce God's rules because when marital life becomes differences, wars, chronic hatred, a hell, a disease and unbearable unhappiness, and God Almighty has warned and prohibited the continuance of such a living, the husband has to divorce her willingly or the marriage contract will be dissolved by the court.

The clerk wrote everything said while both lawyers spoke, the seasoned Judge listened. Eve stood and all the people sitting behind her watched on. To Eve's disappointment the Judge stated though it was illegal to have entered Eve into marriage while she was only fourteen, the thirteen years of marriage had validated the marriage contract (which shattered Eve's hope (and heart) of a one hearing divorce based on that fact, for where was validity when this injustice had been impaled upon her?).

*

THE NEXT HEARING, ADAM'S LAWYER INSISTED EVE WAS MADLY IN love with Adam, then and now. Did she love the plaintiff, the Judge wanted to know from Eve. Nope, she couldn't stand him. But they were claiming they loved each other, insisted the Judge. If it were true, responded Eve with the obvious, then why was he dragging her through court, they had reached court publicly displaying sensitive issues which should've stayed private because they hated each other. Adam's lawyer counter attacked (with lies) the proof of his client's love for Eve was in the fictitious fact that he provided her with everything she needed, sends a large monthly allowance and furnished the house with the most expensive furniture. Eve explained the real situation.

"My client requests she stop working with immediate effect so she can free herself to take care of her children," said Adam's Lawyer "He didn't give her permission to work."

"My client informed the plaintiff of her studies so she could find a job later," said Ismael "He took no legal action to stop her. She also informed him she was looking for work and when she found work she told him, it's been more than a year since she started employment and he didn't take her to court over it, why is it only now he has a problem?"

"She works a morning shift and a night shift," said Adam's lawyer "She confirmed this in the last hearing."

"Do you work two shifts?" said the Judge.

"I start work at eight a.m.," said Eve "and finish five p.m., I…"

"Ah, you see!" interrupted Adam's lawyer "She throws her children and neglects them all day!"

"He interrupted me." said Eve quite flabbergasted by the rudeness of the opposing lawyer.

"Be quiet, let her finish." said the Judge.

"I leave for work the same time my children leave for school," said Eve "They come back home at two p.m., I come back at five p.m. We only have three hours apart when I'm at work and they're at home. My mother lives with me, she brought me up and now she takes care of them while I'm still at work for three hours. My mother is as if I'm at home with them."

"I demand she be made to leave her work." said Adam's lawyer. They obviously wanted her self-sufficiency taken away thinking she would return to Adam if penniless.

"I have to work," said Eve "My so-called husband doesn't provide for my children nor does he provide for me. I don't do anything forbidden. If I don't work, my children and I will end up on the streets and be exposed to dangers."

Adam had been wasting both his time and energy thinking about her too much, sending text messages since the court case began: either poems about how much he 'loved' her which amused her because if he lied to people, lied to his lawyer—alright, but why was he fabricating an existence between them when they both knew the reality of their relationship? Sending messages how it was other people tricking Eve and deceiving her out of loving him, how 'jealous' people were using magic to make her hate him. Then there were the disturbing messages of abducting and killing her and the children so she asked her lawyer if she could use them in court, but he replied there was no way of proving they were sent from him despite being sent from a Saudi number. And with his continuous threats she became extremely paranoid over her children's safety—as what father could think, let alone type such terrible things about his own children, she knew they meant nothing to him, which he had proved time after time, but to threaten them was just despicable and her worry for her children's safety would become an unhealthy paranoia she would forever be unable to rid herself of.

The court hearings never seemed to end and Eve attended every single one. Her pensive eyes noticed all the women with court cases were accompanied by at least one male companion, while she was the only female arriving and sitting alone. Though now a strong and independent individual known in her community for her tenacity and ability to handle and cope with tough living situations and anything life threw at her, seemingly sangfroid in dangerous situations, capable to rear three children single handedly leaving nothing unattended to or unprovided for; known as a tough (but fair) leader at work now in charge of a team of thirteen (and initially uncooperative to being bossed by a woman (especially one whom had begun work at a much lower position than they)) men, supervising they implemented her marketing and sales strategies, how lonely she felt in court, unloved by her own family. They used to love her, all of them. They used to be so proud of her too. Where had it all gone? She could trace where it all went wrong; when her family became dismembered and numbed, it began after her marriage, her brothers had become bitter and violent towards each other from the roughness of the mountains, they just couldn't handle the harshness and immense difference of way of life from Britain. Then Suleiman and his family started whispering poisons into Morad's ear, when Morad became wealthy, and his heart and blood clouded with hatred and his soul distanced from his family, starting with Father, Mother and eventually even Eve; Father had made things worse by mistreating Morad and it helped Suleiman manipulate the latter to Suleiman's own benefit. Then as her brothers left the mountains, one by one, the distance and time seemed to create a much greater aloofness towards her and a rift between them which would never seal. She was no longer the loved daughter, nor the cherished, dear sister. There was always too much time and loneliness waiting for the courtroom to open and she was unable not to reflect on how she had gotten here. Sometimes older men carrying documents approached her, sitting at a respectable distance, asking for advice on legal matters, and if she could represent their case. Only for her to inform them she wasn't a lawyer.

"You have a case?" said the stranger "What case could you have? Aren't you too young to have problems?"

Eve chatted with a lady whose case coincided with the dates of her hearings. Nagat was also trying to get a divorce, her husband never paid for his daughters' expenses, aged twelve, fourteen and seventeen; on the contrary he went to their school whenever he wanted money from his wife, he beat and humiliated them in front of the whole school and took them away, disrupting their lives. She had sold her gold and opened a beauty salon to avoid him draining her resources so she could take care of her children.

Most of the time Eve sat in the back row of the courtroom observing everything. A couple who had been arguing in the waiting room, still argued in front of the courtroom door. The wife was completely covered in black, but Eve could tell from her tiny figure and the tone of her voice she couldn't be older than sixteen or seventeen years of age. The balding husband slapped her across the face then punched her in the stomach, nobody moved a finger to stop him assaulting her, not even the armed guard; not even when she was on the ground being kicked in the stomach. Eve got up, Nagat grabbed her by the arm, pulling her back into her seat as an old lady said: "No, no! Don't interfere! They're family."

"He's beating her!" said Eve.

"It will affect your case and what the Judge decides about you!"said Nagat.

The clerk called out the same pair of names four times. The man left his wife on the corridor floor and walked in, pulling down at his shirt and huffing, as if beating her had been an inconvenience. The young wife followed and stood before the Judge, shaking and crying, doubling over as she clutched her stomach in pain.

"I want a divorce," said the young wife "I want a divorce!"

"Be quiet!" said the Judge.

The young wife continued to babble, she was trying to say something, but was so hysterical nobody could understand her.

"Shut up, you stupid woman," shouted the Judge "You don't even know how to speak!"

The majority of men in the courtroom laughed, including the violent husband. All the heads covered in black veils and niqabs lowered slightly, their shoulders rose and dropped with a deep sigh; the blade of insult and unfairness stung them too. Eve was furious and helpless, she felt muscles in her body twitch involuntarily as she suppressed her anger from translating into speech. She had noticed although the Judge always remained polite and civilised with her and other women whom remained calm, with others who became agitated or hysterical when provoked, he dealt with roughly. Maybe because they interrupted and didn't wait until the other person finished speaking, or did not wait until they were asked a question. Maybe because when they spoke they went off-point or became so shy they hardly said anything at all. Or maybe because they fell into the trap of the 'husband' or husband's lawyer whom purposely provoked them and they reacted shouting, but it was no excuse for them to be treated with less patience. This young girl had been beaten outside the courtroom door and now she was being humiliated. No wonder so many women give up on court and end up living a whole life of misery and drudgery, with no way out of a bad marriage. Adam's lawyer was a sly, uncivil person, he even looked as if he'd walked straight out of a cave and put on a garish shirt and trousers, he always tried to needle Eve, but she always kept her cool (while fuming internally and wanted nothing more than to beat the crap out of him). During one hearing he was able to goad Eve's lawyer, so it diverted from the divorce and marital obedience and became a loud contest about which lawyer knew law better, it concluded with a fight to be held outside the court yard which, as Eve was leaving saw, the subordinate lawyers of Ismael dragged their boss away from to prevent him engaging in fighting. It annoyed her, there was definitely a double standard, the Judge had two different styles for dealing with the same incident: if men shouted or ranted, he used the ink pad like a gavel to quieten them down, but if it was a female outburst he shouted at her. Demeaning. Women were always made to feel wrong. This atmosphere created by male dominance could be felt throughout the court. Wrong that she was in court. *Wrong* to speak out. *Wrong* to want divorce. *Wrong* to defend herself. *She shouldn't be here.* She should be at home, taking care of children, cooking, cleaning, serving her ungrateful husband, even if he was a violent, good for nothing piece of trash. Away and hidden from the eyes and ears of justice. If she was so brash as to want to divorce, then she had better be prepared to go through hell to get it. Or give up and go home, obedient wife. This projection of women requesting divorce as immoral was applied onto women throughout society, not just in court; even other women made females feel bad about seeking divorce. But once you were in court they spewed it until a woman wasn't just covered by her cloaks and sharshafs, but an invisible coat of slime. Of immorality. It always felt wrong to be there. All a man had to do was say 'You are divorced' to his wife and it was the end of the story, he didn't have to be dragged through years of court to prove why he wanted divorce, it was not for women to question; he said it was the end, and that was it. But a woman to want a divorce, what was she up to? How dare she embarrass her husband and family by requesting such a thing? Did she have lovers? Wanted to run away with another man? Was she possessed by a devil? Or did she want to disintegrate the very fabric of society founded on marriage and staying at home? Surely she had followed the path of the Shaytaan, or someone was playing with her mind. How wicked and disgusting for wanting to break the laws of Islam. These men failed, became blind, to the fact Islam gave women the right to a fast and peaceful divorce. If justice were blind to ensure fairness in other parts of the world, in Yemen justice had become blind only to women's rights, unable to serve them any form of justice without making them jump through hoop after hoop of fire.

*

NONE OF EVE'S LAWYERS SHOWED UP.

"I'm going to be late," her lawyer said over the phone "I have a hearing at a different court. Ask him to make us the last."

Eve had seen Mahmood delay hearings when his lawyer was absent, when the clerk announced their names, Mahmood approached the bench and told them his lawyer would be late and to make their hearing the last and the Judge always agreed. The clerk called out their names. Eve approached the bench.

"My lawyer is late," said Eve "But he will be coming. Can you make our hearing last, please?"

"No," said the Judge sternly "Let us proceed."

Eve was shocked (you could tell by the funny (maybe not for you Eve) circular shape of her eyes and open mouth), she could not help but feel something was wrong, and they were to carry on without her lawyer present. She looked towards the door. No lawyer.

"Sir Judge," said Adam's lawyer "I request you reject the claim to dissolve the marriage and endorse the marital obedience claim immediately. My client is a good husband and his wife is following the way of the Devil. She is compromising herself by working with men, my client disapproves of it, his blood boils because of this mingling. She's neglecting her children, throwing them all day with an old woman who can't take care of herself, we demand she stay at home or the children be placed in their father's custody."

"The children are with their mother's mother," said the Judge "If the father was to take custody, and he's in Saudi, who would take care of them?"

"The mother of my client," said Adam's lawyer "My client and his wife are in love, but somebody is playing with her head. It is the duty of the court to enforce our Islamic way of law and make her leave her job, stay at home, take care of her children and most importantly, obey her husband. If you don't stop her, you will be allowing the intrusion of strange ways of life into our Islamic community and our society will rot with intrusive new trends, not part of our culture."

Eve's frustrations fumed inside her, the hearings were not about presenting facts, Adam's amoral lawyer always made them about Eve's morality where he tried to paint her as ethically weak (if spontaneous human combustion were real she would have burst into a veritable ball of flames).

"Do you have something to say?" said the Judge.

"Sir Judge," said Eve "I work in a respectful company, with respectful people. I earn a living to provide for my children. There are women working in every part of Yemen alongside men in every kind of activity, but because we work it doesn't mean we're immoral. Should women who have to work stay at home and let their children starve to death just because the father chooses to neglect them? My mother is strong and in good health, just like she took care of me when I was a child, she will look after my children for the few hours before I return from work. Their father doesn't love or care for them, he's only trying to get custody to hurt me and I don't believe it's his idea to ask for their custody because he always tells me they're not his responsibility. He thinks if you give him custody of my children I'll go back to him. He doesn't care about his children's wellbeing, he never sends them money. His mother claims to be blind and cannot take care of herself, and she never took proper care of her own children even when she could see."

"Is it true?" said the Judge "Is your mother blind?"

"Yes." said Mahmood.

"I'm a good mother," Eve continued "My children are doing very well in my custody. I take good care of them and they're happy. Please don't make my children suffer just because Adam can't accept I'll never be his wife."

"Ha! You are his wife!" said Adam's lawyer glaring at Eve.

Eve kept looking at the Judge and replied with equanimity: "Just because there's a piece of paper saying from a certain date I'm married to Adam, it doesn't mean I'm his wife. I was forced into marriage."

"If she doesn't love him," said Adam's lawyer "Where did the children come from? The children are proof of love!" someone in the audience laughed.

"I was a young lady in a closed room with a strong man," said Eve "Love has nothing to do with it."

"Sir Judge," said Adam's lawyer "I demand this woman be made to obey her husband and satisfy his wishes!"

"I will never," said Eve "I hate him."

"Sir Judge I have spoken a lot with my client, his wife doesn't treat him like a husband—he couldn't even stay in the house he's renting!" said Adam's lawyer "He arrived the last day of Ramadan and they argued all day and all the next day and he ended up leaving the house because she doesn't obey him and they argue all the time!"

"Yes, that's right," Eve said, failing to conceal a smile as his last comments were proving her point, "We argue all the time. We can't stay under one roof because we hate each other. What he just said is true, Adam had to leave because we argue until it becomes unbearable to stay in the house. But *I* pay the rent."

"Sir Judge, women are to satisfy their husband's needs," said Adam's lawyer "My client hasn't been allowed to approach his wife since the year 1998! How can this be allowed?! She's his wife and she must come to his bed!"

"Is this true?" said the Judge sternly looking at Eve.

"Yes, I can't sleep with him," said Eve hating to talk with males about taboo sex in the male filled courtroom "My skin crawls when I see him."

"Do you know the angels curse the wife all night until morning if she refuses to sleep with her husband?" said the Judge.

"It's different in my case Sir Judge," said Eve, exasperation building in her chest, "I didn't agree to be his wife, I don't want to be his wife, I just need to make it official on paper. I can't be in the same room as him, how do you expect me to allow him to touch me?"

Eve always went home after the hearing to change, too depressing to stay in the same clothes she wore to court. She told Mother what happened at the hearing as she changed, and Mother would say a strong prayer for her before she headed off to work.

Court hung over Eve like a dark cloud. The day before going to court she was agitated and the morning of the hearing, depressed. She had thought it would take two or three hearings to get the divorce with all the abundant evidence at hand, but the hearings went on and on, with no sign of ending. The Judge allowed Adam's lawyer to delay and keep the hearings lingering on by introducing nonsense without a shred of evidence. Hearsay was allowed as was repeating issues already discussed. Eve was distressed why the Judge allowed for too much nonsense and irrelevant issues to be deliberated.

*

LIGHT FLASHED THROUGH THE GAPS OF THE PHOTOCOPIER LID. Eve's colleagues drank coffee and read the newspapers in the morning as she made copies of documents. Sabeel sipped at his tea and said: "Ah, have you heard about this, the judicial change?"

"What?" said Zaki.

"A judicial change," said Sabeel "There's going to be a complete change."

"Oh no," said Zaki "I've been in court forever with our case, now it's going to start from scratch again?!" Alarmed, Eve left the copier and took the newspaper

"Here, see…" said Sabeel.

Eve read the article, the government was trying to tackle corruption and improve its judicial practice by changing out the judges and court employees to different areas than their current.

"They'll finish the cases they're already in the middle of, right?" said Eve.

"Probably not." said Sabeel.

"But any new Judge will start from the stopping point of the previous Judge," said Eve "They wouldn't waste people's lives."

"You know," said Sabeel "Here in Yemen everybody new wants to scratch everything and start from the beginning, it's why our country's so behind…the new ministers don't follow through previous ministers' projects and start again. Of course the new Judges will want to hear the cases from the beginning."

News of the change of Judges spread, people worried their time spent in court was all in vain. Every honest person who wouldn't buy a ruling with money, those who had no money or had no strong connection with high officials, were worried if a change of Judge happened, what if the replacement Judge was corrupt? What if the replacement judge was an unjust dictator? The next time Eve attended court, it was what all the people in the yard, in the stairs, corridors and waiting rooms talked about. It had always been loud and bustling in court, but with an undertone of dejection and helplessness, but today the undercurrent was full of agitation and concern. Eve had asked her lawyers about it the same day she read the article, they confirmed if a new Judge was appointed for the area, the case would most probably be heard again from the beginning, as a new Judge would not want to take the history from the records, but to hear everything himself, to form his own opinion of the case. It did worry Eve, at night she prayed to God asking Him the court give a ruling before the Judge changed, it seemed such a great waste of life, all those unpleasant hearings to become meaningless. Not just for her, the court was always overflowing with people and their cases, people and their lives. The problem in the courts of Yemen was once you entered, you never seemed to leave, a throbbing headache which never dulled and never went away. The court system, judges and pugnacious parties unnecessarily prolonged cases, which is why many people used traditional channels to resolve issues regarding divorce, land and inheritance outside of court—it was quicker and more efficient to use the noble, tribal arbitration method. Court was an unpleasant, dragging, life consuming whirlpool, you only entered if left without option or dragged into it by the opposing party, as was Eve's case. She would have been happy to stay out of court and keep Adam away until he divorced her, or dropped dead. He would have had to, eventually. If only you could see kind hearted and morally infused Eve writhing in remorse and repentance after asking God to dispose of her husband for she wanted him out of her life, but without dispatching him herself (Oh the duplicity, Eve!), whether by accident (they do happen all the time) or a swift disease (as painless as possible God, if you please). Deep down she knew this wasn't true because he would have constantly kept bothering her, even if she was only a wife on paper—now she could keep him out of the house even if he came to Yemen so this bad thing he had done to her by requesting 'marital obedience' through court had actually turned into a good thing: after all the terrible things she'd heard about courts and seeking divorce and corruption, she probably would never have initiated at the current time a divorce in court and would be waiting for it to just happen and from her own fear, she would have prolonged her own suffering. Her children's suffering. Now she had been thrown into the sea of court to swim, she was determined to emerge with her divorce. Her freedom. An unpleasant experience, but a necessary one. Too many people coming to court with cases were uncivil and so different to the people Eve worked with so she started arriving early, before the yard and stairs crowded with men whom only made way for men. She took her training manuals and college books to read, to kill time and make use of the long wait, not to mention to avoid the stares.

A few weeks passed and the newspapers still spoke of the change of judges. Eve arrived at court, outside and in, unusually empty.

"Are you sure?" she had said over the phone to No'man "We've never had a hearing on a Wednesday."

"This is the date they provided at the last hearing," said No'man "I'll be in a different court and as soon as I finish, I'll meet you there."

Sumaiya arrived, she'd met Eve a few weeks ago in the waiting room. Sumaiya was also seeking divorce having married a person whom turned out to be different than how he had presented himself prior and during the engagement.

"He was polite and kind," said Sumaiya "He seemed to be decent, after we married I found out he drinks. I thought he would straighten out. We had two children and he got worse, he became a drunk and he wants anal sex!"

"Do you let him?" asked Eve, quite shocked.

"No of course not!" said Sumaiya squirming in her seat "But that's not why I want divorce. It's because he doesn't provide for me or his children and he beats me!"

"Do you have a good lawyer?" said Eve.

"I don't," said Sumaiya "I can't afford one. That's my father over there, do you see him? I work in a hotel and my father's trying to suck me dry because I need his help. The money isn't enough for my own needs, I've even given my children to my mother in Hodeida, but she wants to send them back."

"Your children aren't with you?" said Eve, feeling terribly hurt for her, "That must be hard for you."

"Not really," said Sumaiya "I'm a child myself! My mother can have them."

Eve wondered how a young lady in her twenties could consider herself a child, maybe she just wasn't prepared to be a mother.

Thinking about people in much more unfortunate positions made Eve appreciate her blessings more deeply. She worked, her little income was enough to provide food, clothes, rent, school for her young children. Eve had the sensibility to administer the money she made to be able to buy presents for them when birthdays and Eid came, and when the school year ended with successful reports. If a child was sick, she could afford medical treatment. Maybe it was unfair of her to judge Sumaiya who said she could hardly feed herself (it's not fair of you Eve to judge others just because you willingly do what you think is right).

Eve no longer felt the bitterness and unfairness of what had befallen her. This, she had let go of some time ago. It had been quite dramatic when it happened, when she left the past behind: every few months she felt the pain and unfairness plague her mind and soul and she would open the school assignment autobiography, read her outstanding school reports with the teacher's predictions of a great future, look at the photos and remember the buoyant memory. Finally, she would end up weeping, lying on top of all the photos and reports spread around and under her. Hours of horrible, ugly, bitter crying and bawling over the unfairness of what happened to her at the age of fourteen, asking God why had it happened? Why hadn't she been allowed to continue with her life as it had been? Wanting to go back in time so she could refuse to come to Yemen for a holiday. At some point during this howling and lamenting of what her life should have been, she would regress into the mind-set of a fourteen-year-old, fantasising what she wanted to be, study, do, and the painful sobbing continued until she calmed—which is when it became physically impossible to cry any more with the inside of her chest feeling like cut up raw meat. Until one day, the wailing and mourning turned into such anger, all she could think was, it was over...*that* 'possible' life was over and would never be. There was no point in mourning over it, she would never be the person she was meant to be, but she was who she is now. She tore up the autobiography and the majority of childhood photos she could lay her hands on. It was a miracle cure, she never grieved over 'the life that could have been' again. She had received a lot and been through a lot, but it didn't break her—well, it did break her life, surely changed who she became, but it didn't break her spirit or will to live. Outside of court she was always happy, content was the biggest blessing, she still had ambition to rise to a higher position in work, to get a bigger salary which she deserved, she wanted always to give her children better than what she already provided if it became possible, but she knew this would be achieved in the future if she continued to work hard, and was content with now and how they lived now. She knew she never wanted to be married, this dream the majority of women and girls have, did not appeal to her (who could blame her, she was forced as a child). She was loved, but never allowed herself to fully love, men asked for her hand in marriage unaware she was a mother of three and legally still a married woman.

Eve came out of the reflective reminiscence the arrival of Sumaiya in court on Wednesday had put her in, thankful that after everything, life was still good.

"I found some court employees outside," said Sumaiya "They asked me why I came, they said there aren't any hearings for us today, do you think it's true?"

The usual people with cases arrived, but there was a long wait in the waiting room on the other side of the building as the usual waiting area had not been opened. People muttered about the Judge being later than usual. No'man called Eve to tell her he was on his way. Sumaiya went to follow up court employees for a document she needed, Eve watched from where she sat, and saw Sumaiya promiscuously uncover parts of her body. Eve looked the other way, pretending she had seen nothing, maybe she was showing them new bruises from her abusive husband. A sound of a crowd loudly shuffling up the stairs and the courtroom door opened, Eve placed the books into her bag and went to the other side of the building, eager to enter the courtroom. She stood at the door, but did not venture in any further. Seated in the old Judge's place was a younger man who seemed to have donned his head with one of the onioned domes of Saint Basil's cathedral, Arabian Nights popped into Eve's head. He had a thick neat black beard, narrow moustache, his eyes were small, and a cold expression gave him a mean complexion, he looked the complete opposite of the paternal looking Judge whom oversaw her case. Her forehead creased at the thought the change of judges had been implemented, and this judge who looked like an evil Sultan would be judging her now. Eve snapped out of the stare and looked at the men in the courtroom whose cases were to be heard and her mouth dropped open and she gasped upon seeing their hands and feet chained. They were going to try them with criminals? This was the 'new and improved' system?! How could they sit next to people whom needed to be chained?

"Eve?" No'man whispered standing next to her, Eve turned her head.

"Is this the new judge?" asked Eve with sincere shock on her face.

"No," said No'man "Step outside."

Outside the door, Eve asked again, still in shock: "This is the new Judge? The old one is gone?"

"This Judge," No'man stopped to laugh then continued with a broad smile, "Is for criminal offenses, those are men being tried for serious crimes. He's not our judge, we haven't been notified of any change."

"I was going to have a heart attack," Eve said and laughed in relief "I thought they were going to try us with criminals!"

"Let's go check with the clerk why our Judge isn't here," said No'man "They probably mixed up the dates at the last hearing."

The clerk opened a large register, yes there had been a mistake, no personal case hearings today. A crowd of vociferous men entered the clerk's office objecting with speech and angered hand gestures to their day being wasted, demanding a re-schedule. Eve waited outside the office while her lawyer rescheduled the hearing, Sumaiya joined her. Eve offered to drop her off at work so with their hearings rescheduled they went down the stairs and into the taxi.

"That's where I work," said Sumaiya, pointing at a grey four-storey hotel whose exterior to be clad with variegated limestone was suspended at half-completion, "They don't know I'm married, if they did they'd expect me to do things…"

"What things?" said Eve.

"You know," said Sumaiya "Sex with the guests. If they knew I wasn't a virgin, they'd make me." (Building the hotel façade must be expensive.)

"They can't force you to do anything whether you're virgin or not." said Eve.

"Yes they can," said Sumaiya "They take advantage of girls, especially when they know how much we need the job. I know girls who do this there."

"Have you tried looking for a job somewhere else?" said Eve, concerned.

"Yes," said Sumaiya "But it's impossible to find a job."

"Goodbye," said Eve "Take care of yourself."

Eve took a look up at the hotel as the taxi pulled away. What a grim place to work.

*

DURING THE FOLLOWING HEARING, THE JUDGE REQUESTED EVE and Mahmood each bring a senior family member to talk to him, one of the final steps where elders of both wife and husband's families try to reconcile the differences between the couple to get them back together.

"Can you bring a wise family member to represent your brother?" said the Judge.

"Yes," said Mahmood "I'll bring our father."

"Can you bring a wise family member to represent you?" said the Judge.

"Yes." said Eve, her mind frantic, she hoped it didn't show on her face. Who could she bring? Her brothers never stood by her side and had refused to attend even one hearing with her. Her father had gotten her into this mess, if he came to court he would only make things worse. She walked through the court yard trying to think how she could convince Yusef to attend this one session, and if he refused what would she say to the Judge and what impact would it have, not having a male family member represent her? She walked down the street searching for a taxi, in oblivion to the soldiers flirting and verbally harassing her as she lifted the mobile to her ear.

"Hello Yusef," she said "How are you?"

"I'm fine. What do you want?" he said, with a hint of irritation.

"The Judge wants me to bring someone from my family," she said "You know like the verse in the Quran 'a referee from his family and a referee from her family'. Suleiman's coming to represent his son. I need you to represent me."

"I can't." said Yusef bluntly.

"Yusef please," said Eve "Only this once."

"No, I can't." he said.

"It will only take twenty minutes," she said "Please, this is the last time I will ever ask for your help. Please, all the women in court have a brother, or father, an uncle or cousin with them in every session. I'm always on my own and I'm asking you just this once to come because the Judge has requested it, just twenty minutes…twenty minutes?"

"I can't, I'm really busy." he said, and hung up.

Eve got into the car, troubled. She had no one. This meant the court case could be kept pending or worse, used against her. She called her lawyer.

"You have to find someone from your family to come," said the lawyer with great concern—if no male relative represented her their unwillingness would fallaciously indicate to the Judge something unsavoury about her—"This is an important step."

Extremely depressed, she called her manager to let him know she'd be taking the rest of the day off. Eve swallowed her pride and called Yusef again, this step was too big of an impact to the case than to give up without a fight.

"I'll call dad," said Yusef "And tell him to come."

"You know how crazy and evil dad is," said Eve "He'll screw up everything and I'll end up killing him in the middle of court."

"No, I'll talk to him," said Yusef "I'll make him understand, if he goes psycho—he'll be answering to me."

CHAPTER TWENTY-FOUR

EVE WAS MORE NERVOUS THAN EVER; SHE HAD TOLD FATHER, repeatedly, not to ramble, not to say anything other than answer the Judge's questions. She warned him not to allow Adam's lawyer to provoke him, to ignore him. Father always harmed his children, well known for turning against them for no reason; he had a way of turning one hundred and eighty degrees at the last moment, always doing the wrong thing, thinking he was right. As they waited for the courtroom to be opened, Father fidgeted.

"I want to ask a lawyer for some advice about the inheritance case of our land." said Father looking around at the men milling about, as he tried to distinguish which was lawyer and which was client.

"Wait until my lawyers come," said Eve "When we finish my hearing you can ask them."

He continued to fidget, irritating Eve. She wished the courtroom be unlocked so they could get it over with, before he said or did something detrimental to her case. Mahmood, Suleiman and their lawyer arrived. For the first time after six years of escaping his penitentiary Suleiman laid his eyes on her again, a glimmer of paternal affection passed through his expression.

"Aah, aah!" Suleiman said loudly from the waiting room door "My *Eve*! My runaway *Eve*!", but the genuine cheeriness was no longer in the voice of her once captor, a tinge of bitterness had taken its place.

He came forward and kissed her on the forehead, she made no effort to get up—he had orchestrated her captivity and been the gate keeper preventing her from accessing both law and life, and she was still suffering the lifelong consequences of his actions. Adam's lawyer, with a look of aggravation, ushered Suleiman back into the corridor. Suleiman had aged, his face sagged and his posture was no longer upright and lean as he had been when she lived with them in the mountains.

"Is the bearded man Adam's lawyer?" said Father.

"Yes." said Eve.

Only moments passed after the question and Father got up saying: "I'll go ask him for some advice."

Eve got up and stood in front of him. "Don't you dare talk to the opposing lawyer!" she whispered in his face, her eyes glaring, "He's the enemy, *my* enemy. Do you understand? If you talk to him now, tomorrow, the day after or *ever*...I'll tell Yusef and he will be so angry with you!" Father returned to the bench and sat quietly. No more fidgeting.

The courtroom opened and filled with people. The clerk called out their names, Suleiman and Father stood side-by-side in front of the bench and Eve next to Father.

"You can sit down," the Judge said to Eve "It's him I want to talk to."

Eve was not prepared to leave Father's side just in case he went into family destruction mode. "He's a bit deaf," she said "If he can't hear you properly I can help him understand your question."

"Is it true," said the Judge "You can't hear properly?"

There was a hesitation, then Father replied: "Sometimes." The courtroom crowd laughed, Eve smiled and looked down at her shoes.

"You have been chosen to be referees for your son and daughter as per the holy Quran," said the Judge "If a couple cannot settle their differences we bring a referee from his side and a referee from her side. You are requested to do your best to reconcile their differences so they continue to be husband and wife. I want you to come back with a report of the meeting. I don't want separate reports—one unified report. Do you understand?" Both men understood. "Then do your best to fix their problems," said the Judge "And make sure they continue to be husband and wife."

Eve and Mahmood talked as they went down the stairs.

"In my house, we'll sit," said Eve "And have the meeting."

"Alright," said Mahmood "When?"

"Now." said Eve.

Suleiman was still the shrewd, sly man, getting older had not lessened his scheming. He wanted the meeting to happen without Eve's presence so he could manipulate Father and prevent her divorce.

"No," said Suleiman "We'll go to the hotel and her father will come with us and so will Adam's lawyer."

Poor Suleiman, he thought it was like the many meetings in the mountains he and the Uncles held, when they discussed and decided Eve's life without her.

"This has nothing to do with the lawyers," said Eve firmly "It's family only. You're coming to my house. Why go to a hotel when we have the privacy of my home?"

Suleiman was in a stubborn mood, he sat on a bench in the court yard.

"Then we will not meet!" he said and thumped his staff on the ground.

"You have to," said Eve seating herself next to him "The Judge ordered you to do so."

"I will not help you get a divorce!" said Suleiman.

"The meeting doesn't help me get a divorce," said Eve "It's your chance to convince me *not* to get a divorce."

"Will you agree to what we say?" said Suleiman peering at her through his clever, and now she noticed, clouded eyes.

"I haven't heard what you have to say yet." said Eve.

"You're trying to trick me," said Suleiman "This meeting and report are important to you."

"Listen," said Eve "The Judge requested this meeting, not me. If you won't come to my home, now, I'll go back upstairs to the Judge and tell him you've refused to meet and in this way you'll help me get a divorce quicker, because *you* refused to meet."

A man sitting on the bench shouted to Suleiman: "Do not listen to her, she's trying to trick you! Do not listen to women, they only know the way of Satan!"

"You mind your own business, you busybody! You don't have a life so you have to butt into somebody else's business? Stop interfering before I bring someone to break your teeth!" said Eve turning to face him, raising her voice, a dominant animal baring teeth attempting intimidation (such perfectly aligned, pretty white teeth), the man slouched and became silent.

"You'd better convince your father to come," she said to Mahmood "Or I'm going to the Judge right now to tell him you've disobeyed his orders! Is your father saying you know how to do things better than what God has put in the holy Quran?"

Mahmood turned to his father. "She's right," he said "The Judge wants this meeting and for us to go against what God says will weaken Adam's case and be good for her."

A determined Eve got into the taxi with Father, Mahmood and a grumpy Suleiman. He was still upset she had left them all those years ago; still inclined to believe she would return to the mountains. His body language, the way he spoke to her, the look in his eyes, the way he slightly turned his stiff body away from her when he spoke, all said he was hurt and upset; that she should kiss his hand and head and ask for forgiveness. That *she*, should say sorry. This amused her greatly, after all those years, everything they had done to her and all these years apart, he still held it in his heart that she had *wronged them* by leaving the mountains. Leaving them. If he could, if he had any authority in the city, he would tie her up and bundle her into the car and back up to the village in the clouds.

They sat in the diwan. Suleiman watched her with half closed eyes as she poured tea and served them dates and biscuits, when he opened them to speak to her, he spoke with a tone and cross expression of disappointment in a child.

"You've embarrassed us," said Suleiman "The whole village is talking that you don't want my son and that he's clinging on to you."

"He should respect himself and divorce me." said Eve.

"You'll never get a divorce," said Suleiman "If you do, I'll take my son's children with me—you'll see!"

"They're my children," said Eve "And they'll stay with me."

"Now, what does the Judge want?" said Father interrupting before the to and fro between the two friendly nemesis could get ugly.

"He wants you and my father to convince Eve to remain Adam's wife." said Mahmood.

"Yes," said Eve "The Judge wants you to do your best to persuade me not to go ahead with the divorce," she paused then smiled and said: "Come on, try."

There was a lengthy discussion, Suleiman confirmed his son Adam had committed to paying for all his children's needed expenses, all his wife's expenses, to be a good husband and to treat her right and give her all her rights, on condition Eve stays at home. When Suleiman repeated Eve should leave her job, it was unacceptable that she works, he shook his finger at her, his eyes full of disdain. Father reiterated the same offer Suleiman had made. Both Father and Suleiman emphasised they did not want her to divorce Adam, they wanted her to remain his wife, and Suleiman said he would *make* Adam be a good husband (as if it were possible to give him a personality transplant).

"I reject this offer," Eve replied "I don't want Adam as a husband, I want to divorce him."

"Are you sure?" said Mahmood.

"I'm positive," said Eve "Now let's make the report, the Judge wants one report signed by both parties."

"Should we bring someone to write it?" said Mahmood, already thinking he could get Adam's lawyer involved.

"No, you write it," said Eve, nipping his blossoming plan in the bud, "You were here and heard the whole thing."

Eve dictated the report and Mahmood wrote and modified it to suit both parties with input from Suleiman. Then both Suleiman and Father read, signed and thumb printed it. She submit the report to the Judge during the next hearing.

"We have no knowledge of this report," Adam's lawyer objected "It's forged!"

What an obnoxious, disputatious being.

"Sir Judge," said Eve "This report is the result of the meeting held at your request. It's signed by both chosen referees and it was written by Mahmood, Adam's brother, and they have a copy of it."

"Did you write the report?" said the Judge "Do you have a copy of it? And has your lawyer been given a copy?"

"Yes, I wrote this report," said Mahmood "I did have a copy and I gave it to the lawyer." The Judge gave Adam's lawyer an admonitory look of disgust.

In the following hearing, Adam's lawyer accused Eve of wanting to run away with her children to Britain. She replied she had no intention of leaving the country, her children had been added to her passport so they could go to Saudi and back, Munwa had a temporary passport so they could return to Yemen which had already expired. Layth and Nadine had also been removed from her passport by the embassy pencilling a line through their names. Adam's lawyer insisted she was trying to abscond with the children so she was requested to bring her passports to the next session where she showed the Judge and clerk the crossed-out names and corner-cut cancelled passport (and shrewdly neglected to inform them each of her three children held their own valid British passports—Eve had learnt her lessons from life, she and her children needed a way out if need be (finally Eve, you're learning)). Notwithstanding, Adam's lawyer requested a notification be sent out not allowing Eve to leave Yemen.

"My client is not a criminal whom needs to be stopped from travelling." No'man objected. However, the court issued an order that neither Eve nor the children travel out of Yemen, and a notice be sent out with their names to Sana'a airport and all points of exit, not allowing them to leave.

Adam's lawyer attempted to repeat matters already introduced and dealt with from a long time ago, to have them processed again. No'man objected, the opposing lawyer was only trying to keep the case dragging in court.

"I would like to reserve the case for judgment." said Eve. The clerk wrote down her request which meant she demanded a ruling be made based on all the hearings and the evidence provided throughout—it had gone on long enough.

Eve attended the hearing, hoping it would be the last. The Judge tried persuading her to go back to her marital life and remain the wife of Adam; he tried so hard to convince her, but she replied how much she hated Adam and how much she wanted the divorce. "I request to be allowed to announce dissolvement of the marriage contract." she stated. The Judge gave her permission and she said out loud three times: "I, Eve Zakaria, dissolve my marriage from Adam Suleiman because I hate him." It was a relief to say it, but she would be more relieved once she heard the official ruling.

After spending almost a year in court, Eve's name was called. Worry tinkling in her chest, nervousness churning her stomach she approached the bench with her lawyer as did Mahmood and Adam's lawyer. The Judge read the ruling: Eve's divorce was endorsed and legal; she had custody of her children; Adam was responsible for paying child support; what the Judge ruled as an amount for child support was minuscule compared to what Eve spent on them, but it didn't matter to her (Adam would ignore the ruling and not pay a penny). What she cared about, she had achieved: her divorce and custody of her children. Eve didn't care today, squeezing between the men to get down the stairs nor did she notice the stares and remarks men made as she walked past them, which she usually pretended not to notice. She walked out of the gate, relieved she would never need to come here again. She didn't feel like taking a taxi from in front of the court, she wanted to walk for a while. She looked up at the sky, it seemed bluer than ever, the sun was shining and its kind warmth wrapped her. Eve experienced breathing in fresh air as if she had been unable to for a long time. She stepped out of the dust coloured realm of court and back into multi-coloured life. Life inducing sun penetrated through her black cloak and warmed her clothes, touched her skin. Her senses which had numbed through the dragging, nerve racking, long court trial had come back to life. Her ex-husband had brought her to court under a request of 'marital obedience' a year ago, she remembered dreading coming to court for the first time after everything she'd heard about it, and now she emerged with what she had always wanted—her freedom from an unwanted marriage. She was free. She called her mother and texted the good news to her friends whom always prayed for her and supported her, and went home. What a relief! The nightmare of court was over. The fear of being forced to remain his wife hanging over her head, removed. The dread of Adam ever entering their home again, banished. Now she could take care of her children without any worries. Absolute peace.

CHAPTER TWENTY-FIVE

THE COURT-FREE MONTHS CAME TO AN END BY A SUMMONS TO attend the Court of Appeals where her case ruled by the Primary Court would be heard again. Her lawyers assured her the divorce could not be reversed as it was already done and final. But she asked herself, if it was so, then why had the Court of Appeals allowed for the trial to go on?

There was no need for Eve to actually attend court until the end of January because the Judges were being won over by Adam's lawyer's constant ranting that the Primary Court ruling was anti-Islamic, rotting and decaying to Yemeni society and encouraging to women to leave their houses, husbands and children to pursue a life taboo to Yemeni tradition. Her lawyer objected, and requested they hear Eve's story directly from her. She worried, no matter how much Ismael reassured her he would take her case all the way to the Supreme Court if he had to, but Eve had borrowed the money to pay for their services in the Primary and Court of Appeals and she would not be able to afford lawyers if the case continued to be strung on. Even worse than the money worries, if the Court of Appeals revoked the Primary Court ruling then Eve's case would return to be tried and heard all over again at the Primary Court, more years in courts, not to mention there would definitely be a different judge by now and if the new Judge was a woman-hater or corrupt, it would be easy for Adam to win.

It was a long travel to the Court of Appeals. The guards at the gate searched Eve's handbag, then made harassful comments about how good she smelt, she took the bag from the guard and entered the yard. This court was much larger than the previous one, its buildings were of current architecture, but bleak; the steely grey exteriors and glum interiors darkened the hallways, or was it Eve's eyes darkened by worry? She entered the main building, searched the boards showing which building was for what purpose. They were to be heard in an external building. Eve entered a large hall with the Judge's podium elevated at the end of the room, a few people had already arrived. Eve left the courtroom to search for her lawyer and as she walked along the paths in the yard a woman walking alongside an old winter-white-haired man approached her.

"Eve?" said the woman from behind her face veil "What a nice surprise to find you here!" (It wasn't nice at all for Eve to be here actually) They greeted each other, to her delight it was Nagat her courtroom compatriot.

"My ex-husband appealed the case months ago," said Eve "This is the first time I've been asked to attend."

"You have no idea how happy I was for you when the Judge announced your ruling," said Nagat "I wanted to get up and hug you to say congratulations, but you know…with the court in session and the Judges not wanting us to be happy about divorce. You looked so happy when you turned around and walked out, your face was glowing!"

"It was a happy moment," said Eve "A big relief. I thought it was the end, but here we are again! How did you do in your case?"

Nagat went on to tell her how her ex-husband had waited a long time to appeal the case, during which she had married (the fluffy desiccated coconut); she told how the Court of Appeals accepted her ex's appeal and returned her case to the Primary Court where a new (and biased) judge had wanted to return her to her ex and called her an adulteress for marrying although she had waited the set period by religion (this judge had been removed due to many complaints about his misconduct). But now Eve was highly alarmed at how many times the same case could be batted from court to court, what happened to Nagat meant she too was still in danger of the court returning her to the ex.

"The judge had ruled I have sole custody of my daughters because their father was so bad to them," Nagat went on "But I said to myself, he's still their father no matter how bad he is, they should take breakfast and lunch to him."

"That's big of you," said Eve "Especially after how he attacked them in school and disrupted their lives."

"So my daughters took turns taking food to him," said Nagat "Until one day my eldest was taking breakfast, he knew when she was coming so he waited in the street for her and started to beat her there. The lowlife pulled her cloak off shouting to people 'look at her wide chest, it's just like her mother's' then he pulled out his jambia and stabbed her!"

"No!" exclaimed Eve.

"A taxi driver who'd stopped to watch grabbed him before he could stab her again," said Nagat "The police took him and she was rushed to hospital."

"How is she?" said Eve.

"She's better now," said Nagat. "Her wound needed a lot of medical care and now she's always scared...we all are. We filed a complaint against him, but before he was to appear in court he was allowed to escape from jail!"

"How could he escape?" said Eve.

"The usual way," said Nagat "With an acquaintance and money. He didn't break out, the doors were opened and he was allowed to leave. Everything in Yemen happens with bribes. Now we don't know where he is."

"That's terrible," said Eve "What if he comes back to kill you or your daughters? How could they let him out?"

"We requested an investigation as to how he got out," said Nagat "But they wouldn't listen to us. We're in Yemen, this country's corrupt."

Corruption was rife and those with more money or stronger acquaintances bought rulings as easily as bartering for a product. Thankfully, good judges existed, though it was your address and luck which determined your case was assigned to which judge.

The courtroom filled with people and the judges sat in their seats, Eve came to learn this court had three judges, one senior to the two: one looked like a young Islamic scholar wearing a white dress, a short crimson fez-like hat with a creamy white turban around it and glasses; the second was an older version of the scholar, he was old with a long henna-dyed beard and a bigger turban around his head, and the Senior Judge was middle aged, silver haired, wearing western shirt and trousers.

"You're the witness?" said the Senior Judge.

"Yes." replied an old man requested as a witness for one of the parties of a case regarding the disputed sale of land, he was so frail his body trembled while leaning on his cane for support.

"You were requested as a witness by the buyer?" said the Senior Judge.

"Yes." said the old man.

"Can you tell me the names of the people whom witnessed the sale from both parties?" asked the Senior Judge.

"I don't remember…I remember I was there, but not the names of people."

"Do you remember the date the land was sold?"

"No."

"Do you remember the name of the seller?" said the Senior Judge.

"No."

"Do you remember how much was paid for the land?"

"No."

"Do you remember anything regarding this case at hand?" said The Senior Judge, smiling kindly while wondering what kind of a witness this was.

"I don't know. They insisted I come, but I don't remember anything." said the old man.

The Senior Judge looked towards the party whom insisted on bringing the old man to court and said: "In the future you may want to bring witnesses whom actually *witnessed* something regarding your case." The court room filled with the tired laughter of men whom wanted their own cases heard and solved. Eve's case was up next. Ismael got up with her. The Senior Judge asked her a series of questions which she had already answered many times over in the Primary Court: why she wants a divorce after such a long time? If things could be fixed between her and the husband would she agree to be his wife? Is he a good or a bad person? Did he provide for his family or not? Who takes care of the children while she's at work? Does she know that God, although He allows divorce, Has named it 'the most hated of allowed deeds'?

"She loves him," said Adam's lawyer "She loves my client. She's crazy in love with him!"

"I hate him," said Eve "If I loved him like his lawyer describes would he be dragging me from court to court trying to force me to stay with him?" A few men chuckled behind her.

"Sir Judge," said Adam's lawyer "If she doesn't love my client, then ask her how come she has three children from him? The three children are the fruit of their *immense love* for each other!"

The two turbaned judges nodded their heads, leaning in towards each other they had become one body with two heads, peering at Eve through sly eyes and thick lensed glasses as if she had been caught out by the question.

"You have three children from this man," said the Senior Judge "How can you say you don't love him? You love him and it's why you have three children from him."

"My children are a result of sex." said Eve coolly though this insinuation always irritated her, what did they know about her life or how her children came to be.

The two turbaned judges became flustered, the one writing looked confused as if he didn't know what to write as her statement, as if he could not write what she had just said. As if the word 'sex' should not be mentioned by a woman. Eve's lawyer seemed embarrassed too, he'd turned around, detached from planet Eve and entered his own orbit walking in small circles, his hands clasped together behind his back.

"Women can be raped once and become pregnant from it," Eve continued "Love has nothing to do with it, it's biology. I was in a confined room with a grown man."

"This is true, Sir Judge," said Ismael, now facing the bench, "An example are the girls and women raped in the Bosnia and Herzegovina war and became pregnant. Their pregnancies were a result of rape. Although ordinarily marriage and children are a result of love, in my client's case it was not."

The two judges were in a bit of a pickle, they still didn't want to write down Eve's exact words. The Senior Judge interrupted their whispering and hand turning, and dictated to them what to record. Several more hearings and the Senior Judge made it clear to Adam's lawyer and brother, Adam had come to Yemen to be in court for the next hearing. Adam's lawyer objected and said it was not possible for his client to be in Yemen anytime soon.

"Your client should have thought about that before taking his ex-wife to court," said the Senior Judge "He's the husband and he's the owner of the case so he has to be here by the set date."

*

EVE WAS UNCOMFORTABLE TO BE IN THE SAME PLACE WITH ADAM as much as she had always been uneasy with his presence. The thought of seeing him, hearing him, sickened her. Arriving early for the hearing, she entered the courtroom. A man shadowed over her as she sat reading from a booklet of prayers, she looked up to the sight of Adam, who had slightly gained weight and his hairline receded, gazing down at her and extending his hand. Was he pretending to be civil, putting on a show for the Judge? Well he shouldn't have bothered, the judges hadn't entered.

"How are you?" said Adam genially smiling as if they were on a pleasant date.

Hate gushed through her being and veins and overflowed. "You keep away from me," she said getting up, raising her index finger at him, "Don't you dare talk to me."

"I just want to speak with you." said Adam, shaken by the hostility in her voice, when all he wanted was to take her somewhere private, remove her cloak, then her dress, kiss her plunging a thousand metres deep into her soul and sweetness, look into the depths of her brown eyes wondering what was inside her pretty head and watch her eyes blur with bliss, while he melted and melded into her.

"There's nothing to talk about," said Eve "We've been talking through court for two years. You're not my husband, not even on paper, you're a stranger—so keep away from me."

She kept her finger raised towards him as he walked backwards and stepped aside and she stormed out of the door, angered and agitated by the pretence he always put on in front of others. He always did that. He even had a different tone of voice when pretending to be a good person in the presence of family. He had made her spend two years, and a lot of money which she could have spent on her children's future, in court and *now* he wanted to talk? If he had wanted to talk, he could have when she tried time and time again over the years asking him to divorce her, begging him to get married to another and leave her be. She didn't return to the courtroom until it was full. One of the Judges was missing, but another person had taken his place, for a judge, he should have shown more interest in the cases playing out in front of him than playing with his phone. Eve and Nagat asked if he was a replacement judge, the reply returned he was not a judge at all, but an important person with a high government office. Adam was nowhere to be seen, only his lawyer and brother stood to one side leaning against the wall. When their names were called out, Eve approached the bench as did Adam's lawyer and brother.

"My client is too embarrassed to speak about his personal life in front of all these people," said Adam's lawyer "We request a closed session."

"Granted," said the Senior Judge, he looked at Eve apologetically, "You'll have to wait until all the cases have been heard."

Eve returned to the back of the courtroom where she usually sat. Aggravated—no consideration had been made towards her embarrassment when she had to talk about private matters. Irritated—now she had to sit here for hours, when all she wanted was to get it over and done with. She had attended almost two years' worth of hearings and wanted it to end. No more court. No more him. The last hearing finished and the Judges came down from their platform.

"Follow me to my office." said the Senior Judge to Eve whom waited for the rush of men to pass first.

Eve frowned as the man sitting in the missing judge's seat held hands with Adam's lawyer as they walked across the yard and whispered into each other's ears. Obviously, this man was here for no good. In front of the Judges' office many men waited and crowded around the Senior Judge when he arrived, all talking at the same time, all with the same tired, exasperated expression on their faces. She could feel the same expression on her own face. He shouted at them to wait until the closed hearing was over. Eve, Ismael, Mahmood, Adam's lawyer and Adam followed the Judge into the office, furnished with three desks, one desk had a visitor's chair in front of it, next to the door was a dark green synthetic sofa. The men stood looking around at each other, Eve sat on the sofa seat nearest to the door. The Senior Judge turned around to face them.

"You, you and you—out." he pointed at both lawyers and Mahmood and gestured with his thumb towards the door.

"We have to be present." said Adam's lawyer.

"I said wait outside," said the Senior Judge with a canny smile "I want to talk with them both, without anybody's interference."

Ismael glanced at Eve and wore a concerned look as he left the office. To Eve's surprise, the door re-opened and 'The Man' from the judge's panel joined them, he winked at Adam before sitting behind one of the desks. Adam sat beside Eve on the sofa, she immediately got up and sat on the visitor's chair across the desk from the Senior Judge, and a sour look came over Adam's face.

"We've heard a lot from her, but nothing from you," said the Senior Judge "What do you have to say?"

"I really love my wife." said Adam.

"Excuse me," said Eve "I'm no longer your wife, don't call me that."

"I really love her," said Adam "I'm a good husband. I've given her everything she's ever wished for. I've let her live a life full of luxury and I've given her all the love a man can give his wife. I demand you return her to my home." (Captivity, starvation, cockroaches—how could any woman resist?)

Eve seethed inwards, annoyed by the false tone and the lies…*the lies*! A luxurious life?

"I hate you," Eve said calmly, suppressing her anger, "I do not love you. I do not want you. Respect yourself and leave me alone."

"I love her," said Adam wearing his sincerest face, looking at the Senior Judge, "I gave her the best life she could ever wish for. She's my wife and I'm taking her home with me to my village. I don't have a house here in Sana'a, I can no longer afford rent and I no longer wish she stay in the city, she must return to my village."

"What part of: I'm not your wife, do you not understand?" said Eve "I can't stand the sight of you, the sound of you makes me want to throw up. I hate you." she still talked calmly and clearly.

"I love her, she *is* my wife and I'm taking her home to my village today," said Adam, lifting his shoulders and extending his arms looking towards the Senior Judge again, "I love her, I'm crazy about her. I'm *crazy* about her!"

"We get it, *we get it*," said the Senior Judge wincing "You love her. The problem is—*she* doesn't love you. We can't force her to love you."

"No, wait…she loves me," said Adam "Hold on, let me shout to my lawyer to come, he can explain to you."

"What?" said the Senior Judge "You're going to ask a stranger to explain how much you love your wife and why you should keep her? Or you want him to force us to believe she loves you when we can see she clearly doesn't?"

"She's my wife," said Adam, his voice getting louder, "And I'll take her by force! I'm taking her home with me!"

Eve looked to the Judge, he turned to look at her and reassuringly said: "Don't worry, there's not an authority or power on this earth that can force you to live under the same roof with a man you hate and cannot stand."

This comment enraged Adam, he dropped the false affection and shouted: "I want my children! I want my children right now! They're not staying with her, they're coming with me!"

Nervousness crept into her voice as she said: "The Primary Court ruled they stay in my custody. While he's in Yemen, he can see them once a week under my supervision." Life had toughened her up, and for their sake she had become stronger, but they were her whole life and her biggest weakness; her children were the arm others could twist.

"They're his children too," said The Man "He can take them if he wants."

It was now crystal clear, 'The Man' was here to use his influence to sway the Judges to Adam's favour, Adam failing to make his own impression on the Judges they would now use her children to pressure her into returning to him. For this man to be allowed to sit in a Judge's seat during a hearing, for him to be allowed into a closed session when the lawyers had been thrown out, he had to be of powerful connections. Eve had observed him during the hearings, he wasn't paying attention to any of them, fiddling with his phone, he had come solely to be of assistance to Adam, and now he was whispering into the turbaned judges' ears reassurances, thumping his open palm on his chest, a gesture declaring with his honour he was guarantor of Adam being in the right, of his dishonest integrity, there was no such traditional gesture for women to make (or Eve would have jumped onto the table beating her chest with both fists like a silverback). A sign of corruption—danger. Her children's safety was being compromised, she feared the worst—they'd take her children away. She feared what the displacement would result in, the impact on her innocent young children, mentally and emotionally, and possibly physically if he carried out the threats he used to send.

"I want my children now!" Adam demanded "I only have a short stay and I want to take them with me. Judge, bring them to court in front of you and ask them if they want to come with me. I'll give them everything they want, bring them to court!"

"Sir Judge, please listen to me," said Eve fearing Adam would lure them with sweets, treats and toys, "He doesn't love his children. From the beginning of this hearing, did he make any request for their custody? He never asks about them. I've kept my children out of court, I don't say bad things about their father or talk in front of them about court because I don't want to damage them, don't you see…he's only asking for them because he's angry you said there isn't a power in this world that can force me to live with him? I'm begging you don't put my children in danger." Eve was now crying, big tears rolled down her cheeks as she spoke.

"I want my children NOW!" Adam shouted.

"They're his children," said The Man, looking at Eve with piercing hate, "Let him take them for three days and he'll bring them back to you."

"In three days he could hurt them," said Eve "I've been taking care of them for years," her voice rose "And you think I'll allow him to destroy them in a day?! I won't let anyone harm my babies!"

"I'll take his passport and keep it with me as guarantee he doesn't take them out of the country…" said The Man, with alacrity Adam whipped the passport out of his pocket and into The Man's open hand. "Now do you agree?" said The Man.

Eve could not believe this man, bargaining with her children's welfare. Did he think she was stupid to trust someone who came to corrupt and sway the case? It would be enough to take them to the mountains where no authorities existed and she *would* follow her children there, never to be seen again.

"The passport only guarantees he doesn't leave the country," said Eve "No piece of paper will prevent him from harming them. He used to send messages saying he'd kidnap them, that he would kill them and kill me. I will not give my children to this criminal!"

"Why didn't you mention these messages in the hearings?" said the Senior Judge with concern.

"Because it happened while I was in the Primary Court," said Eve "I asked my lawyer, but he said there's no way we can prove it's his number."

"I'm taking my children today." threatened Adam not even attempting to deny his previous threats.

"I'll keep his passport and you give him his children," said The Man "One week and they'll be back with you."

"No. No. No, I will not let him hurt my children!" she shouted out the words, crying harder.

"Calm down, calm down my sister," said the Senior Judge observing her heightening anxiety "You've been so calm and in control and patient throughout the hearings...why are you so nervous and hysterical now? Why have you lost your calm?"

"My children...are," said Eve, between gulping sobs, "In danger—you can't see...you haven't seen what I've seen and you don't know what I know...he will harm them, he won't take care of them. I'm their mother...I kept them...safe...and now...he wants to take them because he can hurt me... He doesn't care about them... he'll hurt them to hurt me. You're going to help him harm...my children. My children...I kept them safe."

The sobs became so big and strong she was unable to continue talking and had to allow them to flow so she could catch her breath again, then said: "I'm their mother. *I'm their mother.* I've been responsible for their safety since the day they were born. I've been taking care of them since I was twenty and now he wants to hurt them to get back at me for divorcing him. How can I be calm when you're all saying let him take them for a few days he's their father? You don't care...they're my children, if he harms them in any way, I can't help them and *neither can any of you!*"

"They're my children," Adam shouted "I'm taking them with me!"

"It's agreed—he'll bring them back in a few days." said The Man as if his word were royal decree.

"NO!" shouted Eve.

"Everybody calm down," said the Senior Judge raising his palms in an effort to placate everybody "My sister...my daughter, listen to me...he's their father, *no father could harm his own child*, a few days and they come back to you."

"No, you don't understand," said Eve, hot tears streaming down her face, "He doesn't want them, he wants to get back at me! If he loved them, how come he starved them in Saudi? If he cares, why does he not ask about them, ever? He only ever asks for me. All these years he sent no money to support them, not even after the court ruling. He never asked and didn't know if they were eating or starving, clothed or naked, he didn't care or know if they had a roof over their heads or were sleeping in the streets."

"Why should I send money?" said Adam, snorting, "For you to spend on yourself?"

"I don't need your money," said Eve, her eyes spitting despise at him, "Now I can provide for myself and my children. If you want to believe he didn't send money in fear I spend it on myself, then how come he never sent them clothes from Saudi like the rest of the fathers whom work there? What's he going to say about that? He wouldn't have had to send clothes to fit me, he could have sent small clothes to fit his children. If he was worried about the money going to the wrong place, why didn't he have his brother who lives here in Sana'a buy canned food to deliver to his children to make sure they don't sleep on empty stomachs? Can't you see he doesn't love or even care about his children? *He doesn't even know who they are.*"

"Yes I do!" he retaliated.

The Judge picked up the case file, he ushered Adam to come closer. The Senior Judge looked up at him. "What are the names of your children?" asked the Senior Judge.

"Layth, Munwa and Nadine." replied Adam. That was easy, of course he would know their names, Eve was certain he didn't know anything about them. He was unable to get the order they were born in correctly, or their dates of birth at all while the Judge's face winced and Eve held him with a gaze of pure hatred, although good for her argument, the fact he couldn't get their order correct still hurt (it wasn't as if there were ten of them); knowing her children had an uncaring father, still hurt. He was unable to get their age right nor could he tell the Judge where they went to school nor the years they were in.

"That's it," said the Senior Judge "You wait until there's a ruling, and meanwhile they stay with their mother."

"I'll take them by force!" Adam said.

"He'll return them to their mother in three weeks' time." said The Man.

"Who are you?" said Eve looking fiercely at the meddling Man, "What are you doing here? Why are you trying to help him take my children? They're *my* children. No one in this room cares about them other than me and *I won't let anyone take them!*"

Adam forwarded towards her menacingly. "I'll bring the police to break your door down and we'll take them by force," he threatened "You'll see!"

"You see?" Eve shouted, frantically looking at all three Judges, "He'll go bribe the police and take my children by force and terrorise them! Who's going to stop him bribing the police? You see?!"

The Senior Judge came out from behind his desk and put his face into Adam's.

"The police cannot break anybody's door or take anybody's children by force," said the Senior Judge, slowly and squarely, "If you have the right to take the children with help from the police, you have to come to me to issue an order for the police to do so and: it-is-not-going-to-happen. You just proved you don't care about your children."

"What if he bribes policemen and they come and kidnap my children?" said Eve genuinely afraid and certain it was to happen "Who's going to stop him?"

"He wouldn't dare," said the Senior Judge "If he does, he'll be going to prison." turning to Adam, he added "Do you understand?"

Adam gulped, enraged, and nodded understanding. Eve left the office walking hurriedly, weaving her way through the crowded corridor, tears rolling down her face. She didn't feel her children were safe, Adam had brazenly announced his intention to take them by force. Her worst fear intensified with him being in Yemen, she knew for sure he would attempt to kidnap them to hurt her, to twist her arm into going back to the mountains. The damage it would have on them. But she wouldn't let it happen. Ismael ran after her as she walked briskly through the yard.

"What happened?" he asked "We heard you shouting." Eve informed him, she didn't slow down and she didn't stop crying.

"What the Judge said is true," said Ismael struggling to keep her pace "Calm down, he can't take them by force."

"We all know with a simple bribe the police will do anything." said Eve.

"If anyone knocks on your door, just call me and I'll bring the real police to deal with them," said Ismael "I'll go now, to see when the next hearing is scheduled and call you."

There was no reassuring her, she got into the taxi and burst into a frenzied cry, sick and tired of being caused problems from a past she had left behind. Why couldn't they let her live and bring her children up in peace? It was all she wanted: to be allowed to live in peace. Moneer, the taxi driver whom she'd done business with for years, was worried having never seen her in such a state.

"Calm down," said Moneer "You've brought up his children better than two parents together…He should be kissing your feet, not causing you problems, but this is life…God made this life a test for good people. All these problems and patience you survive with, God will compensate you. Don't worry, he might have strong people helping him, but God will be helping you."

Eve on verge of a total nervous breakdown, oversaturated by God's testing, pulled herself together and called the school, she explained to the Deputy Principal what was happening and told her she'd be keeping the children at home for a few days.

By the time they reached school Eve was completely composed, at least on the outside. But inside, her soul was shattered (shards of a slim bottle among bubbles fizzling out on a cold marble floor) by a never-ending worry she had to live with, he would hurt her children if he could. Life would never be wholly peaceful, this past was always going to be part of her present, and she would constantly be looking over her shoulder. She smiled as her giggling children got into the car, but all she wanted to do was bawl and lament the dirge of her life. It wasn't fair, she too had been just a child when this injustice had been heaped upon her; now an adult, but still its problems dogged her. She called work and explained briefly what happened and informed them she would not be coming to work until she was sure her ex-husband left the country and her children were safe to go back to school. Eve had an exit plan, how to get her children to safety if they tried to take them away from her, wasn't prepared to send her children to a painful life of suffering with her ex-in-laws just because of a court order. While her three loved ones mirthfully watched cartoons, blissfully unaware of the dark clouds gathering around them, she packed a suitcase with just enough clothes and hygiene products, passports and all their important documents: if they needed to take off to safety, they had all the necessities they needed in one place. She called her best friend, to let her in on the plan, as she would need her help.

Adam sent a text message from a Saudi number. Nevertheless, she kept the children at home an extra two days and using the help of her friends confirmed he had definitely left Yemen so the children returned to school and Eve to work. In a few months the Court of Appeals had a verdict, endorsing the Primary Court's ruling. Again Eve felt relief and left the courtroom smiling, happy, once again, she had won her case.

As her lawyers predicted, Adam took the case to the Supreme Court.

"You have nothing to worry about," said Ismael "The Primary Court ruled in your favour and so did the Court of Appeals, the Supreme Court will look at all the facts and of course they'll rule in your favour."

Eve smiled, but her expression conveyed her doubt. Ismael read her face and added: "After this, he can never appeal or take you to court regarding the divorce. After this, it's final! He cannot take you to court about marriage—ever!"

Eve sighed inwards, hoping the third time would be the knock out round.

CHAPTER TWENTY-SIX

A T THE END OF THE YEAR, THE COMPANY SHE WORKED FOR had a management change, all the senior employees searched desperately for employment elsewhere, as did she, as the new management had an aversion to subordinates with more experience than they held themselves. Eve had been accepted into employment from the first work interview in her life and had continued to work for the same company for four years. She hadn't searched for work since then, even when work offers had come her way over those years she always declined out of her love and loyalty to the place she worked, despite the growing needs of her family and the increasing high costs of living in Yemen should have made her accept those offers long ago. But no, she felt a loyalty so deep towards the company (and would forever be grateful to the place that allowed her independence and gave her the opportunity to gain skills and experience) and she loved the work she did and people she worked with, it felt as if the company was hers. Back scimitaring in the forest of advertised vacancies she found finding employment had become even harder. Mother requested Yusef to come visit them, and explained to him Eve was on the verge of unemployment and needed him to give out her CVs (now an impressive resumé filled with experience and qualifications) to help her find a job. He enthusiastically agreed (the magical healing power of time), Eve gave him eight CVs backed with copies of her qualifications. Shortly after Yusef left she went to buy groceries and to her dismay, found her neatly prepared CVs, in their lovely pastel coloured, clear cover folders, sticking out of the neighbour's trash on the pavement. A neighbour heard Eve was searching for work and said her husband's friend worked for a foreign company currently looking for a secretary and to give them her CV, which she did.

There was no reply for weeks, until the same day she received calls from two companies for an interview. One was from the largest gas company in Yemen, to which she had applied for several different positions advertised. The second was the foreign multinational company which the neighbour had given her CV to. The interviews were set for the same date and were two hours apart.

"I have one more question," said the HR manager of the foreign company "How did you know about this vacancy? Did you see the advertisement?"

"I didn't," said Eve "My neighbour knew I was searching for a job and her husband heard from a friend about a position here, so I gave them my CV."

"I like your honest answer," said the HR manager "Your CV arrived late, I'd already begun interviewing, but it was the best. When can you start?" Eve wanted to resign and take a month off to revive. "No," said the HR manager "I'd like you to start as soon as possible." They spoke a little more about her work duties, it wasn't the position of secretary vacant, but a receptionist. Eve didn't mind, she knew as long as she entered the company, she would eventually be promoted with all her skills and experience.

"Zakaria… Zakaria," said the HR manager as if the name was familiar "Do you know a Yusef Zakaria?"

"He's my brother." Eve replied in a flat manner, trying to hide her discomfort.

"The Yusef Zakaria married to Noora is your brother?" said the HR manager surprised.

"Yes." said Eve, her heart turned grey and hoped her face hadn't.

"I know his wife!" said the HR manager now smiling brilliantly while Eve's soul grimaced "We used to be colleagues in a different company, a long time ago."

Eve asked her a few questions about the company to change the subject.

The difference between the foreign and gas company was huge, you could tell as soon as you entered the latter's premises, they were larger and more organised, where she was to be interviewed first by the Procurement Manager then the HR Department and an exam was to be sat. The first lasted an hour, the Procurement Manager was doing a professional job with her conduction of the interview, Eve did most of the talking and the Procurement Manager was impressed. The interview with the HR Department lasted just as long who in turn set her another interview later in the week with the Departmental Manager with whom she was supposed to work with directly, it went extremely well too. Both companies offered her a position, the foreign company was the first to respond, she was to meet the General Manager, but before she met with him the HR manager wanted to see her again.

"I made the decision to employ you after I finished all the interviews and *you are* the best," said the HR manager "Your experience, the interview, and your references—they spoke highly of you and they're sad to see you go." She was silent for a moment, and it was obvious from her facial expression she wanted to say something she was uneasy with, "I need to tell you something, I contacted Noora…to tell her the good news that you've got the job—I didn't know you and your brother and his wife haven't been in contact for years," she waited for Eve to say something, but Eve stared back poker-faced so the HR manager continued "So I thought by telling her they'd be happy to hear the good news…but…she had a lot of bad things to say about you and…uh…she warned me not to employ you…she even said you're a snake! And I should beware of you, that if I employ you I'll be making a big mistake…"

"Samar, I came here for a work interview and I came looking for work," Eve interrupted her and did not let her finish "I'm not interested in what my brother and sister-in-law have told you. I can see you're professional so if you're giving me the job based on my capabilities and experience so be it, but if you're saying it depends on what my sister-in-law is telling you—I'm not interested." Eve picked up her purse and got up to leave.

"No, I'm sorry," said the HR manager looking worried she had offended Eve "Please sit down, I didn't mean to upset you, I did say you were chosen because you're the best out of all the candidates. It's just…when I found out, by accident from her, that you're not on good terms…I wanted to say, but you didn't let me finish…if I can mediate a reconciliation between you all. You know—get the water running back on its right course, and it has no bearing on my choice if you get the job or not because she called me several times to say bad things about you, and to warn me *not* to employ you, but you're still my choice…I want you to join us."

"Good," said Eve "Because I don't mix my personal life into my work."

It was only two months and her experience and skills were noticed, and several departments were vying to get her to join them giving her a number of promotions to choose from and plenty of time to wait for the best promotion to come her way.

She instantly made good friends with her colleagues, Najla, a sweet Yemeni, Tigist a young Ethiopian, Iliyana the Eastern European, and many more good people Eve became acquainted with.

Eve glanced at the clock on the opposite wall as she straightened documents she had been sorting, almost the end of working hours. Tigist and Iliyana stood in front of Eve at the reception desk, both with the look of tired relief at the end of a day's hard work with the foreglow of looking forward to getting home on their faces. They chatted and asked Eve about her life, her children, how old she was when married so the conversation became Eve summarising her life story. Najla joined them.

"Start from the beginning so Najla can hear." said Iliyana.

Eve started again, the three ladies stood around Eve's desk, glued to her story, drawn to every word and experience she mentioned. The women were riveted and awed by Eve's life, according to them, all those troubles didn't show on her, nobody could tell she had been through so much.

"That is a lot," said Tigist "No wonder you're so strong, you survived all that, you can survive anything!"

"You've had a very interesting life." said Iliyana.

"What I can't understand," said Najla "Is how you can be normal as if nothing happened? I've only been through a divorce recently, and I was only married a few months, and I feel I can't live anymore.

After all you've been through, how do you carry on? How can you smile and laugh?"

Eve laughed, remembering something she had read as a child in the newspaper funnies a big eared rat-like creature had said, it represented what happened to her life and what she had done about it. She looked Najla in the eye, smiled and said: "When life gives you lemons—make lemonade." (Oh Eve, you'd need several shots of vodka to go with it to forget your traumas). The women laughed at the exceedingly banal cliché and left the office together.

*

IN THE DISSIPATING HEAT OF AFTERNOON, ON AN ASPHALT ROAD below a towering mountain situated behind the Presidential Palace, on her way back home from work, she was stuck in a traffic jam at the worst possible place to be caught—underneath one of those huge trucks loaded with cuboid rock building stones, each rock the size of an industrial washing machine, and perilously overloaded, it was a wonder the rocks heaped into a peak hadn't already tumbled causing a tragedy—which sometimes happened. The bumpy hewn edges reminded Eve of her village, they were the same colour and texture and her thoughts went to the beautiful rock houses built in the mountains, and she could still hear the clink and thump of Uncle Suleiman's sledgehammer against basalt boulder. Eve always admired the intricate patterns on some of the older clay coloured buildings laced with white gypsum, in markets and residential areas in Sana'a, even many modern builds continued to use the same patterns to decorate the houses. The country was a fountain of culture descending from ancient empires, and you could still see what ancient civilisations had left behind, not just in the protected World Heritage sites, but also the architecture and patterns, the crafts, clothes and traditions which carried on; in the people and their ways, none more so than the mountain people she had lived with for eight years. When she had first begun work in Sana'a, she was surprised no one understood many of the words she used, which she had learnt from the village, although many of the employees came from many different villages all over the country, some from mountainous communities too, they had never heard of her village in the mountains. It wasn't whole sentences they didn't understand, just some nouns, verbs, adjectives and they questioned whether these words were Arabic, some older people said it sounded like an ancient Arabic of Yemen no longer in use.

Eve watched the changing of seasons, noticed the slight changes during the day and cherished the diversity, quirks and unconventional ways of many of the city's residents going about their daily lives. There was a number of different dialects spoken, and traditional and western clothing donned, styles both outdated and modern; people from all walks of life mixed throughout society. Even the buildings and architecture seemed to follow no civic planning, but most residential areas were a pastiche of mismatched traditional buildings surrounded by modern builds; grandiose villas next to a humble cement block house; magnificent mansions next to small metal shops used as dwellings or a bland multi-storey apartment block, but in the chaos there was a unity, for the pattern carried on across Sana'a— according to legend the city founded by Shem son of Noah (of the Quranic and Biblical ark). Near home they were intersected by three smiling men riding a motorcycle suited only for two, with a live goat sandwiched between the last and middle passenger, the goat looking outwards through stoned eyes at fellow road users with a relaxed expression on its face of taking the ride (and life) easy. The taxi overtook a small family car on its way to the theme park with the sole male hunched over the steering wheel, while grown women sat in each other's laps their necks bent and heads pressed against the ceiling of the car, their three pretty children, two girls in identical pink dresses and hats and a boy, all under eight years of age, seated dangerously, but gleefully delighted, in the open boot of the car smiling at the people in vehicles behind them, its hood bouncing up and down above their heads as they sped down the lane. Yemenis were the friendliest of people, happy to welcome visitors no matter where they came from, if you were to look beyond the black cloaks, head and face veils, the men in white dresses and colourful skirts, it wasn't much different than any other country in the world. Like any country, it had its traditions, the beautiful, the non-sensical, but all deep-rooted. Otherwise, the people were the same as any other nation, they experienced the same joys, disappointments, successes and frustrations experienced by everyone on both hemispheres; they had the same desires wanted by people all over the world: they wanted their children to have an education; to become doctors, architects, engineers, politicians. As a community and individually they strove for a better future, for their children, and wished to provide the best for their loved ones. Those whom could afford it sent their children to private schools. Teenagers, youth and adults had relationships without marriage, even though it was disdained. Married people cheated on their spouses, even with the risk of severe criticism and shame if caught. No one was ever stoned, the worst to happen if caught—the culprits receiving a severe beating behind closed doors by their own family members; legal action was only taken if someone had tipped off the authorities, and even then officials strove to find a lesser punishment or way out for the accused; flogging and despicable 'honour killings' did not happen, it was simply swept under the rug. Even pregnant unmarried young ladies only brought great shame and distress to their family whom would deny the scandal: the young girl never ventured out pregnant and was never seen in public until after the baby was born while rumours swarmed around; usually the new-born was left at an orphanage or someone's doorstep and the young lady reappeared into society in total denial, her reputation as white as the cloth on a virgin's marriage bed. Men and women wanted to start families and there were those whom did not. Only girls in some rural areas were not allowed an education, and in cities it was forbidden by the few closed-minded families whom hadn't opened up to the benefits of education, but it was being tackled by organisations. Yemeni women worked side by side with men, breaking the male dominant set traditions and attitudes a woman should stay at home or only be employed as a teacher or secretary—which had never been the case in Yemen, for since antiquity women had been its queens and rulers and under their reign during ancient and more recent history Yemen had flourished. Although Yemeni women had to work much harder than their male peers to reach high positions, they had made it in all professions and trades, from small kiosks to owners of large private companies, from actresses to academicians, from sports to Ministers (though many debated the latter was a token appointment), a continuance of Yemen's open-minded and energetic civilisations.

Everybody always claimed and complained the government officials and their network of cronies were siphoning off the country's money into their own personal, secret bank accounts abroad. Eve could see the country's fortunes from finite resources were being wasted instead of being invested into the infrastructure, it could have been such a strong country had it not been devastated by previous occupation, dictators, backwardness and now, corruption. Yemenis suffered from inadequate education and health services. Whilst private schools provided better education than public, the standard was much lower than a state school in the west provided; pupils were packed like rice in overcrowded public schools, making it impossible for teachers to give all the pupils the needed tuition and support in such conditions. Yet Yemen and Yemenis were more active, open and tolerant than any of its rich Gulfan neighbours; Yemenis had more freedom of speech, a lively and diverse political make-up; a tolerant multicultural society made up of multiple religious, political and social schools of thought—all striving towards a democracy, desiring a civil institutions-based governance, albeit with a planted dictatorship keeping the country behind and democracy at bay. True stories throughout all levels of society spoke of misdiagnosis; unnecessary surgeries by unethical doctors commercialising on people's bodies and simple surgeries gone wrong at the hands of unqualified doctors—qualified by a purchased degree. Not all doctors were incompetent, but a large number were and you had to go through a lot of bad ones until finally finding the good. It was good to have faith as God looked over Yemen to protect its people from the lack of real medical services and treatments available (plus human resilience is an extraordinary thing).

Yemen's biggest ailment by far, was corruption, monetary and administrative. This destructive disease manifested in the academic and judicial system, into companies, private and public. Into every aspect of Yemen. Those not corrupt were considered fools for not taking advantage of their influence, while those in important government posts who stood against corruption were attacked and made to leave their positions.

Eve observed everything through eyes much older than her age, this country could have been great. It was beautiful, it had retained its culture and had history, yet its nation as a whole would never reach full potential because of the chaos, corruption and randomness. Nothing was ever fully under control or seen to the end. Haphazard and half-assed seemed to be the ruling tone. People whom didn't earn positions in university, public companies and government, made it to the top while hardworking students and employees who deserved it were denied their places to make way for those 'with connections' and money. A government unable to manage and prosper from its country's human and physical resources, it was no mystery why this country had become so poor, while surrounded by its rich gulf neighbours whom took care of their own people.

Corruption you could keep away from, it was only a path for those whom chose it, but political unrest was always on the horizon, sending fear into a country already unstable from troublemakers (rebels in the north and separatists in the south) funded by rich regional countries trying to divide it; if it blew out into full scale war, it would destroy this already complex but beautiful country; and open the doors for terrorists to enter.

*

AT LAST, EVE WAS DELIGHTED TO RECEIVE THE RULING FROM THE Supreme Court. Her ex-husband could no longer drag her from court to court for the rest of her life as he had vowed, her divorce was final and could no longer be appealed. Finally, she would bring up her children in peace. This year was a good one for Eve, she finished her fourth year of studies with an international college and graduated. In work, she performed so well she took over one of her expatriate boss's position. Eve continued to work hard and was able to buy a small house to provide permanent safety of shelter for her children. Again she felt the agreeable, swelling satisfaction of achieving another goal she had set for herself in the past. She enjoyed the experience of completing the house, choosing the paint, buying the tiles, checking on the builders; even if it meant long hours in the freezing cold and dark, after the end of a long day's work.

At the beginning of the year Eve and her family moved into their new home. In the evening after all the workers had left, Eve prostrated to God in a prayer of thankfulness for this blessing. Then she and her children danced all over the house to the sound of Eve singing a song.

*

EVE LOOKED OUT OF HER OFFICE DOOR TO SEE IF ANYONE ELSE had noticed, distracted from the contract she had been reviewing by the sound of heavy artillery coming from not that far away. She went to the Security Manager's office.

"Jim, can you hear that?" she said "Is it construction work nearby or is it a war?"

She hoped he would say heavy construction, but it was the sound of battle at the outskirts of Sana'a, where rebels from Sa'ada had arrived. Heart pounding in her ears, the feeling of making a big mistake swirling in her chest, she called Mother to carefully find out if she could hear anything from home without alarming her. There was nothing. She had made a mistake and should have long gone to Britain.

"Have faith in God," Najla said smiling "You know it's destiny."

"I have faith in God," said Eve "But I can't just think of myself, I have to think about my children. I can't subject my children to a war or losing limbs from war, I feel petrified and agonised when I see what happens to those families in the news. *Yes, I know we can lose limbs in an accident*, but it's not like sitting through a war. I've never been in one, I was in the mountains when the civil war happened and we weren't reached."

"They won't enter Sana'a," said Najla "Word has it, they'll be crushed in a few days...but there's no full-scale war."

Najla smiled as Eve gazed into the distance.

"What's wrong?" said Najla.

"I think I made a mistake in buying the house," said Eve "I've bought a house and have to pay back over years and what do you know—a war breaks out!"

They both laughed at the risibility of assessing the war around her house purchase, but Eve was worried. She had never witnessed a war, other than what she saw in the news, and it terrified her sick.

Najla was right, the rebels were defeat in a matter of days and normality returned.

*

"WHY DON'T YOU GO BACK TO THE UK?" SAID IAN, AFTER ROBERT, her supervisor, finished telling him how well Eve had coordinated the delivery of several international shipments, some local shipments to the Rig, while executing various tasks and sorting out problems with customs clearance and issuing a whole load of paperwork at the same time "I can't understand why someone like you would choose to stay here. You can do very well if you go back home."

"This is my country. I can't leave my country." said Eve, she eerily sounded to herself like Suleiman and the others in the village, when they wouldn't let her leave the mountains.

CHAPTER TWENTY-SEVEN

T HE EMPLOYEES POURED OUT OF THE CONFERENCE ROOM, after a meeting. Eve, Najla and Masmooh the IT guru stood in front of the reception desk while he finished telling them about an amusing incident at work. Najla slid towards her a newspaper which lay on the counter of the reception desk, a photo of three young girls on the front page.

"Oh my God!" exclaimed Najla reading the article "This one was eight when forced to get married!"

Najla and Masmooh discussed how terrible and tragic these girls were forced into marriage as young children. Eve heard the discussion, but her eyes were on the young faces. They were saved, she thought, thrown back into the feeling of the frightened fourteen-year-old girl she had been on her so-called 'wedding day', her neck stiffened as she experienced the fear, confusion and helplessness she had felt, as memories flooded back. They were saved and could finish their childhood…why wasn't she saved? She knew it was because they were in the city and had people supporting them and fighting for their freedom, it had made all the difference for these girls: somebody on their side. Eve closed her eyes and felt the years she spent as a child in the mountains with no one listening or trying to understand her; her only hope, a prayer to God; her only brief escapes, singing songs as loud as she could, forgetting where she was, its words and rhythm transporting her soul out of confinement and into memories where she ran, danced and flew in bliss like a bird escaping its cage and freely soaring through the skies. She opened her eyes and smiled at the photo.

"You've been saved." she said in a low whisper so nobody could hear her.

She felt a connection to the printed faces for she knew what they had been through and she knew what they had been saved from and, hopefully, never experience. But what about the thousands of girls whom the floodlights of the media would never shine upon and the world would never know about? Her long-lashed sepulchral eyes blinked, for the voices of these girls would never be heard, their songs shall never be sung, their faces and chatter would never be bright and uplifting; the light of their souls had been dimmed, body and mind burdened and traumatised; no nightingale would ever mesmerise them into forgetting their own tragedies at having been an ululated, celebrated child-bride. Eve read the article and imagined how her life could have been had someone saved her eighteen years ago. How were helpless young Yemeni girls in rural areas to access help or even be aware of the law? Why didn't the British government have a system in place to stop its young British citizens from this peril? Could they stop it from happening even if they tried? It was too late for her. Too late and too painful dwelling on it. She snapped out of the reflection realising she would not have these three amazing children had this not happened to her, with a sense of guilt she always felt after wishing she had never been married for she couldn't imagine not having them in her life, or she not being in theirs. Eve now believed in destiny, but she knew whatever direction chosen and choice made created your destiny: three hundred and sixty degrees of options, each one leading to infinite possibilities, but it was up to you, and sometimes interference from others, which direction to take and what to make of it. Her father had made choices and put her in a place which changed her life; changed how she thought and reacted, but she too had hesitated and made mistakes when presented with choice. Eve was now certain, faltering going back to Britain from Saudi had been a wrong decision, but she fully understood the direction she took into getting control of her life back here in Yemen had given them a good life and was right in so many ways, even if it hadn't been the best thing to do. Maybe others were right in their beliefs that everything happens for a reason—for she would not let her son grow up as a shepherd, or her daughters be forced into marriage as children or adults. To give three young lives an opportunity of a normal life, was more than reason enough for her destiny to take her through this journey.

Her reasons for staying in Yemen, a product of her own fears and flaws. She knew what they were and how they came about, and did not expect anybody to understand them.

No song, poem or story will ever immortalise our Eve, but within her the fourteen-year-old lives on forever wanting to live, flooding our Eve, taking over her mind and senses, returning her to the point to which she could never really return—except, when she sings her woes away trilling like a bulbul.

About the Author

Hawaa Ayoub, author of *When a Bulbul Sings*, has experienced the traumas of forced child-marriage first hand. She hopes to raise awareness through writing about child-marriage.

She lived in Yemen for nineteen years, the first eight years in a remote region whose inhabitants hadn't changed their way of life since ancient times, an area at the time inaccessible to outsiders including Yemenis from outside the region.

When a Bulbul Sings is her first novel.

For more information about the author and upcoming books please visit: www.hawaaayoub.com

Lightning Source UK Ltd.
Milton Keynes UK
UKHW04f1808130918
328851UK00001B/10/P